I0773557

hate you later

Lit Lovers Book 1

ciara blume

copyright

Hate You Later by Ciara Blume
Published by Dolce Villa Press

www.ciarablume.com

Copyright © 2022 Ciara Blume

All rights reserved. No portion of this book may be reproduced in any form without permission from the publisher, except as permitted by U.S. copyright law. For permissions contact: author@ciarablume.com

For Brian, who is the yang to my yin. You are my romantic hero GOAT.

"I wanted it to be you so badly." — Kathleen from You've Got Mail, cowritten by Nora and Delia Ephron.

prologue: georgia

. . .

I listen while I prep the Celestial Pets Boutique for the day.

"Welcome to episode twenty-seven of *Lit Lovers*," a male voice announces. "We're your hosts, and this week, we're talking about friction in the fiction. You know what we mean—enemies to lovers, cats and dogs. It's a classic trope, and there are almost too many books and movies to talk about with this one."

"*Pride and Prejudice*," chimes in one of the other hosts.

"*You've Got Mail*," says another.

"Ooh … ooh … *The Hating Game*!" shouts the fourth.

"That's right. We're talking about love/hate relationships today," the first host speaks again. "This week's episode is sponsored by The Grumpy Stump Axe Lodge, where *Lit Lovers* listeners enjoy 20 percent off all lanes on Saturday night. That's less than a buck per chuck. Drink and throw responsibly! Now let's get lit after the jump."

The show's theme music comes on. I put away my old sewing machine that I use to finish my custom pet costumes, and sweep up the fabric remnants and stray threads. Then I make my rounds, filling a hand thrown, ceramic pet bowl with gourmet dog treats to sample. I fluff the clothing on the round rack and straighten the selection of dog booties on the shoe shelf.

Above the shoe shelves are two ledges holding miniature hat and wig stands. I smooth the peacock feathers sticking out of a green, velvet top hat and bite my lower lip to contain the dopey smile that's threatening to bust out. Is there anything better than pet headwear? Probably not. Tiny hats and wiglets for pets are one of the few things truly right with the world. Anyone who's seen an iguana in a toupee will surely back me on this.

    "So, enlighten us, Jackson," a woman's voice teases from the podcast. "Why are so many people turned on by people who piss them off?"

    "It's elemental, Sis," the host replies. "Ones and zeros. Some of us are just programmed that way."

"Not me!" I talk back at the podcast.

I would describe my love life to date as tepid. At the ripe old age of twenty-seven, the one long-term relationship I've had was with one of my braided leather leash vendors. It had ended perfectly amicably. We'd fist-bumped over our mutual breakup. And we're still Facebook friends. He's engaged now to a nice girl who breeds collies.

The last thing I want in my life is drama.

My phone vibrates, and I check the screen. It's a message from Oliver, my Petfluencer Challenge buddy.

> Don't forget to play around with portrait
> mode when shooting the lighting prompt
> today. Can't wait to see your photos!

Suddenly, my Boxer mutt, Cookie, darts to the front of the shop, her hackles raised and ears twitching. It has to be a cat. Probably the stray that frequents the nearby alley. I stuff the phone in my back pocket and walk toward the windows.

"Poor Cookie … don't worry. I'll protect you," I say.

I may only be five foot two, but I'm scrappy. Some people might think I got a dog for protection, but with a black belt in Krav Maga, I'm perfectly capable of defending myself.

As I stand by the door, I stretch and gather my tousled, black hair into a topknot. I push up my sleeves, exposing the tattoos twining up my left arm. Of all the designs, the tiny paw print made up of stars that decorates the inside of my wrist is my favorite. It's my own original design and also the logo for Celestial Pets.

Cookie lets out a small, nervous whine as she paces from the glass door to the shop window. Then she freezes by the door, staring out into the street. Creamy autumn morning light is streaming through the glass. It bathes her in the kind of warm, golden glow that Instagram dreams are made of.

I slide my phone from my back pocket. Quickly, I tap the screen, firing off a number of shots, zooming in and then pulling back.

The moment doesn't last long. Perhaps the cat has moved on, or perhaps I've distracted her with the photos, but a few seconds later, Cookie's tension abruptly falls away and she relaxes. She glances back at me, tail pumping when we make eye contact.

"C'mere, good girl!" I pat my legs, calling her over.

With her tongue hanging out, and the entire back end of her body wagging, Cookie dashes to my side, gazing at me with pure and utter devotion. Her hind leg jerkily thumps the floor as I scratch her, and then she rolls over onto her back for belly rubs. I shoot a few more pics, capturing her, belly up, in a delicious slice of sunshine.

Dogs are so much better than people, I tell myself for the billionth time.

georgia

· · ·

BECAUSE MY HAND is curled into the perfect fist—thumb outside, fingers straight—it really doesn't hurt too bad when my knuckles slam into Bryce Holm's jaw. Actually, it feels good, really good. Cathartic even. He picked the wrong day and the wrong girl. That motherfucker had it coming.

Let me back up about twenty-five minutes.

We arrive at The Onion fresh from work. Kenna drives because the "unicorn," my ancient, white Prius, is completely full of dog hair and Kenna is wearing black. This is fine with me. I suspect I'll need more than one drink tonight.

The Onion is exactly the sort of place you want to go to when you need to bitch about something. The booths are a little greasy. The bar is a little grimy. The floor is a lot sticky. The bar food is not so great, but it's also not so terrible. It's exactly the sort of place you want to go to drown your sorrows. And since misery loves company, it's always packed.

There's always a battle over the playlist on the old-fashioned jukebox. But one thing everyone can agree on is their universal loathing of anyone who wears "positive vibes only" tees or employs a life coach.

I love The Onion. The Onion is a safe haven from the plague of toxic positivity afflicting my generation. Which is not to say I'm pro-negativity. I'm just a realist. No bullshit. No false hopes waiting to get dashed against the cliffs of reality.

Kenna slides her skinny, Levi's-clad ass onto the barstool beside me. She's shed her barista apron and traded her colorful daytime scrunchie for a black bandana that matches her simple, black sweater. Her silver stud earrings are mismatched. There's a coffee cup on the right and a camera on the left. And she has on an elaborately knotted friendship bracelet that I'm pretty sure I made for her a decade ago.

This is about as fancy as my beautiful friend gets. There's a charming simplicity to her minimalist style.

Kenna orders two micheladas and pays the bartender in cash, tipping generously.

"So, what are we going to do about the rent hike?" she asks.

"Hmm. Rob a bank? Turn tricks? Buy a lottery ticket?" I offer flippantly.

Notice about the rent hike had come around noon today. It landed like a carpet-bombing. Email and text messages blew up my inbox mere moments before the perky FedEx guy showed up at my door with the written notice. I'm certain there will be a certified letter arriving at Celestial Pets via snail mail as well. No claiming I didn't get this.

It's a significant increase—nearly 30 percent—starting on November 1st. Just a month and a half away. Is that even legal?

I'm livid but not entirely blindsided. Ever since the rumors started about the Farm & Holm Company doing some upgrades to the dump of a historic building, where we've both been working since we were teenagers, this sort of scenario seemed inevitable. Who needs mom-and-pop shops when you can rent to Starbucks and Urban Outfitters?

"Can't you ask Xander for help?" Kenna suggests.

I shake my head and fold my arms defiantly across my chest. Not happening. I'm not going to beg for charity from my little brother.

It isn't just the rent. It's everything. Celestial Pets is a philanthropic shop. This means most, if not all, of our profits go to support our local pet shelter, Kismet Rescue. And at the moment, Kismet is in dire straits. They've been displaced by another one of the Farm & Holm Company's renovation projects over in the industrial part of town.

"This sucks so much." Kenna drums her fingers on the bar. "You just finally worked out the relocation plan for the shelter."

I'd found the perfect property outside of town at a farm that had a barn with existing kennels. But there is a lot of work to be done to upgrade the kennels for year-round use and to set up office space. Expensive work. Work that Kismet is relying on my shop to fund. Work that I've already taken out a mortgage on my house to fund.

It's something I cannot think about right now without risking a full-blown panic attack. My heart beats jumpily, a caged bird.

"I'll figure it out. I'll just have to cut something." As if there's anything left to cut. Or borrow against.

"Seriously, Georgia You should at least let Xander know." Kenna fixes me with the exasperated look of someone who's well aware her advice will probably be ignored.

"Xander and Mac are already doing so much." I fold my arms across my chest. My brother's partner has been keeping several homeless pets at his veterinary clinic. He even set up a temporary desk in the office for Angie, the shelter's admin, to use to make calls and work on placements.

"You'd think that with the Holm family's history of selling pet supplies, they might have given a little more time and warning before evicting an animal shelter!" Kenna shakes her head.

I can't argue with that. But the Holms had hardly seemed to give a shit. Bryce Holm's heartless tweets were all over the local news.

My phone dings with a text, and I reach around for my bag. It's hanging on the back of my barstool, along with my favorite shaggy, faux fur jacket. Pro tip—the best way to disguise pet fur is to wear faux fur.

I dig around to retrieve the phone in the depths of my cluttered, vegan-leather bag.

The message is from Xander. He's sent a link to his latest viral video and a paragraph's worth of star and champagne bottle emojis surrounding the text.

One million views!!!

Holy shit. That dog he groomed to look like a Pokémon character has received over a million views? As usual, I'm completely baffled by social media, but I'm so thrilled for him.

Before putting my bag back, I collect three weeks' worth of loose change from the bottom to toss in the tip jar. My oversize ring catches on a crumpled-up flyer for the online Petflu-encer Challenge I am doing with my dog, Cookie. The challenge is being run through a local pet fancier's group and is sponsored by a high-end pet food brand that we carry in the shop.

I smooth out the flyer on the bar. I'd agreed to help distribute the flyers, but then I'd signed myself up on a whim. It couldn't hurt to play along. They have some mega-influential moderators dishing out the weekly tips and post prompts.

I'd love to grow a following for the shop and my original pet clothes designs.

"How's that challenge going?" Kenna asks.

I groan. "Uggggghhh."

It hasn't been going great, actually. In fact, it's been a month since I started, and Cookie's Instagram account is still struggling to get follower numbers beyond the double digits. Part of me wonders why I'm bothering. It's embarrassing, especially considering the wholly organic, viral success of my mega-influential little brother.

I have stubbornly refused to ask him for help. I don't want to grow a following via pity follows from his adoring fans.

"I just don't think I'm cut out for social media success."

"You could just ask …" I know Kenna is about to say Xander, but she holds her tongue when I turn my head to glare at her. She sighs. "Fine, then. If you hate it so much, I don't understand why you don't just drop it. Nobody would blame you for tabling that challenge for now. You have enough on your plate, don't you?"

She's right, of course, but I can't quit. Because it's not just my account at stake. The moderators assigned us all buddies, and if I fail, so does Oliver. The ridiculous cat. I can't let that furball down.

I resist the urge to check if I have any messages from him. Texting daily has become part of our routine.

"So, what about you guys? Will the rent hike hurt the diner?" I attempt to steer the conversation away from myself.

"We'll be all right," Kenna says. "The uncles are going to have to raise prices some, but they said they think they'll be okay. Especially if the renovations bring more foot traffic. They're really looking forward to the building being upgraded." She looks almost apologetic. "You know, my photography side hustle pays for my drinks, and I earn good tips at the diner. I could probably kick in some cash for you if you need it, Georgia."

"No, stop it. You're already donating all your free time to take pictures of the animals. I don't need your tips. It's going to be fine. I've got this," I lie.

It won't be fine. The money I borrowed against the house is barely going to cover the shelter's moving and renovation expenses. I was counting on the shop's income to bridge the gap and guarantee that Angie still gets paid.

Poor Angie. She's not getting any younger. I'm sure she relies on that meager salary.

The bartender, a rangy, forty-something guy with a graying soul patch, places our drinks in front of us. "Can I get you ladies anything else?" he asks.

"Chili fries," we both say, almost, but not quite, in unison. The bartender nods his approval before sending the order ticket on to the kitchen.

"Back to that Petfluencer Challenge," Kenna says. "You need any help with the photos?"

"No, it's all gotta be me. They want organic images. Simple stuff."

I take a sip of my drink, enjoying the way the salt, spice, and acid feel in my nearly empty stomach. Tomato juice, lime, and beer. Whoever came up with this recipe is a genius.

"Most of the prompts have been pretty casual so far. But if you've got the time, I could use a favor. That reporter who's doing a story on Celestial Pets asked for a few shots of the shop and my pet costumes. I'll pay you, of course."

"You got it." Kenna nods. "And your money is no good with me. Are you excited about the press?"

I've been trying not to put too much stock in it, but my one and only bright spot right now is that a nationally distributed pet magazine is doing a story on the shop, my designs, and the way we support local artists while funding our sister shelter.

"I guess. We'll see. Hopefully, it will help move the needle." Honestly, I'm not sure what to expect, and I don't want to get my hopes up.

Kenna gives my arm a fast squeeze. "It's gonna be okay, G. We'll figure something out."

I wish I had her confidence. I know she means well and genuinely wants to help, but it isn't her problem. It's mine. The weight of it all—the promise I made to the shelter, the commitment to keep up my mother's legacy, and ultimately, the duty to make sure none of those animals end up in a kill facility—sits squarely on my shoulders.

I take another long sip of my drink and scan the bar for a distraction.

"So, this challenge …" I tap the flyer in front of me. "Want to hear the craziest part about it?" I ask.

"Yes, please!" Kenna replies, leaning forward and taking a big swig of her drink.

"Since it's online and we don't have any IRL interaction, we were assigned buddies. It's supposed to get us to engage more. We leave comments on each other's posts, and we help each other with the prompts."

I pull up my buddy's account on my phone and hand it to her. "Check out my buddy. He's the weirdest cat. His personality is like a stuffy, old-fashioned butler. Like this really proper little old man."

"Oh my gosh, this shit is funny." Kenna scrolls past a photo of Oliver the cat rejecting second-rate caviar, and another of him fussily inspecting the hospital corners on his owner's tightly tucked bed.

"Where's his owner?" she asks. "I don't see anything about whose cat this is."

"That's the crazy part." I smile. "We're not allowed to reveal who WE are. We signed a contract at the start of the challenge to only interact with each other in the persona of our pets. It's like a whole method acting/language immersion thing. No revealing our true identities."

"Really?" Kenna quirks an eyebrow at me. "So let me get this straight. You do Cookie and this other person does Oliver in all your messages? What are they, like texts? Please tell me you're not talking on the phone doing a dog voice." She is looking at me now like I've lost it a little.

"No, we don't do voice chats. Mostly, we leave each other messages in the challenge portal. But sometimes we chat too," I explain.

Kenna bites her lip. This is clearly very amusing to her.

"I'm just trying to picture you pretending to be Cookie, G. I mean, you're just such a badass, and Cookie is just so … not." Kenna has tears forming in her eyes as she attempts to stifle her laughter.

"Hey, now," I defend my dog. "We're working on Cookie's image. Have you checked out her account?"

Kenna shakes her head.

"I know, it seems a little weird. But it's actually been a lot of fun so far. Almost like doing improv. And therapeutic, in a weird way. I feel like I can say anything as Cookie."

"Mm-hmm," Kenna says. "So, tell us where the naughty doggy sniffed you."

"Not like that!" I swat her with my napkin. "Oliver is so uptight that I can't resist winding him up. I keep making Cookie's posts edgier and edgier just to see how he'll react."

"Oh yeah. Testing boundaries. You definitely would like that, you freak." Kenna leans forward and places her hand on her chin. "This plays right into your whole bad-girl-wannabe thing."

"What do you mean, wannabe?"

Kenna snorts and rolls her eyes. "You don't fool me. I know that deep down, you're secretly a big softie, G. I don't know why you want everyone to think you're such a badass."

"Stop trying to fix me, Kenna." I exhale. "I am what I am."

She doesn't seem to get it. There's no room for weakness in my life. Helpless animals are relying on me. I might be able to stand letting down people, but not the pets.

"So, are you going to show me your texts with this Oliver?" Kenna asks.

"No!" I object, sliding my phone into my pocket. "Definitely not. It's private."

"Oh really." Kenna presses on with renewed interest. "This is sounding a little kinky, actually. I'm getting soft-core porno vibes here. Maybe you should submit this story to the *Lit Lovers* podcast for an episode. I bet they'd have a field day with it." She sets down her phone.

"You've been listening to too many episodes," I chide.

"Maybe." She shrugs. "But tell me, have you given any thought about what Oliver's owner is like IRL? What if it's that guy over there? He looks like he might have a high-maintenance Persian cat in his life."

Kenna tilts her head toward a grizzled, bandanna-capped biker who's arm wrestling in the corner. "I think he's got room for an entire litter of kittens in that beard."

"Stop!" I try not to snarf my drink.

The truth is, I have wondered about Oliver's owner. But that's beside the point.

"I can't go there," I say. "It's probably a little old lady or some nerdy teen. It doesn't really matter."

I push the flyer away from me to make room for the bartender to set down our chili fries.

Before I can even lift my fork, Kenna snakes her hand under mine, spearing the first fry.

"Too slow!" She laughs and bites into her chili-sauced French fry. Her eyes half-closed, she moans with delight. "Oh God. I wish I could date these fries."

"Those fries are totally your type." I laugh. "Dirty, spicy, terrible for you …"

"They're perfect," she agrees. "Wouldn't change a thing."

"That's probably why you wouldn't date these fries. You'd have nothing to fix," I point out.

Kenna shrugs. "Then I'd marry them." She holds up a fry, mouths the words "I do," and then proceeds to kiss the French fry before popping it in her mouth. She has sauce drippings on her chin and winks as she accepts a napkin.

Suddenly, she freezes, mid dab. "I've got it. The solution to all our problems! You should marry a Holm!" Kenna punctuates her proclamation by shaking another chili fry at me. I duck to avoid an airborne droplet of meat sauce.

"Hear me out. You could take over the company, save the shelter, and get some help in the shop so you'd be free to live a life of luxury and leisure." She pronounces leisure like "lez-zure" with a fake British accent.

"I'd rather marry that biker in the back corner than Bryce Holm!" I gag for effect.

Kenna and I went to high school with Bryce Holm, the entitled, pompous, arrogant stepson of the head of the Holm company. He was a couple of years ahead of us and infamous. The perfect amalgam of every teen movie villain, minus the good hair.

"Doesn't Bryce have an older brother? His dad was married before Bryce's mom. European woman? I think she went back there with the kid."

"Don't know, don't care." I shrug and shudder. "Bryce Holm. Blech."

As if on cue, summoned from the murky depths, I spy him coming toward us. Seconds later, I feel his hot, boozy breath on the side of my neck. Talk about manifesting. Is nothing sacred anymore? What the hell is *he* doing in The Onion?

"Did I hear someone say my name? Can I buy you ladies a drink?"

I sneak a glance over my shoulder. It's been a decade since high school, and the lights in the bar are dim, but I recognize Bryce Holm all the same. He's fatter and his hair is thinning, but the signature swagger hasn't changed. Same old smug-ass douchebag. His golf polo, pressed and creased jeans, and flashy watch are ridiculously at odds here in The Onion. I don't know if he remembers us. But we certainly remember him.

Kenna and I exchange a look. Her eyes are wide and horrified. "Sorry!" she mouths, as if she'd conjured him up with that chili fry.

Bryce insinuates himself into the narrow space between me and the empty chair to my left.

"No thanks. We're all good here," I say, refusing to meet his eyes. Not that I'm in any danger of that. I'd have to have eyes in my DDs to meet his present gaze.

"Come on … whatever you want, Princess." He smirks, snapping his fingers officiously to get the bartender's attention.

The bartender looks my way with a wary glance that asks, "You okay?" I can tell he's struggling to remain impassive as I nod almost imperceptibly.

It appears that Bryce Holm has leveled up on the douchebag scale. His left hand, casually placed on the bar, sports a sausage-like ring finger with a diamond-studded wedding band. It's so ostentatious it almost looks fake.

"I'm surprised you aren't trying to get us to pay for you," I mumble, still refusing to turn to face him. I can feel moist heat radiating off him as he angles himself toward me. I instinctively lean away, toward Kenna.

"Come on, Princess, don't you remember who I am?" He leans in closer. He's wearing too much cologne. Barf. I count to five, taking stock of each of my fingers as I arrange them neatly into a fist. Try me.

"Uh-oh," Kenna mutters under her breath.

I'm more than ready when Bryce Holm places his right hand on my shoulder, spinning me out to face him. His lizard eyes dart between my mouth and my boobs, and his hand slides down my spine to the small of my back. He licks his lips.

And then he's down.

The pain blooming in my knuckles is nothing compared to the satisfaction of seeing the befuddled expression on Bryce's face as his precious, denim-clad ass makes contact with the beer-tacky floor of The Onion. I shake out my hand and blow on my knuckles to cool them off.

Bryce's face is a roadmap of shock. Pure shock. Then he squints, revealing rivers of pain. Finally, his face floods red. Anger.

"What the fuck?" He grabs on to a table to pull himself up and snatches a napkin, sending silverware flying dramatically. He spits into the napkin, inspecting it, looking for blood.

"Oh, come the fuck on. I didn't hit you THAT hard," I say. His balance just sucks. But there'd be a bruise. For sure, there would be a bruise.

"Did you see that?" Bryce gestures to Kenna and the bartender. The bartender shrugs impassively and fills a plastic cup with ice, which he then hands to Bryce.

"I think you kind of asked for it, man," he says. "She's a black belt. You're damned lucky you still have your balls."

Kenna sighs. She puts a twenty-dollar bill on the bar and then pulls on her coat before laying a tentative hand on my shoulder to get my attention. She holds out my furry coat.

"Let's get out of here," she says. My heart is still pounding and, if anything, I'm overheated. But I humor her and slip into the coat.

"You stupid bitch. Don't you know who I am?" Bryce says again. With a sullen huff, he plonks himself down at the bar in the space we've vacated, ice pressed to his jaw.

"Oh, I know *exactly* who you are." I sneer, picking up the remains of my drink, ready to pour it on him if the opportunity arises. The bruise will heal, but there's no way he'll be able to get a michelada stain out of his pressed pants.

"Isn't he that loser who barfed all over himself at homecoming?" Kenna speaks loudly enough for half the bar to be reminded of one of Bryce's less proud moments. She takes the cup out of my hand and nudges me toward the door. "C'mon, G," she pleads, "it's not worth it."

"But the animals," I say. "What about his tweets about the shelter pets!" I'm this close to throwing the drink in his face.

It's at this point I realize that all around us, people are holding up their cell phones, filming us.

"You're not going to be able to help any animals from a prison cell." Kenna speaks low and calm into my ear and places my bag on my shoulder.

"Fine," I say begrudgingly. I pause to glare one last time at Bryce. He's using one hand to hold the cup to his jaw and is furiously texting someone with the other.

"I have witnesses," I warn. "You've clearly never heard of personal space."

Kenna grabs a fistful of fur and drags me to the door. It reminds me of the way a mother cat moves her kittens.

"Time to go, G!" She firmly shoves me through the exit.

I'm expecting a rush of cold night air as she pushes me. A sharp contrast to the heat radiating from me and the close atmosphere inside. But instead, my breath is knocked out of me as I run smack into a wall—a solid wall of a man sheathed in a dark-gray sweater.

The sweater is soft, at least, I note as my cheek slides across his chest. Cashmere. Has to be cashmere.

Oof.

"Hey! Watch where you're going!" he says. Only when he notices I'm not breathing does he ask, "You okay?"

I gasp. His large, warm hands come to my shoulders to steady me, but they don't linger there long enough to give me any excuses to swing. I shove him back instead. My head is swimming. I'm feeling a little disoriented, which I chalk up to having the air knocked out of me, plus the michelada and too much adrenaline in my system.

"She's fine," Kenna says, squeezing out the door behind me. "We were just leaving."

"Or trying to," I croak.

The man and I do that thing where we both step in the same direction in an attempt to get around each other and end up colliding again. What the hell?

He looks annoyed. Does he think I'm doing this on purpose? Is he?

"Maybe pick a side?" he suggests haughtily.

Because he's backlit by the blinding neon sign just outside the door, I'm seeing more silhouette than details. I can't quite make out his face beyond the impression of chiseled features. He's slim, but solid. Slicked-back, medium-length hair. Clean. He smells great, actually. Shampoo, woodsmoke, and a hint of wet wool. He's so tall. I'm not so sure I could take him. But I'd really like to try, I suddenly think.

Woah! Where did that even come from? Must be all the adrenaline. This is a totally different of thinking. The of thinking that has me wrestling with this stranger and not minding if he ends up on top. Inappropriate thoughts that I have no space for.

My heart is still pounding wildly. I have to get out of here.

I duck past him and race-walk toward the parking lot. But I swear I can still feel his eyes on me, all the way to the car. And somewhat perversely, it's not a problem. I actually like the feeling of him watching me, laser-focused, like a cat hunkering down and following its prey. I shouldn't like it so much, should I?

Kenna and I sit in the car and catch our breath in the quiet for a moment. She shakes her head and turns to look at me. I rub my sore knuckles and stare at my hands. They're shaking.

"You sure you're okay, Georgia?" Kenna asks. I shove my hands into my pockets.

"Yeah, I'm fine, totally fine." I bluff. "You know me. I've always hated the Holms."

"Yeah, I know." Kenna puts the car in gear and spares me her knowing gaze. "Plus, that hottie in the doorway really blew your big, dramatic exit, didn't he?"

hudson

· · ·

I DON'T EVEN MAKE it past the threshold of The Onion before getting walloped by a pint-sized, fur-clad pixie.

She's flustered and clearly seems upset. I suspect I've added to it somehow just by being in her way, but is that my fault? It's not like she owns the place!

"Hey! Watch where you're going!" I say. Then I notice she's not breathing. "You okay?"

"She's fine," her friend says.

I reach out to steady her, then think better of it when her hands connect with my chest, giving me a sharp, angry shove. The neon lights reflect off her glittery fingertips, tricking me into seeing sparks. My eyes travel to her face where her plummy, red lips are tightly pursed. Her lipstick is sparkly as well. Her brows are furrowed, drawn together under thick, black bangs. This does nothing to mar how incredibly pretty she is, though, I note. Long, black lashes and a delicate upturn to her green eyes. Eyes that are presently narrowed, scrutinizing me with what seems like an unfair amount of suspicion.

Quickly, I take a deep breath and hold my hands up by my sides in the universal I-am-not-a-threat position to indicate my neutrality. The last thing I need tonight is another scene in this town involving a Holm. I recognize that I'm much larger than the average man, and that fact alone can be intimidating to certain women in certain circumstances. And particularly, to such a tiny, fairylike one, I imagine.

Facing each other, I step left and she steps right. I step right and she steps left. Now it's like we're doing some of ridiculous square dance, and it's starting to annoy me. Is she punking me? I don't have time for this.

I pinch my brow. "Maybe pick a side?"

I'd been driving for several hours already, and I'm not looking forward to this meeting. I just want to get in, get out, and get it over with.

She deftly ducks under my still-raised left arm, making a run for it. Okay then!

I turn to watch her as she flits off into the night, trailed by her tall, blonde friend. I am surprised to realize that I'm turned on. It must have been the contact. The sudden body slam. She was soft and warm. Also, the smell of her. Maybe the lipstick. Whatever it was, she caught me totally off guard. My eyes stalk her all the way across the parking lot, clocking her confident gait and appreciating the way her shiny hair catches and throws back what little light the night has to offer. Then, just like that, she disappears into the passenger side of a parked car.

I shake my head to clear it and steel myself before heading in to meet my train wreck of a younger stepbrother.

Bryce wanted to do the handoff at some fancy wine bar, but I'd insisted that he meet me at The Onion. Nobody gives a shit about whether you're a Holm or Smith or even a Kardashian at The Onion. It's where I almost always get together with my one remaining childhood friend, Jackson, on the rare occasions when I'm in town. I make a mental note to call him to catch up just as soon as I'm settled.

The interior of The Onion is warm and steamy with people enjoying the generously poured drinks and the savory bar food. A crowd is gathered around the pool table in the corner. Assorted drinkers and diners are scattered around the wood-paneled interior at haphazard intervals. The servers hold trays over their heads as they dance their way around all the makeshift table formations. They aren't even going to try to contain the chaotic arrangement of dragged-together tables and chairs that their patrons come up with. It's all good, as long as it stays friendly.

It takes me a minute to locate Bryce. He's sitting alone, hunched over his phone at the bar, and … is that a cup of ice I see him holding on his jawline? Oh shit. What did that idiot do now?

Last month, Bryce tweeted that there were "more than enough dogs in the world, so nobody should miss a few strays," referring to the animals in the shelter that we'd evicted from the former Farm & Holm warehouse space.

Smooth, especially for someone whose family runs a large, famous, online pet supply website. Make that infamous, now.

In retrospect, we should have anticipated this. The shelter had been operating in our empty warehouse for over a decade. Practically rent free! Not that we're getting any credit for that now. But there's a limit to charity. We couldn't halt the whole project for them. What good would it do anyone if the entire building collapsed?

Of course we could have handled things a lot better. For starters, someone could have—should have—put a muzzle on Bryce. The real estate side of the family business isn't even his area.

Bryce's tweet had a domino effect. It spooked our investors in the warehouse reno, creating cash flow issues. Protesters showed up at the construction site. Reporters are still hounding us for an official response.

Our father, Walker, is right about one thing. The sooner we get Bryce away from Ephron, the better.

I ease into the barstool next to him, pushing aside a nearly full plate of chili fries that smell absolutely delicious. They're still warm. What a waste.

"What's this, now?" I point at his jaw. "Let me guess … you tweeted that drowning kittens is a fiscally responsible solution to feline overpopulation?"

Bryce appears to consider this as an option for a moment before glaring at me.

"Shut the fuck up. I was minding my own business when some psycho bitch attacked me. You just missed it. She and her friend lit out of here!"

"Wait. Was she wearing a black-and-white fur coat, by any chance?" Realization dawns on me. I bite my lip.

"Yes! I think so. Tough girl. Real Amazon type?"

"Hmm … I believe I saw her on my way in." I smile, adding, "She was actually shorter than Lilly." Our little sister, Lilly, is still twelve, but she has the tall genes. Thinking of her makes me smile.

"I don't think so." Bryce freezes, deflating a bit. "But even if she was, you know size doesn't really matter."

"Yeah, some people say that, but I don't buy it." I pull the cup away from his jaw to examine the damage. There's a little swelling, but nothing serious. "Why do I have a feeling that whatever went down, you probably had it coming?"

The bartender chooses this moment to clear away the chili fries and nudges his head in Bryce's direction with a scornful look before addressing me.

"Dudes best learn to keep their hands to themselves, if you know what I mean. I told him he's lucky he's still got the ability to make babies."

Something catches my eye as the bartender goes to wipe the surface in front of me, and I reach out to peel a damp sheet of paper from the bartop. It's a flyer for the same online Petfluencer Challenge I've been participating in for the past month. What are the odds?

"What's that?" Bryce asks.

"It's a flyer for that challenge I told you about. The pet influencer one?"

"Oh, right. That stupid masterclass for crazy cat ladies." Bryce rolls his eyes. Now I'm tempted to deck him.

Months ago, long before the situation blew up about the shelter, I'd tried to get Bryce interested in learning about influencer marketing. His response? Ranting publicly on social media about "all the greedy freeloaders."

Sales on our pet supplies' website have been plummeting. We almost lost one of our top pet food vendors when Bryce mocked their spokesdog—the same spokesdog that's serving as a moderator for the Petfluencer Challenge.

But there's no point in trying to reason with Bryce now. I close my eyes, inhale and exhale deeply, then roll my neck to release some of the tension from my long drive.

"Listen, Hudson, I know what you're thinking," Bryce asserts. "But quit being such a worrywart. That whole influencer thing's going to blow over. And nobody cares about a few dogs in a Podunk town shelter. Wait till we start getting press on the new pet clothing line I just launched. The leeches will be begging us for free samples again, and nobody's going to be talking about that stupid shelter anymore."

"Clothing line?" I ask. Last time I checked, we'd backed off from manufacturing. Too much risk. "Who approved that?"

"Nobody. I don't need to get approval at my own company. Manufacturing is MY area, if you recall. Pet owners go gaga for that shit. Speaking of which, how's your little kitty cat?"

Bryce asks this question with all the condescension a man who's just been decked by a tiny girl can muster.

"Oliver isn't my cat. I'm just watching him for a friend back in Seattle," I state blankly.

"Right." Bryce snorts. "She's gone, Dude. You are such an idiot."

I hate that he has a point. I should have seen the red flags sooner with Ashley.

Ashley works for the company we use for managing and staging our properties. She was living at a hotel near my place in Seattle while getting one of our projects ready to show. What I'd thought might be a perfect, short-term, 'friends with benefits' situation turned into her showing up at my apartment with a suitcase and a cat carrier the morning after an awkwardly aborted one-night stand.

When I'd politely informed her that we were not, in fact, in a relationship—nor was I interested in cohabitation—she had freed the portly, elderly Persian cat from his cage.

"How can you say that, Hudson? We have a cat together!"

She'd then placed her hands over the cat's ears while she played her ace. "I can't take him back to the shelter. They said they'd put him down."

The cat, no doubt sensing imminent doom, had promptly commenced hacking and hawking until he regurgitated a golf ball-size hairball on my white carpet.

At least he'd looked genuinely remorseful about it afterward.

In the end, I'd sent Ashley packing but agreed to keep the cat until she found a more permanent place to live.

"Ashley will come get Oliver when her schedule settles down," I tell Bryce.

In the meantime, it hasn't been so bad for me. Oliver and I have an understanding. He lets me take photos of him for the pet influencer challenge where I'm learning a lot, and I let him stay with me. Occasionally, he gets caviar. He hasn't had any more issues with hairballs since I got him on a healthy diet and regular grooming schedule.

"Sure, sure." Bryce rolls his eyes and presses the sweating cup back against his jaw.

I notice he's still got his wedding ring on. Maybe that's a good thing. Grief about his recent divorce is the angle we're going with in the press release, apologizing for all the tweets. I wonder if anyone will buy it.

"Are you getting back together with your ex, or are you planning to keep that thing on forever to scare away your overeager suitors?" I ask, pointing at the ring.

"Stupid ring. It won't come off!" he complains.

I'm willing to bet that the girl he'd hit on saw the ring too. What a tool. Good for her for punching him. I'd like to shake her hand.

Actually, recalling the feeling of her hands on my chest, I'm thinking I'd like to do more than just shake her hand. Perhaps I'm not so much better than Bryce after all. I'm just better at avoiding messy situations.

And cleaning up after other people's messes.

I push all thoughts of the feisty, sparky woman out of my mind. Back to business. What a mistake it had been to let Bryce stay in the warehouse lofts after he broke up with his wife. He'd offered to "keep an eye on construction" and "make sure things stay on track."

Instead, he'd nearly derailed the entire project.

"Did you bring the laptop and the company phone?" I ask.

Bryce shakes his head. "No point in bringing that stuff. I told my assistant to leave everything at the loft for you." He reaches into his pocket and pulls out a key ring with a key card and a small, electronic fob. "This fob will get you into the parking garage and the elevator. The key card will open the door to the loft. There's a binder on the kitchen counter with all the information you'll need for the coffeemaker, the Jacuzzi, and the security system, etcetera. You'll love the glass-fronted Jacuzzis. I had them installed in the two model units." He looks so pleased with himself as he talks about his completely unauthorized design whim.

"Thanks," I say and pocket the key. We never should have let him stay in the lofts after his wife left him. I rub my temples in an attempt to ward off the tension headache that's looming. Those damned Jacuzzis. We'll never recoup the money and the additional time spent getting permits and modifications together that were done to make sure they were installed to code. By the time I found out about it all, it was too late to turn back.

What's done is done. Tomorrow is a brand-new day. A day when I won't have to worry about any more of Bryce's questionable design contributions. No more Johnny-on-the-spot overstepping his bounds.

The real estate side of our family business is my area, and it's up to me to get things back on track. Hudson to the rescue.

"Still planning to set sail on your little rumspringa tomorrow?" I ask.

Bryce puts the ice cup down and runs a finger along his tender jaw, grimacing then smirking. He seems to think he has the right to gloat about this trip. "Yeah, that's the plan. My driver will take me back to my place in Seattle tonight. I'm flying out in the morning, and I'll meet up with Dad in Bora Bora."

"Sounds super," I say tightly, doing little to hide my disapproval.

Nothing like a little father/son yacht time to celebrate Bryce's latest fuck up. Good thing I'm here to clean up the mess while they take their extended bachelor trip.

"Is there anything else I need to know about? Any other surprise 'executive' decisions you've made? You left me the contact info for the foreman and copies of all the documents for the permits?" I ask.

The warehouse conversion was already well underway when Bryce moved into the model unit, but finishing is often the trickiest part, I know, and it's where budgets can spiral out of control.

Bryce waves a hand dismissively. "Yeah, yeah. Whatever. The lawyer's got all that info. And I'll bill you for my design input."

"The hell you will." I snort.

"Gotcha." Bryce smirks and points his finger at me, imitating firing a gun.

"What about the Feed Co. building?" The original HQ of the Farm & Holm empire has been leased out to local merchants for the past three decades and is long overdue for renovation. It's up next, as soon as we finish the warehouse conversion. "Anything happening that I need to know about over there?

Any blowback from the rent hike notices that went out today?"

"No clue, Dude." Bryce shrugs. "I never go over there, to be honest. People see me and they act like I'm supposed to fix their Wi-Fi and pipes and stuff. Not my problem. I leave that stuff to the management company, and I guess to you. You're the big, important real estate Dude, right?"

"Right," I say. Why should Bryce give a shit about preserving the historic HQ, the building that our family empire was founded in? There are no Jacuzzis or dedicated parking spots for his Ferrari there. The comment about the pipes is a bit worrisome, though. I make a note to follow up with the tenants as soon as I'm settled.

"Well, that's it, then," I say, standing up and offering Bryce a handshake. "Give Walker my regards, and safe travels to you both."

"You're not even going to stay for dinner with me?" Bryce asks petulantly. He feigns being wounded. He's not above playing the wounded orphan card. Both of Bryce's parents abandoned him. First his birth father and then his mom, our former cleaning lady. She'd cleaned out one of my dad's bank accounts and fled the country not long after marrying him. Nine year old Bryce got left behind. Walker adopted him.

That's how I ended up with a stepbrother who is four years younger than me.

Bryce spent his entire childhood in Ephron. He's the one who got to grow up in *my* house. He slipped easily into the role of heir to the Holm dynasty. He's still the one who calls my father "Dad," while I struggle to bring myself to call the man anything but "Walker."

Bryce doesn't feel like he's got anything to prove. Quite the opposite. He's cocksure that no matter how much he screws up, he'll continue to be blessed and accepted, just as he is. My stepbrother is the one who was actually abandoned by his biological parents yet somehow, I'm the one with the abandonment issues.

"I'm sorry, man. I've actually got the cat in the car," I explain. "I want to get him settled in the loft and have a look through that binder you left me before it gets too late. And you probably want to get on the road back to Seattle, too, right?"

"Right," Bryce says. "Hey, I'll send you a selfie when I get to the yacht."

"Be good, Bro." I clap him on the back in a halfhearted half hug. It's all I got.

"I won't be." He laughs. He probably won't be good. At least he's being honest.

"You're going to rock this, Hudson," Bryce says mock-encouragingly as I pull away. And then, as an afterthought, he says, "Don't go taking all the credit though."

"As if you'd let me," I reply over my shoulder.

There's no sign of the sparkling battle pixie or her friend in the parking lot. There's just the moonlight, reflected in the glowing, amber eyes of a large, furry cat waiting patiently on my dashboard.

georgia

. . .

"INCOMING! WITH MUFFINS!"

The bell on the door chimes, and Kenna breezes into Celestial Pets, followed closely by Xander.

Kenna is holding a coffee caddy with three white paper cups in one hand. She has a brown bag full of pastries in the other. Xander is freshly showered, shaved, and impeccably groomed as usual. Not a single fuchsia (this month's color) hair out of place. No doubt he's been up for hours. He's probably gone for a run already and made breakfast for himself and Mac too. All before 10 a.m. Lucky Mac. It's been lonely for me since my little brother moved out of the house we inherited from our adoptive mom. The house I've borrowed tens of thousands of dollars against. I can't even think about it now.

"Oh my God, you smell good." I inhale the scent wafting around Kenna. "Coffee and blueberry muffins should be your signature scent."

"You really could use someone to feed and water you. Too bad I'm not your type," Kenna says. "I brought you a triple shot."

She gestures at the cup, holding three shots of espresso. Kenna is famous in Ephron for knowing exactly what beverage you need on any given day. Her uncanny ability to prescribe the perfect drink has led to a loyal following at the diner. Her barista apron reads "Coffee Witch."

"You should also eat though. I'm assuming you haven't had anything to eat yet this morning," she says.

"No, and I'm famished," I admit. "I was up finishing the mural till 4 a.m. last night."

It's finally done. Just in time to make it into the photos for the article in *Pet Friends* magazine.

"What do you think?" I gesture to the freshly painted south wall of the shop. It's the first significant change I've made to the store since my mom passed two years ago.

Xander stops in his tracks to admire the transformation.

The mural extends from floor to ceiling. There's a starry sky full of pet-themed constellations, each with their own "zodiac" caption. The Milky Way, on closer inspection, is actually a school of tiny fish. "Tag Us!" is spelled out across a sparkling shooting star. Our social media handles are detailed in the tail.

At the center of it all, looking down from above, there's a winking, friendly-faced, smiling moon with the face of Joan Starr, our foster/adoptive mom and the founder of Celestial Pets.

"You know," Xander whistles, gazing at the moon, "Mom would have loved this." He does nothing to hide the tears in his eyes, which of course have the effect of making my eyes leak too. I look away and busy myself, rearranging the muffins on the paper take-out bag.

"Seriously, G, bring it in." Xander holds out his arms. I hesitate, still feeling the burn of a lump forming in my throat. It's too early in the morning to get all emotional.

"Dude, you know you're getting hugged, right? Resistance is futile." Xander tilts his head and flashes his most magnetic smile.

"Fine." I roll my eyes and capitulate. Coming out from behind the counter, I let my not-so-little bro wrap his arms around me. He squeezes me tight in a bear hug. I find myself hugging him back, enjoying the burst of brotherly affection despite my natural inclination to deny myself. It feels so good to get a hug from him.

Xander has always been a force. Everyone loves him. Dogs, cats, small children, grumpy old ladies, hunky philanthropic vets …

"Tell me your secret, Xander," Kenna says. "You're the only one she actually lets hug her." She hands him his usual—an Oat Milk Matcha Latte.

"I just like to keep YOU on your toes so you keep bringing me muffins." I point at Kenna, stuffing a huge bite of muffin in my mouth. "Mmm … you are a goggess," I muse, my mouth too stuffed to properly pronounce my ds. I wash the muffin down with a generous gulp of coffee.

"How many dogs are on your schedule today, Xan?" I ask.

Xander always parks one of his mobile grooming vans in front of the shop on Saturdays, which is a great source of foot traffic for us. Even more so since he has become TikTok famous. People actually follow his van, like a food truck, dropping in to watch him work his magic.

My baby brother is an artist. He has a way of seeing each pet's inner personality, and then bringing that to life in his sessions. Video game characters, super heroes, film classics …

he pulls from it all. You never know "who" is going to emerge from his van. This is exactly what makes his videos go viral.

Xander checks his schedule on his phone before answering. "Six dogs total, counting the stray that got brought into the clinic last night."

I know Xander won't be charging a dime for that one. Kenna will donate the photos, and I'll supply an outfit or two for the cute factor. It's a winning formula for getting pets adopted —fast.

If only I had the winning formula for raising cash fast. I tamp down the tide of worry. There's still a month to go. Maybe I can somehow make the Petfluencer thing pay off?

"So, G ..." Xander pulls his phone out of his pocket and taps and scrolls for a moment before finding what he's looking for. His forehead wrinkles as he frowns and places the phone on the counter. "You want to talk about this?"

I glance warily at Kenna before checking the screen, but she looks mystified and shrugs.

The image is blurry but immediately recognizable. It was taken at The Onion two nights ago. Bryce Holm is sprawled on the ground, and I'm standing by the bar, holding my fist. Kenna is sitting right behind me, eyes like saucers. It's already a meme. The caption is: "This one really hit Holm."

I sigh and push the phone away. "Picture's worth a thousand words, don't you think?"

"Does this have anything to do with the rent hike?" Xander asks.

Now I'm caught off guard. I spin to face my friend and confidante. "Dammit, Kenna! Did you tell him?"

But Kenna holds up her hands defensively. "Wasn't me, G!"

"It's all over the local merchant Facebook group, Georgia. What the hell? Did you think you were going to just keep that from me?"

"It's not your problem, Xan," I say. My cheeks are burning, and I can feel my entire body retracting, tension returning as if the hug never even happened.

"The hell it isn't. This shop may be in your name, but it and the work we do with Kismet is our family legacy. Yours and mine. I'm setting up a GoFundMe right now!"

"No, you're not. I don't want your charity. Plus, it isn't sustainable, we both know that. What happens after we run through that money?" I argue.

And what happens when I can't make the mortgage payment?

Just then, the bell chimes again, and we all look up to see who is stopping by this early. Cookie rushes to greet Kismet's sole, full-time employee. Sun-kissed, no-nonsense and kind faced, Angie was one of my late mom's best friends. She has worked for the pet shelter since the very first day it opened. She's saved thousands, if not tens of thousands, of pets.

Angie is wearing a tennis skirt, a terry cloth sun visor, and a faded sweatshirt with the shelter's logo. Naturally, it's covered with dog fur.

"Uh-oh. Am I interrupting something?" she asks, swiftly reading the room.

"Not at all." I smile at her. "I've got your things in the back." I'd set aside a tiny, tooth fairy cat costume and a bag of gluten-free dog food for her to deliver to a couple of the foster families who were keeping the shelter afloat during the relocation.

"Thanks, Georgia. I thought I'd play fairy godmother and run the supplies by the fosters on my way to my match this morning." Angie smiles. And then she sees the mural. Her whole face lights up.

"Well, would you look at that!" she exclaims. "That's a masterpiece! Georgia, honey, your talent knows no boundaries! Can you believe this girl?" Angie gestures at me, looking for corroboration from Xander and Kenna. "She is an artist, I tell you! A natural artist. As if that clothing wasn't enough." Angie points at the rack where my handmade pet clothing is on display.

Angie has a penchant for dressing up her pets. She loves to feature her own dogs—all seven of them—wearing my designs in the weekly *Kismet* newsletter. She's one of my best customers.

"I'm just going to have a little look through …" Angie picks up a Cinderella Coach-themed pumpkin suit. "Oh, my goodness, Georgia, these just keep getting better! You really ought to do something more with these costumes. You could start a whole clothing line. Maybe once we're settled at the new location, we could plan an event. Like a fashion show. Or a masquerade! Your mom would be so proud of you, Georgia. I know she would!"

But would she? If she knew that I'd mortgaged the home she was so proud to own free and clear, would she still be proud? There's no way I can make the mortgage payment, plus pay Angie's salary, with this rent hike. The rent hike is almost as much as the two other figures combined.

Yet, I can't bear to even think about having to let Angie go. The thought makes me feel sick and dizzy. I duck into the back room to retrieve the items I've set aside for her.

From the back, I hear Kenna offering Angie a muffin. And then Xander pipes up.

"Tell me more about this masquerade idea, Angie," he says. "Sounds like it would be a great fundraiser, actually."

"Absolutely!" Angie enthuses. "We could sell tickets!"

"Ooh! You know what? We could make it a catered event," Kenna chimes in. "Maybe do a live auction?"

"Oh, my goodness! I love this!" Angie exclaims. "We should make it an annual thing! A tradition!"

"Just what I was thinking," Xander says. "It could be a truly *sustainable* way to raise money for the shelter going forward." He speaks louder as he enunciates the word sustainable, making sure he's projecting his voice into the back for me to hear.

As if there's any question about whether I can still hear him in the tiny back room of my tiny shop.

By the time I emerge with the bag for Angie, it's as if the whole thing is decided.

"Georgia, honey, how are you at making flyers?" Angie asks. "We gotta get the word out and put together a planning committee ASAP if we're going to target the week before Halloween."

"But we don't even have a venue!" I protest. "Where are we going to hold a party that size with people and their pets?"

Angie waves a hand, shuffling off this concern as if it's nothing. "Oh, don't worry about that. Something will turn up!"

"So, it's settled, then." Xander winks at me. "We're throwing a Pet Masquerade!" He looks genuinely excited.

"Let's do the planning meeting on Friday. We can meet at the diner," Kenna suggests.

"Sure." I take a deep breath and exhale, smiling politely until Angie leaves the shop and we can talk more reasonably.

"It's not charity," Kenna blurts out the minute Angie is out the door. "We all want to do this AND it could really help."

"C'mon. This could really be good for my grooming biz too. Don't be a spoilsport, G," Xander cajoles.

I can't help but think that this might keep them busy and out of my hair while I figure out a real solution. I throw my hands up in mock surrender.

"Fine. I'm not entirely convinced that this will be the answer to our prayers, and I'm not sure how you think we are going to pull this off without a venue, but I won't stand in your way."

Kenna and Xander exchange a look and a fist bump.

"You two are the worst," I say.

"And by the worst, I know you actually mean the best." Kenna grins.

Abruptly, and probably wisely while they have me where they want me, Xander changes the subject.

"Hey! Did you two catch *Lit Lovers* yet? The 'Enemies to Lovers' episode is out."

Xander is the one who got us all hooked on the local podcast that is about all things romance related. He started listening to the show in the van while he was working, and now he's fairly obsessed.

"I haven't listened to the whole thing yet," I say. "I never know where they're going to go with stuff. It gets pretty colorful at times. I can't safely listen when there are customers in the shop."

"You know," Kenna says, "that episode a made me think about you, Georgia. They were talking about *cat* people and *dog* people." Kenna snickers, and I've got a bad feeling about where she's going with this.

"Wait, what? What's up?" Xander asks, looking from me to Kenna. "Spill."

"She hasn't told you?" Kenna asks Xander. I set down the coffee cup and shoot Kenna a warning look. It doesn't faze her in the least.

"As you know, my big sister tends to tell me nothing."

"I tell you what you need to know," I defend myself. "And this isn't something you need to know about."

"Oh, I definitely need to know now," Xander says, leaning in and urging Kenna to continue.

"So, you know the Petfluencer Challenge Georgia signed up for with her dog?"

"You signed up for a Petfluencer Challenge? With Cookie? And you didn't tell me?" Xander looks incredulous. "Is there a prize or something? Can I give you a shout out?"

"No, Xan. There's no prize, and I don't need your help. See! This is exactly why I didn't want you to know. I'm just doing it to learn the ropes. I thought it would be good for the shop and my clothing line."

"She's burying the lede." Kenna laughs. "She has a *pen pal*. Georgia's got a whole pervy, private chat going on between her dog and some cat in the group. It's just like something off the *Lit Lovers* podcast."

"Ooh, now that does sound spicy! Totally enemies to lovers!" Xander teases, reaching for my phone. I pivot, holding it out of his reach.

"Lies!" I protest, feeling myself blush. "Please, Xander ... I don't have any enemies OR lovers. Who has the time for relationships?"

"He does, apparently." Kenna jerks a thumb at Xander, who smiles and nods like the cat who swallowed the canary. If he wasn't my brother, I would probably want to strangle him. He makes falling in love look so easy.

"It really doesn't have to be that complicated, G," he says. "Why do you have to make everything such a struggle? Let me fix you up with one of my and Mac's friends."

"So I can double date with my little brother?" I roll my eyes.

"I mean, why not? Would that really be so awful?" Xander challenges.

"Xander has a point. You really do need to get out and date more," Kenna says.

I narrow my eyes at her. "Traitor!"

"Okay, then. Maybe you just need to get laid?" Kenna flops into a large, faded and weathered, red plaid wing chair in the corner near the counter. My mom put the chair there years ago as a place for shoppers' plus-ones to land. The fidgety kid, the bored spouse. But it's always sort of been Kenna's chair. She's here so much, she might as well have her place to sit.

Xander leans against the counter, watching us spar, with a this-is-gonna-be-good look on his face.

"Put away the popcorn, Xan," I say. And then I turn to Kenna. "How about you tell me who your date is for tonight?"

"No time. I have to edit this week's photo sessions." Kenna shakes off my question matter-of-factly.

"So, who's the workaholic now?" I hold out a hand. My point has been made.

"But," Kenna amends, holding up one finger, "I'd make time for a date if I was asked. I don't think I've ever had such a long dry spell. I'm starting to have fantasies about the diner's Uber Eats drivers."

"Stay away from the Uber Eats guys, Kenna. I don't think any of them are over twenty-one," I say.

"I'll have you know that Carlos is in his seventies," Kenna informs me. "I bet he was very hot in his thirties."

"Maybe ask his wife." Xander puts an end to the speculation. "Weren't they high school sweethearts? Doesn't she still pack love notes in his lunch?"

Leave it to Xander to have the inside scoop on everyone's love story.

Xander checks his watch and appears to have come to a decision. "I think I'll leave you two to discuss your dream men while I get the van prepped for the day. Kenna, I'll text you to come shoot a few 'before' photos when that stray gets here, cool?"

Kenna holds up and waves her phone, holding it up to indicate she'll be on the lookout for his text.

After Xander is gone, Kenna slouches farther into the worn chair. She opens a dating app and proceeds to swipe.

Swipe, groan. Swipe, groan.

"I don't know why I even bother," she laments. She holds up the phone to show me a badly lit bathroom selfie of a short, hairy, middle-aged man who has somehow managed to match with her.

"Do you see what I see?" she asks.

"The tampons and makeup brushes all over the bathroom counter?" I venture a guess.

"This dude is probably married. Ugh! Dating apps are so depressing! I can't even fantasize about any of these men. You want to have a look?" Kenna holds out the phone.

"No thanks." I refuse to let her pass that grenade. "Something tells me they aren't my type either."

"That guy in the doorway the other night was your type though. Didn't look familiar. Wonder if he's from here or just passing through," Kenna says. "Too bad you were in such a huff about Bryce Holm. You could have asked for his number."

I slow-blink at her and pointedly straighten the "Dogs Welcome, People Tolerated" sign on the counter.

But I can't help thinking about the guy in the doorway at The Onion. He was so solid. So steady. He'd barely budged when I slammed into him. And he was tall. Larger than life. I have a thing for tall guys. Tall, muscular, capable guys who show up and know how to get shit done. Most of my fantasy fodder comes courtesy of my favorite, bingeable show, *Vikings*.

IRL, Ragnar Lothbrok probably doesn't live in Ephron though. He's not out shopping for cat food on a Saturday morning. Anyway, everyone knows that Vikings don't shop, they raid. I imagine Ragnar stomping in and raiding my shop for catnip treats. Highly unlikely, but not a bad daydream. What kind of cat would he have?

My brain immediately furnishes an image of Oliver, my buddy cat, and yet again, I find myself wondering about his owner. What does his owner look like? I can't quite picture him. Or her. Although I'm pretty sure he is a man, since Oliver has described his home as a bachelor pad.

I'm dying to know. What kind of grown man owns a judgmental Persian cat with a penchant for propriety and a stuffy British accent? A nerdy loner? A precocious ten-year-old? Carlos Diaz, the Uber Eats driver? Ragnar Lothbrok?

If only. Whoever he is, he is making the challenge fun. And he makes me laugh.

"So … um … Georgia … helllooo?" Kenna turns on her phone's flashlight and aims it at my face to get my attention.

"So, the 'enemies to lovers' thing. Maybe there's really something to it." She stretches out her long limbs and draws herself back up in the chair. "It's the old opposites attract. Like I'm so boring and so nice. Maybe that's why I am so drawn to bad boys. And you're a dog person, which is probably why you need to date someone with a cat. Maybe a *Persian* cat?"

"Oh sure." I smile cheerfully, all the while shaking my head no.

"Can you imagine me dating a cat owner, considering how Cookie feels about cats?"

Kenna shrugs. "You never know. Has your buddy posted anything else interesting? I'll let you see my Tinder inbox if you let me read your texts with Oliver." She holds out her phone hopefully. "Pretty please?"

"No thanks. I'm not in the mood for dick pics." I decline her generous offer. "And I told you, it's nothing scandalous. Just stupid stuff."

"Fine, but you have no idea what you are missing. One of the dicks has freckles in the shape of a penguin." Kenna sighs disappointedly and pockets her phone. She stands and stretches. "I spoke with Mac this morning. Sounds like that stray is a peekapoo. The poor thing is insanely matted. Should be a huge transformation. Can I pick an outfit for him?"

"Of course!" I wave an arm at the pet clothing rack. "Have at it. Pick some small and medium size options. Pekingese and poodle combo might be either."

Kenna peruses the rack, considering the assortment of my handmade outfits. We're pretty well stocked at the moment. There's the usual assortment of pirates and fairies, but I'm most proud of my outfits that capture pop culture human looks from different eras.

Kenna spins the rack, stops it, and snort-laughs as she pulls an outfit out from the center. "This! This one. This is IT!" She's chosen a mini karate gi and headband a la *The Karate Kid*.

"Please, God, let this suit fit and make sure this dog has a pronounced underbite." Kenna holds her hands together, only half-joking with this prayer, I suspect.

I have to laugh. "Take it. I could not have chosen better myself."

"You know, Georgia, we may not be so lucky in love, but this little dog is about to get lucky. When we're through with him, it's going to be a love match with his forever family for sure!" Kenna clutches the outfit to her heart, grinning.

This … this is why Kenna is my best friend.

hudson

. . .

I'M out for an early afternoon jog on the waterfront when the phone in my armband starts playing the *Pirates of the Caribbean* theme. It's the ringtone I've set up for Bryce and Walker. They're FaceTiming from the yacht.

I settle myself on the cement stairs that lead down to the water, push my sunglasses up onto my head, and take the call. It's still morning in Bora Bora, and Bryce and my father are both wearing colorful, Polynesian-themed shirts and holding breakfast cocktails served up in hollowed-out pineapples. Oh boy.

"Morning," I say. "How's it going?"

"Can't complain." Walker toasts to the camera, then sets down his drink, trading it for a cigar. "We've had decent weather, and the chef is doing a helluva job."

"That's great," I say, feigning interest. I picture the chef cutting octopus-shaped hot dogs for Bryce and arranging my father's breakfast plate to look like a smiley face, complete with eggy eyes. They are both such children.

"Well, it would be great if you'd joined us for once, Hudson!" Walker leans forward, blowing smoke at the camera. Bryce leans back and fans the smoke away.

"Someone's gotta stay home and keep an eye on the business." I keep my tone neutral. We all know that my dad doesn't mean it. He counts on me *not* to come along on these little trips.

"How's the loft?" Bryce asks. "Pretty sick sound system, right? You been in the Jacuzzi yet?"

"I haven't even turned the Jacuzzi on," I say. "Looks like we're a little behind schedule here. I can't see us launching the coworking spaces before the New Year. I think we're going to have to bump the grand opening of the workspace to February and release the residential in waves. The holiday launch sequence was a little overambitious."

Walker looks quickly at Bryce and sets aside his cigar before leaning in. Bryce turns away from the camera. I can see the shadow of a bruise on his jawline. It's hard to read his expression, though, because he's wearing dark sunglasses.

"Okay, Son. I'm glad you're on it. We'll make it work."

"It's a great project," I state. So great that even Bryce's meddling can't screw it up.

It doesn't escape my notice that Walker just called me "Son." I think it's supposed to convey his confidence in me or something. But the word rings hollow and a tad manipulative. I'm here to save the day, doing things and working hours that no regular employee would ever put up with.

Bryce lowers his glasses and leans forward, slurring a bit. "Hey Huds. I'm dying to know. Is your cat trending on TikTok yet?"

Jesus. Is he drunk? It may be the weekend, but it's not even noon there.

"Since when do you have a cat?" Walker asks.

"I'm watching him for a friend," I say.

Bryce snorts.

"I never pegged you for a cat person," Walker muses.

"Right?" Bryce sneers. "He takes pictures of that cat all day long."

"We've had this conversation, Bryce," I say. "The challenge is providing me with vital market insights. Despite your prejudices, pet influencers are critical for driving sales. We need to understand our customers and their problems if we want to sell products that solve those problems." I swat a gnat away.

"Shouldn't you just focus on being Real Estate Jesus?" Bryce asks.

"There's nothing wrong with Hudson taking an interest in all aspects of the business," Walker interjects.

"Don't worry. I'll be sure not to run up any marketing or production bills and derail your projects, Bro. You just enjoy your big-boy Slurpee there." I check my watch. This conversation is getting tedious, and I can feel the resentment seeping in again, darkening my day. I know it's not good for me—or the business—to let Bryce get under my skin like this.

"Uh-oh, Huds. What's that? I think you're breaking up." Bryce slurps his drink loudly as he taps the screen.

"Okay." I stand up. "Just email me your itinerary. Have fun, guys."

"Wait …wait …" Walker stops me before I end the ridiculous call. "Can you give your sister a call? I know she is anxious to see you."

"Already did," I say. "I'm seeing her soon."

"Oh good. Some of her friends are giving her a hard time about the shelter closure and the whole stupid Twitter thing. She was saying she wanted to do something to raise awareness for homeless animals. I don't know. Maybe you can help her think of something?"

"Explain to me again why we aren't just paying to relocate the shelter?" I sigh. It's been bothering me since I heard about the eviction notice. Not that I think we owe them anything, or that we have so much excess cash to throw at this, but the solution to the PR problem seems rather obvious.

"Because we don't have to," Walker says, puffing his cigar. "They already have a benefactor, Celestial Pets. They've been covering the shelter's operating expenses for years."

"But what about their physical location? Haven't we been donating the space to them forever?"

"Yes, we have, and it's been a sweet write-off. But I don't want to open a whole other can of worms when we've already got so much going on. Fact is, we've done plenty for that little shelter, and it's not part of our mission statement to make sure they stay open," Walker says.

"Right? Who cares about a few lousy strays?" Bryce scoffs.

Walker turns to stare at Bryce, incredulous, and looks for a moment as if he might smack him upside the head.

"Are you a moron, Bryce? That is NOT what I said. I said it's not OUR problem to solve right now. We can send them some complimentary supplies or something when they get back on their feet."

"Celestial Pets is the little pet boutique in the Feed Co. building, no?" I ask.

"Correct." Walker nods. "Interesting inventory. Lots of local artists. I'd love for us to carry more of that of inventory online, but you know that folksy stuff doesn't scale."

"Just wait till my new pet clothing line gets some traction, Dad!" Bryce looks smug. Walker looks doubtful. We both ignore his non sequitur.

"Interesting about Celestial Pets. I'll make a plan to stop by and see how they're doing," I say.

I have to wonder how a tiny shop like that generates enough money to support a pet shelter. Even a small one. I feel a momentary ping of guilt about the rent hike notices that just went out. That couldn't have been a happy surprise for them. But just like everything else, the rent hike was necessary. Rates haven't increased for years, and as a result, the building is starting to fall into disrepair.

"Okay, keep me posted. Tell Lilly to text me if you speak to her first," Walker says, and then we really do sign off.

"I'm back!" I call out as I come into the loft. "Come out, come out, wherever you are!"

———

It takes a moment to locate him. He's asleep on an oversize, leather ottoman in the living room. From the entryway, I see the tip of his tail flicking as he dreams. It's stirring up the dust particles, making them sparkle in the sliver of afternoon sun.

"Look what I got for us, Buddy!" I make my way through the living room toward the kitchen, pausing to hold out the bag for Oliver to sniff. "It's fresh salmon." I shake the bag. I'd stopped at the fish market on the way home.

Oliver arches his back and stretches, unimpressed. If anything, he looks annoyed that I've disturbed his nap. He rolls onto his back and plays dead.

"Seriously, Dude? That's all you have to say about this?" I give the bag another shake. Oliver opens one eye and stares at me with an icy look of disdain. The effect is only mitigated by the fact that his tongue is sticking out. Classic Oliver. I snap a pic.

I'm still chuckling as I put the fish away. Oliver rouses himself, jumps up onto the counter, and paws at me to pet him.

"Oh, now you want my attention?" I ask.

He looks expectantly at his bowl, a parting gift from Ashley, along with promises to come back for him as soon as she can.

It's been a while since she's checked in on her cat. I consider sending her the hilarious photo I just took but change my mind at the last minute. She doesn't deserve this photo. Instead, I compose a caption and send the photo off to my Petfluencer Challenge buddy, a punk rock Boxer named Cookie. The caption reads: "You can rest when you're dead."

Cookie responds almost immediately with a picture of her laying splayed, belly up, luxuriating in a pool of sunshine. The light throws rainbow prisms from her bejeweled collar. The caption says:

"I wasn't really naked. I simply didn't have any clothes on."

I laugh out loud. At first, I thought it was weird being paired up like this, but now I'm enjoying the daily exchanges. And I am beginning to see the point. Building an online persona is easier when you have someone to bounce your ideas off. Cookie is the perfect foil for Oliver.

How would I describe her, exactly?

Cookie is a sort of female rebel without a cause. Rock and roll. Rage against the machine. She likes clothing with holes and bright colors. Leather and lace. She eats whatever trash she craves and always says whatever is on her mind. She doesn't take shit from anyone. She isn't afraid of anything.

Oliver Abercrombie Westerhaven Von Dutch Kitty, however, is the absolute polar opposite of Cookie. Maybe that's why the moderator paired us up?

Oliver is exactly as snooty, judgmental, and upper crusty as his purebred Persian pedigree suggests. He eats his food from a custom-engraved, silver-plated, paw-shaped bowl. No dramatic license needed here. Of course, he prefers caviar to kibble, if he's the one choosing. His hair is always perfectly brushed and tangle free. His claws are trimmed regularly, and he would never resort to clawing the furniture.

That part is a flat-out lie, actually. Bryce won't be so thrilled with me when he sees the state of his favorite leather club chair. Oliver has decided to use it as a scratching post, and I can't bring myself to stop him.

Oliver, we've discovered during our daily exchanges, has a very judgy personality. He doesn't approve of torn jeans, foul language, loud music, bright colors, or slobbery dogs. All the things that Cookie loves best.

At the moment, what I love best, apparently, is using my Oliver voice to wind Cookie up.

For some reason, every time I chat with Cookie, I feel seventeen again. She brings out the smart-ass, contrarian me. She says up, I say down. It's a little absurd, but I enjoy the jousting so much that I get a thrill every time my phone pings with an incoming message.

It's possible that it's time for me to seek out other extra-curricular activities. Ephron is a smaller town, but that doesn't mean I have to live like a monk. Surely, there's got to be some women around who aren't looking for anything too serious. Just some fun for a month or two?

I wonder if I might run into the woman from The Onion again if I head back there, say, tonight?

My mind, and then certain other parts, flash back to the visceral reaction I had when she slammed into me. I can still conjure the way she smelled—lemon and white flowers. A hint of something cool, like mint. Mmm. Head back, eyes closed, I take a deep breath and let the image float there a second before wafting away.

Something tells me that she isn't the type to seek out a one-night stand. She'd be all or nothing. Women with that much confidence and fire usually are.

This, of course, only makes me lust after her more. But women like her are dangerous for guys like me. I'm not about to repeat my dad's mistakes.

Typically, when women hear I'm a Holm, they see dollar signs and power. Favors granted. Gifts given. Doors magically flying open for them with VIP valet parking and room service on the other side of the velvet ropes.

This is not what I see. I see freeloaders. More people who expect me to oil the machine and keep everything running perfectly in their lives so that they can keep playing while I pay the bill. What's really in it for me? Besides the sex? Not a heck of a lot.

Fortunately, getting sex without messy commitments has never been that much of a problem for me.

I push the thought of the woman from The Onion out of my mind. Best not to get in over my head. Better to stay focused on the business.

But no harm in chatting anonymously online with a dog, though, right? I pull out my phone.

I hope you're behaving yourself, Cookie.
Doing anything special tonight?

53

georgia

. . .

I SINK into my overstuffed couch with a mug of SpaghettiOs, a remote control, and a much-loved quilt emblazoned with stars and dogs. The shop had a really good day today. Double my usual sales.

But even if I have those kinds of sales for the rest of September, it still isn't going to be enough. I'm dubious about the masquerade. If push comes to shove, I'll just have to sell my car. It will make it hard to get to work, but I'll figure something out. Too bad I can't take Cookie on my bike. Or maybe I sell the house and rent something closer to the shop.

The thought of selling the house hurts my heart. I feel a stab of real, physical pain. It's the only real home I've ever known. Prior to being adopted at fifteen, my entire childhood was a study in impermanence. A half dozen foster homes, some decent but short-lived. Some were not so decent. I learned to make do. There was one short stint with a bio aunt, until she got deported. She hasn't stayed in touch.

Kenna, who was adopted at birth, has often asked me what I recall about my birth mom. But the truth is, not much. I can barely recall living with her before she and Xander's dad died on his motorcycle.

What I can recall is my anxiety when nobody came home that night, or the next day. I was five years old, and I'd never been left alone with my infant brother for that long before. I had no idea what to do. I warmed milk in the microwave to make him a bottle when we ran out of formula. I'd eaten my cereal dry to make the milk last.

This isn't a memory I like to dwell on. I pull the quilt up and around my shoulders and conjure a different flashback. Choosing fabrics with my mom. Cutting out the stars and dogs. She'd signed us both up for a quilting class, and it really wasn't her thing, or mine, at the time. But she'd insisted we stick with it, leaving the design to me, as well as a fair amount of the stitching. It was how I learned how to sew. Wrapped up in the quilt, I can almost still feel her presence. Almost. Even after two years, I miss her so tangibly.

I shovel pasta in my mouth, pausing to rewatch Xander's TikTok transformation of the stray dog from earlier today.

The rescue peekapoo, whom we all agreed to call Mr. Miyagi, had indeed had an adorable underbite. Xander was able to salvage enough long fur at the top of Mr. Miyagi's head to give him a canine man bun. That little dog had *owned* the karate suit. We'd uploaded the photos on Petfinder immediately, and by the end of the day, there were already fourteen applications from families wanting to adopt him.

This is such a win. This is what makes it all worth it.

Cookie curls up beside me as I scroll through some of her photos, cropping and adding filters. I select a shot of her with her head sticking out the car window, tongue out and cheeks flapping in the wind, and add a funny caption: "Good girls go to heaven, bad girls go everywhere."

"Okay, Cookie, let's see what Oliver has to say about that," I say before checking my messages in the challenge portal. There's one new message in my inbox.

I hope you're behaving yourself, Cookie.
Doing anything special tonight? It's been a
quiet day here. My flatmate was out for
several hours, leaving me to my own devices.
I took the opportunity to make a detailed list
of all shelves that need dusting, clothes that
need ironing, and silver that needs polishing.
The bachelor pad is in quite the
unacceptable state. My human's standards
are slipping.

Silver that needs polishing? What a little weirdo.

        I'm surprised he doesn't polish the silver with
        you, Furball.

I start to reply in the messaging center, but before I can hit send, a message pops up inviting me to chat live. Apparently, Oliver is online too.

Eight o'clock on a Saturday night. Interesting. I guess we're both dateless losers. I smile.

Good evening, Cookie! I'm surprised to catch
you at home. Have you been naughty again?
Are you grounded?

        Who says I'm not going out, Oliver? It's only
        8 p.m. Last call's not till 2 a.m.

Well, don't let me keep you from your revelry,
though I do worry about a vulnerable, young
lady such as yourself finding herself alone at
such an hour in a disreputable tavern.

        Relax, I'm not going anywhere tonight,
        Furball. Last night was a late one. I've got a
        hot date with the sofa and a can of
        SpaghettiOs.

May as well play it safe and stick close to the truth, I figure. But it's more my own truth than Cookie's. In real life, Cookie is on a special diet, and SpaghettiOs would wreak havoc with her guts—certain doom for my new rug. Fortunately, my iron constitution is A-OK with the Os. I scoop around the tiny frankfurters, saving them for last.

> Do you really think that's prudent, Cookie?
> I'm concerned you aren't getting proper
> nutrition. Surely, your owner has some sirloin
> somewhere for you.

> Yeah, right. What's cooking for you tonight,
> Oliver?

> My owner is preparing us pan-seared salmon
> with a garlic and tomato reduction, blanched
> broccolini with sage brown butter, and garlic
> mashed potatoes. Unfortunately, we have run
> out of caviar, but we are making do.
> Desperate times ...

> Wow, fancy-pants!

> Cookie, please tell me you are not eating
> your meal straight out of the tin again.

Guiltily, I glance down at my favorite oversize coffee/soup/pasta mug. Ridiculous. Of course I wasn't eating my food out of the tin.

> No, silly, you can't put the can in the
> microwave.

The three dots indicating that Oliver is typing appear, then disappear, then appear again. In the meantime, I flip on the television and type *Pride and Prejudice* into my streaming TV's search box.

So, what else is on tap for you this evening,
then? Planning any home piercings?

> Tattoos, actually. I thought I'd tattoo a big
> heart with your name on it across my left butt
> cheek, and it's going to say: 'I heart Chonky
> Cats.'

*Oh, dear. Do Boxers even have butt cheeks? I do hope you
are taking precautions to sterilize everything.*

> Good point, Furball. I guess I won't be inking
> your name on my furry bottom after all.
> Actually, my owner is putting on a movie.
> Something about a podcast she heard earlier.
> Pride something?

You aren't referencing Pride and Prejudice,
are you?

> Uh … maybe?

I look at the search results that come up. That Jane Austen
book is popular! There are at least a dozen movies and mini-
series versions to choose from. Or, I could just watch *Vikings*, I
think, missing my nightly Ragnar time already. Why did I
have to pick *Pride and Prejudice*? Jane Austen isn't particularly
edgy. Why hadn't I told him I was watching a horror film?
That would have been much more in keeping with Cookie's
voice and would certainly get more of a rise out of Oliver.
Stay in character, Cookie, I remind myself. He's typing a
response.

> Well I certainly hope you are watching the
> 1996 BBC production with Colin Firth. As far
> as we are concerned, there really is no other
> modern production that quite does the book
> justice.

I click on the information button next to the BBC version's thumbnail. Four episodes? Six hours? I might as well read the book. Hard pass. And then I see the perfect title. Just what I need.

> Actually, we'll be watching Pride and Prejudice and Zombies, Oliver. Have you seen it?

Zombies? Oh, my. I don't think I have seen it. And here I thought I'd seen every modern film version of the Pride and Prejudice oeuvre.

Oeuvre? Did he really just type the word oeuvre? For the hundredth time, I wonder who the human behind the voice of Oliver really is. I want more. I *need* more. I fish for a clue.

> Um ... Oliver. Can I ask you something personal?

That depends. A gentleman has his secrets.

> What's an oeuvre?

It's a body of work.

> Yeah, I know. But I can't believe you just used it in casual conversation. Will you take my SATs for me, Oliver?

You know I would never stoop to participate in such a sordid deception, Cookie.

> Ok, but how about your owner? Would he?

I wait and hold my breath as the three dots come and go again. There are no explicit challenge rules about not talking *about* your humans. You just can't speak AS your humans. Surely we can reveal some minor details without giving up our real identities? I had deliberately called Oliver's owner a "he." At the very least, I'm about to suss out if my assumptions are correct about that.

> What makes you so sure my owner is a man?
> Oliver calls me out on my move.

> Well, you called your place a bachelor pad.

> And your owner, Cookie? I'm assuming she
> is a she?

> Oh yeah, she is, Oliver. She's as badass as I
> am, and we like to party together.

This is true if you include watching Netflix and eating SpaghettiOs from a chipped mug while wearing old sweats and a Joy Division Concert tee in your definition of partying.

> Ah ... well, my owner is indeed of the male
> persuasion, Cookie.

I compose my next question and then tap my fingers slowly and wickedly, considering it for a moment before I commit.

> So, Oliver, would you describe him as hot?

Asking Oliver whether he had a hot owner is totally something that a direct, in-your-face Cookie would ask, right? It isn't like I, Georgia Starr, am sending a so-what-are-you-wearing text, is it? Honestly, I feel about twelve years old right now.

I take a deep breath, hit send, and squeeze my eyes shut. He pings back immediately, and I open one eye to read.

I don't know, Cookie. I do suppose he cleans
up well. He doesn't seem to have any trouble
getting dates. Not thatI've been terribly
impressed by them. Lately, it's just the two
of us.

Interesting … very interesting.

And what about your owner? Is your mommy
betrothed or otherwise engaged?

I smile, seeing what he's doing there. I have to give him
props. In one short sentence, he'd asked my age *and* marital
status. Possibly because of Cookie's youthful and rebellious
voice, he's picturing her owner as an angsty teenager. He is
about a decade too late for that.

She's single. Very single. And all she does is
work. When she's not partying with me, of
course.

Hey Cookie? Are you watching your
movie yet?

Not yet, Oliver.

My owner is sitting down with our dinner, and
he's been surfing for something to watch. I'm
not so sure I approve of him partaking in a
meal on the sofa, but he does look tired, so I
suppose I'll allow it just this once.

It's ok if you have to go, Oliver.

The stifling silence of the room I'm sitting in suddenly settles
around me. Back to my lonely Saturday night, basking in the

ghoulish glow of my Roku search screen. I'll probably be asleep by ten.

> Actually that's not what I had in mind. I hate for my owner to have a hole in his Pride and Prejudice oeuvre expertise. I thought we might watch Pride and Prejudice and Zombies … dare I say … together?

> Are you asking me on a date, Furball? Don't you have to get permission for that or something?

> Oh heavens, let's not get ahead of ourselves, dear Cookie. We're just two domesticated animals watching a movie together on a Saturday night. Let's not put a label on it, shall we?

> It's a deal. Hit me when you're ready.

And then I lean back, cue up the movie, and wait to hit play.

———

Several times during the movie, I find myself reaching for my design sketchbook. The costumes are exquisite. Right up my alley with their Victorian sensibilities crossed with a twist of badassery. It gives me ideas for a Steampunk collection. I can totally imagine Cookie in a corset with a holster. I wish I had more time to sew.

I set the sketchbook aside when we message.

> She really shouldn't have gone off with that Willoughby rogue

> Who the hell does Darcy think he is, anyway? Lizzie doesn't need his protection.

I am never eating another housefly again.

Oliver writes this last message during the scene when they use houseflies to suss out the Zombies. I have to laugh at that.

Curled up on the couch beside me, Cookie twitches and trembles restlessly. She's probably dreaming about running away from cats. I feel slightly guilty to be impersonating her so shamelessly. And I'm surprised at how easy our conversation is. At no time during the film did I feel lonely or weird. I should feel weird, shouldn't I? This isn't exactly a normal interaction. But watching a movie with Oliver is so fun!

I'm not even sleepy. I seem to have found my second wind.

Things only get a little awkward when the credits roll. The film is over and, now what? Time to go for a walk? I don't want to stop chatting. I feel like I have to say something after five minutes of silence. The credits are going to end soon.

Well, Furball ...

I begin to type in the chat box, preparing to wish him a good night. Or peace out. Or whatever Cookie would say. Smell ya laters? See ya, wouldn't wanna be ya?

Oliver texts before I can hit send.

You still there, Cookie? I just checked the challenge prompts while the credits were rolling. Have you had a chance to peruse it? This week's posts involve costumery. We have been advised to "dress for success." I do hope you'll find yourself something befitting/appropriate to wear.

I will wear whatever I damn well please, Oliver. You're not my boss, and you probably wouldn't recognize fashion if it landed in your cat bowl.

If he only knew! Of course, I'd been looking forward to this week's assignment, pulling some of my favorite handmade outfits for Cookie to wear. A hot-pink wig, a leather jacket … I am pretty sure I'll be photographing Cookie in the "Boss Bitch" T-shirt I made for her at some point this week. In fact, I was planning on having her wear it when the reporter came in for the interview.

> I daresay I might regurgitate some of the getups that you call fashionable, Miss.

Rude.

> Well, I do prefer wearing nothing at all, of course, if you would rather see me that way.

I can't resist a saucy smile when I hit send. Oliver responds with a cheeky blushing emoji.

Suddenly, I remember the shot I sent him earlier, with the quote about being naked. Sparring aside, I was proud of that one. I don't want to end the chat without hearing what he thought.

> What did you think about that shot I sent earlier today? The one in the sunshine?

> Interesting capture. Was that for the natural light prompt?

> Yes! We shot in morning light and used portrait mode to get the blurry effect in the background, outside my shop window.

> Your shop, you say?

I smack myself on the forehead. Stupid, stupid, stupid. And I was doing so well. I can't believe that after an entire night of chatting without messing up, I would slip out of character now.

Um ... yeah, whatever. My owner has a shop.
She keeps me there. I'm her bodyguard.

Interesting. What kind of shop is this? Would
I have heard about it?

Never mind. Doesn't matter.

I have a keen mind for business myself. If
you should ever feel yourselves in a pinch.

The thought of him advising me out of my current predicament is just ludicrous enough to refresh my mood.

As if I would ever take advice from a CAT!

Well, you seemed to like my advice when it
comes to your photography.

Technically, he is right. He's given me some great tips on how to get better shots from my phone.

Fine. You do have a knack for phone
photography, Oliver.

Well, then I suppose I can concede that you,
my dear, DO have an eye for pet fashion,
Oliver writes. Which leads me to a request.
Perchance you might do me a favor?

Hit me.

This next assignment seems like it's more up
your alley. Got any wardrobe suggestions for
a crotchety, old, Persian cat?

Might I have any suggestions? How ironic.

I had just successfully avoided telling "Oliver" the details about my shop. So, what if I recommend Celestial Pets to him now as the perfect place to purchase an outfit? Where to start? Surgeon cat? Salty fisherman? Those would be freaking hilarious on Oliver. I can think of a half dozen ideas for him—some that he might even think are "suitable." I'm itching to start designing something right now.

But of course, if I invite him to shop at the store, I might figure out who "Oliver" really is. Would I be violating the rules of the challenge? What if I don't like him as much in real life and I still have to work with him?

Too risky.

I'm not sure I want him to know who I am in real life either. I'm not looking for his pity purchase. Best not to tempt fate.

> I have one piece of critical advice for you, Old Man.

> Pray, do tell.

Oliver shoots over a cat emoji and some praying hands.

> Check out some sites like Etsy. Buy handmade. There's nothing worse than showing up in the same damn outfit as every other cat. You're better than that. Plus, big-box companies and fast fashion are killing small biz.

> Sounds expensive!

I hope I'm not laying it on too thick.

My face gets hot. I can actually feel myself blushing. Once more, I resolve that I will never *ever* let Kenna read these texts. She'd have an absolute field day and for sure accuse me of being a closet furry. I've said enough for one night. Time to wrap this up before it gets any weirder.

hudson

. . .

"RODNEY! Stop splashing your brother! He's already soaked!" a young mother admonishes her son as he dashes around the fountain, pausing to throw water at a smaller sibling who is careening after him.

I pass the plaque and dedication to my great-grandfather at the center of the square, beside the large gazebo. Despite my long absence, Ephron, WA still feels like home to me. I have to begrudgingly admit this.

Perhaps it's the familiar imprint of making most of my earliest memories here. Park bench picnics with my mom. Watching fireworks in the town square. The "before" days. Before my parents divorced, before I got whisked away to a Swedish boarding school at 12. Before my father remarried his cleaning lady, then the au pair, starting his second and third families.

The park is full of afternoon visitors. The benches are populated by clusters of gossiping moms pushing strollers. Bouncy toddlers eat snacks off their trays while older siblings run and play together.

There are some teenage boys by the gazebo stairs, doing tricks on their skateboards in a blatant attempt to impress a group of girls sipping brightly colored smoothies. Although they're a few years older, the girls make me think of my sister, Lilly.

Except, if Lilly were here, she'd probably be the one showing those boys how to land their jumps.

Perhaps if I'd spent a little more time here, that would have been me and Jackson skateboarding in the park. I snap a photo of the town square and text it to my old friend.

> Same old Ephron. Weird to be sitting here. Get together soon?

He responds immediately.

> At a conference this week, but next week for sure! You should come on my podcast. We can riff about prodigal sons returning.

He punctuates his text with a devil and winky emoji.

This reminds me to add Jackson's podcast to my queue. Apparently, he has a wise-cracking podcast that is all about romantic literature and culture. I haven't had a chance to listen to it yet, but it doesn't surprise me at all that my tech-guru friend is into romance novels and has a literary podcast.

Jackson's always been a bit eccentric. As a kid, he liked to run statistics for superhero story arcs. In his late twenties, a very successful IPO on his first startup made him wealthy. He's now free to do whatever he wants, which, at the moment, includes teaching logic at the local college, building new apps, and apparently, this podcast. I add *Lit Lovers* to my queue before I forget and then look for a place to sit for a moment. I need a few minutes to process and just be here.

There's one mostly open bench a few yards away from the fountain. A tall, angular blonde girl in an apron is sitting alone, off to one side. Her blonde hair is twisted in a curly topknot, held together with a pen. She's entirely engrossed in whatever she's doing on her tablet. It looks like maybe she's editing photos.

"Mind if I take a seat?" I ask.

"Sure, sure." She waves a hand magnanimously without taking her eyes off her screen.

I sit down and relax a bit in the sunshine. If you've lived in the Pacific Northwest long enough, you know what comes immediately after these idyllic fall days. Long, dark, wet winters. Best to soak up as much vitamin D as you can while you can.

Light filters through the sprawling sycamores, dappling the ground. The air smells of earth and juniper. I watch as the mom of the splashing boys hands them shiny, copper pennies to toss into the fountain.

That fountain's been refurbished recently, I note. Gone are the elaborate, bronze downspouts and copper snails I recall loving. Now, the water pops up from hidden jets, at irregular intervals, landing with a sploosh. The smaller boy shrieks with delight when a sudden spurt startles his big brother.

I recall tossing pennies here as a child, too, though I can't imagine what I might have wished for at that point in my life. Everything was pretty idyllic back then. I do recall believing my great-grandfather was the one who granted the wishes. I'd half-expected him to pop up out of the fountain himself, like a dungaree-clad, mid-nineteenth-century version of a genie.

"Hey." The girl suddenly looks up from her tablet, scrutinizing me. "I think I know you."

"I highly doubt it." I smile, lowering my sunglasses and leaning back with my eyes closed. I fold my arms across my chest, enjoying the warmth of the sun on my face. She couldn't know who I am, could she?

It isn't all that often that I get pegged in the wild as a Holm. But when it happens, it makes me uncomfortable. Every time. I'm not interested in celebrity, local or otherwise. Given my family's recent bad rap, and the local merchants' reaction to the rent hike, it's not necessarily a good thing for me to be recognized.

"No, really," the girl says, and I can feel her gaze still on me. "I *know* you. You ran into my friend outside The Onion the other night. That was you, right?"

I open one eye and turn my head to get a better look at the girl. She's staring openly at me with wide, cornflower-blue eyes and a completely guileless smile.

I sit up a little straighter and raise the sunglasses.

"That human missile was your friend?" I ask. I'd noticed the battle pixie wasn't alone, but frankly, I was so taken by her, I'd barely taken stock of anyone else.

"Ha! Human missile!" The girl snorts loudly. "Love that. I'm Kenna, by the way," she says. She sticks out her hand.

"Hudson." I extend my hand to shake hers. Just Hudson, for now.

"So, Hudson, you live around here?" Kenna asks, and I can tell she is fishing for something. Perhaps she's just curious about the new guy in town? I'm definitely not getting any flirty vibes from her, which is just as well. She seems perfectly nice, but not really my type.

Her friend on the other hand …

I *have* to stop thinking about her friend. I'm not looking for a relationship, I remind myself. I think of my dad's multiple marriages. Bryce's imminent divorce. It's a family curse. I have no desire to jump out of the frying pan and into that dumpster fire.

But a part of me still wonders. What if … what if I were to meet someone who has no idea who I really am? Will I still have to be that guy? I haven't felt such a strong and instant spark of attraction in a long time. It's difficult to just let it go. Had she felt it too? And if she finds out who I am, will it still feel the same?

Probably not, considering she decked my brother. Clearly, she is already plenty familiar with my family.

Just like that, my fantasies of meeting someone new without having to unpack the Holm baggage evaporate in the late-afternoon sunshine.

"I'm in town for a few months," I say. "We'll see after that." This is the truth. I'm not going anywhere for at least six months. Not until after I've cleaned up Bryce's meddling with the new construction and fully launched the warehouse loft conversion.

It's going to be a long, lonely stretch if I don't start making some friends besides Jackson. But how exactly am I supposed to do that in this town where everyone literally already knows—and loathes—my name?

"I hope you like soup," Kenna says.

"Soup?" I give her a quizzical look.

"This great weather's not going to last, Bud. Come November, it's going to be serious soup weather."

I smile. She's right. "Actually, I'm quite fond of soup. And I make a mean bowl of chili."

"Can't be better than the diner's famous black bean chili," Kenna argues. "Although word to the wise? Take some beano before you eat it. Your whole family will thank you."

"Ah!" Understanding dawns on me as I take in her apron, the small notebook in her apron pocket, and the pen in her crazy bun. "You work over there?"

"My uncles own the diner. I help them out. I'm their barista." Kenna grins.

"Coffee Witch?" I read the words embroidered on the front of her apron. "What exactly does that mean?"

She raises her eyebrows and smiles enigmatically.

"It's just a thing I do," she explains. "I can intuit the perfect drink for people just by looking at them. And when they drink it, everything in their life goes a little better."

"I imagine that's pretty magical for business," I agree. "But do you think it's the caffeine or the power of suggestion?"

"Oh ye of little faith." She shrugs again and smiles mischievously, suddenly reminding me of Lilly. "Some people say it's life-changing."

"Just don't call me a flat white," I say.

She makes an apologetic "eek" face, as if that was exactly what she was about to say.

"Stop!" I laugh. What a curious conversation this has turned out to be. No hidden agendas that I can suss out. She doesn't seem to need anything from me. It's refreshing. But bound to be short-lived. It's only a matter of time before she learns who I am. And tells her intriguing friend. It's a pity, really. A part of me wishes I could stay incognito. Just for a few more days …

"Sorry, Hudson. My powers don't always work outside the diner."

"Right, of course." I laugh.

"I have to get back to work now. But stop by for a coffee later?" She suddenly stands up.

"Maybe I will. After I run my errands," I say.

"Make sure you check out the pet store." Kenna smiles knowingly at me. How could she know I was headed to the pet store? Perhaps I'm not flying as far under the radar as I think I am?

"Why is that?" I ask, a little suspiciously.

"Because you've got a little something there." She laughs and points.

Gazing down, I see a clump of tan cat hair clinging to my pants. I vaguely recall Oliver winding around my legs while I was on my Zoom calls earlier. I pick the fur off, letting the breeze take it. And I make a mental note to get myself a tape roller.

"It's a super-cool store!" Kenna says over her shoulder. "You don't want to miss it!"

"I'm headed there next." I smile.

"Café Vienna?" Kenna calls out, momentarily walking backward, then shaking her head to veto it. "No, no … that's not it. I swear the magic doesn't work outside the diner."

"I'm just a regular Joe!" I laugh.

"Yeah, we'll see about that," she says with a final wave as she spins and strides off back to the diner.

As I stroll across the square, I text Lilly's mom, Mel, to confirm the details for picking up my sister tomorrow night. I suggest I meet her in Holm Square by the fountain.

> Lilly is SO excited to see you. Mel texts back
> and adds in a smiley face emoji, a flower, and
> three pink hearts. And so am I. I can't wait to
> see my favorite stepson.

Winky face. Flames. Red heart. Eggplant. I sigh.

My father's third wife stands a little too close and hugs me a little too long. I'd call her a cougar, but she's the same age as me, thirty-five. This isn't the first time she's sent me a string of confusing, potentially inappropriate emojis. When called on it, she acts shocked, feigning wide-eyed innocence.

> Any ideas about what Lilly would like for her
> birthday? I'm out shopping, and I want to
> pick something up.

I text Mel back, ignoring the eggplant in the room and bringing the conversation back to my soon-to-be, thirteen-year-old sister.

> Graphic novels? Video games?
> Skateboarding stuff? I've tried to get her into
> clothes and makeup, but she's not
> interested.

Sad face. Faceplant. Rainbow. Easter Island Guy.

Easter Island Guy? Perhaps she doesn't actually know what she's doing with the emojis. At least I hope that's the case. The thought of a sinister, sexual, hidden meaning behind the Easter Island Guy is going to haunt me now.

> Thanks, Mel. Tell Lilly I'll see her tomorrow.

I slide my phone into my pocket and cross the street.

Most of the Main Street businesses opposite the park-like town square are largely unchanged, still familiar to me from my childhood. You can't miss the iconic Ephron Diner, with its striped awning and sandwich board specials out front. Celestial Pets, the tiny pet store, still has pride of place—front and center in the block-long, two-story Feed Co. building.

I browse the other shop windows before making my way in. The florist shop is selling some nice home decor items, succulents, and potted plants in addition to the standard floral arrangements and bouquets. A gourmet wine and cheese shop has replaced the candy store. There's still the same toy store on the corner. I remember pressing my nose against the glass at Christmastime, gazing at the holiday display. It's a little early for that right now, but the store window is full of skateboards and penny boards.

As I'm gazing at the rainbow-colored decks and fluorescent-colored wheels in the toy store window, a twenty-something man in sweats and a beanie jogs past me. I spot the reflection of the dog running alongside him. It's a Boxer and looks just like Cookie.

I spin around, just in time to catch one last glimpse as they round the corner. Could it be? But this dog's owner is very clearly a man. So, no. Not unless I'm being catfished. Which seems unlikely.

I dismiss the thought. There are probably dozens of Boxers in the Ephron area. It's a relatively common breed. I just haven't ever noticed before.

I run a hand through my hair and turn back toward Celestial Pets. The sign above the door is weathered and the awning is faded, but the items in the window are unique. Everything looks fun and colorful. It's the sort of place I might want to shop, if I had a pet.

I can see there's a rack of pet clothing in there. It occurs to me that maybe they'll have something for Oliver to wear for this week's challenge prompt. I might pick a few things up. Even though he's not technically mine. I'd probably prefer this stuff to anything in Bryce's new collection, even without Cookie's "shop local" lecture.

Suddenly, I'm excited to check the place out. I want to learn more about their relationship with the shelter, maybe feel them out about how they are doing in light of the recent rent hike. I want to understand how they've managed to fund the shelter and stay afloat for the last twenty-five years. I'm curious to speak with the owner. According to my records, the name on the original lease is Joan Starr.

I head into the pet store, picturing an older woman as the eccentric owner. A real pet fanatic. Hopefully, not the type who knits items from salvaged pet hair.

But there's nobody in there who fits that description at all.

The only person in this store is the battle pixie, and she's looking even more luminous in the light of day.

georgia

. . .

IT'S JUST a normal Tuesday afternoon when Ragnar walks into my shop.

Technically, this dude is not a legendary Norseman, but damned if he doesn't look like one. He confidently strides in —sort of like he owns the place—pauses, and has a look around. He turns to look at me, and a hot shiver snakes its way down my spine. His eyes travel around the shop slowly, devouring everything in sight. They seem to say he is satisfied with what he sees and he will claim what he wishes.

I think that I might have binged a few too many episodes of *Vikings* last week. Time to move on to something else. Superheroes, perhaps. Of course, the first one that springs to mind is Thor. I've clearly got a thing for Norsemen. Chris Hemsworth has nothing on this dude.

Ragnar turns to face me. "Is the proprietor of the shop here?" he asks. "Joan Starr, I believe?"

I narrow my eyes. The proprietor? What is he, some kind of salesman? Is he here to hand me some kind of legal notice? There's also something vaguely familiar about this guy ... his voice.

"Joan passed away a couple of years ago," I say matter-of-factly. "I own the store now. But we've tried to keep her spirit alive here."

Ragnar studies the star-studded wall and Joan's portrait on the moon. "Hmm … interesting mural," he says. He glances back at me again for a minute, then continues looking around, really examining the various items in the shop, picking up things, one at a time, and looking them over. It's as if he's taking stock. Surveying. Calculating. It's almost as if he's doing mental profit and loss statements in his head, deciding what might be the most valuable commodity to fill his boat. Should he go for the hand-tooled, leather leashes or the cast-pewter collar charms?

How odd.

Stealthily, I watch him, playing a little game I like to call "Guess the Pet." It involves trying to guess what kind of pet —species and breed—a customer is shopping for. I am usually pretty good at this game. Aside from the clues that make it easy, like a pug-themed keychain or a sweater full of cat hair, most people have a pet personality tell of some sort.

The cat shoppers are more aloof, taking their time, making circuitous loops around the store. They don't really want suggestions, just to be left alone to make their choices. The dog shoppers head directly to the products they need, asking enthusiastic questions and lapping up advice.

Small pet people are harder to suss out. The rabbit and guinea pig owners vs. bird and lizard people can be tricky. We don't get many fish people. The store is too small to stock aquarium supplies.

I don't see any visible pet hair on Ragnar's clothing to indicate what sort of animal he owns. His own hair is also impeccably groomed. Medium length, streaky blond, with a slight wave. Surfer hair in another place or season. He wears it swept back from his face. There's no hiding those deep, deep-blue eyes and strong, sculpted features. Even though he's blond, he's not too fair. This makes his blue eyes stand out all the more.

He is also very tall. His larger-than-life presence practically fills the entire shop. I can see the shape of hard, lean muscles through the wool sweater he is wearing. Hang on … is this the guy from The Onion? Could it be? My mouth drops open, and I forget to look busy while I'm checking him out.

Ragnar notices me staring and meets my eyes, smiling slightly. Knowingly. For a long moment, he holds me in the tractor beam of his gaze. Then he turns and takes three long-legged steps, crossing the store to the clothing rounder.

He's moving fast like a big cat, but directly like a dog. Still can't tell, dammit.

I get a glimpse of his butt and catch my breath. I shouldn't be staring at a customer's ass, should I? In my defense, between his height and my seated position on the barstool, his ass is right smack dab in the middle of my line of sight. Plus, it's perfect. Round. Firm. Seaworthy. I can picture him standing at the helm of a bucking ship.

What the hell is wrong with me?

"Um … can I help you with anything in particular?" I offer. Dog or cat? Which would it be? I shake my head, trying to dislodge the inappropriate thoughts and return to a safe, professional space.

One thing's for sure. There's no way he's a snake guy. I can always spot them a mile away.

"Do you think this would fit a small dog?" Ragnar holds up a British judge costume from the cat costume section. "And these?" He pulls out several options, including a cop suit, surgical scrubs, and a wizard's robe-and-hat combo I'd sewn tiny, star-shaped beads onto.

"It depends on the breed. Do you have a dog?" I ask, abandoning my guessing game.

"Um … Affenpinscher? No, wait. Brussels Griffon? I always get them mixed up. Sorry, it isn't my dog. It's my little sister's," he says.

"I think they would be fine," I say. "The important thing is that they aren't restrictive or uncomfortable. It's essential that your pet is happy in their costume. We have a generous return policy if the clothing doesn't fit or if your pet hates it. Is your sister local?"

"She's not too far," he says, "but she doesn't drive."

"Well, if you're not too far, you could always bring them back for her, as long as it's within our thirty-day return window," I say.

"Thirty days!" he exclaims. "That's awfully generous." And then he takes another look around at all the stuff in the shop again. "Seriously, thirty days? For everything?"

"We want our customers to be happy and feel confident about their purchases." I fold my arms across my chest and raise my eyebrows. What's his problem with our return policy?

"That's definitely generous for pet supplies," he says. His eyes are twinkling, but there's no mistaking the strong note of Judgy Mc Judgment pants from him. He walks over to the wall and examines Joan's face in the moon.

"Is this Joan?" he asks. "She looks familiar. I think I remember her. She was nice to me when I came here as a kid."

"You came here as a kid?" I ask. This is surprising. I certainly would have remembered if a teenaged Ragnar had walked into the shop while I was on duty. He has to be what, mid-thirties?

"Yeah, when I was a preteen. I lived Ephron till I was twelve." He smiles. "We didn't have pets, but when my parents first split up, my mom got a dog. I thought I won the lottery."

"That's sweet," I say, further studying his openly handsome face and dreamy eyes. I try to imagine his younger self coming in for dog treats, and Joan extolling the virtues of pumpkin purée and coconut oil for a dog's digestive tract.

"Not really. They sent me off to boarding school a couple of months later. So … no pets for me!" He holds up his hands, empty palms, to the ceiling for emphasis.

"You can still always adopt," I point out. "There are plenty of animals around here that desperately need good homes."

"I prefer to keep things uncomplicated," he says. "But it's nice to see the shop is still here. How's business these days?" There it is again, that slightly calculating, stocktaking interest. Not like a normal customer. He places ten outfits on the counter, along with some freeze-dried salmon nibbles. Ten outfits! Who buys ten fifty-dollar pet outfits all at once?

Then again, who am I to question a massive sale? Mama needs rent money. Literally.

"We do okay," I say. "You do know these treats are supposed to be for cats?"

"Yeah, but they say right on the package that dogs love them, too, right?" He holds up the package. It says that the treats are beloved by dogs as well and are safe for human consumption, but I've never been tempted to try them.

"True." I nod slowly. Ragnar picks up a Lucite standee from the counter. It's a permanent display detailing the importance of our work with the Kismet Shelter.

"So, a little shop like this must make a decent profit in order to be able to do such significant charitable work," he says, making a question sound a lot more like a statement. He is still looking around the place like he's planning a heist, but then his eyes shoot back to mine and he smiles quite warmly and genuinely, as if he actually cares. It disarms me.

"I think it's amazing that you're doing this," he says. I feel a sizzling sensation in my belly, like I've just swallowed a scoop of pop rocks. My hands shake a little as I remove the hangers from the costumes.

"It's always a struggle being a small-business owner," I admit. "Our rent is going up at the end of next month, and we'll have to hustle a bit. But this place is practically a landmark. We have a loyal customer base. Good people who know we support good causes and who believe in shopping local."

"Shopping local …" He repeats the phrase. "I've been hearing that a lot lately. I guess it's nice if you have local options and can afford them. But you know, some people can barely afford the cost of regular kibble, let alone vegan dog biscuits. What about them?" he challenges, a hint of disdain in his tone. It's as if he thinks vegan dog biscuits are the most ridiculous idea in the world and shops like mine are frivolous. But then, why is he even shopping here?

He pulls out his wallet and counts out a stack of hundred-dollar bills. "Cash okay?"

Seriously? Who the hell walks around town looking so damned hot, then ambles into a pet boutique and peels off six hundo, all the while acting like he's the Robin Fucking Hood of dog snacks?

He shocks me—literally—when he hands the money to me. There is an actual spark of electricity that travels between us. I jump back. He laughs.

"Damn, woman." He shakes his head with a wry smile. "You okay? That's some high-voltage carpet you have in here. Or maybe it's just you?"

Okay, I totally hear it now. The voice sounds similar. I really think it might be the same guy from The Onion. I wish I'd gotten a better look at him. All I'd really clocked was his height. I'd been too amped up after hitting Bryce to notice much else.

I raise a brow, starting to get suspicious. Had he come in here looking for me? "So, what brings you back to Ephron?"

"Work. Probably be here a few months at the very least," he says, eyes twinkling. "Maybe we'll *run into* each other again?"

He continues to look directly at me in a way that's giving me thrills, and then chills. I'm having temperature regulation issues. Is he or isn't he that guy?

"Maybe." I tear my gaze away and shrug, doing my best to look noncommittal.

As I wrap his pet costumes in tissue and place the rest of his goods in a gift bag, he peruses assorted flyers on the counter and bulletin board. I steal a few more quick looks at him, doing my own stock check. He is not merely handsome. He is also well put together. I watch as he takes one of the flyers that Kenna made for the masquerade planning committee meeting on Friday. He folds it carefully, tucking it into the back pocket of his well-tailored pants.

Everything he is wearing is expensive. There's no obvious labels or brands that tell me this. It's all about the materials. Even as an amateur designer, I can spot this. His shoes are high-end leather, probably Italian. The sweater has got to be merino or cashmere. And all credit to his perfect ass, his pants fit like they were made for him. Then again, given his height, he probably has to have all his pants custom altered.

I look down at my own outfit, feeling underdressed.

I'm surprised that this man is so openly flirting with me. My combat boots, tattoos, hand-knit, black tunic, and tiny nose ring usually tend to ward off the more affluent, polished, corporate types. Why me? Shouldn't he be out hunting for a trophy wife? Some lulu lemon-wearing, Gucci purse-carrying, Range Rover-driving type who will hang on his every word and book reservations for them both at all the right restaurants?

I am not that girl, I think. That is not my comfort zone. But what exactly is my zone, then?

I recall my recent virtual "date" with Oliver. That had felt totally comfortable. I am a SpaghettiOs, on-the-couch kind of girl.

Ragnar leans across the counter to take my business card and adds it to his bag. I notice that he also smells really good. So good. Woodsy. Clean. Sexy. Oh, wow. I'd seriously like another hit of that. I want to inhale him deeply and savor that smell.

But what I really need is to hear him speak some more so I can figure out if he really is that dude from the other night. As if there is really any question. My body is already telling me he is. I am having the exact same, totally uncharacteristic reaction to his nearness. It's like I'm turning into a werewolf, and he is a big, juicy steak. This isn't normal.

I take a step back. I need to extricate myself from this situation before my hormones and brain conspire to make me even crazier. I can't afford to have these kinds of feelings. Ragnar is fire. A fantasy, for sure. But only that. And probably, my reaction is due to how long it's been since I've hooked up with anyone. Maybe Kenna is right. Maybe I just need to get laid. I can feel my heart thumping and try to put the thought of wrestling with Ragnar out of my mind. Way far out.

The problem is, now that he's in there, I can't seem to evict him. It's like he, and he alone, is fully occupying the lust apartment in my imagination. Shit. I can't handle IRL Ragnar. He's too much. He is the polar opposite of no drama.

Perhaps I can go back to wondering what Oliver's owner might be like? As ridiculous a notion as that seems, it feels a whole lot safer.

I hold out Ragnar's bag and he takes it, his fingers grazing mine. No shock this time, just a compelling warmth I'd like to lean into.

"That diner next door any good?" he asks. "I could use some coffee …"

"Um … yep, sure is. It's the best," I say, shoving his change at him now. I have to get this guy out of here—and fast—before I lose my last scrap of sanity.

"Can I grab anything for you?" He raises his eyebrows, and his eyes glint mischievously, inviting me to engage in this dance. I am tempted, so tempted, even though I know it probably would never work. I know I need to resist. Even if it's just sex. Looking at him, I have the uncanny feeling that a one-night stand with him wouldn't be enough. I'd want more. Much more.

Shut that down now, Georgia!

Emotional attachments, even far-out, fantastical, potential ones, are a luxury I cannot afford right now. I can't afford to open my heart up again just yet. Or possibly ever. But certainly not when I've already leveraged myself to the hilt in order to save the people, places, and things I already love. More emotional attachments = more risk.

There's too much at stake with the store, the shelter, and my house to even indulge in this fantasy for a second longer.

My hands drift to the pawprint constellation tattoo on my left wrist, and I rub it absentmindedly, a habit I've had for years when I'm nervous.

He's still waiting for me to answer his coffee offer.

"No, thanks." I smile blandly, retreating into a robotic shop-keeper persona. "I'm good."

"Okay, if you say so," he says. He looks a little disappointed but recovers quickly. "Thanks for the help here." He holds up the bag and waves before ducking out the door. "See you around!"

And then he's gone.

The bell's tinkle seems to reverberate in the air for a moment before everything becomes still again. I'm not sure if the lights are suddenly dimmer or if I'm imagining it. Perhaps the sun has just slipped behind the clouds.

Thirty minutes later, my phone buzzes with a flurry of incoming texts from Kenna.

> So … what did you think? Tell me everything!

> About what?

> About the MAN, Georgia. The tall, sexy, Viking man who was just in your shop!

> Oh. You saw Ragnar?

> He just left the diner. That's not his real name, btw.

> I don't know his name. I just call him Ragnar in my head.

You recognized him from The Onion, though,
right? Did you apologize for running into
him? Get his number?

Of course he was that guy. Had to be.

Nope. Man drama is the last thing I need
right now.

Are you crazy? He's 1000% your type. I
couldn't have ordered a more Viking-y guy
for you from a catalog.

What kind of coffee did he get?

Suddenly, I'm dying to know what our resident coffee witch prescribed for Ragnar.

Hold on. Give me five. I'm coming over

Before Kenna has a chance to get over here, Xander jogs into the shop with Cookie. Her bright-pink tongue is hanging out, and she is panting hard. After slurping up a bunch of water, she makes a beeline for her dog bed behind the counter and collapses.

"Looks like you two had fun at the dog park?"

"I ran into a few of my customers and got roped into a discussion about the ethics of pet hair dye," Xander says.

That explains why he was gone so long. Xander could give a Ted talk about pink poodles.

I bend over and give Cookie a pat. "Thanks for taking her. I know it's your day off. She gets so bored cooped up here sometimes."

"No worries. I love going to the dog park." Xander grins.

Suddenly, the bells shake so hard they clatter, and Kenna bursts in, holding a cup of coffee like it is the holy grail. She holds it out to me. "You have to taste this."

"What is it?" I ask.

"Just taste first, then I'll tell you."

I sniff the coffee. It smells delicious, actually. Smooth and roasty, but not overwhelming.

"Are you sure you want caffeine this late in the day?" Xander raises his eyebrows.

"Shut up, Grandpa." I roll my eyes and take a sip. Oh, that is good. Even better than the usual Kenna stuff.

"What is that? What did you do to that coffee?"

"Right?" she says. "I think I'm calling it Ragnar's Gift."

I stop inhaling the brew. "Wait, what? Why Ragnar? What does he have to do with this?"

"Seriously? I cannot keep up with you two." Xander holds up his hands in protest. "Who is Ragnar, and what does he have to do with coffee now?"

"Ragnar is a character from Norse legend," I tell Xander. "Just try the coffee." I pass the cup.

"Mm-hmm … you're not sick or anything." He looks dubiously at me.

I roll my eyes again and shake my head. "No, and I didn't backwash either."

"Fine." He sniffs and takes a cautious sip. "Ooh. That IS really good."

"You are not going to believe what's in it," Kenna says, looking smugly from Xander to me and back.

"Uh-oh." Xander pushes the cup back at me. "Do I actually want to know?"

"Eggs!" Kenna laughs.

I attempt not to do a spit take. Eggs? What the …?

"By the way, Ragnar asked me to make this one for you, G. He asked me to bring it over too."

"Back up." Xander spins a finger as if he can rewind our conversation. "Who is Ragnar, and why are there eggs in my sister's coffee?"

"His name is not really Ragnar," I tell Xander. "He's just some random guy who came into the shop earlier today—"

"She's only telling half the story," Kenna interrupts. "He's a really HOT guy. Totally G's type. The whole Viking package. And it's not the first time they've met. She slammed into him when we were leaving The Onion the other night. And now they're going to fall madly in love and make a tribe of terrifyingly good-looking Viking babies!"

Kenna grins, sighs, and clutches her chest as she collapses into her chair in an exaggerated Disney princess swoon.

I ball up a paper napkin and chuck it at her. She catches it and lobs it back at me, hitting me in the face.

"So, spill. What kind of coffee did you make for him?" I throw the napkin away.

"He didn't order anything for himself," Kenna says matter-of-factly. "He perused the entire menu and quizzed me about all the drinks, and then he asked me if I'd ever had Fika with eggs and we got to talking."

"Fika?" Xander looks at me. I shrug.

"Fika is the Scandinavian term for a coffee, usually enjoyed with friends." Kenna sighs. "I already knew that. But what I didn't know, and honestly, this is a little embarrassing, professionally, was the proper method for brewing Fika."

"Which is? Don't just stop there," Xander prompts, suddenly onboard with the whole story.

"The eggs!" Kenna practically jumps out of her seat when she blurts this out, like she's just guessed the winning answer on a quiz show. I suspect she may have had a little too much coffee herself today. "You put a whole egg, shell and all, in with the coffee grounds. It's alchemy. No bitterness whatsoever. A little extra work, but really unique and special. Don't worry, the egg actually gets strained out before it's served. I can't wait to add it to the secret menu!"

"There's a secret menu?" Xander looks stricken, as if we've been holding out all these years.

"Basically, it's a list that only exists in Kenna's head." I snort. Not that it matters. Everyone over there is pretty accommodating when it comes to special requests.

"So, this mysterious Ragnar clone pops in, teaches you how to make this magical egg coffee, and then has you bring it over for Georgia?" Xander asks. "Now I'm swooning. It's like something from a movie."

"It's pretty amazing, right? He said he wanted her to have it, with his compliments."

"Hmm," I say, taking another sip. Dammit, it is good. So good. But none of this makes sense. "Did he say anything else to you?" I ask. "Like, did he ask you any questions that seemed unusual?"

"You are so suspicious," Xander accuses. "Isn't it possible that the dude was just into you, G?"

"Maybe," I say. "But he was asking a lot of questions about the shop when he was here. I got a weird vibe. What else did he ask you?" I grit my teeth and set the coffee down.

"He asked how business was, if we were busy. And if I liked working in the diner. And he asked about YOU," Kenna recounts. "He wanted to know how long you've been the proprietor of Celestial Pets."

"I think he's scoping us out," I say, feeling the pilot light of my temper about to get lit. I knew it. Someone like him would never simply flirt with someone like me. "He probably works for some big chain store that's just waiting to swoop in and take over our space when we can't pony up for the rent hike."

Anger surges, filling the empty spaces left behind by all the other feelings that stretched me out earlier. By comparison, anger feels safer. More comfortable. It gives me something to do. A problem that I can solve.

"Calm down, G. Nobody's kicking us out. We have a lease, remember?"

"Tell that to coffee guy. He's breathing down our necks, just waiting for the chance to jump in and take over our spaces. He was probably spying on us the other night. He's … he's a bad egg!"

"Jeez. I really didn't get that impression, G," Kenna says. "He actually seemed pretty nice to me."

"Well, you trust everyone!" I argue. "Haven't you said that's your whole problem with dating? You're too nice and you just keep attracting assholes?"

"Thanks for the warning, G, but it wasn't me he was into. For some reason, he seemed really anxious to get to know you. But we all know you don't DO relationships, right?" Kenna prickles.

That's the problem with best friends. They always have your number. Instantly, I feel a twinge of conscience for my harsh words. She didn't deserve them.

"I'm sorry," I mouth at Kenna.

"I know," she replies, forming the words without sound.

Xander sighs. "Look, we're not accomplishing anything with this speculation. It's almost five. Are you guys doing anything tonight?" He checks his phone. "Let me call Mac and Angie. I'm going to head home for a quick shower, but maybe we can meet back at the diner and get some more of the details for the masquerade hammered out over dinner. We can nail down the catering and call some of the vendors to see if they want to participate in the silent auction."

"I'm in. We can brainstorm potential locations too," Kenna suggests.

"Definitely. And come up with a plan about how we're sharing this shakedown on social media?" I say, looking at Xander.

"OMG. So now you're cool asking for my help?" Xander looks shocked.

"We need to leverage every advantage. I'm not going to just roll over and let Ragnar ruin everything!" I say. "We have to update the website too—ASAP. Do you know how to do that?" I ask.

"Yes, ma'am!" Xander nods happily.

I'm suddenly feeling so much more empowered. I'm going to do what I do best. I'm going to come out swinging.

"By the way, dinner is on me tonight," I announce.

Smiling victoriously, I reach into the cash drawer and pull out the stack of hundred-dollar bills, fanning myself dramatically.

Big mistake.

As I wave the money around, I catch the briefest lingering whiff of Ragnar. Not Ragnar the enemy, who I'm presently poised to vanquish. Ragnar with the smiling eyes and solid chest … the fantasy man whose flirting and mere presence had nearly driven me to dive under the counter and hide from the possibilities.

I really hadn't wanted to want him so much.

I inhale deeply, trying to remember and record his smell, but it's so faint. It's already gone. A familiar song you're trying to recall in a passing car. The ice cream truck heading to another block on a blazing-hot summer day.

Ragnar smells like all the things I'm grasping for that I can never have. He's just out of my reach.

hudson

. . .

WHEN I GET out of the shower, Oliver is there, sitting on the back of the toilet. He's staring disappointedly at me and the towel that's on the floor.

"Okay, I'll hang my towel properly this time." I pick it up.

He hops down and follows me into my closet, looking doubtful as I choose my clothing for the day.

"It's perfectly acceptable to wear sweats when you work from home," I say. "Besides, you're just going to shed all over me anyway. I'm not getting dressed up for that."

This is getting ridiculous, I think. He's not even my cat.

I pull up Ashley's contact info and text her a photo of Oliver attempting to groom himself while sitting in a shoebox in the closet. It's way too small for him, but he seems to think he fits there.

Your cat is nuts.

She gets right back to me.

95

I pull on a hoodie.

Surprisingly, I feel a wave of relief washing over me. October is not too bad. It means that I'll be able to finish up the influencer challenge. And at least Oliver will get to spend some quality time here in the loft. He really seems to like it here. The oversize windows are perfect for birdwatching and napping under.

"C'mere, Furball." I scoop Oliver up and carry him down to the kitchen to feed him his breakfast. He purrs loudly as I get out the bag and tucks in while I'm still pouring the kibble.

I pour myself a cup of coffee and add some almond milk. The color is almost exactly the same as Oliver's fur. This gives me an idea, and I play around with perspective a little, snapping photos from different angles. Finally, I get the one I'm trying for. It looks like Oliver is sitting inside the coffee cup. Even funnier than a too-small shoebox. I think the technical term for photos like these is "getting mugged."

I send the message and coffee photo off before settling into the chaise lounge by the window. I've got a clear view of the river and mountains in the distance. Even though it's only been a little over a week, I'm enjoying watching the season shift. The leaves are starting to change colors. Sitting here and sipping my coffee while instant messaging with Cookie is becoming my new morning ritual.

> Hey Oliver. What mischief are you up to
> today? Closet org?

> You know me so well. I've got a full workday
> ahead, but I thought I'd check in with you
> first. How's it going?

> Big day tomorrow. I'm trying on outfits. What
> do you think? Dressed for success?

Cookie shoots back a photo of herself in a "Boss Bitch" tee and a pair of heart-shaped sunglasses.

> Such language!

I add a shocked-looking cat emoji.

> Hey, where's your "dressed for success" pic,
> Furball?

I realize that I've been calling Oliver "Furball" a lot lately, and it's probably because of her.

> Still working on it. But I promise it's going to
> be great.

> Better be, she says. Our next prompt is …
> interesting. A little weird. Maybe we should
> talk it out. Are you ready to explore your dark
> side with me?

> Please, I'm perfectly well adjusted.

Am I? Am I really? I consider the fact that I'm having a conversation with a dog right now. But it's for work. I'm exploring the world of pet influencers. This is what I keep telling myself, anyway.

> Ha! I'm not buying it. You didn't get this
> uptight by accident. Spill, Ol. Tell me your
> deepest, darkest fears.

She's referencing this week's prompt. In order to make our characters more believable, we're supposed to create some posts dedicated to their flaws, their deepest fears, and their guilty pleasures. We are essentially creating our pets' back-story. This is where we learn why they are the way they are.

I'm drawing a blank on this one. Since Oliver appeared in my life at the ripe old cat age of eleven and came from a shelter, I don't have many details to work with. I could make up a story for him, but it doesn't feel quite right. Plus, I've already established him as a persnickety eater, a clean freak, and a stickler for following the rules. What kind of kittenhood trauma might be responsible for all that? My fingers pause over the keyboard while I try to compose something witty or funny, worthy of this cat.

> Does my coffee addiction count as a deep,
> dark secret for this assignment?

> No, Oliver. Your coffee confession is lame.
> Everyone is addicted to coffee.

The cat jumps up to nestle beside me, tucking his head under my arm and rubbing his whole face enthusiastically on my elbow.

> Ok then … if you must know, I'm afraid of
> being forgotten.

I improvise, imagining a past life for Oliver where his owners moved on without him.

Who could forget a cat like you? she replies.

You'd be surprised. Out of sight, out of mind. Does anyone wonder how their butler is doing while they're on vacation?

That's a weird analogy.

Not really. I'm here to serve and amuse my humans. Until they get bored with me, and ... I don't know, replace me with a kitten?

That's really shitty of your owners, Oliver. They should have more respect for you and value you much more.

Thanks, Cookie

I feel strangely gratified. Cookie is good people. Or rather, good dog. She's a good dog.

So, what happens when they get the kitten? Do they leave you by the side of the road?

Oh, no. Nothing that dramatic. They just ignore me till the cute, little kitten makes a mess. Then they remember me and how great I am at cleaning up messes.

How does the thought of being replaced by a cute, little kitten make you feel, Oliver?

Invisible? Used?

That's so wrong. You should crap in your owner's laundry basket. That would get their attention.

I would never do anything so inappropriate! If anything, I go to the other extreme. The more they ignore me, the more compelled I feel to curry their favor. I'm constantly torturing myself with my shortcomings. Like, maybe if I had opposable thumbs and could actually fold the laundry, they'd be more likely to bring me on vacations with them.

Do your owners know you feel this way, Oliver? And have you considered that they might be afraid of you? I mean, you are pretty perfect. I've never met a more competent cat. It's intimidating. I'm scared of you.

How could a badass "Boss Bitch" like you be afraid of a stuffy, old cat like me? Your type eats cats like me for breakfast.

Looks can be deceiving.

…

She sends this message and then types some more. The three dots come and go, and after a bit, it's clear that whatever she was about to say, she's changed her mind.

Tell me more, Cookie. What is it you're hiding?

Oliver, this can go no further than this chat …

Pinky Swear

I follow up with a pawprint.

Well … I'm afraid that everyone will figure out I'm not really so tough.

I'm nothing special, just your run-of-the-
puppy-mill stray. I know how to take care of
myself because I haven't really had any other
choice for most of my life. And I look out for
my people too. But it doesn't mean I don't
get scared. I'm so scared I'm afraid I'm going
to let my people down. And if I don't take
care of everything, who else will?

You know I've got your back if you need
anything, right? Not that I don't think you're
up to the task. I'm just worried that you're
not sufficiently supported.

I pat my pocket, feeling for my keys. As if I'm going to jump
in the car right now and go rescue her. From what? Or whom?
A thousand silly scenarios flash through my imagination.

Ok, but you don't count. You're a semi-
fictional cat.

Fair enough. So why don't you ask for some
help? I'm assuming you have family and
friends. Isn't that what they're for?

I ought to know. Saving the day for my family is my full-time
job. Not that it brings me joy most of the time. It actually
brings me a fair amount of bitterness and resentment. But my
family is hardly typical. And it's hard to know who your true
friends are when you come from a family dynasty like mine.
Everybody wants something. A piece of the Holm pie.

I find myself scowling, and I stop petting Ollver. He nips me
gently, hoping I'll continue. I lift him up and remove him to
the floor. Then I picture myself growing old, alone, and bitter.
It's not a great vision.

Ironically, I didn't feel bitter or resentful when I just offered to help Cookie out. I'd meant it. It was a genuine offer. This is a surprising gut check. Almost as surprising as the realization that I am kind of dying to help out this anonymous fictional dog. Some crazy part of me wishes I could rush in like a hero and fix all her problems.

Not because I have to. Because I *want* to. I really want to.

Cookie starts typing again, and I wait for the three dots to disappear as her message comes through.

> I guess I don't want their help because I don't want them to have to worry. I want them to feel safe and protected. I want them to rest easy.

> That's really sweet in a way, Cookie. Who knew what a big softie you are under all that studded leather.

> More like control freak! But I'm also afraid that the minute I let my guard down, something really bad will happen, you know? It usually does.

> Like what?

I have this overwhelming desire to give Cookie a hug right now.

> You know what's worse than being ignored, Furball?

> Finding cat crap in your clean laundry?

> Nope. Guess again, sir.

> I give up, Cookie. What's worse?

NOT being ignored, because there's literally
nobody out there to ignore you.

I scroll back to the goofy, cocky photo of Cookie that she sent at the beginning of this conversation and try to will the sentimental lump out of my throat. Who could ignore a lovable dog like that? What a crime!

She's right, actually. Being ignored isn't so bad in this context.

Are you still afraid of being abandoned,
Cookie?

You never know. People change their minds
and make stupid decisions. They kick the
bucket unexpectedly. Shit happens. Real shit
you can't fix. Not just the kind in your laundry
basket.

Shit indeed. Our usually fun conversation has taken a decidedly dark turn today. And yet, I don't regret a thing. If anything, I feel closer to Cookie than I've felt to anyone in a long time.

You know what? At least we have each other.
I'm not going anywhere, and I've got your
back. From now on!

I insert a smiling cat emoji in a sad attempt at levity.

About that. That's the other thing…

Please don't say you're planning on ghosting
me the minute the challenge is over?

No, it's not that. It's just that I'm not sure if
our relationship can stand the test of time. I
wasn't joking when I said I was afraid of you.
It's not just you though. It's cats in general.
Cats scare me silly.

It's true. My other secret fear is that I'm afraid
of cats IRL. I can't deal with your species,
Furball.

I'd never hurt you, Cookie. And I'd never
abandon you either. I happen to be rather
fond of your kind.

It's not lost on me that I'd never make these kinds of promises
to a woman I was casually texting with. But Cookie is not a
human. She's safe from the Holm curse.

Thanks. You're pretty ok for a weirdo. For the
record, I'd also never ignore you or crap in
your laundry basket. I think your family
sucks. You're too much of a national treasure
to be ignored or taken for granted. Save your
energy for the people who will appreciate
you. Cats like you don't come along
every day.

Validation hits me like a revelation. It's ridiculous, really, how
"seen" I feel. Actually seen. Not as Oliver, but as myself.
Years of therapy and it comes down to this. What finally hits
home is the simple wisdom of an anonymous Internet canine
oracle.

You know, you can just say no to them.

I think for a moment before typing my reply, hoping to be as
useful to her as she has been to me.

I think you are wise beyond your years,
Cookie. Not sure what circumstances made
you that way, but don't forget that you don't
have to do it all alone. You're pretty lovable,
and you might want to consider letting others
take care of you. Don't rob them of the
chance to demonstrate how much you mean
to them.

Feeling a bit drained, I get up to pour myself another cup of coffee and process the conversation. A few minutes go by. Neither one of us types again.

I sit back down on the chaise and scroll through Instagram, catching up on my feed, liking reels, and leaving comments on a few other hash-tagged pet feeds. Then I click back to Cookie's profile and scroll back through some of her posts, revising my impressions based on this new information about her. If anything, I think I like her more.

I notice her follower count has almost doubled.

I see you've gained several new followers
this week, Cookie. Well done.

Thanks, Oliver. I promise I'll still be your
friend when I'm instafamous and fielding all
the collab requests.

Collab? Pardon? Is that a Collie or a
Labrador? Or both. Heavens, Cookie. Are
you sure you're up for a threesome? It
sounds like exploitation!

I smile as I tease her. Our usual banter-y conversation is back on track. Why do I love winding her up?

Collab = Collaboration. That's when big
brands pay you to rep them, Boomer. Why
are you even doing this challenge?

Not too far from the truth, actually. Cookie would probably make a great mascot for the Farm & Holm website, if she were so inclined.

Abruptly, Cookie quits the chat, leaving me wondering what exactly her duties are. I'm more curious than ever about her owner. Who is she? What does she do?

But of course, when I try to picture a face on that owner, the only face that comes up for me is the woman from The Onion and the pet boutique. I'm still stuck. I still can't stop thinking about the battle pixie.

I can't help imagining what it might be like, for example, if *she* were up for a totally different type of collab.

———

Later that afternoon, I head back to Holm Square to pick up Lilly. It's quieter today. Most of the moms and kids have already gone home to make dinners and do homework and whatever other mysterious routines rule in suburbia. I can barely remember.

I observe my sister from behind as I sneak up on her. She's sitting on a bench, tossing coins into the fountain. She's inherited the Holm height and has the same blonde hair as me. I'm struck by how much she's grown since the last time I saw her. That chubby toddler I remember so fondly, and who seemed to morph overnight into a sporty little spitfire, is now a lanky tween, poised on the cusp of something else. There's nothing "baby" left, but Lilly's also still very much a girl. She isn't trying to look older than her age like so many tweens do. She's about to turn thirteen, which I know, from friends and past girlfriends, can be a tricky time. Lilly seems to be weathering it better than most, and for this I am grateful. I feel a surge of protective brotherly love.

I've never begrudged Lilly anything. From the moment she was born, I've adored her. Despite the fact that we've never lived in the same house and that her mother has always been such a problematic presence for me, we've managed to forge a bond. Weekends at my place in Seattle and holiday visits with her have been supplemented with FaceTime and online gaming. She got me hooked on Animal Crossing.

Maybe it's not the most typical sibling bond, but I wouldn't trade it for anything. As far as I'm concerned, Lilly is one of the best things that's ever happened to this family.

"Penny for your thoughts!" I pluck an AirPod from her left ear and place it in mine. "Woah, The Cure? Since when are you into them?" I keep the AirPod in and listen to the chorus of "Love Cats."

"The Cure is classic!" Lilly jumps up onto the bench, turning to face me. Standing there, she's practically the same height as me.

I embrace her in a bear hug.

"What have they been feeding you?" I ask. "You're huge!"

"Hudson." Lilly frowns sternly. "Hasn't anyone ever told you that you aren't supposed to comment on a preteen girl's body and size? You could give me a complex. I could spend years in therapy, explaining that my body dysmorphia started when my big brother called me huge."

I clap a hand over my mouth. "OMG, Lilly. I am so sorry. I didn't mean it that way. I mean, all of us Holms are tall."

She laughs and jumps down, pulling a skateboard from under the bench. "Shut up! I'm just messing with you. I love being taller than half the boys in my class. Keeps those mouth breathers in their place!"

I heave a sigh of relief.

"Make any good wishes?" I ask. "Has Great-Grandpa popped out yet to grant any of them?"

Lilly laughs. I'd shared my childhood fantasy with her when she was very young, and she'd fallen for it hook, line, and sinker.

"No, it was more like target practice," Lilly says, rolling her board under one foot. "I try to get the pennies to land in the jets. It's fun to watch them shoot up with water when you do. I was thinking, more than wishing."

"Wishful thinking?" I ask, sticking out a toe and stealing her board.

"Hudson!" she protests, but I can't resist. I take the board for a lap around the fountain.

"Not bad, old man," she says.

"Don't forget who got you your first deck," I say. "And you should be wearing a helmet."

"It's in my backpack." Lilly rolls her eyes and pulls a black-and-white marbled, sticker-covered helmet from her bag. "You want to borrow this before you give yourself a head injury?"

Sheepishly, I step off the board and hand it back to her.

"How about we buy some ice cream, and I take you back to my place for dinner? There's someone I want you to meet."

"Oliver!" Lilly looks excited. "Is it Oliver? OMG, I can't wait to meet your cat."

"He's not my cat," I say. "I'm just watching him for a friend till she gets settled."

"Right, sorry," Lilly corrects herself. "I can't wait to meet your temporary houseguest. He's a shelter pet, right?"

She kneels to put the helmet back in her backpack and pauses for a moment, staring across the square toward the Celestial Pets pet shop. Then she cocks her head at me.

"What do you think about the situation with that pet shelter, Hudson? Don't you think we ought to do something about it?"

"I dunno, Kiddo. I spoke to Walker about it, and he seems to think the situation is already being handled by our friends over there."

"Yeah," Lilly says doubtfully. "I heard the owner of the pet store decked Bryce last week. Not that he didn't have it coming."

"How did you hear that?" I ask.

"Social media." Lilly rolls her eyes at me like I'm her grandfather. "Heard of it?" Even as she ribs me, Lilly can't hold back a smile.

"Anyway," Lilly says, "I'm not so sure how handled the situation really is. I saw this flyer on the door over there." She takes out her phone and pulls up a photo of the same flyer I'd pocketed in the shop—the one for the masquerade planning committee. I grab the phone and study the photo while she zips up her bag and slings it over her shoulder.

"If they've got it so handled, how come they're planning a fundraiser all of a sudden?"

"Dunno." I shrug. "It's not our problem though, Lill."

"Fine. Maybe it isn't our problem," she says, "but it sure as hell is our opportunity!" Lilly reaches into her pocket and tosses another coin in the fountain, waiting expectantly for a moment. "Damn. No luck."

"What'd you wish for?" I ask.

"I wished that Great-Grandad would pop out and smack you upside the head for not seeing the most obvious solution in the world to our family's massive PR problem," she says.

"Which is?" I look from Lilly, to the fountain, to Celestial Pets, and back again. The store is still open, and I wonder if the woman's there again. I'd love to know what she thought of the coffee. Had I overdone it? I'm dying to stop back in. But it's probably too soon. Or maybe it's already too late. It's only a matter of time till she figures out who I am. I frown.

"Oh my God, Hudson. Are you really that stupid?"

I shake my head at her, distracted and a little frustrated. "Apparently, I am. Enlighten me, please."

"We get involved with that fundraiser—"

"Not our thing." I shake my head, interrupting her. "At best, it's slapping a Band-Aid on things. At worst, it might backfire. Like we're trying to whitewash the problem. It won't look sincere. It'll look like we're just trying to buy our way out of a PR mess."

"No, duh." Lilly shakes her head at me. Impatiently, she spins the wheels of the skateboard under her arm. "Buying our way out would be a total Bryce move. Which is why I'm not suggesting we do that." She sighs and reaches out a hand for her phone, which I'm still holding. She then enlarges the image on the screen and points at it, holding it up for me to read what she's pointing at.

"Look here … it says they need a venue."

"Yeah, so?" I'm still not getting it.

"Who has an entire, big, empty, refurbished warehouse space beneath the lofts they are trying to sell?" Lilly looks truly exasperated now.

"The co-working space isn't done yet, Lill. It's bare bones over there still."

"That makes it even more perfect for an event like this! You can fix the PR problem AND use the op to show off the lofts." Lilly presses a button and the screen goes black. She drops her phone back into her pocket. "Not to mention that it's kind of the right thing to do." She raises her eyebrows reproachfully.

"I don't know, Lill. You have no idea how much I already have on my plate just trying to get the place habitable."

"Look, this is a premium marketing op, and if you're too dumb to take it, I don't know what to say. I thought the company was in better hands with you than Bryce, but maybe I better start looking for a part-time job so I can begin saving up for an Ivy League."

I ruffle her hair. "Let me think about it," I say, glancing back at the shop. Getting involved with the fundraiser might make sense for the biz. But it would also give me an excuse to get to know Georgia a little better. That makes the idea more attractive. Dangerously so.

"Oliver would want you to do this, Hudson," Lilly says. "Think of all the shelter pets who might *die* if we don't do anything!" She pleads passionately now, saving her most compelling argument for last, like a true lawyer.

"You should probably text your mom to let her know I'm here and will bring you home by nine," I suggest.

She rolls her eyes. "When did you get so boring?"

"Think about what flavors of ice cream we should buy. We don't have to tell your mom that we're skipping dinner and going straight to the sundaes, do we?"

"Absolutely not." Lilly grins. "Now you're speaking my language."

georgia

. . .

THE MORNING OF THE *PET FRIENDS'* magazine interview arrives as gray and lackluster as a bowl of overcooked oatmeal. It's a dismal reminder that winter is coming to the Pacific Northwest.

My car fills with fog as Cookie pants in the passenger seat and the windshield wipers quit on me. I have to roll down the windows and freeze my ass off just to see where I am going. Cookie seems amused by the idea of me hanging my head out the window and tries to make a twosome of it, climbing on my lap and pushing her head out beside mine. It's a short distance and I take it slow, but it's still a miracle that I don't crash.

Outside the shop, I am greeted by a flock of cackling grackles that have congregated on the trees out front. When I look up, one of them promptly baptizes me with birdshit.

"Are you assholes kidding me?" I howl into the tree as I unlock the shop. It's only seven, and I haven't had my coffee yet. The interview isn't for another hour, but I'm here early to straighten up and rehearse my speaking points.

Whoever said bird poo is good luck wasn't wearing a dry-clean-only biker jacket. I scrape off most of the gunk with an old, plastic loyalty card and eliminate the rest with antibacterial pet wipes.

I attempt a reset. Today is going to be a good day. Celestial Pets is getting featured in a nationally syndicated pet magazine. The article is going to include a link to our website, and people are going to see the photo op wall and … Actually, I'm not exactly sure what to expect. We've never been profiled like this before, but I'm hopeful. It can't hurt.

I review what I've been told about the journalist who's writing the piece. Her name is Emily Romano - she's a freelancer. She's local to Ephron but just moved here in the last year. She doesn't have any pets, but her neighbors adopted their bichon from Kismet. Xander is their groomer, of course.

When I talked to Emily on the phone, she'd sounded like she was around my age. She seemed friendly and let me know the visit to the shop was mostly a formality as she'd already done her research. But she wanted to meet me, ask a few questions, and see my pet clothing collection for herself before finishing the piece. Maybe shoot a few photos in addition to whatever I could send over.

Nothing to be nervous about. Nothing to lie awake half the night making mental checklists about, or anything.

I tap my studded cowboy boot against the edge of the counter. The metal makes a satisfying sound, clinking out an audible "check!" as I run down my pre-interview list:

Peppermint and Basil Air Freshener Spray … Clink!

Clothing straightened and organized by breed and collection … Clink!

Shop vacuumed and dusted … Clink!

Fact sheet printed … Clink!

I skim the one-page "About Us" sheet, skipping to the end. It's a good reminder of why we do what we do:

> *Since opening our doors, Celestial Pets has supported the placement of over two thousand pets—cats, dogs, birds, bunnies, lizards, and even a few chickens—into loving homes.*
>
> *At Celestial Pets, we believe that pets are more than animals who live with us. They are our soul mates. Our pet connections are "written in the stars."*

The primary focus of this article is going to be the shop's connection to local artisans and causes. But with Halloween coming up, and a tight deadline, Emily said she also wants to be sure to feature my handmade costumes.

I deliberate a bit before finally pulling two costumes for samples. I choose a small, frothy-topped, puppuccino coffee costume, and a soft, cotton, velvet pumpkin suit sized to fit a larger dog. These are outfits I've made multiple copies of. I've been sewing much more than usual lately, both at home and in the shop, making sure the rack stays packed.

I fold the costumes into tissue paper and place them in a bag stamped with the Celestial Pets logo. I also include a few cards and brochures from our artisan vendors. Last, I pop in a small baggie full of dog treats for Emily to share with her neighbors.

Now there's nothing left for me to do besides check my own appearance.

My simple, black-knit mini dress was thankfully spared the wrath of the grackles. It pairs well with the studded boots. For luck, I piled on a stack of my mom's signature silver bracelets. My nails are done. My hair was flat-ironed, but the morning mist took care of that. It's a hot, tousled mess again. I do what I can to smooth it down.

My mom's likeness smiles down at me, silently keeping me company. I wish she was actually here right now to savor this moment. She would have loved getting press. But she isn't here. I'm alone.

Not totally alone though. I watch Cookie, who is sprawled out behind the counter. She's wearing the Boss Bitch T-shirt I made for her, and is happily working away at a new bone. Not a care in the world.

I could also use something to distract myself with. I may as well finish last week's episode of the *Lit Lovers* podcast.

I cue up the episode to where I last left off and curl up in the arm chair.

"I don't know, I don't get the whole hate sex thing. It just seems so negative attention seeking to me," says Chelsea, one of the female hosts.

"That's because you're such a goody-goody, Chels. But whatever. I don't need to know what YOU'RE into, Sis."

"It's your podcast, Jackson. You're the one who invited me on here."

"I don't think it's really about HATE hate," purrs Alexis. She always likes to take things up a notch. "It's that forbidden fruit thing. The more we deny ourselves, the more we start to obsess."

"And by we, Alexis, do you mean you?" asks Jackson.

The four podcast hosts go on to discuss one-night stands and pontificate about which Disney villains they would and wouldn't sleep with. I laugh and shudder when the hosts unanimously decide that Jafar from *Aladdin* and Ursula the

Sea Witch from *The Little Mermaid* are probably two of the most unfuckable characters ever, which is why they'd make the perfect couple.

"Can you imagine if they were your parents? And you caught them having sex?"

I die a little. How do they come up with this stuff?

I'm so caught up in the episode that I don't even notice at first when Emily shows up. She taps the glass door to get my attention, and I jump up and rush to let her in.

"Oh my God. So sorry!" I hastily unlock the door. "I was just listening to a podcast."

It's still playing, actually. I hadn't turned it off in my mad dash to the door. Emily smiles sympathetically and steps into the shop, looking all around.

"I'd have to say, Maleficent is on the table," Jackson jokes.

"You wish you could have Maleficent on a table, you perv." Em, the most conservative of the four says.

"I guess I'd consider Gaston if I was desperate enough," Chelsea says.

"No one thrusts like Gaston," Alexis sings.

"Gross! That's my sister you're singing about. Stop that immediately," groans Jackson.

Two of the hosts, Jackson and Chelsea, are siblings. This makes it awkward for them when the show inevitably turns to the topic of sex. Which is often. I scramble to the speaker and hit the off button.

"So, *Lit Lovers*?" Emily raises one brow and bites back a smile.

"Do you listen to it too?"

"Actually, I try not to. I can't stand hearing myself."

"What?" I look at her, then back at the now-silent speaker. "I mean … you? You're one of them?"

Emily unwraps a big, beautiful, paisley pashmina from her shoulders and sets her oversize bag down on the counter. She's blushing a bit.

"It's primarily Jackson's podcast, but I got roped in by Alexis. She's a mutual friend who works with him. Long story. But yes, I'm one of the four hosts."

"I'm probably going to have to interview *you* now," I say. No joke. Xander is going to freak out when he hears about this.

Emily is a little older than me, but not by much. Early thirties, I'd guess. She's average height and unapologetically curvy. Her long, brown hair is worn loose, curly, and cascading. It frames her expressive hazel eyes. The cabled sweater she's wearing appears to be hand-knit. There's something slightly old-fashioned, natural, and wholesome about her. She seems genuine and unpretentious.

Emily's eyes crinkle when she smiles. "You can interview me about the podcast after I interview you about the store, but I'll go ahead and apologize in advance. I'm pretty boring. I'm the resident square on the podcast. I wasn't even down to have a one-night stand with Gaston, let alone let Scar be my sugar daddy."

"That's a really good call." I bite back my own smile now.

Emily nods gravely. "I'm glad we're on the same page."

I like her immediately. Aside from being thrilled to get this interview, I am suddenly and unexpectedly delighted to be making a new friend. It's the last thing I expected today.

"Please, sit." I encourage her to take a seat in the plaid chair, and I sit down behind the counter at my stool.

"I don't have to open for another hour. Can I order you some coffee? I can call next door. The diner next door has the best!"

"Oh my God, I know!" Emily says. "I've been there a few times. But I'm good. I've been up for a while. I think I've hit my caffeine quota already."

Emily settles herself on the chair and opens up her bag. She dives in and proceeds to sort through the contents, pulling more items out of the mid-size satchel than seems reasonable, or even possible. A beat-up looking computer, knitting needles and a ball of yarn, a tangerine, a red, sandwich-size Tupperware container, a Van Gogh-printed travel umbrella and a self-help book titled, *Go Your Own Way: The TrailBLAZ-Er's Guide to Love* by Blaze Smith, are all set aside before she finds the items she's looking for.

She emerges victorious with a small, black, moleskin notebook and a fountain pen. "Mind if I take notes?"

"Not at all," I say.

For the next hour, Emily and I chat about the shop, drifting in and out of side conversations about Ephron, tacos, travel, and dating. She tells me the story of how she was recruited by her friend Alexis for the podcast, and I tell her about my hopes for Cookie's social media account. We talk at length about the peekapoo and his Mr. Miyagi suit. Before I know it, sun is streaming through the front window and it's almost time to open.

"Okay." Emily sets down her pen. "I think I have what I need about the shop. I just want to ask you about these two specific outfits. I have screenshots from one of the *Pet Friends'* message boards.

She holds out her phone to show me the suits. "Your prom queen dress and this chef's toque?"

"Um … wait a minute." I take the phone from her and zoom in on the photos. They are the same colors as my outfits and the same general styles. But they are NOT my costumes. "Where exactly did you say these were posted?"

"What? On the *Pet Friends'* boards. Let me see if I can pull up the posts."

I hand her back her phone and pick up my own. Dread is coursing through my veins. "Let me do an image search," I say.

I hold my phone over one of the images on hers and snap.

Immediately, my screen fills with catalog images of dogs in costumes that are incredibly like my own. Same colors, same characters … but these are not my handmade creations. These are shoddily made, mass-produced knockoffs. The dollar amount they are selling for wouldn't even cover my materials.

I click the link to see where it will take me.

When I realize that I have just landed on the home page of the Holm family's flagship website, Farm & Holm Pet Supplies, I gasp.

"Are you okay?"

A lava-like pustule of outrage begins to form beneath my surface. I can feel it bubbling as I struggle to maintain my calm. I cannot let it ruin this interview, this opportunity.

"Those aren't my designs," I state, working overtime to keep the emotion out of my voice. "It appears that I've been copied."

"Oh my God! I'm so sorry." Emily's face shows true horror. "Now I feel awful. I didn't know."

"Well, you know what they say about imitation …" I force my lips into the world's least sincere smile and resist the urge to wipe away the sheen of sweat gathering on my forehead. Must keep my shit together! The last thing I need is for this article to suddenly turn into a puff piece about the adorable, cheap pet costumes available on the Farm & Holm site.

"I won't link to them," Emily says, reading my thoughts. Clearly, I'm not as good at hiding my emotions as I should be. "That's really shitty of them to knock you off. You should probably get a lawyer."

"Honestly, I'm not sure I can afford one," I admit. "Or that it would do much good."

Odds are I'd spend more than I would recover. I am not the first designer to be knocked off. I've been hearing stories like this from our artists for years. Those who pursued legal action were rarely successful against corporate giants like Farm & Holm. Proving your idea is the original is an expensive and lengthy process. Crushingly so for small, independent artists like me.

Any last hopes I've been holding on to that the article will somehow mitigate the effect of the rent hike evaporate.

"Thanks for not linking to them." I force myself to meet Emily's concerned hazel eyes. "I appreciate that." She returns my gaze then looks down at her watch.

"Look at the time! It's almost time for you to open. I'm sorry I kept you so long."

Emily begins stuffing items back into her magical bag. It's really a marvel. Like something out of *Harry Potter*. If only magic were real. Then I could conjure up a way to repay the mortgage while still making rent and paying for the shelter.

"For what it's worth, I love what you're doing here," Emily says, as she shakes out and refolds her beautiful scarf. "Let me know if there's anything I can do to help."

What I want to say is, "You can write an exposé on the evils of Farm & Holm Co." But I keep my mouth shut. I know better. Farm & Holm is a major advertiser in *Pet Friends* magazine.

Emily picks through the handouts on the counter, stopping when she gets to the masquerade planning committee flyer.

"Actually, you know what? Maybe I can help with this! I'd love to join the planning committee. I'll talk to Jackson too. He might want to do an episode about romantic comedies involving pets. And just thinking out loud here … but is anyone livestreaming the event for you guys?"

My jaw drops. "You would do all that for me? For us? Why though? You just met me. You hardly know me."

She pauses and puts a hand on my shoulder. "Okay, I realize this is not entirely professional, but I'm relatively new in town, and I don't know, you seem cool. I'd like us to be friends. It's not like you're asking for a kidney. This seems like it'll be fun."

Emily folds the flyer in her magical bag.

I look into her earnest face, searching for signs of subterfuge. Then I recall my conversation with Oliver and his advice that I accept help from friends and family. Why is that so difficult? Why must I always be looking for ulterior motives and reasons not to accept any offers of help?

I believe that Emily really means it, she actually *wants* to help. Suddenly, I'm seeing things in a different light. My natural inclination to shrug off and reject her offer isn't only stupid, it's rude.

I wonder if that's how I appear to people? Proud to the point of being rude? It may be a lost cause, but I'm not going to turn her away.

"Okay." I exhale. "Thank you. Thanks so much. I guess I'll see you at the meeting on Friday, then."

"It's a date!" Emily says, turning to leave.

"Hey! Don't forget your goodie bag!" I hold out the sample bag.

Emily pauses by the door.

"I'm so impressed. Even more so now that I've seen this place. You're a real force, Georgia. A font of creativity and a beacon of light. I hope you know that."

Her praise seems so sincere. So why do I still feel like such a fraud?

hudson

. . .

"STAY, OLIVER, STAAAAYY."

On Thursday morning, I get out the bag of clothes from Celestial Pets. I can't procrastinate any longer. I've got to get Oliver's costumed photos done so I can check that prompt off the list.

The session is not going great. I just want to finish up so I can text with Cookie for a bit. I'm surprised I haven't already heard from her. But she did say that something important was happening today.

What constitutes a big day for her, exactly? What sort of occasion calls for a dog in a Boss Bitch tee?

I have fifteen minutes to wrap this up before my next Zoom meeting.

"That's it. Good kitty. Don't move a muscle …"

I look sternly at the cat and back away slowly. Who am I kidding? He doesn't give a shit. He's going to stay if he wants to stay and go if he doesn't. I have no control here. I should have attempted this last night when Lilly was here. An extra pair of hands would have been a good thing.

Being a pet influencer is hard work. Actual work. There's the planning and scheduling of themed content, shopping for props, shooting and editing the shots, posting them at the right time, engaging with other accounts, and tracking your growth. You have to stay ahead of constantly changing trends. And you have to do all of this—build this brand —*before* you're even getting paid to do it.

People really have the wrong impression about this petflu-encer thing. There's so much more to being a pet influencer than snapping a few cute photos of your hedgehog.

Presently, Oliver is sitting like a statue, on top of the fridge. He is wearing a British robe, and it fits his personality perfectly. The robe drapes nicely, and the tightly curled matching wig … well, the wig is just hilarious. It makes the costume. I shoot in burst mode, hoping at least a couple of the shots will work out.

"May I approach the bench, Your Honor?" I ask. He's flicking his tail agitatedly.

Oliver looks pretty pissed off under the wig, but he has a resting asshole face. He always looks pissed off. The fact that it's still on his head tells me it can't be all that uncomfortable for him.

I place one of the salmon treats on top of the fridge for him and consider trying another one of the other costumes. I'm just not feeling it though. I can't come up with a scenario for the other costumes I've purchased. I wonder if I should just return them, which would mean seeing Georgia again, or just let Lilly have them for her dog, as I had originally intended. There's no way I need this many costumes, especially since Oliver won't even be here anymore after next month.

While the prospect of seeing Georgia thrills me, I quickly dismiss it. The shop probably needs the funds. I can always donate the costumes if they don't fit Lilly's dog.

I also shouldn't be looking for excuses to go back to that shop. It can't end well.

"Mrrrrrow?" Oliver shoots me an impatient are-we-done-here-then look from atop the fridge.

"You're so right," I tell him. "I have to focus on the reasons I'm back here in Ephron. I can't let myself get so distracted."

I sweep the wig off his head and hold out a couple more tiny chunks of freeze-dried salmon, for which I am rewarded with a head bump and purr.

"You're done for today, Buddy." I unsnap the robe, and he gingerly pulls out his two front paws, like he's used to being undressed. Then he arches his back and allows me to stroke him along his spine.

Quickly, I edit the photos. It doesn't take much. They're good as is. I've captured him gazing down from on high in one or two of them, and the angle just works. Judge Judy has nothing on Oliver. He could be a meme. He just needs a tagline.

I can't wait to see what Cookie says. I'll wait for her feedback before posting. Maybe she can help me come up with the caption.

Without warning, my phone erupts, blaring the theme to *Pirates of the Caribbean*. Startled, Oliver jumps down to the counter, then leaps to the floor, shooting me a disparaging look before slinking off toward the living room. Add the *Pirates* franchise to things he doesn't approve of.

It's early for a call from Bora Bora. What is it there, 8 a.m.? Hastily, I swipe up on the screen, hoping nothing's wrong.

"Hello, son!"

"You're up early, Walker."

"Just got off the phone with Lilly. I think it's wonderful we're hosting that masquerade fundraiser at the lofts."

Oh, Lilly. We'd left off the discussion with it still being a maybe. But Lilly isn't one to take no—or even maybe—for an answer when she's determined to hear a yes. I shake my head.

"I didn't agree to that yet, Walker. I only told her I'd speak with the crew and look into it."

"Well, shake a leg. I've already called legal to look into event insurance and see if they have to pull any permits. And I spoke to someone over at the shelter, Angie something. Told her to get in touch with you. She suggested you attend a planning meeting at the diner. It's tomorrow, by the way."

"Where's Bryce?" I ask, suddenly aware that my dad is missing his sidekick. Probably sleeping in.

"I don't know. He's spending a few days at the Four Seasons with a bride who got dumped at the altar." Walker shrugs. "Gotta hand it to him. Kid works fast."

I rub my temples. I'm not even a little bit interested in Bryce's stolen honeymoon.

"Anyway," my dad continues, "do whatever you have to do to make it happen. Also, I told Lilly I'd be back for her birthday party. Might just stick around for this fundraiser too."

When it comes to Lilly, Walker actually is a pretty dedicated father. I have to give him that. He takes a real interest in her life. Perhaps it's because they're so similar? There's no saying no to either of them.

I was on the brink of agreeing already. So, what's the holdup? Professionally, it seems like an excellent idea. Out of the mouths of babes, as they say. With the right staging, we'll be able to show the completed units to potential buyers next month. Which works out perfectly with the timing of the masquerade. But personally, it makes me uncomfortable.

I keep thinking about how Georgia is going to react if I show up at that meeting and she realizes who I really am.

Why? Why do I care? Why am I hand-wringing about such an obvious decision? And why have I allowed this woman—who isn't my usual type and who doesn't even seem interested in me—to get under my skin like this?

I don't even know what I was thinking, sending that coffee over.

May as well go ahead and rip off that Band-Aid. It's not like I can continue to keep my identity a secret indefinitely.

"Okay." I surrender. "I'll figure out how to do it. For Lilly."

georgia

. . .

EMILY WALKS OUT THE DOOR, and I count to ten in an attempt to calm myself. One, motherfucker. Two, motherfucker. Three … Never mind.

I'm picturing that painting *The Scream* by Munch. *The Scream* is how I feel right now. Just superimpose a photo of my foreclosed house in the background and a bunch of stray dogs, colorful cartoon legs sticking straight up in the air to indicate their demise.

I walk to the window and flip the sign from "Closed" to "Open" and dismiss the idea of getting some sewing done this morning. Not today.

So, I'm being knocked off. It happens. I pace angrily back and forth in the small shop.

It isn't actually surprising that someone is making similarly *themed* pet costumes. The shocking part is that these designs aren't merely similar. They're almost identical, until you look closely.

I make my way back to the counter and retrieve my laptop from beneath the register. A few jabs at the keyboard, and I'm on the Farm & Holm Supply website, ready to assess the damage.

Usually, I ignore their site. Mom always said, "Comparison is the thief of joy."

But today, Farm & Holm is clearly the thief, and I'm not feeling any joy whatsoever.

It is impossible to live here without knowing about the Holm family and their flagship company. The Holms are the most successful residents to emerge from Ephron, the town's biggest claim to fame.

But Farm & Holm Pet Supplies is everything Celestial Pets is not. They don't treat pets like family members, they treat them more like possessions. Like livestock.

"To each their own, Georgia," my mom had said. She was never bitter about the Holms. "There's plenty of room for us to coexist. The universe is abundant."

My mom was so kind, so caring, so … *naive*, I think.

I straighten the flyers on the counter as I take stock of the situation. The same unscrupulous company that booted the shelter and spiked my rent is now knocking off my designs.

The rent hike affecting all the tenants may just be "business." We all feel the squeeze. But this part? This feels personal. I can't coexist like this. I can't even exist.

"How do you expect me to do this alone?" I shout at my mom in the moon.

I click through to Farm & Holm's pet costumes page and flinch. There are a dozen options, and each of them—every last one—appear to be copies of one of my designs.

"So, what should I do, Mom?"

The winking woman in the moon remains mute. But of course, I know what she would say.

"Breathe, Georgia, just breathe."

I attempt to take a deep, cleansing breath. I try to use it to push back my anger, frustration, and feelings of helplessness. I tell myself I am not helpless. I just need to remain rational to come up with a plan.

I'll talk to the bank. Maybe they'll give me more time?

Perhaps there's a way to send a boilerplate cease and desist letter? I have design notebooks with fabric swatches. Would this be enough to prove the designs were knocked off? Where would I even send the letter?

I click on the "About Us" link at the top of the Farm & Holm website and land on a page with the story of the company. There's a link to an article about the warehouse conversion. No mention of the animal shelter that they booted from the site, I note.

Another article suggests that Walker Holm is considering stepping aside and passing the torch to his son.

Blah, blah, blah, bullshit PR, blah. I scroll down to the bottom. Who's in charge of Farm & Holm right now? That is what I need to know and all I care about!

Please don't let it be Bryce, I think, feeling like gagging.

At the bottom of the Farm & Holm Supplies home page are a bunch more links, including customer care, which I am pretty certain will be useless. The "Contact Us" link dumps into a form.

Damn. I'm not getting anywhere.

I resume my pacing until another idea comes to me.

"Alexa," I say, calling up the one helper I have no guilt about tapping on a regular basis. "Who is the current head of Farm & Holm Supply?"

"Here's what I found on the web," Alexa says in her robotic voice. "The current COO of Farm & Holm Supply Co. is Hudson Holm. Hudson Holm was born in 1986. He attended the Wharton School of Business. He lives in Washington State."

Alexa pauses before asking, "Does this answer your question?"

I run-hop the five steps back to my laptop and type Hudson Holm into Google. Who the hell is this Hudson? I haven't heard the name before. If Hudson is thirty-five, he would have been done with high school before I even showed up here.

Could he be the missing son from Walker Holm's mysterious first marriage? Kenna mentioned something. She might know. Or her uncles certainly would.

One thing's for sure. If he'd grown up here, surely I'd have heard something about him. I would have run into him. I've lived here for twelve years, and with the exception of douchey Bryce and Walker's tween daughter, who lives with her mom in the family mansion here in Ephron, I haven't run into any other Holm heirs.

I type the name Hudson Holm into the Google search box, and immediately, my screen fills with links to articles in business journals and professional organizations. Where to click first? Instead of choosing, I click the "images" link at the top of the page to filter the search results.

The screen refreshes, filling up with a virtual gallery of photos.

Hudson Holm, smiling and accepting an award. Hudson Holm at a ribbon cutting, arm draped around a tall, thin, glamorous blonde woman. Hudson in a yurt, attending some sort of corporate retreat.

My blood runs cold as a Viking ice storm because I do know Hudson Holm, and I've most certainly run into him before. I know exactly who he is.

Hudson Holm is Ragnar.

———

By noon, the shit is really starting to hit the fan. Literally.

My eyes water as I pass a plastic baggie and disinfecting wipes to an older gentleman who is wearing his sunglasses indoors. He's accompanied by a very overweight Newfoundland that has just relieved his bowels in the middle of the shop. The massive dog looks far more ashamed than his unapologetic owner.

"Trick's tummy is so sensitive, isn't it, Tricky? I guess I shouldn't have shared that pastrami sandwich with him." The man shifts his weight uneasily before handing back the proffered baggies and wipes. "I'm so sorry, but I have a bad back. Could you maybe …" A loud farting sound comes from their vicinity. To be perfectly honest, I am not entirely sure who is passing the gas.

Forcing a civil look on my face, I bag up Trick's poo and throw a few wipes down on the polished cement floor. It's bad. So bad. I'm going to have to fumigate the shop. At least this didn't happen before the interview.

"Oh, thank you. You're so kind. So, tell me, do you have any recommendations for sensitive tummies like ours?"

I try to channel my mother. She wouldn't have judged this man for feeding his dog pastrami. She'd relish the chance to teach him about the merits of probiotics and high-quality kibble. But I am not my mom, and today is not the day. I package up some food and probiotics and ring the sale as quickly as possible.

"You think it will help?" the man asks hopefully.

"I know it will," I say. "Let me get that door for you and Trick."

I walk past him to the door and open it under the guise of being helpful. Fresh air streams in. Sweet, sweet relief! Thank you, baby Jesus.

Cookie's dog tags clink as she rises, stretches, and shakes herself. She's as desperate to get some fresh air as I am. Maybe even more.

Finally, the man and his dog lumber out of the shop. I watch as they cross the park in Holm Square and turn up Main Street toward the boarded-up, beat-up building that was once a church, and more recently had been used as a community center. The real estate sign out in front of the building has a big "Sold" sign on it. According to the rumors, it's about to become a fancy theater. If that's true, it will be great for local business. But all the more reason to raise our rent even higher.

Cookie whines plaintively, looking desperately at the door.

"I promise I'll take you for a walk in a few minutes, Cookie. Let's just get some fresh air in here first." I prop the door open and spritz my trusty basil peppermint room spray around, misting generously.

Normally, I'd have been texting with Kenna all day, venting about what was happening. But Kenna is on a pet portrait shoot today, and I don't want to break her flow. Xander is also away. He and Mac are in Seattle attending a dog show.

This just leaves Oliver. I haven't had a moment to message him all day. But I'm looking forward to finding a way to tell him about Trick's tricky tummy.

But first, I realize I should eat something. It's past noon, and once again, I've neglected to feed myself. Stress never seems to diminish my appetite. Despite the day I've had, I'm starving. Hovering on the brink of being light-headed.

I root around in the darkened back room, using my flashlight to locate something edible. My shin slams into a shelf. I yelp in pain. This situation with the lights not working in my storeroom is getting ridiculous. The mini fridge holds the wilted remnants of yesterday's salad. Cup O' Noodles it is! I drag the electric kettle to the bathroom sink. Lunch will be ready in five minutes.

I set the kettle back on the stand, flip the switch, and wait. Within ten seconds, there are sparks shooting out from the base, followed by a small puff of smoke. Then the kettle's light blinks off.

"You're shitting me," I grumble, rubbing my still-throbbing shin. But I'm not giving up. I'm hungry. Not quite Donner Pass hungry, but getting there. "Guess we'll heat this up the old-school way."

Cautiously, I unplug the kettle. I peel back the Cup O' Noodles lid and pour cold water in. Then I put the cup into the tiny microwave perched on top of the mini fridge.

"Can this day get any worse?" I whisper into the shadows cast by the woeful, tiny microwave light.

This is the moment when Cookie makes a noise that I've never heard her make before. Part howl, part bark, part whine. The noise is followed by a loud crash. And then the sound of something shattering. And a different, more feral and ominous-sounding growl that I don't recognize.

What the hell?

I burst through the door in a crouched stance, scanning for the dog. The clothing rack is knocked over. A tower of stacked pet treat boxes has toppled over. There's a ceramic dog bowl in pieces on the floor.

Cookie is still exactly where I left her—gated in behind the counter. She's trembling, crouching in the farthest corner of the small space. Her tail is between her legs, and it's apparent she's peed herself. She doesn't seem hurt. Just terrified and possibly embarrassed about the pee. She is staring up at the counter above her, whimpering faintly.

I follow her gaze to the source of the problem. The chubby tomcat leaps up onto the counter and greedily gobbles up some of the sample treats I always keep there. He pauses warily for a moment when he sees me, as if weighing his options, then decides I'm not enough of a threat to deter him from his feast.

"Nice kitty," I say, slowly easing myself around to the front of the counter. It isn't that I don't like cats. I just don't understand them like I understand dogs. Cats are so unpredictable.

I take a step toward him and lay a hand on the counter. He doesn't seem fazed. Good. This is good. I am almost close enough to pet him. Would he let me pick him up? What am I going to do with him?

I try to remember what the pet rescue people always say about cats. You're supposed to throw a towel over their head? Or was it just the body and not the head? I glance around. I don't have a towel anyway. Maybe I could take off my shirt? I quickly dismiss this idea. I'm not about to man the shop wearing only a bra.

Her courage bolstered by my presence, Cookie chooses this moment to bark. Before I can even figure out what is happening, the cat is airborne. A brown ball of fur launches toward me, claws out, scrambling for traction.

White-hot pain grips me as the claws graze the flesh of my right hand. The cat is sailing through the air and out the door before I can take another breath.

"Mothereffingeffer! Fuck! Shit! Damn!" I yell. My hand feels far worse than it looks, but with this being a stray, I'm going to have to clean it off thoroughly. And my first aid kit is in the car.

Five minutes ago, I was thinking that this was a pretty shitty day. I hadn't even been bleeding then. What a fool the five-minutes-ago version of me was.

This calls for a plan. I take a deep breath, leaning into my well-developed ability to navigate a crisis. And as crises went, this isn't the worst, right? Nothing truly tragic has happened. Just a little pee and blood and broken glass. I can handle it. No problem. Having a plan of action always calms me in a crisis.

Step One: Clean hand in bathroom. Temporarily bandage with toilet paper.

Step Two: Sweep up broken glass.

Step Three: Walk Cookie to car. Get first aid kit.

My phone dings with a notification. Maybe Kenna is back? Using my uninjured hand, I flip the phone over.

It's from Oliver.

> You haven't posted anything today. Were you
> going to do the cliché prompt today?

Shit. I had totally forgotten to post. We're supposed to choose a common phrase or a cliché and use it as inspo.

Step Four: Cliché prompt?

THWOMP! Something explodes in the back. The microwave comes to an abrupt stop, beeping forlornly. I lean over and peek through the doorway.

The microwave is flashing feebly in the dark, a beacon of hopelessness. I can just make out the worm-like noodles plastered to the steamy interior.

No soup for you, Georgia!

Step Five: Deal with noodle-pocalypse.

I wash and wrap my hand in toilet paper. Before leading Cookie out of the shop, I tape a note to the door saying that I'll be back in ten minutes.

Cookie tugs me toward the grassy, town square park. "Nope. Sorry girl. We're going to the car first. Do you not even see the state of me?" We cut through the alley to the lot behind the building where I usually park.

Except something is extremely wrong. The unicorn isn't where I'd left it. My Prius has simply vanished. I can't believe it. First my designs, and now someone has stolen the unicorn? Why would anyone want to steal a ten-year-old Prius? It's not exactly a Mercedes. It's an old car. Its plates aren't even current.

The plates.

I'd been so busy worrying about everything else that I'd let almost a full year go by since the tags expired. Ruefully, I remember the "fix it" ticket that I shoved in the glove compartment three months ago. The same week I'd taken out the mortgage, so I'd been distracted.

The police officer *had* warned me that normally he'd tow a car with plates that far out of date.

I smack my forehead with my injured hand and wince. The toilet paper from my back-office bandage is already starting to disintegrate. Blinking back tears, I sink to the curb and sit there for a moment, kicking crumbs of asphalt with the pointy toe of my boot.

How had this day degenerated so far so fast?

My cheeks burn with shame. Cookie sits down beside me, watching me anxiously. I lean into her, and she licks the tears right off my face. She's still wearing her Boss Bitch tee.

"I'm sorry, Cookie," I whisper. "This—all of this—is my own damn fault. And I'm going to fix it, all by myself. Because that's what I do." And then I get up.

Step Six: Figure out how to get car back.

I stop by the diner to borrow some Band-Aids, but of course, Kenna's melodramatic Greek uncles want to make a fuss. Old Georgia wouldn't have let them. I'd have made up an excuse about why I have to get right back to the shop and insist that I can bandage myself. But new Georgia sits on a chair in the alley outside the kitchen, allowing Nick to assess my wounds.

Stavros peeks his head out and then goes back inside to pack up a doggie bag of leftover grilled steak bits for Cookie.

As Nick rewashes and bandages my scratch, he regales me with tales of the legendary Athens Street cat colonies.

He applies enough betadine and antibiotic ointments to eradicate a pandemic.

"Thanks," I say. "This is above and beyond, you know. I just needed a few Band-Aids."

"No. Thank you for letting me," Nick says, holding my good hand in his big, warm one. "Listen Georgia, you have to let people take care of you sometimes, and it's our pleasure. Tell me. Are you eating enough?"

"I'm fine, Nick," I assure him, but my stomach growls, giving me away.

"Stavros, make sure you pack up something for Georgia!" Nick yells into the kitchen, but he needn't have bothered.

Stavros emerges with two bags—a sandwich and chips for me, and a bag of cut-up steak cubes for Cookie. She's getting her sirloin after all. Oliver would appreciate that.

"You're spoiling us!" I take the bags gratefully and thank them again. It isn't actually so bad being taken care of. I'm just not used to it. A warning bell goes off in my head. I probably shouldn't let myself get too used to it.

Finally, I take Cookie on the walk she's been waiting for. We circle the square twice, then I sit on a bench near the fountain for a moment so I can scarf my sandwich. It's close enough for me to keep an eye on the shop in case anyone shows up.

Cookie sits beside me, impatiently nudging the paper bag full of steak bits.

"You think that's for you, huh?" I reach into the bag with my uninjured left hand to get a little cube of the meat for her. She impatiently slurps it out of my hand, not close to actually biting me, but making me jump, nonetheless.

"Hey! Don't bite the hand that feeds you!" I say.

Light bulb moment. Don't bite the hand that feeds you. This is my "cliché" shot. Easy-peasy for once.

I pull out my phone and open the camera. I gingerly dip my fingertips back into the bag of treats, then I cup a piece of meat in the palm of my left hand. Cookie is already salivating, and I'm ready to capture it.

"Wait!" I command, slowly unfolding my fingers to expose the treat.

Cookie stares walleyed at the morsel, drool trailing from the corners of her mouth. For once, she's making it easy for me.

I snap a few shots and then finally release her when she starts to shake. Poor Cookie. I laugh as she gobbles the treat up, washing my whole palm clean with her tongue.

Relieved that I have this assignment in the bag, I post the photo to Cookie's Instagram account. Then I copy the link and shoot it over to Oliver's inbox.

Cookie nudges my sore hand, hoping for another treat.

"Noooo!!!!"

The phone slips out of my grasp in what feels like slow motion. It hits the edge of the fountain with an ominous, cracking sound before landing in the water.

Step Seven: Booze.

hudson

. . .

MY PHONE PINGS with missed calls all day long. I see flashes from Lilly, Walker, Jackson, and a local number I don't recognize. Possibly the pet shelter? I'm so busy, I don't have a spare moment to play the messages back. I keep getting pulled into one meeting after another.

Good news, mostly. Since announcing Bryce's leave of absence "to do some important post-divorce healing," most of our investors are back on board for the warehouse renovation. This is a huge relief. We're still a little over budget, but I'll find more corners to cut.

I'm optimistic about how the finish details are coming together. My meeting with the landscape architect is particularly gratifying. He has some suggestions that will significantly lower the costs for the patios and roof decks. We switch from slate surfaces and irrigated planters to heat-resistant, recycled concrete pavers and xeriscape.

We also decide to move forward with artificial turf areas and eliminate potentially toxic plants. This pivot makes the entire project more cost effective as well as more pet friendly.

"You know," the landscape architect enthuses, "this is such a landmark project for us. It'd be great press."

"Excellent idea! I'll have our team pitch that," I say.

After I meet with the foreman to do a rundown of all the recent eco-conscious and sustainable changes I've made, I feel particularly proud. Not just because we're delivering this project closer to on time and under budget. I actually believe all of these things will make this a better place to live—for everyone. It's a great feeling to be a part of a project like this. Something I actually care about.

The warehouse is exactly the sort of place I'd want to live if I were putting down roots in Ephron. It's not just apartments. It's going to be a community. A work/live mecca that honors its residents like family with a built-in sense of belonging. Why hadn't Bryce been able to see and appreciate that?

To my stepbrother, this building was all about showing off. He'd argued for valet parking with extra spaces out front to showcase his luxury cars.

I nixed that in favor of more room for outdoor seating, facing the river. It'll be a great place to gather at sunset.

To me, this project isn't about showing off. It's about showing up. I just wish Bryce had kept his nose out of my part of the business.

Then again, if Bryce hadn't meddled, I wouldn't have made it my priority to be here, living on-site right now. I wouldn't have this time with Lilly, and much as I hate to admit it, there's something nice about being in Ephron again.

My phone chirps with a preset alarm reminding me to post today's Petfluencer Challenge photo. Fortunately, this prompt is easy. I already have the perfect photo. I won't fall further behind.

For the "What a Cliché" prompt, I scroll back and click a picture of Oliver sitting precariously on his haunches, grooming himself. His hind legs are pointed to twelve and three o'clock, and his tongue is hanging out. I caught him with his nose nearly buried in his own crotch. Any other cat would look ridiculous in this pose. But somehow, the little bastard has managed to look like a haughty aristocrat, even in this ignominious moment.

I caption the post "Cleanliness Is Next to Godliness" and throw in a few hashtags for his breed. The post gets a few likes almost immediately, and I get the dopamine hit of social media success.

Though I'm not sure five likes actually qualifies as "success." Once again, I note that this stuff is harder than it looks.

I grab a cup of coffee and head back up to my loft to reply to messages and catch up on my social media. Lilly has left me three messages to call her so we can "strategize" about tomorrow's planning meeting.

In the elevator on the way up, I try to imagine what I'll say to Georgia. What will she do when she finds out I'm Bryce's brother? *And* the guy who raised her rent. Will she even want our help with the fundraiser? Then again, how can she say no?

Will she take a swing at me too?

I don't think her attack on Bryce was unprovoked. But there's something about her that strikes me as feral, almost. The mere fact that I cannot begin to predict how she might react has me on my toes, second-guessing everything I might say to her.

I'm transported back to The Onion, that sensation of stepping sideways, repeatedly, trying to get around each other and failing.

Meanwhile, my whole body seems to echo with the memory of her hot, soft body slamming into mine. Her sparkling fingers on my chest. The curve of her long, black lashes and her wild, green eyes glowing under the fringe of her bangs. She'd still been flushed from her fight. Those lips.

I'm aching to know what they feel like smashed under mine. I shift uncomfortably and groan as the door dings, grateful both for the comfort of my jogging pants and the fact that there's nobody else living up here to witness the fact that I'm stepping out of the elevator with a hard-on.

It's become so difficult to stop thinking about Georgia. Sparkling, sparky Georgia, backed up against the starry wall of her shop.

I shake my head and consider sticking it in the freezer. Why am I even entertaining these thoughts when she clearly has a problem with my family? Why am I ignoring such major red flags and indulging in this fantasy? I give myself a tough talking to.

I am not here to save homeless pets. Helping the shelter might be the "right thing to do" as per Lilly's admonition. But why does it always have to be me doing the right thing? Ephron's problems are not my problems.

Furthermore, I'm definitely not here to start something with someone who inevitably would want more from me than I have to give right now.

A second, more stubborn voice in my head argues with the first. This voice sounds a bit like Cookie. It says,

"Is that what you're really afraid of, Furball? Or are you actually afraid that you're the one who'd want more? If you never ask for what you want, you can't blame anyone else when you don't get it."

"What I want," I argue back, "is to complete this project my way. To turn this waste of space into something I, my entire family, and future generations can be proud of."

"I just hope they appreciate you," the Cookie voice comments.

"Oh, shut up!" I say out loud to nobody as I exit the elevators. "I am here to see this project through, profitably. Nothing more."

And then I'm struck again by the altered view. It still hits me fresh every time I come up here. Pride. I'm proud of this place. And not just in a dollar-sign way.

The roofline of the original warehouse has been dramatically changed by the multi-level penthouses, each with their own balconies and decks. A breezeway between the units leads to a lush roof garden with a view.

I can imagine a crowd of people enjoying the roof garden area. Such an inviting spot, with its sweeping riverfront views. There's a circular firepit, a small bar, and several cocktail-style, cement tables sheltered beneath a portico. My mind paints in the twinkling lights and space heaters we'll be adding in order to make the space functional nearly all year round.

It will be the perfect place to host friends or for neighbors to dine together.

Who am I kidding? This project isn't like all the others. It's special. You can take the boy out of Ephron, but apparently …

I settle myself at one of the small tables and scroll through the messages I've been avoiding all day. The first one is from Jackson.

Hey, I'm home. Ready for that drink?

Want to meet at The Onion? I'd love your
opinion about something. I'm hosting an
event at the warehouse next month.

Pet masquerade fundraiser?

Yes.

I answer, wondering how he knows.

I wouldn't put much past Lilly, but she doesn't really know my friend.

Lucky guess. My cohost from the podcast is
volunteering. She asked if I'd help get the
word out.

Interesting. Talk over beer and burgers?

The emptiness in my gut announces itself with a growl. Jackson thumbs-up this message.

I can be at The Onion in twenty.

I slip my phone back into my pocket and head back to the loft to grab my car keys. But before I can get through the door, the phone dings again. I check to see if Jackson has changed his ETA, but this time, it's Cookie.

Relief washes over me. It isn't like her to go the whole day without a single post or text. I was actually starting to get worried. I read her message.

I finished the assignment, Oliver! Let me
know what you think? Do you drool on your
human like a little savage too? Xoxo, C

I follow the link and read the caption before studying the image. It reads: "Don't Bite the Hand That Feeds You."

In the image, Cookie is cross-eyed, staring at a treat being held out in front of her. Long rivulets of drool appear to be suspended, midair.

I can only assume the outstretched hand belongs to Cookie's owner. I study the woman's palm, because it *is* clearly a woman.

Her hand is small and delicate. The focus is on the dog's face, so the hand is slightly blurry. The details are softened. I follow the lifeline crease in her palm down toward her wrist. There's a tattoo there. Most of it is covered by her sleeve, but there are tiny shooting stars peeking out. They remind me of sparks.

> Is that your human in the photo, Cookie? She has a tattoo?

I settle back into my chaise lounge and open the challenge portal to chat, but almost as soon as I do, I realize that I really can't do this now. I've got to go if I'm going to be on time to meet Jackson. My stomach rumbles, reminding me that I'm starving.

I send a brief text, promising Cookie that I'll be back later. Then I take one last look at her photo before heading out.

georgia

. . .

SOMEHOW, I make it through the rest of the day, phone free and with a bandaged hand. I use a landline to call a cab to get me home. I'm lucky to find someone who's okay with my dog accompanying me in their vehicle.

"Tough day?" the taxi driver asks.

"You have no idea."

Sitting in the back, I open my laptop, hop on the cab's free Wi-Fi, and review the slobbery cliché photo I posted earlier. It's such a glorious shot. It might be my favorite yet. Cookie looks possessed. Her eyes are crossed, and you can see actual strings of saliva. Gross but cool. I check the likes and comments. This one's getting traction.

But weirdly, nothing from Oliver. Either he hasn't seen the photo or he wasn't particularly impressed. I decide to give him a nudge.

> I finished the assignment, Oliver! Let me know what you think. Do you drool on your human like a little savage too? Xoxo, C

Despite my bad mood, I smile a little. Oliver will surely be horrified by how undignified and slobbery Cookie looks in that photo, and his response will be a pick-me-up after my super-shitty day.

Immediately, a chat request pops up.

> Is that your human in the photo, Cookie? She has a tattoo?

This is not the reaction I was expecting. Does he not see the copious amounts of spittle? The crossed eyes? The extended tongue?

> Yeah, that's my owner. You have a problem with her tattoo now?

> I'm so sorry, Cookie. I've got to meet a friend right now. But can we please talk about your vulgar public slavering later?

Abruptly, he leaves the chat.

"Okay fine, Oliver," I say out loud, slapping my laptop shut, "be that way." The cab driver looks in his rearview mirror at me and raises his eyebrows.

"Your kid?" he asks.

"No." I let out the breath I was holding. "Long story. It's a cat."

———

As soon as I'm home, I kick off my boots and flop on the couch with a generous pour of my favorite boxed red wine. I'm too tired to do anything functional, but I'm so tempted to get back online right now to do some more research. There are things I need to know. Like who's the blonde in the photos with Hudson Holm/Ragnar?

That woman looks like what I imagined was his type. Right down to her invisible pores and expensive, balayage-tipped tresses.

Not that it matters. She is more than welcome to him. I should feel sorry for her, dating a Holm. Hudson might even be worse than his brother. He's the devil in deceptive packaging.

Which is just another way of saying he's the devil, I realize.

Thank goodness I resisted his attempts at flirting with me. Who knows what else he thought he could get away with?

He isn't going to get away with anything, I vow. I recall how satisfying it was, punching his brother. For some reason, I can't imagine decking Hudson though. I *can* imagine ripping his clothes off. Just tearing them off. Right. Off. His. Perfect. Body. And then sinking my nails into his flesh. Maybe biting him too. I bet he'd taste delicious. He'd certainly smelled good.

The bastard.

Maybe I should check if there are some shirtless photos of him online? I could print one of them out and throw darts at it.

I'm spinning, and I have to put a stop to it. I will not think about Hudson Holm anymore. Not even for a minute. He is officially banished from my brain. I will not waste another moment imagining him striding into my village wearing deerskin pants and a horned helmet.

I hate him. I hate Hudson Holm!

I polish off my glass of wine and refill my cup.

Perhaps Emily was right, and I'd be better off phoning a lawyer? But of course, the only lawyer I know well enough to call is the one who managed my mom's estate.

And what good would it do to call him, really? Even if I had the cash to pay a retainer, I'd be pitting my hourly-rate estate attorney up against what was likely a whole team of sharky, in-house counsel.

Good luck with that.

Time to regroup. I'll need to come up with a new plan. Tomorrow. Tonight, I just need time to sink my sorry, tired self into a steaming-hot bubble bath.

I fill the tub with hot water and drop a hot-pink, jasmine-scented ball in, watching it fizz and turn the water a violent shade of pink. Then I lower myself in.

One of the perks of being only five foot two and living in an older home is that I can practically swim in my oversize bath-tub. This is something I indulge in on a regular basis. Scented candles and bath bombs are my love language. And after a childhood of deprivation, there will always be a small part of me that can't believe I have a whole bathroom and bathtub to myself.

For now, anyways.

I cannot think about this at the moment.

My Alexa speaker is on the nightstand just outside the bath-room door.

"Alexa, play my music!" I order from the tub. A moment later, though, displeased and impatient with her inappropriately perky selections for me, I change my mind.

"Alexa, call Kenna!"

Kenna's phone rings and rings, until it goes through to her voice mail. I vaguely recall she said something about a date tonight. I just hope it's not one of the Uber Eats guys, or worse, one of the dick pics ones. But I can't blame her for trying. Her eternal optimism and unflagging belief in happy endings are two of her most endearing traits. Two that I wish we shared.

How long has it been since anyone touched me?

The thought of Bryce's hand sliding down my shoulder still makes me shudder.

Next question.

Who was the last man I touched? Not counting my brother and Uncle Nick from the diner?

It was Hudson Holm, of course. Full-body slam.

And now he's back in my head. We're going there—again. I replay the sensations of crashing into him and find myself enjoying it a little too much. If I'm being honest, I enjoy it even more than the memory of punching his brother.

Honestly, how can those two even be brothers?

Rolling onto my stomach, I stretch out my limbs and attempt to practice gratitude. I'm grateful for this bathtub and my entire house. The roof over my head tonight. Even if it doesn't last. I'm grateful to have my brother and my best friend in my life. I take none of it for granted.

But I'm still so lonely, I say to myself, hugging myself under water. Acknowledging the feeling, it feels like probing a bruise. A bruise that refuses to go away. It lingers in the places where comfort used to live.

People say they will be with you always. And then they leave.

I hear Oliver's voice in my head. *"All the more reason to hold tight to the people who matter most, Cookie."*

That's weird. But no weirder than the fact that I'm also really grateful for Oliver. A coffee witch, a man impersonating a Persian cat, and a dog groomer. These are my people.

Flipping onto my back, I duck my hair under the water and turn on the tap with my toes. Hot water swirls around me, almost but not quite as good as an embrace. I sit up to swig another gulp of my wine.

"Alexa, call Xander!" I demand.

He picks up on the first ring.

"Hey, G! Everything okay? I'm at a restaurant on Front Street, so it's a little loud here."

I can hear music in the background and people laughing.

"Um … yeah. No big deal. It can wait. Just wondering how your trip is going." I sink back down into the water. "How was the dog show?"

"Can we catch up tomorrow at the planning meeting? We'll be back by noon. Oh, and I have news about a venue for the masquerade. I think we might have the perfect space lined up."

"Okay!" I dunk my head under the water again. First good news of the day. When I come up, Xander is speaking low and rapidly. I can picture Mac beckoning him back to the table. I feel the stab of my loneliness jabbing me in the ribs again. I miss half of what he's saying.

"And there's plenty of space for everything we want to do. It's fire! We'll talk more when I'm home. See you tomorrow?"

"Sure, okay, Xan. Catch you then. Get back to Mac. And be good," I say, careful to keep my tone as neutral and as upbeat as I can muster. I don't need to drag Xander down with me. I'm happy for him and Mac. Truly. As he would be for me. If I was into relationships.

We hang up and I let myself drift in the cooling tub, determined to empty my mind of all troubling thoughts for the remainder of the night. Cookie wanders into the bathroom and attempts to drink bathwater.

"No, Cookie!" I admonish. She barks, looking over her shoulder hopefully. She's hungry, I realize. And so am I.

I pull the plug and step gingerly out of the tub. Given the day I've already had, and the effect of the alcohol on my empty stomach, I'm not taking any chances. The last thing I need now is to slip and fall and be forced to call the paramedics to save my naked ass.

Hudson Holm would make a super-hot paramedic.

Dammit! I have to get that man out of my fantasies. Hudson Holm is not a Viking fantasy, sparring partner, or a paramedic. He is my enemy.

I pull on my favorite pair of vintage silk pajama bottoms, slip my feet into thick, chenille slipper socks, and pull on a vintage tee. I am not going to wallow. I am going to make dinner. And then I am going to hate-watch *Vikings*.

Tonight, instead of rooting for Ragnar, I am going to take great pleasure in watching each and every scene in which he gets his ass kicked. I might even imagine myself doing the ass-kicking.

I pad down to the kitchen, humming and singing the *Vikings* theme song lyrics.

"More … give me more … give me more …"

Cookie trails behind me, tail wagging excitedly. I set my empty wine glass on the counter before making our dinners.

First, I open a can of wet food for Cookie. I scoop it into a bowl and mix in her dry food. She wastes no time, bolting her meal in minutes and then chasing the bowl around the kitchen as she licks it clean.

I don't even want to mess with a microwave tonight. I pour myself a bowl of cereal and take it to the couch. With my dinner, drink, and the remote lined up in front of me on the coffee table, I cue up my show.

But before I hit play, just in case anyone wants to get in touch with me, I open my laptop and place it on the side table.

It dings almost immediately with an incoming message from Oliver.

> Hey, Cookie, can we talk?

I try to type my response with one hand, missing letters. So instead of "Sure, what's up?" I send,

> Sr. wat p?

> Hmm … everything ok there?

I retrieve the laptop and prop it on a pillow on my lap.

> Sorry, Furball. My owner had the world's shittiest day. Broke her phone. Had to get out the laptop.

> Is she ok?

> Right as rain, Oliver. Drowning her sorrows. Best foot forward.

> Pardon?

> Ugh, sorry, Furball. Clichés on the brain. Such a bad day at work. But you know, it's always darkest before the dawn.

What other clichés could I use to describe my day? I run down a list in my mind.

> Did you see the comment I left on your post, Cookie?

I pull up my account in another tab and scan my post for Oliver's comment. He's written, "I think your bark is worse than your bite, Cookie. But you might want to consider finishing school. Good girls don't drool over their sirloin. Xxoo, O." I bite my lip. It's so sweet and so dorky. Especially the way he's signed it.

> Good one. Now go check mine.

I laugh a little and sip my wine, imagining him reading what I've written in response to his "Cleanliness Is Next to Godliness" post. I've commented: "Seems like you're entirely tongue in cheek." Xoxo, C

> A bit on the nose, don't you think?

> I give as good as I get, Furball.

> I am sorry about your bad day though, Cookie. I'm assuming this is some kind of a business problem? Maybe I can help?

There he goes, offering business advice again.

> Really, Oliver? Do you have an MBA from the Cat Fancier's Association? Are you going to catsplain the solution to us?

> Very funny, Cookie. We both know it's not actually Oliver doing the typing here.

My heart thumps in my chest and I sit up straighter. Touché! Bluff called!

> Well, well, well. Aren't you afraid we'll get
> kicked out of the challenge if we break the
> rules?

Some rules are meant to be broken.

> You certainly don't beat around the bush!

Perhaps I'm barking up the wrong tree,
Cookie, but I had the impression you enjoyed
playing with fire.

> Careful what you wish for.

Seeing is believing. Put your money where
your mouth is. Shall we tempt fate and meet
at last?

Holy shit! What's happening here? Is he for real? My eyes bug out rereading that last message again and again as my fingers hover over the keyboard. I look down at my nearly empty third cup. Does he actually want to meet up?

Maybe a hookup isn't such a bad idea. Maybe it's the perfect way to blow off steam.

But no. No freaking way. Even if I had my car, I'm not in any condition to drive. In my pajamas. With a towel on my head. Nope-a-roony. I'm not going anywhere. Not even to meet up with Oliver's owner. Who I'm just dying to meet, aren't I? How many times have I fantasized what he might look like?

At this point, I'm just drawing a blank. His face is a big old blank for me. I'd walk into The Onion—in my imagination it was always The Onion—and then what?

How would we even know each other? Would we need to bring our pets along to recognize each other? No. That would be silly. I am just being silly. Neither of us are dragging our pets to a bar.

> Maybe we should tell each other our
> humans' names before we consider meeting
> in person? I'll spill the beans if you will.

It occurs to me that Oliver could be a real creep. He could be catfishing me. What if he is a serial killer? I have no way of knowing he isn't a serial killer.

My fingers are poised and ready to Google whatever name he feeds me. I click over to the second browser tab. It's still full of images from the last name search I ran. Hudson Holm. Grrrr.

I fight the urge to get out a sharpie and scribble a mustache on him directly on the screen. I scroll slowly down the page. Nope. No shirtless photos. Pity.

> Sorry, Cookie. I'm just yanking your chain.
> Though to be perfectly honest, you are
> growing on me.

> You may eat those words.

I breathe a sigh of relief, followed by a sharp stab of disappointment.

The three dots come and go again. Finally, a message appears.

> Real talk, Cookie. Can you just look away for
> a moment and show a message to your
> owner?

> Are you pulling my leg, Oliver?

Hand her the laptop, Cookie. THIS
MESSAGE IS FOR COOKIE'S HUMAN'S
EYES ONLY!

.

.

.

Hi there, Cookie's person. This is Oliver's
person.

Maybe it's the wine, but I find myself giggling.

Hi there, Oliver's person. This is Cookie's
person typing.

I have a very important question for you,
Cookie's person. I'm dying to know. Do you
ever wonder about me?

All the time, Oliver's person, I think.

You know what they say about forbidden fruit

I bite my lip.

Same. Ok, you can put Cookie back on now.
I just wanted to tell you that I liked your
tattoo. Bye.

.

.

.

Oliver?

I type cautiously.

I'm back, Cookie. Thanks for letting me talk
to your human.

Maybe you tell your human that I'd like to
know a little bit more about him? I think he's
got a bit of an unfair advantage now that he's
seen that my human's an actual girl.

My human isn't what you'd expect.

Are we talking Beauty and the Beast ugly?

Heavens no! He's just not someone you'd
expect to have adopted an old, crotchety cat
like me. But it just goes to show you.

You can't judge a book by its cover?

Humans are complicated.

They sure are, Furball.

Good thing we're not humans, Cookie.

Birds of a feather, Ol.

We're a little more warm-blooded than that.

How am I going to manage without you when
this challenge is over?

I stifle a yawn.

Also, Furball, I have to confess that right
now, I'm about three sheets to the wind.

And yet you manage to amuse me so.

                                        Same.

I propose that when the challenge is over, we
throw caution to the wind.

            You aren't afraid that curiosity will kill
            the cat?

Are you telling me to let sleeping dogs lie?
Shall I go lick my brokenhearted wounds?

                No, I'm in. In for a penny, in for a pound.

My heart is pounding, but I can barely keep my eyes open. I
haven't solved any of my problems tonight, but somehow, I
feel a thousand times better.

    You know what they say, Cookie. Good
    things come to those who wait.

                            Mm-hmm … so sleepy, Ol.

Get some shut-eye then.

                            Later, Hater! Xoxo, C

Hate You Later! Xxoo, O

I fall asleep with the laptop on the floor beside me.

hudson

. . .

HOW DO I prepare for my lunchtime meeting with Xander and Georgia?

By getting up early and rereading last night's message thread with "Cookie." It's still funny. Stupid, maudlin, and funny. Ten minutes after I go back over the transcript, I'm still grinning like a fool. I can't stop thinking in clichés. Hopefully, this doesn't mean I am one.

I'd had a couple more beers after I got back from The Onion—no Georgia this time—and I'd been feeling lonely. Part of me was wishing that my Petfluencer buddy would take the bait and agree to meet up. Another part was glad she didn't. Either way, it was fun to flirt.

My phone rings and it's Lilly, FaceTiming. She's probably at school, getting ready to start her day. From what I can see, she's sitting on a bench near a playground, flanked by two friends I don't recognize.

"Hey, Lill! How's it going?" I walk out onto my balcony and she stands to walk as well, leaving her friends on the bench behind.

"I just want to go over the speaking points for your one o'clock with Georgia Starr and her brother, Xander," she says. "I had Dad's assistant loop me in on your planning committee meeting. I just got the calendar notification."

"Why on earth would you do that?" I ask.

"One, because this was my idea to begin with. And two, do you know who Xander Starr is? His TikTok videos get a million views!" Lilly says. "I want in on that meeting. I have a favor to ask of him."

"Wait, what meeting is this again?" I feign ignorance, just to wind her up. What's the point of having a little sister if you cannot occasionally wind her up?

Lilly lets out a long-suffering sigh and says my name in a reprimanding way.

"Hudsonnnnn."

"Lillyyyyyy."

I'm pretty sure that Lilly will take over Farm & Holm someday. She's intense. In the best way.

"Cut it out," she says, looking down her nose at me exactly like Oliver.

"Fine … yes, I'm going to the masquerade planning meeting today, Lill. What is it you want from this Xander guy?"

"He's a groomer. Does radical pet transformations. I can't believe you haven't seen them?"

I shake my head to indicate I have not.

"So, here's the thing. Don't agree to anything unless Xander comes to my birthday party."

"Pardon?" I ask, genuinely confused.

"Don't let them have the space for their event unless Xander Starr agrees to come to my birthday party. My friends are obsessed with his feed. I'm hoping he can teach us some cool transitions, maybe give us ideas for original audio, and share his thoughts on how to find the best-trending hashtags?"

"English, Lill."

"I thought you were up on influencer culture, Hudson. This is all pretty 101."

"Baby steps. I'm still learning." I'm pretty sure my sister already knows more about influencer marketing than most of our social media team. "Besides, is this a birthday party or a TikTok masterclass?"

"Both," she says with zero irony. "Do you have a problem with that?"

"Okay." I smile wryly. "I'll try and work it in. And here I was under the impression that we were offering them the space because it was good PR for our family business and, oh yeah, because it was the *right thing to do*."

"All of these things are true, Hudson," Lilly says. "Which is why this is what we call a win/win/win." She counts the wins off on her fingers as she says the words. "Three wins!"

"#Winning?" I offer. She scrunches up her face in response.

"Hey, you know what, Huds? Maybe you should just Face-Time me in later? My schedule is pretty light. I have a 1 p.m. English class, and I've already seen the movie version of *Holes*. I could take an extended bio break."

"How about I text you if I have any questions," I say, firmly

One of her friends from the bench approaches, gesturing urgently. Lilly frowns, then turns back to me, distracted.

"I gotta go. See you next Saturday! Bye, Hudson!"

I don't even have time to respond before she hangs up. And before I can move, Oliver jumps into my lap, pinning me down on the chaise with his preternatural, human-immobilizing cat powers. I use my time as a hostage to learn more about Xander Starr.

There's a brief bio and a photo on the Pawsome Mobile Grooming site. I search for the resemblance to Georgia. They share the same green eyes, but that is about it. While Georgia has fair skin, Xander's skin is dark. Georgia is tiny and curvy, Xander is tall and lean. Her hair is black and tousled. His hair in the photo is bleached blond. He looks younger than her. Early twenties?

I click through to his TikTok account next, watching one video after another. The creative transformations he does really are incredible, and I love how he shares pet care tips, personal stories, fun facts, and statistics in every video. Watching these is addictive. Before I know it, a half hour has passed. Honestly, that guy actually could teach a masterclass on social media. I kind of wish he was the one moderating the Petfluencer Challenge I'm doing with Cookie.

But if he was, I might not have been partnered with her.

I'm still thinking about her owner's tattoo and our cliché convo as I get in the shower.

georgia

. . .

CAN you get a hangover from three large glasses of wine? The answer is yes, when you drink cheap, boxed wine and you are as much of a lightweight as me.

I wake up facedown on the couch, cheek covered in slobber sauce. Cookie is licking me and nudging me with her nose.

"Back off, Cookie. It's Friday," I mumble into a throw pillow.

The shop is closed on Fridays. It's my only day to sleep in. Fridays are also my days to run errands, clean the house, go to the doctor, and do other important things like … retrieve my car from the impound lot.

The previous day's drama creeps in like a slow tide, bathing my brain with bad news as I wake. I swipe my hand around the coffee table to find my phone and come up empty-handed and sore. Oh yeah. That's right. Injured hand. No phone.

Awareness is overrated.

Sitting up, clutching my head, I locate the laptop on the floor, leaning against the couch. It's resting next to my mug, which has dried spaghetti sauce clinging to the inside. A few fossilized Os are still sticking to the spoon.

My adulting game is not so strong today, I acknowledge as I look up the number for the impound lot.

There's no way I'm making it through the day without a cell phone. I go to the kitchen and rummage through the drawers till I find what I'm looking for.

Mom's old phone. I wrap my hand around the cold, metal square, feeling the squeeze in my heart. Holding her phone reminds me there's no way to call her and there never will be. Despite this fact, the phone lights up the minute I plug it in and starts charging. As if it hasn't sat in a drawer for two years, untouched.

Xander and I always teased Mom about her clunky, old flip phone. We'd even bought her a smartphone for Mother's Day, but she'd traded it back in for something simpler.

I unzip the bag of rice holding my phone, crack the case, and extract my SIM card. Miraculously, the SIM card works in my mother's old phone.

I feel quite victorious until I snap a couple photos and review them. Grainy. Out of focus. Truly bad. This is never going to work for the Petfluencer Challenge. What am I going to tell Oliver?

Perhaps Xander or Kenna will let me use their phone for the challenge if I ask them? I could take the photos of Cookie while they're in the shop and email them to myself. I put that idea on the back burner to percolate for now. Maybe it would be okay to ask for a little bit of help? Maybe just this once.

I leave the phone to charge while I pay my fine online and work out the details to pick up the car. Xander's message pops up on my computer screen, "One o'clock at the diner today—don't forget about the meeting!"

There's no time to linger in the shower. I rush through my routine and throw on a pair of frayed, embroidered jeans with an oversize sweater. I'm going to have to rush if I want to make it to the diner in time for the meeting.

"It's just for a few hours, Cookie. You'll be fine. I'll be back soon, I promise." I hate leaving her home alone. As a special treat, I smear some peanut butter around inside her favorite rubber chewie. That should keep her busy for a while.

On my way out the door, I remember to text Xander to let him know Emily will be joining us.

You'll love her, Xan, trust me.

BTW, Angie can't make it today. One of her dogs ate something weird, but we can fill her in later.

I text back from my cab

See you at one!

Two hours later, I'm circling the block in the unicorn. I feel legit with my shiny, new registration tags freshly applied to my plates. But adulting is expensive, and that feeling is fleeting. It's another eight hundred dollars that I don't have to spare. I'm just digging myself deeper and deeper into this hole.

There's no avoiding it. I'm going to have to set up a meeting with the bank next week. I'm worried they'll call in the entire loan if they find out about the rent hike. And if I have to put the house on the market? Then I'll have to tell Xander. He'll never forgive me for losing the house.

There's no parking in front of the diner, so I turn around the corner to the back lot and hustle. I'm already ten minutes late. That's going to earn me a lecture from my punctual little brother.

Emily's already texted that she is there. Hopefully, she's proving to be a distraction.

When I finally arrive, I spy Emily and Xander, settled in a large, semicircular booth in the corner. Kenna's seated with them, wearing her work apron. Emily and Xander are passing a phone back and forth. She's laughing so hard that she has to put the phone down and wipe her eyes.

Xander is probably showing her one of his pet transformations. Maybe Mr. Miyagi?

Accepting her help was a good idea, I think.

"Oh good, you're here! Emily just arrived too." Kenna sees me and waves, then slides out of the booth. She is walking toward me with a paper to-go cup with a lid. I take it and inhale deeply, feeling the last foggy bits of my headache retreat. Oh, sweet caffeine redemption.

"It's the egg coffee again, isn't it?" I say, sipping. "It's good. So good."

The last time Kenna made me this coffee, it was because of Hudson Holm. But is that the coffee's fault?

"You have no idea how much I needed this," I moan.

"You okay, G? You seem a little tired." Xander looks me over.

"I didn't sleep great last night." I wave away his concern. "Nothing that a little bit of Kenna's coffee can't fix right up. I see you've both met Emily?"

"Kenna and I have met previously." Emily smiles at Kenna and holds up her drink.

"London Fog with orange blossom honey," Kenna says, "obviously."

"It's like she sees inside your soul, isn't it?" Xander raises a brow at Emily, who shrugs and nods back in agreement.

"And this one?" Emily points at Xander. "How is it fair that there's so much talent in one family?"

Xander acts nonchalant, but I can tell he is flattered.

There's a loud crash over by the coffee bar, and Kenna rubbernecks to see what the commotion is. She gestures to a confused-looking girl working the espresso maker. "I'll be right back … just going to troubleshoot over there."

Xander turns back to me. "So, G. Why didn't you just tell me that Emily was part of the *Lit Lovers* crew?"

"It was supposed to be a surprise. I was hoping to be here for your inevitable fangirling. Sorry, Emily."

Kenna comes back to the table with a towering plate of French fries and pulls five place settings from the pocket of her apron. "I got these for the table. I took my break early so I can join the meeting."

"Hey, I think you've grabbed one place setting too many," I point out.

"Actually, no." Kenna sets down the fries and looks at Xander. "You didn't tell her about the big news yet?"

"I was just getting to it." Xander finishes reorganizing the stacks of jelly in the condiment holder. They are now perfectly sorted into single flavor stacks of equal height. The extra jellies are set aside. The uncles used to pay him in milkshakes to perform this chore, and he's never stopped doing it.

Xander drums dramatically on the Formica table. "Are you ready for it? The Holms are creating an event space for us in the warehouse reno."

He dumps out the plastic cube holding the sugar packets, methodically separating the raw sugar from the stevia.

"They're super excited about hosting. Might make it an annual thing. Apparently, the idea was Lilly Holm's suggestion. Can you believe it?"

"Lilly Holm?" I ask incredulously. "What is she, ten?"

"That's hardly the most interesting part." Kenna stares meaningfully at me, grabbing a sugar packet from one of Xander's piles. She rips into it and stirs it slowly into her tea. "Lilly's OTHER big brother—the one who is NOT BRYCE—is joining us to discuss the plan."

Kenna winks dramatically at me and turns toward the door, smiling and beckoning to someone.

She stage-whispers, "You'll never believe who it is, Georgia!"

Xander follows Kenna's gaze. "Oh good, he's back. I'll introduce you and Emily."

My heart stops. Everything freezes. There's just me, and him, viewed through the heatwaves rising off the fragrant, steaming fries. I can't look away. The sounds of clinking cutlery and rattling ice cubes echo in the booths around us. My face feels hot, and although I have an irrational urge to bolt, I also feel like I cannot move a muscle.

Emily taps my arm lightly, and I tear my eyes away to look at her. Everyone else is watching him get closer. She is the only one looking at me.

"Do you know him?" she mouths. I nod tightly, almost imperceptibly. My toes are tapping. My fists are clenched. My upper lip wants to curl into a snarl. Even my nostrils feel twitchy. They want to flare.

Fighting to stay calm, I funnel my focus into breath work. How does that work again? Breathe in for five, hold for ten?

I draw in a long, slow breath, counting, and immediately lose track. Instead, I opt to simply hold my breath.

"Sorry, guys. I didn't mean to be rude, but I had to take that call," I hear the man say. "I'm Hudson, Hudson Holm."

"This is Emily," Xander says. Hudson reaches across me to shake Emily's hand. He turns toward me, smiling cannily. "You're Georgia, right? We met at your shop."

Unable to hold my breath any longer, I exhale it in an awkward swoosh. So much for breath work.

It's him, alrighty. Hudson Holm. And he's sliding into the booth beside me. Right next to me. Up close and personal. His leg is brushing against mine. And I can smell him again. What is that scent? I hate him for smelling so good. I want to lean in closer to sample it more properly. I want to get the hell away from it.

"Sorry," he says, looking down to where our legs are touching. "I have a hard time fitting in booths."

"Please," Kenna says. "You should see some of the manspreaders who come in here. I swear I've seen guys half your size take up three-quarters of this booth."

I inch toward Xander, who doesn't hesitate before shoving me right back toward Hudson. As payback, but also as a distraction, I snag the freshly organized jelly sorter, dumping it out, mixing everything up, and then restacking them in deliberately mismatched stacks.

Xander twitches, glaring at my handiwork.

"So, Georgia, as I was saying, Hudson here has not only offered up the event space at their newly renovated warehouse, but he's also joining our planning committee."

Hudson swipes an orange marmalade before I can place it on the mixed-up stack of grape and strawberry and hands it back to Xander, who is currently trying to sequester the orange ones from me.

I tilt my head up to scowl at Hudson. He stares back unflinch-ingly, blue eyes glinting with amber sparks of … something. He almost looks amused. Like he's double-dog daring me to do something, say something.

But in the next instant, he surprises me, reaching out and taking my bandaged right hand.

"What's the story here? What happened to your hand?" he asks. He gently turns my right hand over, trailing a finger across my palm from my bandage-wrapped middle finger, down to my wrist. He studies my wrist, placing his large thumb over the soft flesh, like he's taking my pulse. Which is approximately one hundred billion bpm.

My skin buzzes beneath his touch, and I feel the booth rock as if it's a boat that's just been pushed away from the dock. I could swear the booth is swaying. I almost have to fight the urge to hold on to him, like he's the only solid thing.

What the hell is happening here?

"It's nothing." I snatch my hand away. "Just a scratch. A little work accident."

"You should be careful if you got that from an animal." He places his large, well-groomed hands back on the table. Even his damned hands are attractive. "It's easy for scratches to get infected."

"I'm fine," I reiterate. But am I? I can't ignore this dangerous energy sparking and fizzing between us.

Xander clears his throat. Hudson looks away from me. But he doesn't budge his leg. If anything, he's taking up more space, ceding no territory. And neither am I. I brace my foot against the pillar under the table, kicking Xander in the process.

"Ouch!" he exclaims, shooting me a what-the-fuck-is-up-with-you look.

"So Xander, my sister, Lilly, and her friends are all obsessed with your TikTok. I had a look and I can see why," Hudson says. "Really creative. Your shelter pet transformations are so inspiring. I understand it's made a huge difference when it comes to finding homes for the animals."

What a kiss-ass. Xander practically glows, basking in this praise.

"I can't take all the credit. A lot of the time, it's all down to the outfits we choose. Georgia is the one who makes the pet clothing." Xander puts mayo on his BLT. "Her designs are really special. She's been getting a lot of press lately. In fact, Emily here was just in the shop to do a piece for *Pet Friends* magazine."

Emily nods, looking worriedly from me to Hudson, and back to me, before making room for Kenna to slide back into the booth. She's the only other person here who knows about the knockoff situation, and she's started to put two and two together. Emily meets my eye.

"The story just went to press," she says. "Should hit the stands next week. I was thrilled to write about Georgia's pet clothing. Other companies may try to copy her, but she's the real deal."

I could kiss her.

"I did know about the clothes." Hudson smiles tightly. "I was just in the store last week, remember? I picked up a few pet outfits. Didn't know about the article though. Congrats on the press."

"Wait, you were in the store last week?" Xander looks from me to Kenna, realization dawning across his face in the form of a smug smile. "Hold on. You're the egg coffee dude?"

"Guilty." Hudson grins. "My Swedish grandma taught me how to make it that way."

"I couldn't believe he came up with a coffee recipe I'd never heard of!" Kenna praises Hudson.

Et tu, Brute?

Hudson turns back to me with that blazing, blue gaze again. So knowing. Almost intimate. I hate how it instantly warms me.

"Did you like the coffee, Georgia?" His voice vibrates against me like a caress. Like he's petting me. My body is betraying me and behaving ridiculously. Next thing I know, my leg will start kicking wildly like Cookie's does when I get that spot behind her ear.

"Hated it." I scowl.

Kenna snorts. "Really? Is that why you inhaled that entire cup I just made for you?"

"I was desperate," I say. "I hadn't had any coffee yet today. I didn't want to get a no-coffee migraine."

Hudson's brow wrinkles in such a boyish manner when he frowns, I note.

"Sorry about that, then. I should probably let Kenna stick to the coffee prescriptions, right?" he apologizes.

"Right." I take a bite of my Reuben and a swig of my soda. "So how did your sister like the costumes you bought for her?"

"She hasn't seen them yet," he answers, dipping a fry and raising it to his lips. I can't take my eyes off that French fry. "But I'm sure she'll love them. They are very clever."

Hudson's watch makes a clicking sound, and he glances at his wrist. "I've got to get back to the office for a meeting in forty-five minutes, so we should probably review the details quickly. You're welcome to use the space, but there are a couple of things I'd like to ask in return."

"Name it!" Xander beams.

"The first thing has to do with our efforts to market the property. We'd like to open the model lofts for tours during the event. It's a pet-friendly property, and I think this fundraiser is a great match for the demographic we're targeting."

"Done!" Xander slaps the table enthusiastically. "Mac and I were just saying that we wanted to check out the lofts."

"You definitely should! I'd love to hear what you think," Hudson says enthusiastically. "The second thing is more of a personal favor. It has to do with my little sister. I mentioned she's a big fan of yours, Xander. Georgia's, too, apparently."

The song "Love Cats" by The Cure suddenly trumpets out from beneath the table. Hudson reaches down into his pocket and fishes out his phone.

"Yep. Speak of the devil. This is her FaceTiming right now," he says. Hudson presses the screen. "Lilly? We talked about this. You shouldn't be cutting class."

"Don't worry about me, Hudson. I've got a 4.0 GPA. Everything's on track for Stanford. Are you there with them?"

"Yes, I'm here." He sighs and turns the phone around, slowly rotating it so we can all see.

"Everyone … say hi to Lilly."

A young, freckle-faced girl waves. She seems to be sitting on the vanity of a sink in a public restroom. Probably the girl's bathroom at her school. We're all reflected on the screen in the mirror behind her.

"Let me talk to Georgia first!" she demands.

"I'm here. How can I help you?" I raise my eyebrows and wave. "Why me?"

"I understand you punched my brother Bryce?" she says.

"What! Where did you hear that?" I look at Hudson, but he shrugs. Kenna shakes her head. Xander looks amused.

"It was all over Twitter. Someone texted me a photo. But that doesn't matter. The point is, Georgia, that you are my hero. Bryce is such a jerk. I can't believe he tweeted what he did about the pet shelter. I know how much you and your family have done for Kismet Rescue, and my friends and I want to help. We thought maybe if we got a little assistance from Xander and got better at making videos, perhaps we could mobilize and make a difference."

I have to pick my jaw up off the table. Who is this kid?

"Any friend of the shelter pets is a friend of ours." Xander kicks me gently under the table.

"Okay, but I still don't get why you need me?" I ask.

"Because you're the GOAT, Georgia," Lilly argues. "I gotta get back to English class, but please, please, please say yes? Huds, I'm counting on you to close this deal."

She hangs up abruptly, but we all keep staring at the screen for another ten seconds.

"So now you've all met my boss." Hudson smiles wryly.

"Um … what's the GOAT?" Emily asks.

"Greatest of all time," Kenna answers, still staring at the blank screen.

I turn back to face Hudson, hating it that I have to crane my neck so much to meet his eye.

"Are you punking me? Is this some kind of a setup? Your family are the ones who forced the shelter out. And you have to know that our charitable efforts are being undermined by your rent hike."

Xander looks miserable, but I keep going.

"So, from where I sit, it feels kind of cruel for you and your family to be pretending you care about us and our shelter efforts."

"You think my little sister is pretending?" Hudson challenges.

"She's a kid," I respond.

I'm not really questioning his little sister. She actually seems sincere enough. But I'm definitely questioning him and his hundred-dollar bills, rock-hard abs, and forest-fresh scent.

"Don't confuse me with my stepbrother, Georgia." Hudson's frown deepens. "I'm not going to apologize for having a successful business, but I also don't share Bryce's sentiments about the shelter. It should have been handled differently. I think that's what Lilly was getting at. We both feel that way."

"Really?" I counter. "I might have bought that line a few weeks ago. Before the rent hike on a building that you barely maintain. And before you tried to kneecap me with your new, 'affordable' pet clothing line. Why not throw a flaming brick through my shop window while you're at it?"

Emily stiffens, biting her lip, and Kenna and Xander are frozen like statues, looking shocked and confused. I wish I'd had the chance to speak with them before this confrontation.

Hudson is glaring right back at me now. "Look, Georgia, I won't argue with you about how amazing your handmade clothing is, but not everyone can afford to spend fifty bucks on a silly little outfit for their cat."

"Like you or anyone in your family can begin to identify with that issue." I sneer. "And that's beside the point, isn't it? Let's just speak plainly here, shall we? I know what you're up to, Hudson Holm! I know you've been knocking off my clothes. You ought to be ashamed of yourself!"

I try to stand up in the booth, to even out our height difference, and I knock my plate. Xander scrambles to keep my
drink from spilling, then places a hand on my shoulder,
pushing me back down into my seat.

"What the hell's wrong with you, G?" he hisses in my ear.

"I have no idea what you're talking about," Hudson says.
There's a muscle twitching in his jaw. "But I assure you that if
there is an issue about copyright for any of the items we're
producing, our legal team will be investigating it and getting
to the bottom of it."

"Oh, please, cut the act. Just pull up the Farm and Holm site."
I reach for the flip phone and open it, only to realize I've got
phantom phone syndrome. I'm still feeling an Internet
connection in my hand when there is none.

Hudson stares at the flip phone and raises an ironic eyebrow.

"Seriously? I think you're going to have to find a dial-up
connection to use with that thing," he says.

"Pull it up on your phone, then. Every single one of the pet
clothing designs on your site are obvious knockoffs of my
line. It's causing brand confusion." I point at Emily. "Just
yesterday, she couldn't tell whether a suit she saw online was
yours or mine. I had to set her straight."

Emily shrinks back into her seat, and I apologize for putting
her on the spot.

"It's true," she says.

Hudson speaks cooly. "These are some pretty serious accusations you are making. Like I said, if there's been some sort of
issue, our team will definitely want to look into it. But in the
meantime, how can I be sure your line isn't a knockoff of
OUR stuff?"

"Because my stuff isn't crap!" I growl back at him.

"Well, I'd sure hope not. Not at those prices," Hudson says. His thigh is still pressed hotly against mine, but I refuse to give up any ground. "Just a tip … maybe if you focused on producing something that could scale, you could sell more stuff. You wouldn't have to charge so much."

"You think I should just give up on earning a living wage? Maybe I should skimp on materials like you do? Or maybe you think shelter pets and people like me don't deserve nice things?" My claws are on full display now. "Listen, Mr. Cashmere sweater collection, I'm not going to apologize to you for caring about quality. You can stick your silver spoon—"

"So just to be clear," Hudson interrupts, "you're saying you don't want to use the event space, free of charge, no strings attached? Am I hearing that correctly? Hasn't anyone ever told you not to look a gift horse in the mouth?"

Kenna's head is in her hands. And Emily is still biting her lip, eyes wide, glued to the scene I have caused.

Xander looks horrified. "Nonsense. Of course we want the space. And I'm happy to come to Lilly's party. Let me talk to my sister. I'm sure we can all work this out."

"Great. That's settled. It's a go, then," Hudson says. "Oh, and I spoke to Jackson last night. Thanks for tapping him, Emily. He had to teach today, but he said he's down to livestream the entire event. That should open it up to a much broader audience"—Hudson turns to me, speaking slowly and enunciating as if I need extra time to process—"which will be great for the shelter pets."

Kenna begins to clap her hands when she hears this, then looks at me. The ice lasers coming out of my eyes are enough to pause her hands in midair before they can connect again. She glances down and places her hands in her lap.

Hudson slides lithely and quickly out of the booth. "I honestly think this will benefit all of us and our mutual goals." He smiles warmly at everyone, but his knowing eyes stay glued on mine and only narrow slightly when he says, "Let's stay in touch."

hudson

. . .

I'M NOT ADEQUATELY PREPARED for this.

Sure, I'd braced myself for this meeting with Georgia today. I suspected she'd be less than cordial upon figuring out who I am—Hudson of the cursed Holm clan, brother of Bryce, the dog hater, evil landlord, and all that. But I am not physically ready to be crammed into a booth beside her. Not just beside her. Against her.

Our bodies are touching, hip to knee. Some of this is inevitable. I wasn't built for tiny diner booths. My size tends to turn these seating arrangements into much more intimate encounters. But this is more. This is a battle. She isn't just touching me. Georgia is *pressing* her thigh against me. Is she marking her territory, or is she trying to get rid of me? She's ticking against me like a time bomb that's about to explode.

Why is she so pissed off at me, exactly? I've never done anything to her. Farm & Holm isn't perfect, but we're not exactly evil either. And I'm not my brother's keeper. She's so damn mad. Possibly the crazy kind as well as the angry kind. So why am I so turned on by her again?

Dammit. Damn her. I steal tiny looks at her between pleasantries.

Georgia Starr is wild-eyed and ferocious-looking today. Dangerously gorgeous. No makeup besides that red lipstick. Her hair's a mess, but that tousled look suits her personality perfectly. Nobody tells Georgia Starr's hair what to do. Meanwhile, the baggy sweater may be hiding her curves, but her jeans … the way her tight jeans are clinging to her thighs makes it difficult for me to focus. There's an embroidered vine snaking up her leg that disappears under her sweater. I want to reach under there, run my fingers along its path, and see where it ends.

I know I won't sleep well tonight. I'll be replaying this scene in this booth over and over again in my head.

Is she really accusing *me* of knocking her off?

"How do I know *you* haven't knocked off our designs?" I fire back.

Her look of molten hatred makes me regret saying it the moment it comes out. It's kind of a low blow. But then again, there's no reason she needs to make me her personal punching bag, is there?

I'm reminded of another cliché, one that didn't show up in the conversation with Cookie last night.

No good deed goes unpunished.

Making my excuses, I slide out of the booth. I can still feel the imprint of Georgia's thigh and the smoldering, green heat of her glare when I get in my car.

Could there be any truth to her accusations? I dread the task that lies ahead of me.

———

Oliver watches me pacing, head turning back and forth like a spectator at a sporting event. I take a long pull of my beer, stopping by the floor-to-ceiling windows. It's getting dark out. Twinkling lights reflect off the river. Normally, I love the nighttime view. It's like watching fireflies. But tonight, I'm too unsettled to enjoy it.

My laptop is already set up on a work table next to the chaise. I sigh and speak to the cat. "May as well get this over with, right, Buddy?"

Oliver rises, stretches, and comes to sit beside me, purring his approval. I type in the URL.

The Farm & Holm Pet Supplies site loads quickly. There's our familiar logo, front and center. A pop up chatbot dog named "Max the Retriever" offers me his assistance. There's also a flashing banner advertising "New for Boo!" that links directly to Farm & Holm's brand-new pet clothing collection. Bryce's collection.

Already, I can spy some duplicate themes. I have a bad feeling about this.

I open up a second browser window and pull up the Celestial Pets website, clicking into the album of Georgia's designs, past and present. I recognize the doctor scrubs and a few of the other costumes that I purchased last week in the store. Her collection is larger and more bespoke. Many of her costumes are one-offs. I hold my breath, hoping that my initial impression was wrong.

But when I rearrange my screen and view the two sites side by side, I do see it. I really do.

The similarities are undeniable. Every single one of the twelve designs on the Farm & Holm site corresponds to a nearly identical version of one of Georgia's costumes.

A clammy wave of shame rolls over me, leaving me feeling nauseated. But it doesn't last too long. It's replaced by a white-hot bolt of anger. None of this is my doing.

I screen-shoot the two pages, side by side, and open the images in markup, using different colors to circle and link the matching outfits. It's like I'm doing some kind of children's worksheet where you match the frogs. Except this isn't a game.

Our lawyers are going to make a meal of this. I can already see the bills rolling in. And if this gets out to the press? To our investors?

I save the image I'm working on with all the circled matches and attach it to an email addressed to Bryce, cc'd to Walker.

Subject line: What the actual fuck?

As soon as I hear the whoosh, indicating the mail's been sent, I open my laptop and call the boat.

Walker picks up almost immediately. I can see he's a little sunburned. He's lounging in bed, reading a book. Stone-cold sober. So much for the bachelor party. This looks oddly like a normal vacation.

"Two calls from my firstborn son in one week!" Walker greets me. "To what do I owe the pleasure?"

"We've got a problem," I say. "Where's Bryce?"

"No clue," says Walker. "Fiji maybe? He messaged yesterday that he was meeting up with some friends."

"I thought the whole point of getting Bryce out of Ephron was to keep him out of trouble. Shouldn't you be keeping an eye on him?"

"I'm not a babysitter," Walker scoffs, "and Bryce is a grown man."

I get to the point. "Right. Well, here's the deal. We've been accused of knocking off products. Take a look at the email I just sent you."

I wait patiently while my father pulls up the email, puts on a pair of reading glasses, and reviews the image I've sent.

"Dammit. This doesn't look good," he agrees. "You're going to have to alert legal."

"I know."

"How exactly did you find out about this?" he asks.

"That's an interesting story," I say. "I went to that planning meeting for the masquerade earlier today. It was an ambush. Let's just say that the owner of Celestial Pets would love to plant a stake with my head on it in the town square, right next to great-granddad's plaque. Bryce's head could go on the other side. She'd be happy to make us a matched set."

"We really can't afford a problem like this." Walker sighs.

"I know," I agree.

"Maybe it's just a misunderstanding. Let me see if I can reach Bryce and conference him in."

A misunderstanding? Seriously? I try not to lose it prematurely. I can't wait to hear Bryce's explanation.

The screen erupts with static-y screeches and loud music as Bryce finally joins the conference call. Walker winces and covers his ears.

"Mute button!" we both say, gesturing wildly.

"Sorry, sorry!" Bryce says, his image freezing and coming back. He mutes himself, then holds up a finger while walking indoors, presumably asking us to wait while he finds a quieter place to speak. Silently, we wait.

"Wanker," I say, under my breath. For once, Walker doesn't argue with me.

Bryce appears to be a guest on a superyacht. There are stairs, a hallway, and then suddenly, it appears he's in a private bedroom.

"Hey, hey!" Bryce bounces on the bed and leans back against the quilted headboard.

"You got a thing there, kid." Walker points at a neon-green thong clinging to the upholstery. Bryce reaches up, snags the thong, spins it on his finger, then shoots it away like a rubber band.

No comment.

"How's it hanging, Bro?" Bryce smiles smugly.

"Have you read my email?" I ask, annoyed that he isn't even acknowledging the issue.

"Yeah, I saw it. I don't understand what the big deal is. Why do we have to even have this call? It's DOG clothes." Bryce examines his reflection in his mirrored sunglasses. "It's hardly Dolce & Gabbana."

"The outfits appear to be very similar, Bryce," Walker says.

"Look, they have a pumpkin costume, we have a pumpkin costume. You're telling me that the idea of dog pumpkin costumes is something that people think they own? Pretty ridiculous, don't you think?" He blinks innocently at us.

"It's not the concept, Bryce. It's the execution. The materials. The design," I say. He's making my eyelid tick.

"Oh, stop. How do you even know they didn't knock us off?" Bryce scoffs. "We're a big company with worldwide distribution. Celestial Pets is just a puny, little pet shop in a Podunk little town." He gestures with his hands as if he's weighing the issue and finding one side lacking. "Who ya gonna believe here?"

I hate myself right now for having suggested something so similar to Georgia.

"Who made our pet costumes, son?" Walker cuts in.

"You know we had them made at our shop in Asia, Dad." Bryce's chin juts out.

"And who, exactly, designed them?" Walker asks.

"We worked with the manufacturer on the samples and specs," he says.

"And I assume there's a record of that?" I chime in.

"Well, I guess. I mean, there's the DHL records, I suppose," Bryce theorizes. He's examining his cuticles now.

"What DHL records?" I ask.

"When I sent them the outfits." Bryce rolls his eyes like we're the idiots.

"What outfits?" Walker and I ask, simultaneously.

"The ones from that stupid, little pet shop," Bryce says. "Obviously."

"Hold up a minute." Walker stands up, looking genuinely pissed off now. He paces back and forth in his tiny cabin. "Are you telling me you sent actual outfits from Celestial Pets to our Asian manufacturers?"

"Yeah, but they were just SAMPLES." Bryce grimaces. "I didn't tell them to make them exactly the same. It was just … you know … a general guideline of the sort of stuff they should make. That's how manufacturing works. You send some stuff that people like to the factory, and then your team copies it but makes it way cheaper for a higher profit margin. Do I really need to explain this to you two?"

Our father is silent, for once. I watch him sit down, head in his hands.

"How did you even get the outfits? Did you go into the shop?" I ask.

"No! My assistant bought a few. And she placed a couple online orders." Bryce waves his hand dismissively.

"No wonder that little girl decked you. Jesus fucking Christ on a Tuesday, Bryce. That's it. I give up," Walker says. He wipes his hands together and raises them to indicate just how done he is.

Oliver runs over, jumps on my desk, and plops down in front of the screen, staring curiously at my father and stepbrother.

"It was an unprovoked attack!" Bryce defends.

"Nice-looking cat, Hudson," Walker says.

"Thanks."

"Look, Dad, I'm coming back to our yacht tomorrow and we can talk about this, okay? Maybe it's not exactly what you would have done, but everybody 'borrows' in fashion. There's no reason to get your knickers in a twist."

"The hell you are coming back on my boat," Walker bellows.

"But all my stuff is on there." Bryce pouts.

"I'll leave it in a locker at the port," he says. "And Hudson? I'll see you at Lilly's birthday party in two weeks?"

"Great," I say. "Lilly will be thrilled."

"We'll work this out. But first, you gotta call whoever you gotta call and get all those products down. We'll have to find a way to make it up to that girl."

"Her name is Georgia," I say.

"Right, Georgia," Walker repeats. "There's gotta be something we can do to keep her from suing us."

"Is this all really necessary?" Bryce chimes in.

"Shut up, Bryce," Walker says. "I'm done talking to you. In fact, I'm done talking to both of you for now. I'm just going to read my dumb book … now where is that thing?" He pulls up a copy of what appears to be Blaze Smith's *Go Your Own Way* and abruptly leaves the conversation.

"Bye, Bryce," I say.

Following my father's lead, I slam my computer shut.

georgia

. . .

THE MORNING AFTER THE MEETING, Kenna holds a white paper bag full of pastries in front of the door to the shop and shakes it. It's labeled in black sharpie with the words "I'M SORRY" in all caps.

This is her version of a white flag.

"Permission to enter?"

On Saturdays, I usually like to come in early and spend some time sewing before making sure the shop is ready for the weekend. But today, I have other plans. I'm doing a full survey of all the outfits on the Farm & Holm site that are knockoffs of mine. I've also downloaded a boilerplate cease and desist letter.

"Fine. But that better not be an egg coffee." I gesture at the paper cup.

"Pumpkin Latte." Kenna plunks the coffee in front of me, imitating an obnoxious, over-caffeinated teenager. "OMG, you guys! It's officially PSL season!"

"I can't believe you think I'm that basic." I take a sip of the insipidly sweet, frothy beverage, trying not to wince.

"I don't. I had an extra because the new trainee was practicing, and I was afraid you'd rip my head off if I brought you your regular."

"Egg coffee is not my regular." I force the pumpkin stuff down. "And I thought you had my back."

"I had no idea Hudson was a *Holm* the first time I met him. I just recognized him as the guy from The Onion who had you all flustered," Kenna says.

"I was not flustered!"

"Okay. Whatever you say." She pokes at the flip phone on the counter. "You shouldn't be using this. It's like a historical artifact. It needs to be preserved in a museum."

"I don't know when I'll be able to get a new phone. I have to dig up my insurance."

"How are you going to do the photos for the challenge with that thing?"

"I'll manage," I say. Now is probably not the best time to ask her to borrow her phone for photos.

"Don't be silly. Just use my phone. Or let me take some shots."

"Thank you, Kenna. You're a really good friend."

"Mm-hmm." She sips her hot drink. "So why didn't you call me when you found out about the knockoffs?"

"You were on a shoot," I say. "And then I tried to call you, but you were out on a date. What happened with that?"

"Nothing." Kenna rolls her eyes. "Dude was such a dud. Spent the whole night detailing his skin and hair care routines to me. And then he wanted me to go in on a Groupon with him for laser lipo."

This gets a genuine snort out of me.

"Really? Which part of your skinny-ass anatomy did he suggest you use the Groupon on?"

"My calves." She sticks out a leg.

"The nerve!"

"So, it's back to that celibate life." Kenna sighs. "At least I don't have to have a panic attack every time I forget to take my pill first thing in the morning."

"I'm sorry. That sucks," I say, sympathetically.

"You know … I know you don't want to talk about the Holms, but I just can't stop wondering about that night at The Onion. Can you imagine the conversation between Hudson and Bryce after we left?"

In fact, I can imagine it. I have imagined it a million times and a million ways. I have practically written a choose-your-own-adventure novel imagining all the different ways that conversation might have played out.

"I don't care what they had to say about me," I assert. "The Holms may be our landlords, but they don't matter to me. I don't want to think about Bryce or Hudson or anyone else in that family."

"Lilly Holm seems like a pretty cool kid though. She's certainly your fan."

"Nope. Don't even say their name." I hold up a finger.

"Whose name?" Xander comes in the door, wearing a bike helmet.

"Hey, Xander. Did you bike here? Who's driving the van, then?" Kenna asks.

"Mac is." Xander fans himself. "I asked him to help out. Big day. We've got three strays coming in." He turns to face me. "Did Angie call you, G? She's touring the new location today.

They're putting the new heaters in the kennel and pouring the cement pad for the portables. They should be able to have everything operational by November 15th, barring any more setbacks."

"That's great!" I try to look like I mean it.

If they're pouring cement this week, that means they are ahead of schedule. Great news for the dogs, bad news for me. My checks to the construction company have most certainly already been cashed, and the final bills will be arriving shortly. There's no turning back now.

There's no way I'll be able to pay Angie's salary, plus make the mortgage payments and cover the rent hike, come November.

"I'm excited about the photos today," Kenna says. "You two mind if I shop?"

"Help yourself." I wave toward the clothing rack. Xander takes off his helmet and leans against the counter, doing stretches, while chatting with me.

"So, are you feeling any better today?" he asks. "Thinking more clearly?" He does a lunge and glances sideways at me, warily.

"I was totally blindsided. I will not apologize for losing it."

"Understood. But you might have given him a chance to explain."

"Explain what? Why their shitty management company can't be bothered to fix anything over here? Or how it came to be that my original designs are being copied on their website? He's got a *lot* of explaining to do."

Kenna calls out from the rack, "Yeah, but it might not be Hudson's fault. He actually seemed nice to me."

"Then YOU date him," I snap, and instantly, I feel the bile-green slime of envy sucking me under. I can't bear to picture it. She can't have him either.

"Nope. Too clean-cut and blond. He's not even close to my type," Kenna says in a flat voice without even looking up.

Xander takes me in for a moment, then comes behind the counter to give me a hug.

"Cut it out, you're gross." I make no move to push him away.

"You just looked like you needed it," he says. "You're so stressed." He glances at the cease and desist letter on the counter. "We can hire a lawyer, if you want. I can help out. Bottom line—you need to chill. It's all going to be okay. You don't have to do everything alone."

"What if it's not?" I sniff. How am I going to tell him about the house? At this point, I really don't see any other option. I've got to come clean. At least he'll still have a place to live if I lose it.

"It's really wonderful that Mac is helping you out today, Xander," I say.

"Yeah, he's the best," Xander agrees, continuing his lecture. "But you know what, G? He didn't offer. I asked him. I know you hate asking for help, but people like to feel needed. I like to feel needed."

"Me too!" Kenna calls out.

"That's what friends and family are for … to support each other. You've always been there for me, and God knows what kind of inmate Kenna would be dating if it wasn't for you."

"Hey, now!" Kenna objects.

"You have spectacularly bad taste in men," Xander snorts.

"I like to think of it as faith in humanity," she says.

"There's fixer-uppers and then there's tear downs." He shakes his head dubiously before turning back to face me. "My point is, it's high time you start letting people in. You can't keep it all bottled up. And you're not fooling me with your whole 'it'll be fine' bullshit. I know you need a miracle to meet your obligations with the shelter."

"How do you know that?" I argue stubbornly.

"I helped Mom do the finances on this place for years, Georgia. She had a hard time paying Angie's salary at the best of times. I can't tell you how many times she almost took out a second mortgage."

There's something comforting in knowing my mom struggled too. But also horrifying. Because she hadn't ever resorted to mortgaging the house. My legs feel wobbly, and I have to sit down. I flop into the plaid chair.

"Poor Mom. And poor Angie. I can't even think about what she'd do if we had to lay her off."

"Angie? I suspect she'd do whatever she felt like doing. Play tennis more. Buy more stuff for her dogs?"

"But she needs that job, Xander," I argue. "She's a senior citizen. She's probably living on a fixed income."

"I have news for you, Georgia." Xander snorts. "Poor Angie was an early investor in Microsoft. She's not working at the shelter because she needs the money. She pulls in more interest monthly than we pay her in a year. Can you get off the struggle bus already?"

"What?" I sit bolt upright at this unexpected news. "Are you kidding me? Angie is a millionaire? OUR Angie?"

Suddenly, I can't stop laughing. The whole thing seems so ludicrous. All this time, I was picturing Angie clipping coupons and feeling guilty about charging her anything for the costumes she keeps coming back for.

Kenna and Xander gape at me as I continue to shake and howl with laughter to the point of inducing hiccups.

"Are you okay, G?" Xander casts a sidelong look at me. I take a deep breath and attempt to get ahold of myself.

"I mortgaged the house," I blurt out. "I'm so sorry, Xander. I fucked up. Please don't hate me." I can't even look at him. I cover my eyes with my hands.

A beat goes by, and then I sense them moving closer. Kenna sits on the arm of the chair and rubs my back. Xander kneels in front of me, gently peeling my hands from my face.

"Georgia," he says.

"I don't know how I'll pay it back," I admit. "It was already going to be a stretch before the rent hike."

"Dammit, G. What were you thinking?" Xander sighs.

"That we had to make sure the shelter could reopen in a new space so the animals would be safe and so Angie could keep her job." I hiccup as I justify my decision.

"Okay, but how were you planning to pay it back?"

"Marketing," I say. "I signed up for that Petfluencer Challenge. You've done so well on TikTok." My plan sounds so flimsy to me now. Especially since I still have fewer than two hundred followers.

"That didn't happen overnight though," Xander says. "I've been making grooming videos for years, and it's taken a long time to figure it out. I don't know why you didn't ask me for help."

"I know." I hang my head in shame. "I just didn't want to bug you. I thought I could figure it out myself. I've been so stupid. I've let everyone down. Mom would be so disappointed in me."

"Stop it. Mom would still be proud of you, Georgia. And she'd say the same thing we've been attempting to tell you. Stop trying to do everything alone."

"He's right," Kenna says.

"So, you're not mad at me?" I wipe my eyes and dare to look at my brother.

"I'm not gonna lie. I'm a little pissed that you kept this from me." Xander lets out a long breath. "But I'm not mad at you for trying to keep the shelter open."

"And if it means we lose the house?"

"We're not losing the house." Xander shakes his head.

"But how?"

"We're going to blow out this event. It's not just a local shindig anymore. Between my followers and Jackson's offer to livestream, we have the ability to reach hundreds of thousands of potential donors. We're going to pay for the shelter's renovations and at least a few months of operating expenses."

"And if that doesn't work?"

"We'll figure something else out. But it IS going to work."

I sigh, feeling some of the tension lift from my shoulders. "Thank you for not being mad at me," I say to Xander.

"See how much more you can accomplish when you trust people enough to let them in?" Kenna squeezes my shoulder. "I'm glad you're finally starting to see some sense. Nobody can possibly do it all alone."

"But what about the Holms?" I ask. "What am I going to do about the knockoffs?"

"Let's get through this masquerade. Afterwards we can hire you a lawyer, and you can sue the pants off Hudson Holm. If you still feel like it."

I bite my lip and Kenna punches me.

"You just pictured him without pants, didn't you?" She laughs. "Admit it."

"Never!" I shake my head.

"So, we're all in agreement? We're going to bury the hatchet for the next three weeks and make this event a success?"

"Speaking of burying the hatchet …" An idea occurs to me. A way to blow off steam. "There's something I need to do first. I think it might help."

"What's that?" Xander asks.

"The Grumpy Stump, 8 p.m. tonight. There's a special discount for *Lit Lovers* listeners tonight."

Kenna jumps up. "I love it! Let's goooooo!"

Xander groans. He's not as much of a fan of the place as I am. "Are you really going to make me go there again?"

"It's therapeutic," I say. "You can't expect me to bury the hatchet with the Holms before I get in a few good throws."

hudson

. . .

IT'S TOO QUIET. I check my phone repeatedly on Saturday. Almost forty-eight hours have passed since I've heard from Cookie. She hasn't posted on her feed either. Something's been off since the other day. What if something happened to my buddy? Or her funny, wise-cracking human with the tattoo? How would I even know?

After spending the day wrestling with what to do about the knockoff situation, the only answer is to take Bryce's collection down. I put in a work order with the on call team. But I can't do anything till I go back over it with legal on Monday morning. I'm at the point where I'm about to go stir-crazy. My thoughts keep obsessively pinging between a woman who hates me and my anonymous canine pen pal.

Clearly, I'm in need of a social life. I give Jackson a call.

"Hey, man, you around? Want to grab another drink at The Onion?"

"Oh shit. Look at the time. I've been sitting at my desk working on this damned algorithm all day. It's a good thing you called. I'm supposed to be somewhere in thirty minutes. Have you ever done axe throwing?" Jackson asks.

"Axe throwing, you say?"

Coincidentally, the one sport I excelled at in boarding school in Sweden was axe throwing. It was a pretty common pastime there, long before becoming popular in the States. I was the reigning champion of the boys' dorm. I don't mention this to Jackson, however, just in case I have the opportunity to hustle him. He is a bit of a know-it-all.

"You'll have to teach me," I say innocently.

"There's a newish place, not far from your lofts," Jackson says. "It's a lot of fun. You get a bucketful of axes and chuck them at a target. They've sponsored a few episodes of my podcast, and we're doing a discount for our listeners tonight. Almost forgot I said I'd be there. It should be right up your alley, given your resemblance to Thor."

"I believe Thor's thing was throwing hammers." I correct him.

"Well, you can pretend it's a hammer, if you like. I sort of like to pretend I'm Cupid."

"Isn't Cupid supposed to use an arrow?"

"Arrow, axe … honestly, wouldn't it be more persuasive if he used an axe?"

"No," I state emphatically. "I don't think it works that way, dude. Maybe don't share these theories with your app backers. Or your dates."

"Nobody ever called me subtle. I think if people could just be more direct, there'd be a lot less heartache. It'd be like, whoosh! Kachunk! Bullseye!"

The idea of a chubby, winged, axe-wielding baby seems wrong on so many levels. "Somehow, I don't think this is what the Romans intended. Sounds more like a horror film."

"Nah. It's more like romantic action-adventure."

"Speaking of which, they actually serve beer at an axe throwing place?" I ask. "Is that really a good idea?"

"Probably not," Jackson says, "but statistically speaking, there haven't been too many accidents at The Grumpy Stump."

Without addressing what constitutes "too many" or why the place is named The Grumpy Stump, we make plans to meet there in about half an hour.

Since The Grumpy Stump is in the industrial district, not too far from the lofts, I choose to walk. Fluffy clouds are zipping across the sky, and the smell of wet leaves lingers in the cool, misty air. Jackson passes me in his car, parks, and jogs back to walk the last two blocks with me.

"Sorry I missed the event planning meeting yesterday. How did it go?"

"It went." I sigh.

"Emily said Celestial Pets' primary goal is to raise funds for the shelter relocation?"

"Yep." I nod. "Folks are a bit touchy about that. Bryce hasn't helped matters."

"How are you even related?" Jackson shakes his head.

"Technically, we aren't," I point out.

"Seems like a good idea, giving them the use of your space," Jackson comments.

"It was actually Lilly's idea," I say. "I think she was getting a hard time about the shelter from some of the kids at school."

"Poor Lilly. It's so tough being a kid these days," Jackson says. "Cyberbullying comes up all the time in our dating focus groups."

"You clearly don't know my sister." I laugh. "She's basically a mini-Walker. Nobody pushes Lilly around. Come to the next planning meeting?" I suggest. "We're doing the walk-through next week. You can meet everyone and work out the livestream stuff then. It's coming together pretty quickly."

"Works for me." Jackson nods.

———

The Grumpy Stump sign displays their logo—two crossed axes above a stump burned into a three-foot-wide slice from an old growth tree. Stained yellow and lit from above, it glows golden in the night, gathering locals like moths to a flame.

It's busier than I would have thought. Axe throwing appears to be a hit. It's a younger crowd than you'd find at The Onion. Small groups of hipsters mill around outside, vaping and chatting. There are a lot of interesting tattoos, haircuts, and some truly impressive facial hair. The conversation seems lively.

From the street, I'm startled to see two familiar faces seated inside at the end of the bar. Xander and Kenna are engrossed in conversation. They don't notice us when we come in.

Kenna shouts toward the caged-off area beside the bar, "Just keep going. You can take my bucket. I'm useless at throwing axes."

"Are you sure we should be encouraging her?" Xander speaks loudly to Kenna, voice rising above the din. "She's chucking those axes so hard, I'm afraid she might hurt herself."

"She'll be fine. She just needs to let off some steam," Kenna reassures him.

And then I realize who they're talking to ... and about.

"I heard that!" Georgia's voice yells back from the throwing area. "Guess whose face I'm picturing on the stump?"

"Hi, guys." I step closer and wave.

Kenna and Xander both freeze, looking worriedly at each other.

"Jackson, this is Xander and Kenna. They're two of the key players on the team organizing the masquerade. Do you two already know Jackson?" I ask.

"Double shot Americano?" Kenna asks. Jackson gives her the thumbs-up sign.

"Thrilled to meet you, man!" Xander sticks out his hand.

"Xander is obsessed with *Lit Lovers*," Kenna explains for my benefit.

"Small world." Jackson smiles. "I was just chatting about you and your sister with Emily. You want to come on the podcast later this month, maybe help spread the word about your event?"

"Really?" Xander says. "You'd do that?" Xander's eyes go wide at the mention of the *Lit Lovers* podcast, and he looks excitedly from me to Jackson.

"Absolutely. Hell, you'd be doing me a favor, bro. I hear you've got quite the following of your own. We can talk about rom coms with pets in them. You'd be surprised how many romantic literature aficionados are also passionate pet owners. I definitely think there's some cross correlation there that bears closer investigation." He considers this for a moment. "I should probably train an AI on it."

"This is just … amazeballs!" Xander exclaims. "So how do you two know each other?"

"We went to kindergarten together," I supply. "Jackson is one of my oldest friends."

"I can't believe we've finally lured you back home." He punches me in the shoulder, then turns back to Kenna and Xander. "This guy is really okay. Don't let anyone tell you otherwise."

Jackson flags the bartender and orders a couple of pints. There are at least a dozen locally brewed choices on tap. "He's here just in time to test my latest dating algorithm."

"That is so not happening," I say. "What's Georgia drinking?" I ask Kenna.

"Pale ale," says Kenna. Then she turns toward Jackson. "I volunteer as tribute if you need more test subjects."

"Sweet!" Jackson says. "We're focusing more on male beta testers right now, but I'll definitely be in touch."

"You might want to focus more on the female user experience if you're really serious." Kenna rolls her eyes. "We're not the ones sending the dick pics."

She raises her eyebrows at me when I add a pale ale to my tab. "Oh, wow. I see you like to live dangerously."

From the throwing lanes next door, a hearty thunk is followed by a victorious whoop. "Yessss! Take that, you lousy, Viking POS!"

"How many axes are in each bucket?" I ask.

"Five," Xander answers.

"So, I guess I'll wait till she's thrown four more before offering her the drink?"

———

"No!" Georgia says when I approach her lane. "No fucking way. You are not allowed to be here right now."

"It's a free country," I say, instantly regretting it. Is that really the best thing I could come up with?

Georgia is flushed from the activity. Her hair is still tousled. She's wearing a pair of broken-in biker gloves, which suggests to me she must be a regular. Makes sense for a battle pixie.

"You come here often?" I ask.

"Yes," she says. "Yes, I do, in fact." Her eyes flash dangerously. I set the drink down and back away.

"Fine, fine." I hold up my hands. "I just wanted to buy you a drink and apologize for yesterday. I was a little blindsided by your accusations. I do take them seriously though. And also, as psycho as you seem to be, I'm really glad you decked Bryce. I'm with my sister on that one."

"You're calling me a psycho?" Georgia says, retrieving an axe from the stump.

"Well, if the shoe fits …" I wave my hand in her direction. "I actually thought I was showing great restraint not calling you an axe-wielding psycho."

"Hmph!" she says, dropping the axe back in the bucket and stomping back in my direction. But I can see she is trying not to smile at my joke.

"Look, Georgia. I can't help but think we got off on the wrong foot," I say. "I propose a truce … and maybe a wager?" I hold out the drink.

"You haven't roofied that, have you?" she asks.

"No!" I roll my eyes.

"Prove it."

I take a big swig and hand the drink back to her. She grabs it from me and takes a sip. The foam clings to her upper lip, and I'm dying to wipe it away with my thumb. Or my tongue.

Shit.

"I propose we throw a round, and if I win, you give me another chance. Come to my sister's party," I say. "Your brother's already going, and I know Lilly would be thrilled if you came too. You really are one of her heroes."

"And if I win?" she asks.

"Name your prize," I say.

She thinks about it for a moment, sizing me up.

"If I win, you do the maintenance on the Feed Co. Building," she says.

"Is that really the best you can do?" I ask. "You don't want to aim a little higher? I was already planning on personally overseeing the maintenance."

"No rent hike?"

"No can do," I say. "That's just not in my power. It's been a decade, and the building really needs work, as you know."

"Fine. If I win … you let me make your costume for the masquerade. No questions asked."

"No questions?" I bite my lip. This could be bad.

"What's the matter? Are you afraid you'll lose?"

"Not at all," I say, taking the bet. "I'm in. May the best man win!"

———

A crowd has gathered outside the lanes, and the atmosphere feels taut. Throwing is a great release. Jackson steps up to act as an unofficial judge, prompting us when it's time to throw in our side-by-side lanes. We've agreed to ten throws, and changing lanes after the first round of five. Pretty standard.

I take a few practice throws, gauging the weight of these axes and the feel of the targets. Georgia stretches and rolls her neck and shoulders. I try not to let the sight of her neck distract me.

Jackson calls the first official throw.

Just for fun, I aim the first axe at the outermost ring on the stump. Georgia hits a bullseye. I might have underestimated her. She turns to me to gloat.

"You're going down, Holm." Her eyes are shining with something slightly more than a mere competitive streak.

But her next throw is less lucky. And on the third, her axe clatters to the ground.

"The party is at two," I say, after sinking two consecutive bull's-eyes.

"Fuck you," she says, and her axe finds purchase in the dead center of the wood target. She removes her fleece jacket, unzipping it slowly and fanning her cleavage while staring at me. I miss my next shot.

We trade lanes, colliding into each other in the process. Once again, we can't seem to get past each other.

"Pick a side," Georgia says haughtily. Kenna snorts.

I take my time with each of my next two throws, sharing a detail about the party between each. Georgia glares at me before sinking her throw into the center of the target.

"Dress is casual," I say. "But you'll probably want to cover up a little more if it's chilly." I let my eyes wander unapologetically over her thin, damp tee. Although we've both worked up a sweat, the cool air in the lanes is clearly affecting her.

She stares back at me as I pull off my sweater.

"It's just regular wool, not cashmere," I say. "You want to check?"

She turns to throw, and I notice her pink tongue peeking out between her lips as she concentrates. It's adorable. Her axe hits its mark.

"The outlets in the shop need to be replaced. And the bathroom could use remodeling too," she says.

"Don't feel obligated to bring a gift to the party." I send my axe sailing through the air. "Although if you do, Lilly is really into graphic novels."

"The radiator needs replacing. It's either boiling hot or freezing cold. There's no middle ground."

"That seems like it would suit you."

On the next throw, our two axes sail through the air like synchronized swimmers, both diving into their marks with perfect form and timing.

"Holy shit," says Kenna.

"Two more throws," Jackson calls out. Georgia takes a deep breath and stretches. I can imagine what she's thinking. She can't make another mistake. She has to be perfect or it's all over.

Her entire body tenses when she throws. She grunts, releasing a passionate sound from deep within that guts me. I know with absolute certainty that this is a sound she'd make in other intense situations.

With a primal groan, I release my axe and it lands at an angle —half in the center, half out.

"Last throw," Jackson announces, slipping into a professional announcer's voice. "This could go either way, folks. The pressure is on. It's a draw."

"You got this, G!" says Xander.

Georgia turns to face me. We look at one another for a hot, sweaty second, eyes locked, foreheads perspiring, and we throw, both of us shouting at the moment of release.

Her axe lands in the center of the marker. Mine comes close, but misses. I wasn't entirely sure what I was going to do until the moment it left my grip.

Kenna and Xander let out a whoop and a cheer, high-fiving each other, and hug Georgia. She is grinning now and the smile changes her, opening up her whole face. It's like light is suddenly pouring out of her. I can't get over the transformation … or the thought that I want to give her more opportunities to turn that light on. I want to feel that light shining on me.

Georgia pulls her axe out of the wall and holds it up like a trophy, basking in the cheers and applause before taking a bow.

"Hold on, hold on. It's customary to shake after a duel," Jackson announces.

"What are you doing, Dude?" I ask under my breath.

"I could ask you the same thing, you lousy axe hustler," he mutters back. "But if you must know, I believe I'm playing Cupid."

I reply, "Shut. The. Fuck. Up."

"Shake! Shake! Shake!" Jackson starts the chant. The crowd follows, demanding we end the duel with a handshake.

"Fine," I say, "let's shake then. I'll honor my side of the deal. Just don't make me wear anything that'll lead to an arrest."

"I'm gonna need your measurements, big guy." Georgia's eyes dance a diabolical tango over me as she peels off her biker gloves and sticks out her hand to shake mine. I notice it's still bandaged.

But that's not the hand I'm looking at. Now that the gloves are off, I can't take my eyes off her other hand. My eyes are glued to the pawprint tattoo on her wrist. It's surrounded by some very familiar-looking, tiny shooting stars.

Quickly and firmly, Georgia grips my hand and pumps it. Then she spins on her heel to leave, taking the winning axe with her.

I'd know those stars anywhere.

georgia

. . .

ON TUESDAY MORNING, I finally fill in the cease and desist letter, attaching copies of the printouts from over the weekend.

The lights are still out in the back. Not that I really expected Hudson Holm to do anything about it. But it had been fun imagining him showing up in a toolbelt to "personally oversee" the maintenance. I might also have imagined him shocking the shit out of himself.

It felt so good to beat him the other night. Almost as good as it'd felt to punch Bryce.

Kenna and I spend the rest of the weekend trading costume ideas for him. She's thinking Smurfette. I'm pulling for the Poop emoji.

Of course, there's still that one other idea. It's not as mean, but I can't get it out of my head. I keep imagining it— mentally dressing and undressing him in a Viking costume. Tight leggings. A fur vest. Maybe some lace-up, fur leg bits over his boots.

What a tragic waste of a gorgeous body. For a second, when he'd peeled off his sweater at The Grumpy Stump, I'd thought he was taking off his tee too. I'd caught a glimpse of that hard belly, and it had been almost impossible for me to focus afterward.

But I'd rallied.

Hudson checked me out too. He didn't even bother to hide it. The way his eyes crawled all over me. Not normally the sort of thing I'd welcome. But I liked it. I enjoyed the obvious effect I was having on him. He'd clearly wanted me as much as I wanted him. And we'd both known how impossible that was.

At noon, Angie drops by with great news. All three of the strays from Saturday are being picked up today. She purchases a collar and charm for each of them, using her own money for the gift. For once, I don't feel guilty ringing up her sale.

"Such nice families, Georgia. And I swear, it's all because of those costumes of yours." The corners of her blue-gray eyes crinkle up when she smiles. She pats my hand.

"Don't forget about Xander's transformations and Kenna's photos," I say. "They deserve credit too."

"Of course, but it's you we all rally around, Sweetheart." Angie smiles and reaches over the gate to pat Cookie.

"I'm so excited about this masquerade, Georgia. I've always wanted to go to a costume party. You'll let me know exactly how I can help out?"

"You've always been the shelter's den mother, Angie," I say. "I can't think of anyone else to better represent the shelter at the event."

"Oh, den mother!" Angie claps. "That's it! That's my costume. Thank you, Georgia!"

"Any time." I smile.

"I think I'll bring my photo albums so I can show people pictures of the animals when I tell them about the adoption success stories," Angie muses.

"I think that sounds like a great idea." I finish wrapping up the charms and walk with her to the door. "I don't know what we'd do without you, Angie," I say.

And then I just go for it. I give her a hug. It's awkward at first. She startles, like she's just been tackled. But then she relaxes, wrapping her arms around and hugging me back—hard. We both look at the portrait of my mom, missing her. Angie pats my back in a slow rhythm.

"Excuse me? Mind if I come in? I'm with Farm & Holm ..." We're interrupted by a middle-aged man in coveralls peeking in through the door. He's holding a large toolbox in one hand and a package in the other. "I hear you have some issues with the lights?"

Angie holds the door open for him. He gestures at the box. "Looks like this delivery is for you folks too."

"Leave it on the counter," I say. Angie gives me a little thumbs-up sign and a wave before slipping out the door.

I turn back to the repairman. Could this be Hudson making good on his promises?

"We sure do have a problem with the lights. Let me show you what's going on."

———

Kenna drops by to keep me company as I finish up for the day. She sweeps while I sew the fasteners on three more pet suits. With Halloween so close, the costumes are flying off the rack. Today was another good day. My favorite part was when a group of high school students stopped by to shoot selfies in front of the mural wall.

Kenna pauses by Cookie's bed. "So, Cookie, what's new with your cat friend?" she asks the dog, but she's actually looking at me. "I saw that your buddy Oliver liked your last post."

"I saw that too." I smile, remembering. And then I realize that I haven't posted anything for four days! "I feel so bad that I'm falling behind."

"Wow! That last post totally blew up!" Kenna says. She holds out her phone to show me.

That's when I see it. There are over three hundred likes on my last photo of Cookie! Holy shit.

What happened?

Quickly, I scroll through the likes, and then I notice Cookie's been tagged by Farm & Holm Pet Supplies! They've included Cookie in a Sunday Funday "Cute Dogs to Follow" post.

I hand back the phone, showing the post to Kenna.

"Looks like someone threw you a *bone*," she says, elbowing me like she's a vaudeville comedian. "Get it?"

"Very funny," I say, wrinkling my nose. I'm not sure how to feel about this. Is it possible Hudson Holm has figured out that Cookie is my dog? But how?

"You've picked up over two hundred new followers too," she says, still looking at the phone. She swaps the broom for a sheepskin duster and gets to work dusting off the displays on the counter.

"I'm not sure what's more exciting—the followers or the fact that I no longer have to pee in the dark," I say. "The lights finally got fixed!"

"Hey, you have an unopened package here." Kenna stops when she gets to the box that was dropped off this morning. "Doesn't look like your normal deliveries. Did you buy yourself something? What's in that fancy box?"

"Oh, that box … right. Totally forgot to open it," I say. "It's probably samples from some company that wants me to carry them in the shop. I filled out way too many forms when I was at the pet expo. Some of those vendors can be pretty pushy."

"Hmm." Kenna checks the time. "Well, I'd love to stick around, but I'm having dinner with Uber Eats Carlos and his wife. Homemade tamales. You good here?"

"I'm great. Thanks so much for helping me," I say.

"No plans for tonight?" she asks.

"No, but Cookie and I will be just fine. We're going to watch some TV and get a good night's sleep. I'm just going to finish up with these forms and listen to a little *Lit Lovers* before I head home."

"Okay. Shoot me a message on the laptop if you need anything," Kenna says. "And I mean it, too, Georgia. Xander's not your only family. You're stuck with me as well." She gives me a quick hug.

"Thanks for keeping me from dating serial killers," she says.

"The right guy is out there," I say, believing this for her with all my heart.

I lock the door behind her as she leaves. Then I go back to the counter and open up my laptop to search for the *Lit Lovers* podcast. I still can't get over the memory of Jackson officiating during my duel with Hudson. He'd been even more quirkily charismatic in person than he was on the show. But I'm still having a hard time understanding how the Jane Austen-loving podcast host could be lifelong besties with Hudson Holm.

While the episode downloads, I put away the snaps and Velcro. I'm facing away from the door when I hear the sound of knocking outside the shop.

I turn to see if Kenna forgot something. But it isn't her, it's Hudson.

What on earth is he doing here now? His hair is mussed and he's wearing sweats. He looks a little agitated.

Warily, I unlock the door.

"So," he says. "I've been waiting all day. Are you going to open the box already?"

hudson

. . .

I DRIVE into town as the sun is setting, hoping that Georgia's reaction to seeing me will be less violent than the red and orange streaks slashing the sky. If she doesn't open the freaking box already, though, I'm going to lose it.

It's been two days and fourteen hours since I discovered that Georgia was Cookie and Cookie was Georgia, and for some reason, this information is much harder for me to digest than the fact that Bryce did deliberately knock off Georgia's designs.

Suddenly, everything makes perfect sense:

- Cookie wrote that her owner, who owned a *shop*, broke her phone on Thursday night.
- Georgia was waving an ancient flip phone around on Friday.
- Cookie hasn't posted anything in three days.

I had to do something. Say something. But what? I couldn't just show up and say "Hey, Cookie, I know who you really are!"

So, I went shopping.

As soon as I woke up yesterday, I went out and bought a brand-new, top-of-the-line phone. Georgia/Cookie isn't going to be able to keep up with the challenge assignments (let alone run a business) without a functional mobile phone.

It's a perfectly reasonable thing to do, I tell myself. As buddies, her success and mine are tied together.

Once I started shopping, it was hard to stop.

I wasn't sure what kind of case Georgia would want for her phone, so I bought three from the kiosk in the mall. One with stars. One with dogs. And a third bright-red one that's waterproof and drop proof.

I kept picturing Georgia's winning smile from the other night, and I imagined the photos she'd be able to take with better equipment. This led me to the camera aisle, where I picked up a ring light, a tripod, and a gimbal—just in case she wants to do more video.

When I got home, I unwrapped the phone and got to work planning and making a video of my own. A video that will hopefully explain everything.

The rest of my Monday night was spent messing with tissue paper and packaging and scanning YouTube for lessons on how to tie the perfect gift bow. It was better than ruminating. It was better than tying myself in knots, thinking about how Georgia's thigh felt against mine. How she looked after she beat me at The Grumpy Stump. I couldn't get it out of my head.

I can't get HER out of my head. I know I won't be able to move on until I come clean with her. Explain everything. But then what? Wish her well? Add her to the corporate greeting card list?

Yes, you idiot, I chastise myself. That is all there is to it. All there can ever be.

I know for sure that the electrician hand-delivered the box to Georgia early this morning. He dropped it off while he was there fixing her lights. So why haven't I heard anything yet?

The breeze shakes loose colorful, stray leaves as I cross Holm Square. The path is littered with them. The Feed Co. Building forms an impressive silhouette, backlit by the neon sky. The lights are on inside Celestial Pets, even though it's just after closing time. As I get closer, I can see Georgia and Kenna in there, and a very familiar-looking dog.

I watch as Kenna hugs Georgia, then pats Cookie—it really is Cookie—and leaves. Georgia locks the door behind her. The sign on the door says "Closed."

I scan the store for any sign of the box. Had she just opened it and discarded the contents? Perhaps someone else took it? Finally, I spy it. The package that I so carefully and painstakingly packed was neither discarded nor stolen. It is sitting on the counter. Ignored and, apparently, untouched.

Frustration surges through me. The longer this charade goes on, the harder it's going to be. Enough! I'd really hoped to avoid doing this face-to-face, but it appears I have no choice.

I rap on the window.

Georgia startles and squints in my direction. I can see the moment she recognizes me. She stops, draws herself up another inch, and takes a deep breath. Cookie runs to the door ahead of her and she unlocks it, cracking it open. Her eyes are a query. "What do YOU want," they say. My eyes dart to the mural wall, recalling my fantasy of backing her up against it.

Just a fantasy. Have to put it out of my mind. Now and forever.

"So," I say, "I've been waiting all day. Are you going to open the box already?"

She looks from me to the box, confused.

Cookie takes this opportunity to shove her head through the crack in the door to sniff me. Her big, pink tongue swoops out to lick my hand. Georgia grabs her collar to pull her back, and as she does, I slide into the shop.

"Come on in, why don't you," Georgia says.

She doesn't seem threatened by my intrusion, but then, why would she be? She's already demonstrated that she knows how to defend herself.

"Thanks for letting me in," I say, noticing that the lights are on in the back room. "I see my electrician was here earlier."

"Mm-hmm," Georgia says. She's sizing me up. Her eyes travel over my hoodie and sweats, sweep down to my athletic shoes, and then back up to my face.

"You out for a run?" she asks.

"No," I say, suddenly self-conscious. I didn't sleep much last night, and since I didn't have any video calls today, I hadn't really thought about dressing up. Did I even use a brush today? I rake my hand through my hair and take a step toward her.

She releases the dog.

Tail wagging, Cookie lunges toward me, and I have to swivel quickly to avoid getting knocked in the nuts. Georgia smirks.

"Hey, Cookie," I say, kneeling down and letting her lick my face. "It's so nice to meet you in person."

Georgia taps her foot impatiently. She's wearing Doc Martens. Lace tights. Her arms are folded across her chest, covering a close-fitting dress that appears to be constructed of upcycled concert tees. I see pieces of Kiss, Iron Maiden, and Lilly's fave, The Cure. She's corralled her hair into impish pigtails that beg to be tugged.

Georgia's eyes narrow, taking me in as I check her out. I peel my gaze away from her, give Cookie a pat, and rise.

"Is there a reason you haven't opened that yet?" I gesture at the box.

"So, that's from you, then?" She looks curiously from the box to me, trying to work it out.

"Why don't you open it and see?"

"Should I be worried?" she asks.

"What do you mean?"

"Well, the last time I got a special delivery from Farm & Holm, it was the notice for the rent hike. And given your accusations at the diner, I'm not sure it's legally in my best interest to accept anything from you."

"Just open the box," I say. I watch her eyes dart back to it. "You know you want to."

Georgia pivots and walks behind the counter, toward the box. And past it. She reaches underneath and pulls out a sheaf of papers, which she taps on the counter to square up. Then she marches at me, green eyes blazing defiantly. She takes the sheaf of papers and smacks them into my chest.

"How about I just give you these?" she says.

I look down at her hand, pressed against my chest, and immediately, she withdraws it. The papers flutter to the floor.

"What are those anyway?" I ask.

"All of my designs that your company has copied," she says, chin out. "And a cease and desist letter."

"Duly noted." I make no move to pick them up. Instead, I stick out a foot. "You know, I wore my sneakers to save us from shocking each other this time," I say.

"You probably wore them in case you had to run," she challenges.

"I'm not my brother," I say.

"I could take you." She takes a step toward me. "You know what they say: The bigger they are, the harder they fall."

JFC. Things are happening in my pants, and this is not going as planned.

I say, "Open. The. Box."

"I must admit I'm curious now." Georgia glances over her shoulder. "But is this a gift box that says 'I'm super sorry for being a massive dick,' or is it more like Pandora's box, filled with anthrax and ancient curses?"

"You'll never know unless you open it," I say. She has a point though. It is a bit like the box in the Pandora story. Once that lid is opened, there's no putting the knowledge back in the box.

"Honestly, I've been waiting all day for you to open it, so I'd appreciate it if you'd put me out of my misery. I promise I'll get lost immediately after, if that's what you want," I say.

Her brows raise at that, and she heads back to the counter again.

"And you'll take that letter seriously?" She pauses, her fingers poised an inch from the end of the bow.

"I will," I say, "I swear."

"I'm going to hold you to this, Hudson Holm," she says. And then she pulls the bow.

georgia

. . .

MY NEED TO know what's in the box does battle with the distraction of being alone in the shop with Hudson Holm. His larger-than-life presence dominates the space. As sexy as he was in cashmere and well-cut pants, I have to admit, he's even more appealing in sweats, his hair disheveled, and with the spicy shadow of stubble peppering his jaw.

He's staring at me so intensely that it's making me feel clumsy. A little giddy. My hands are shaking. I refuse to give him the satisfaction of seeing this though. Leaning forward against the counter, I pull the bow slowly, watching the loops fall away.

For the life of me, I cannot imagine what's inside. The not-knowing is excruciating. But in a delightful way. It's not just me. Watching Hudson squirm while I take my sweet time is kind of giving me life.

I tap and flick my fingers slowly on the unopened box, listening for echoes.

"I wonder," I say hopefully, "if perhaps you've brought me the head of your dear brother, Bryce, as a peace offering?" I lift the box to gauge its weight and shake it lightly.

Hudson's cheek twitches, but his eyes sparkle. He bites his lip.

"There's no way Bryce's head would fit in a box that small, Georgia. I think we both know that."

"I suppose you're right. Pity though." Sighing, I sloooooowly open the lid.

There are a number of things in the box, all wrapped in tissue. But sitting at the top is a brand-new iPhone. The newest version, with the biggest screen, the best camera, and the most memory.

"What the?" I push away the box and attempt to pick my jaw off the counter. "That's … an iPhone! I can't accept that!"

"You may as well," he says. "I've already opened the box and turned the phone on, so I can't return it. See the note?"

I look down. There's indeed a tiny Post-it note on the iPhone box, and the outer wrapping has already been removed. The note says, "Look inside."

"Is this some kind of joke?"

"You need a phone, right?" I see him looking at the flip phone on the counter, one brow raised.

"Yeah, but I can't afford THIS phone." I gesture at the box.

"Do me a favor and look inside? I said I'd leave afterward if you want me to, remember?"

"Fine." I open the box and take out the phone. It's gorgeous. Sleek and black, so much nicer than my old phone. Nicer than anything I was ever going to get off eBay to replace my old phone.

Damn him for putting this temptation in my path. Giving it back was going to hurt.

A tiny sticky note clinging to the screen offers up the passcode.

"My street address? Really?" I ask.

"You can change the passcode," Hudson answers.

"Open the photo album," another note says.

Hudson steps closer to the counter. For whatever reason, Cookie has glued herself to his side. Is she sitting on his foot? What the hell, Cookie! Hudson is absentmindedly stroking her.

"Okay, here goes," I say, opening the phone and clicking into the album.

There's only one thing there—a video with the screen title "Play Me."

I look back up at Hudson, who meets my gaze and nods gravely. Then he takes a deep breath. I watch his Adam's apple bob as he swallows.

"What the hell is this?" I hold up the phone. "You're freaking me out a little here."

"Oh, for God's sake, Georgia!"

Exasperated, Hudson reaches across the counter and takes the phone out of my hand. He hits play and props the phone back on the counter between us.

I recognize the song immediately. It's the theme from *Toy Story*—one of my favorite Pixar movie franchises ever.

"You've got a friend in me…"

I feel my breath catch. I look at Hudson for an explanation, but he merely points at the video that is now playing on the screen.

It begins with a montage of familiar photos. Not the Pixar characters though. These are photos of Oliver, my Petfluencer Challenge buddy. There are a few photos of Cookie too. Several of these are shots I've shared on Instagram. But there are also some that I haven't posted. Not on Cookie's account anyway.

The photos of Cookie alternate with pictures of Oliver.

"Where did you get these?" I pause the video. "This is seriously fucked up. It's one thing to steal my designs. It's another to hack me." My palms are sweating now and my heart is racing.

"Georgia." Hudson places his hands on the counter. His eyes meet mine imploringly. "I promise I didn't hack you. Twenty-five more seconds. Just finish the video, please?" He taps the screen, hitting play, and stares down at it. I look down as well.

There's a final short photo of Oliver that I don't recognize immediately. He's dressed up in a judge's costume. The costume is familiar as well. It ought to be. I made it. And Hudson purchased it in my shop a week ago.

The music ends, and the next clip is a video one. Oliver is standing on a couch, kneading the cushion and blinking at the camera. The camera gets shaky, as whoever is holding it approaches him and scoops him up. For a moment, all I can see are shoes, floor, and couch cushion.

Then the camera flips around and it's Oliver again, seated on Hudson's lap. They're both looking into the camera, selfie style.

"No!" I shout, dropping the phone. "No, no, no. No fucking way!"

"Yes way."

"You cannot. You don't even have a cat."

"That's actually a long story," Hudson says.

"And this is how you tell me?" I reach out and poke him in the chest. Hard.

Actually, it's a pretty nice way to tell me, all things considered. But I'm not sure how I feel about it. Or him. Though his chest really is nice.

"I know it's not ideal, but honestly, I didn't know how else to break it to you, Georgia. You clearly hated me the minute you found out who I was."

"How long have you known?" I ask.

"Not long. Just since Saturday night."

"Saturday night?" I ask. "How? Was it something I said?" I don't recall mentioning Cookie or the Petfluencer Challenge at all.

"It was your tattoo." Hudson catches my hand and turns it over, rubbing the tattoo gently. His touch sends shivers to all the right places.

"So, you weren't only buying my pet costumes to knock them off …" I muse. "Let me see that photo of Oliver again?"

Hudson whips out his phone and pulls it up. "Listen, the phone's not a big deal for me, and I know this challenge is important to you. You can't do it without the phone. And I don't think Oliver can do it without Cookie."

"You tagged me from the Farm & Holm account."

"Not me, the social team. It was just a suggestion. They loved Cookie's feed. There's other stuff in the box, too, by the way."

"If you think this is getting you off the hook …" I step out from behind the counter just as Hudson moves forward, and once again, we're blocking each other's way.

"Like what?" I ask, moving left. He moves sideways at the exact same moment, continuing to block me. I'm so close I can see his stubble. So close I can smell him.

"Some stuff for the phone." Hudson holds up his hands as we step sideways again, still squaring off.

"Are you doing this on purpose?" I ask.

"No." He laughs. "Scout's honor. I'm just going to stay right here until you say it's safe to move."

"Why should I believe you?"

Maybe it's the smell of him. Maybe it's the nearness. Maybe it's the revelation that he's been Oliver all along. Anger, wonder, and confusion. Something in me is crumbling. I can't continue to hold up this barrier. I'm shaking with the strain of it.

I want to keep hating him so much. But I can't.

"I also brought you more Band-Aids," he says, pulling a handful of colorful bandages from his pocket.

I break.

I slap at the wall, flipping off the lights. Darkness gives me the element of surprise. Then I take two steps back for momentum and fly at him in the dark, shoving him backward toward the wall.

He doesn't see it coming, but he also doesn't resist me. Is it three steps or ten? I don't even know. We're tumbling together, and physics have stopped making sense. There's just a throbbing beat, quick and slow at the same time. Somehow, we both hear it because we're moving together in perfect sync. Back, back, back until he slams against the mural wall, pinned there.

He pulls me against himself, groaning, and I can tell I've made an impression. A big one. I can feel his need.

"What are you doing, Georgia?" he whispers, leaning down to breathe me in. My hands slide under his sweatshirt, palms grazing the smooth skin of his chest. He sucks in a breath as my fingers glide across his chest and over his nipples, causing my own nipples to sting and harden in response.

"Exactly what I've wanted to do since the first time I saw you." I shock myself with the raw honesty of these words.

"I'm shocked by this behavior, Young Lady, utterly shocked!" Hudson adopts a stuffy British accent, exactly like I've imagined Oliver all along.

And then his lips are on mine. He kisses me softly, brushing his lips from side to side as he samples. Then his kisses grow less tentative. His lips crush mine, hungry, demanding. There's no turning back now. Ragnar has arrived to plunder my village.

Hudson parts my lips with his tongue, probing, tasting, and searching. Around us, the constellations sparkle and glimmer, thousands of painstakingly painted, glow-in-the-dark stars lighting the night.

I'm floating, so lost in the moment that I don't hear the banging on the window till Cookie barks.

Bang, bang, bang.

"What?" I pull away.

"You expecting someone?" Hudson's breath is ragged. His voice is rough. Cookie barks again and whines a little.

"GET A ROOM," I can hear Xander calling through the crack in the door.

I run my hand through my hair and make my way to the door, unlocking it and opening it a crack.

"Everything okay in there?" Xander asks. "You need my help?"

"No, Xander, I don't need your help."

"I didn't think so, but I just thought I'd ask. Mac met me for dinner at the diner after I finished up today, and I parked the van down the street. Thought you'd want to know that it's not as dark in there as you think. The whole square can see someone's getting busy in there. Just a little heads-up."

Xander is grinning smugly, peering over my shoulder. "I didn't think you were dating anyone, G. Who you got back there?"

"None of your—"

"Holy shit! Is that Hudson Holm? Hey, man!" Xander attempts to stick a foot in the door, but I stomp on it.

"Night, Bro," I say, shutting the door and turning the lock the instant he withdraws his foot. I wave goodbye to him, and he shakes a finger at me before turning to go at last.

"Well, that was awkward," Hudson says.

"Ha, you think that was bad?" I straighten my dress and attempt to put my head right. "Just wait till he talks to Kenna and the two of them find out that you're Oliver."

hudson

. . .

THE SPELL IS BROKEN after Xander leaves. Now it's just the two of us standing here, staring at each other, trying to make some sense out of what just happened. Of everything that has happened over the past two weeks.

Even though I've known for two days, I'm still experiencing a fair amount of cognitive dissonance. My brain strains as I try to reconcile this woman with the character of Cookie, the dog, even as the actual dog sits at my feet, panting happily. It's like watching a film about the multiverse, worlds colliding.

"I should go," I finally say.

"What about the phone?" she asks.

We're still standing in the dark. Close enough to touch, but we don't.

"Please keep it?"

Georgia bends to collect the papers she dropped earlier, rearranging them back into a pile.

"It's too expensive," she argues. "And it doesn't change anything about this." She taps the stack of papers, holding it out toward me. This time, I take it from her. I roll the papers up into a tube and place them in my hoodie pocket.

"The phone's a gift," I say. "Consider it a gift from Oliver to Cookie. She needs it to complete the challenge. It doesn't have to have anything to do with us humans."

She turns the phone over in her hand, considering this.

"You should know that Farm & Holm isn't selling pet costumes anymore, Georgia. The whole collection's been removed from the site. We will find a way to make it right. *I* will find a way to make it up to you."

I hold her gaze when I say this. Some of the fight seems to leave her. She lets out a sigh.

"Do you know how it happened?"

"Not entirely," I admit. "But I have a pretty good idea."

"Bryce?" she asks.

I nod.

"But why? Why would he do that?" She drops into a chair by the counter.

"Because you're talented?" I suggest. "You have great ideas. He probably didn't see it as stealing. He saw it as liberating your ideas. Delivering them to a wider audience."

"Is that what he said?" she inquires, lip curling.

"Not in so many words," I say.

"And is that what you think?" she asks, eyes searching mine in the dim light. I have to look away.

"Look, I obviously think it's awful, Georgia. Bryce had no right to steal from you. But is it really the end of the world? Have you thought about the idea that you could reach a broader audience if you were willing to consider outsourcing some of the manufacturing, maybe partnering with a production house? I really think there are ways you could successfully scale—"

"Is this some kind of snow job where you try to convince me you actually did me a favor?" She stiffens. "You can't have my designs. Those ideas are mine. You stole them."

"Not me, Georgia. I didn't steal them."

"Fine, then YOUR family's company! Same thing!" She jumps to her feet. Cookie barks, looking from Georgia to me.

Same thing? Well at least now I know how she really feels.

"I'm doing my best here. Just tell me what you want." I hold up my hands, feeling utterly frustrated. What I want, very much, is to kiss her again. That business feels even more unfinished to me than the matter of the knocked-off clothes.

"Actually, I don't know what I want right now. I need to think." Georgia sits back down and sighs. "But I do think you should go now, Hudson. This …" She gestures at the phone, the dog, the shop. "All of this has been a lot."

"Got it," I say. "I guess I'll see you at the next planning meeting?"

"Sure," she says.

"And online?"

"Maybe. We'll see." She frowns and draws up her knees, hugging them to her chest. All the fight has gone out of her. Folded up like that, she looks so small and so sad. I don't want to leave her alone like this.

"Are you sure you're okay, Georgia?" I ask, taking a tentative step toward her.

"Just go, Hudson. Please? Can you leave already?"

It's the last thing I want to do, but I honor her wishes. I turn slowly and walk toward the door, pausing to pet Cookie before I go.

"Hate You Later, Cookie," I say.

And then I walk out into the night.

georgia

. . .

ON WEDNESDAY MORNING, before the shop opens, I finally show the video to Kenna. I've barely slept at all and have lost count of how many times I've played it.

"Just watch it. Watch the whole thing. Do not comment," I say. I place the phone propped up on the counter.

"But …" she starts to object.

"Zppp!" I make the zip motion, holding a finger over my lips.

"Why are you showing this to me if I'm not allowed to have an opinion? And whose phone is this? Is that the new iPhone?"

"Just watch," I say. "There will be time to discuss later. I just need you to hold your comments to the end."

"Fine. Has anyone told you you're a control freak?"

I nod.

"Go ahead and hit play," she says.

My emotions are all over the map. Every time I watch this, I seem to feel a different way.

Reaction #1: What the hell? How long did he know this before telling me? Was he gaslighting me all along? What's his end game?
Reaction #2: Oliver is adorable. This video is the sweetest thing I've ever seen. Did he really make it just for me?
Reaction #3: Why is he so hot? How bad would it actually be if I slept with him … like just a little?
Reaction #4: Fucking Holms. Business is business. Best to keep it that way.

I study Kenna's face as she watches the video. She seems to be leaning toward Reaction #2, especially when she bursts out with a grinning "OH MY GOD," laughing incredulously and looking from me, to the video, to me again. She claps a hand over her mouth when I remind her to remain silent and refrain from reaction.

"So, you want to watch it again?" I ask at the end.

"No. I mean yes, but why? Did I miss anything?"

"I don't know. It's just that I've watched this a hundred times, and I still can't make up my mind how to feel."

"I don't think that's how feelings usually work, G. There's no 'deciding.' Usually, you just feel how you feel." Kenna studies my face now. "So, how do you feel?"

"I feel a lot of different ways."

"Starting with?"

"Surprised."

"I'll bet!" She shakes her head and laughs again. "Who knew Ragnar was a cat guy?" Then she slaps her forehead. "Oh dammit!"

"What is it?" I ask.

"You're really not letting me read those texts with Oliver now, are you?" Kenna laments.

"Not a chance."

"This is terrible." Kenna sighs. "I was going to submit them to *Lit Lovers* for discussion."

"You wish," I say.

"So, what now? What are you going to do?" Kenna asks. "Seems like the ball is in your court."

"I don't know!" I bury my face in my hands. Cookie nudges me from the side and I pat her, reassuring both of us.

"Let's start with the phone. I'm assuming the phone is from him? How did it happen?"

"It was in that box that was dropped off yesterday. The one that I thought was samples. He came in right after you left and demanded I open it already. Apparently, he was waiting all day for me to open it."

"That's actually quite romantic." Kenna looks impressed.

"I don't know what I thought was in the box, but it wasn't that. There was a bunch of other stuff too." I grab the box from behind the counter where I'd left it. "Phone cases and photography stuff." I pull out the accessories.

"This is great stuff, very thoughtful." Kenna examines the items appreciatively. "Now you can finish the challenge and stay involved in the social media planning for the masquerade. That's a good thing, right?"

I make a face and put the phone on the counter, pushing it away.

"Georgia, you're keeping the phone, right?"

"I was thinking I wouldn't," I say. "These phones are expensive. I don't want to take on any more debt."

"These phones are expensive for you, sure, but I assure you, it's not putting a dent in Hudson Holm's checking account." Kenna looks about ready to wring my neck. "Why must you be such a martyr? You need it to do the challenge. He needs you to finish the challenge. And it's not like he can return it. If you're not going to keep it, I will. The camera on these is awesome." She swipes the phone off the counter.

"Give it back," I demand. Kenna teases me for a moment, then finally hands it back.

"Fine." I sigh. "I'll keep the phone. It still feels weird though."

"Why?" Kenna asks, looking more critically at me now. "Did anything else happen?"

"Maybe," I confess. "Maybe a little bit."

Kenna leans forward. "Keep talking."

"I might have jumped him." I say it fast and groan. My head is back in my hands.

"Oh, Georgia, no! You didn't!" Kenna claps.

"Ugh." I moan. "I mean, at least I didn't deck him."

"Well, thank goodness for that," Kenna says. "But?"

"But I did kiss him. A lot."

"And? How'd he take it? Did he hiss at you?"

"Shut up with the cat references," I warn. "Or else."

"Or else what?" she teases.

"I swear to God, Mckenna Papadopoulos!!" I threaten, using her full name.

"Fine, fine." She capitulates. "So, you made out with him?"

"Guilty." I admit.

"Ah, so it was ... good?"

"So good. Scary good. Cosmic even." I glance at the stars I painted all around the shop.

"So, what happened next? Did you …?" She looks around the shop, clearly trying to imagine where such a deed might be done in the tiny space.

"No!" I shake my head. "Xander banged on the window. He was passing by and he … uh … saw us."

Kenna raises a brow.

"Kissing!" I amend. "That's all he saw! Xander was walking by and he noticed something was going on in the shop and wanted to make sure I was okay. I sent him on his way, but not before he figured out that it was Hudson."

"Oh, Lordy." Kenna is stifling a giggle now and she fans herself. "So, you sent Xander away. Then what?"

"Then I kicked Hudson out."

"Wait. You kicked him out? Why?"

"I don't know. I was just so …" Overwhelmed. Overheated. Conflicted. Confused. Terrified.

"Just so, what?" Kenna probes.

"I don't know how to feel."

I return to my original dilemma. "I'm all over the map, and it's scary. I really think the best thing is probably just to give back this damn phone and keep it strictly business, you know?"

"Holy shit," Kenna says. "Of all the ways that someone could describe you, I never thought 'big fucking chicken' would be the top choice."

"Excuse me?" I bristle.

"You're scared, aren't you?" She folds her arms in front of her.

"Maybe, a little," I admit. "But come on, there's a lot at stake here. My business, the shelter …"

"Oh please. That stuff is not what you're scared of." Kenna dismisses my fears. "You've got a lot of people on your side, and on the shelter's side, Georgia. None of us are going to sit idly by and watch Celestial Pets and Kismet go down."

"How do you know Hudson Holm isn't just snowing me so I won't put up too much of a fight when he leases this place to a frozen yogurt franchise?" I argue.

"I saw how he looked at you at the diner, Georgia," Kenna says. "And at The Grumpy Stump. He's not interested in your space. Unless you count being *in* your space."

I shake my head again.

"How did he figure it out, by the way? The whole Cookie/Oliver connection? Did he see Cookie in the shop?" she asks.

"It was my tattoo," I explain, pulling up the photo I'd posted.

"That one never gets old. Such a great shot." The photo makes Kenna smile. "Do you want my opinion?" she asks.

"I don't know." I shrug. "Do I?"

"I think if you were a real badass, you'd give him a chance. He doesn't seem so bad to me, besides being so clean-cut and preppy. But whatever floats your boat."

"He's a Holm," I argue.

"That's hardly his fault."

"He has a cat?" I offer.

"Is that really the best you can do? I hate to break it to you, Georgia, but most relationships—at least the good ones— don't end with a fist bump. How will you ever know if you don't at least try?"

hudson

. . .

THE GOOD NEWS is that she kept the phone. She's keeping up with all the prompts for the challenge.

The bad news is that she hasn't replied to my messages. It's been a week, and we still haven't talked.

Work is an effort. I'm showing up for calls and making decisions about vendors and contracts. But my mind continues to wander back to the night in the pet shop. My thoughts linger in that magical space, surrounded by the stars, taking my fill of Georgia's lips.

I'm hungry. Starving for more. I cannot concentrate on anything. I'm starting to worry that this isn't going to go away—not unless we do something about this animal attraction we seem to have for each other. But then what? I don't trust myself not to make a mess of things.

My family has already done enough damage. Which brings me back to damage control. I've put together a proposal for Georgia that I hope she'll consider before moving forward with a lawsuit. I'm just not sure when or how to share it with her.

Nobody's heard from Bryce since Walker booted him off the boat. My father insists he has a plan.

Walker is flying in tomorrow—just in time for Lilly's birthday party. He's asked if he could crash with me.

"What do you think about a houseguest, Oliver?"

Oliver is doing his usual afternoon sunbathing by the large loft windows. He doesn't seem particularly motivated to interact with me. Perhaps he's just bent out of shape that I haven't been lavishing him with as much attention or taking nearly as many photos of him since discovering his pet influencer buddy's true identity. I've been doing the bare minimum.

"Do you miss Cookie?" I ask. Oliver looks up at me mournfully from the living room floor, tail swishing. Then, with a world-weary sigh, he lays his head back down and resumes his morose staring at the wall.

"Me too, Buddy. How about we try sending Cookie a photo?"

Quickly, I improvise an idea for a shoot. I tear into a bag of chocolate chip cookies that Bryce left in the pantry and select the most perfect-looking one. Then I lie down on the floor beside him, stretching out on my belly. I set the cookie down on the floor in front of Oliver's nose. When he lowers his head to look at it, I snap.

Got it!

It's so perfect that I'm a little sad that I cannot high-five Oliver.

I open the challenge portal, scrolling down past our last "Hate You Later" sign-off.

I fire off the photo of a somewhat bereft-looking Oliver, staring at the chocolate chip cookie. His range really isn't wide, but that cat has got bereft, bored, and judgmental down pat.

> Can't stop thinking about you, Cookie.

Much to my surprise, she messages me back moments later.

I thought you didn't eat junk food, Furball.

> I'm not eating it, Cookie. I am merely gazing at it. It reminded me of you.

Well, make sure you don't leave any crumbs on the carpet.

> Heavens! I would never allow that to happen, Cookie.

Of course you wouldn't. What have you been up to? I noticed you posted your costume photo. The judge costume suits you. You do seem judgmental AF.

> I was quite disappointed that you didn't like that one, Cookie. I even tagged your owner's shop in the post.

Thanks for that, but she doesn't need the charity.

> Hmm … I'm not sure I understand your definition of charity.

This isn't going well. Time to change the subject.

> Do you think I should check out Jackson's podcast? I'd like something to listen to while I clean the house.

Lit Lovers? I'm not sure you'll like it, Oliver.

Why not?

It gets a bit naughty …

Hmm … what was the last episode about?

Literary tattoos.

Interesting. Such as?

It depends what you're into. There's your
Jane Austen tattoos, your Shakespeare
tattoos …

What's a Jane Austen tattoo?

Mostly phrases from Pride and Prejudice like
"Most Ardently" or "Obstinate, Headstrong
Girl."

One of those tattoos would suit you, Cookie.
If only dogs could get tattoos.

Maybe. My owner has a Shakespeare quote
on her back.

Which quote?

Her tattoo says, "Though she be but little,
she be fierce."

Accurate.

I type the 100 percent emoji.

But of course, now I'm wondering what that tattoo looks like.
Where exactly on her back is it? Does it skim her shoulder

blade? Hover above a hip? How large are the letters? If I were to trace a finger down her spine and lay my palm flat against the small of her back, would it cover the entire expression? I'd like to try to capture her fierceness, though I'm not sure it can be done without injury.

> What about your owner's pawprint tattoo,
> Cookie? What's the story there?

> It's the logo for the shop.

> Great logo. Did she design it?

I don't recall the clever logo from my childhood visits to Celestial Pets, and the matching mural wall with all the additional celestial designs certainly wasn't there before. I have a feeling there's something special about that particular tattoo.

> Yes, she did, Furball. That tattoo is a Georgia
> Starr original. Her first ink, in fact.

> Well, that sounds like a good story, Cookie.
> Would you tell me about it?

She doesn't answer me right away. The three dots come and go a few times, the last time for several minutes. Long enough for me to make myself a cup of Earl Grey tea and settle on the sofa.

Oliver admonishes me with his stare when I set my cup down without a coaster. I go and fetch a coaster for the cup and a saucer for the teabag. By the time I return, "Cookie" is typing again.

> Georgia was seventeen when she got the
> tattoo. She drew it in math class. Mr. Foster,
> her math teacher, was always giving her
> detention for drawing on herself.

Mr. Foster doesn't sound very nice at all.

No, he wasn't. He always said, "Get your
head out of the clouds, Starr!" and then
everyone would laugh because it sounded
weird telling a star to get their head out of the
clouds. Which only made him madder.

I'm so sorry, Cookie. I hope she didn't get in
too much trouble.

Her mom understood. She said that being
creative is just how some people process.

She sounds like a great mom.

She was, but my owner wasn't the easiest
kid. The same week her adoption was final,
she ran away from home. She took a bus to
Seattle and tried to get a tattoo. The owner
of the shop made her choose between
calling the cops or calling her mom to come
get her. She chose her mom.

Was her mom angry?

No. She came into the shop and said, "Ok,
Georgia. You can get the tattoo on one
condition."

What was the condition?

She rolled up her sleeve and said, "You'll just
have to deal with your MOM having a
matching tattoo."

And did she do it too?

I send back my message with the heart emoji.

Yes, and she also made the design the store
logo.

Can I see the tattoo again?

She shoots me back a photo of her wrist, and I can see all the delicate details of the design. It's clever the way the paw print contains a small cluster of stars. My fingers ache to wrap around her wrist. I want to kiss the tender spot, feel her pulse where she was inked.

I bet that hurt!

Not as much as a cat scratch!

Hope she's healing well. No more Band-Aids?

It's healing fine.

Any chance I'll see you anytime soon, Cookie?

What do you mean, Furball. You know how I feel about cats.

Well, I was wondering if maybe you'd make an exception, just this once. I believe that your owner is coming to tour the event space in my building later this week?

It appears she can't get out of it.

Well, my owner would love it if your owner brought you along to see the space. It's quite pet friendly.

We'll see.

I promise to be on my best behavior.

Whatever. I mean, I could probably take you.

I'm sure you could. One more thing, Cookie?
If you don't mind my asking a small favor?

Dude, you bought us a phone. We owe you.

Do you think you could still help both of us
out with our costumes for the masquerade?

Actually, I think I know JUST the thing for you
and your owner, Furball. Prepare to dazzle.

No rhinestones.

We'll see.

Suddenly, I'm afraid. But also, as is my custom whenever speaking with Georgia, slightly turned on.

We end the conversation with our usual sign-off.

Later, Hater! Xoxo, C

Hate You Later! Xxoo, O

georgia

· · ·

EPHRON'S WAREHOUSE district is a light industrial area with many aging warehouses, some that have been converted into workshops by artists and tradespeople. There's The Grumpy Stump, a few auto body shops, a tattoo parlor, and a totally creepy self-storage building.

Easy access to the river and to the train tracks has historically made this a natural place to build warehouses. But times have changed, and many of the old warehouses are empty and decaying. There's graffiti on the walls, and not the artsy kind. We pull into a parking lot that is sprinkled with trash and weeds. It's in stark contrast to the new construction across the street.

"Wow!" Kenna marvels at the sleek, modern structure across the street. "Remember when we were in high school and this whole area was like the *wrong* side of the tracks? Like the forbidden forest?" She waggles her fingers ominously to punctuate this statement.

"So forbidden." I laugh. "That was pretty much my liberal mom's only rule. Stay away from the warehouse district!"

The Farm & Holm warehouses were the largest ones in the district and located closest to the waterfront. Apart from a section that used to house the shelter, the building has been empty for a decade. My recollection of the structure was a façade full of boarded-up, broken windows and flaking billboards.

Not anymore.

Looking at the building now—really looking—I'm struggling to put together which parts remain from the original. It's hard to tell where the old construction ends and the new begins.

The street-facing, block-long façade of the building is fronted with glass and metal. Its dramatic and vast open interior on the ground level reminds me of an urban art gallery. The polished cement floors gleam.

I know, from the development's website, that the plan is to set the space up as a communal workspace. A place where people can work from home without being at home.

"Xander should be here any minute." I check my watch. Cookie pokes her head over my shoulder and noses me, anxious to get out and look around.

"You okay to face him?" Kenna asks.

"It's just business," I say. Every time I chat with Hudson/Oliver, I think maybe there's something there. But then I get scared again. Still, I did bring the dog today. If Cookie can face her fear of cats, perhaps it can inspire me to be brave as well.

"Come on, G, don't pull that business bs," Kenna comments. "You two have some wild chemistry. There are enough sparks there to torch a rainforest."

I ignore her nudge and pretend to check my messages on the phone that he got for me. I'm hanging on to it for now, but

I'm trying not to get too attached. As soon as I can afford a new phone, I'll give it back.

"I get it. You don't want to talk about it anymore with me, but have you talked about it with him?"

"Sort of," I say. And then I see the van pulling into the lot. "Oh look, it's Xander and Emily!"

Xander parks beside us and jumps out, knocking on the passenger window.

"Team huddle, everybody out!"

He's wearing high-tops and a tie-dyed tee made by our mom that takes me back to his high school days. I clip Cookie's leash to her collar. Once I'm sure there's no broken glass in the lot, I let her jump out of the car. Was I crazy to bring her? Did Hudson really mean it when he invited me to bring the dog? Are we really going to introduce our pets to one another?

What was I thinking? There is a fairly good chance that their relationship would be even more volatile than ours.

"Hi, guys." Emily smiles shyly. "Thanks again so much for including me. Jackson is on his way too."

"You kidding?" Xander says. "Emily Romano, you are the bomb. We are lucky to have you!"

"Loved the *Lit Lovers* episode on tattoos, by the way," I tell her. "Totally up my alley."

"Georgia has a Shakespeare tattoo." Kenna volunteers.

"Enough about that." Xander holds out his arms, flapping and gesturing for us to gather round. And, of course, we comply. Resistance is futile.

"Why are we huddling, exactly?" I ask.

"I just want to make sure we are all on the same page. Let's go over our assignments. Kenna, you're checking out the kitchen. Emily is on decorations and PR. I'm working with Jackson to plan the livestream site. Georgia is planning the silent auction—"

"What about me?" says a deep voice from outside the huddle.

We break formation.

"You're supplying the space," I say. "That's more than enough."

He's wearing jeans and a black tee. There's that stubble again, delicious, scratchy-looking stubble that I long to feel against my skin. His eyes meet mine and connect. For a second, we're the only ones in the parking lot.

"Hudson!" Xander grins and goes in for the fist-bump. "We need an MC. Interested in the job?"

"I'd love to MC if you'll have me," he tells the group, but he's still making eye contact with me. His gaze flits to Cookie, and he leans over to pet her.

"I'm so glad you brought her," he says. "After the meeting, you'll have to come up to my loft and meet Oliver."

"Do you really think that's a good idea?" I ask. I'm also giving him the bullet eyes because I still haven't told Xander that Hudson is the owner of Oliver.

Kenna has quickly surmised as much and looks amused. Xander is clearly searching his memory, trying to recall who Oliver is and why that should matter to him.

"Wait a second, you two." Xander's face explodes into a grin, and he busts out in a belly laugh like this is the funniest thing he's ever heard.

"Oh, I see. You didn't tell them?" Hudson looks hurt for a fraction of a second, but then it's gone.

"Turns out we're both enrolled in an online Petfluencer Challenge." I cut Xander off and address Emily in particular.

"Remember I told you I was participating in a challenge so I could build up my dog's social media channels in the hopes of promoting my shop and the shelter?"

"Of course, of course." Emily looks from me to Hudson. Her face is serious and professional, but the instant Hudson looks away, she winks at me. I suck in a breath and shake my head. Not her too!

"Shall we?" Hudson gestures toward the building, and we all follow in his wake. He's striding swiftly.

"It's a funny story." Hudson glances back over his shoulder, not making eye contact with me. "I only just realized this past weekend that Georgia was my challenge buddy. Small world. She's been a great help. I don't think Oliver would have found his voice without Cookie's assistance."

"This is all so fascinating." Kenna takes three long-legged strides to reach Hudson's side. "I would love to hear more about the process, maybe read those messages?" Then she looks back over her shoulder, smiling smugly at me.

"You wish." Hudson smiles.

"Rats!" Kenna scrunches up her face and mutters to herself. I can't help but laugh a little.

Emily loops her arm through mine and leans in. "So, I'm still not sure what exactly is going on here, but I want you to know I've got your back."

"I'll explain later," I promise.

Xander, bringing up the rear, is still cracking up. I shoot him the same dirty look I used to reserve for his crashing my sleepovers in high school, and I'm gratified to see it still works. He shuts up.

Jackson and Angie are waiting when we get there. They are chatting cozily on an old sofa in the reception area.

"The workers brought that couch in, but we'll have other pieces in place on the twenty-eighth," Hudson says.

"Oh, that's too bad. This couch is so comfy," Angie says. She has brought along her photo album and is still flipping through photos, sharing stories. "I was showing Jackson some of our success stories. He said he lives alone. I think he needs a dog. I'm seeing doxie—"

"So, basically, you're a matchmaker," Jackson says to Angie. "We need to talk some more. I'm not sure if I should have you on the podcast or hire you to consult on the dating app." He strokes his chin thoughtfully.

"I've never listened to a podcast before, but I sure do love apps. And romance novels."

Jackson holds out a hand, helping her up, and they join the entourage.

"Don't mind me," Jackson says. He uses his tablet to take photos of everything, noting outlets and access and jotting notes directly on the screen with a pen.

"I like to capture as much visually as possible," he explains, snapping a photo of Cookie. "We should preload photos beforehand of the pets that are participating in the costume contest. We can use them as placeholders to set up the voting," he suggests. "Are you soliciting donations with the votes?"

"We can't make it mandatory, but I was thinking we'd request a dollar a vote." Xander nods his head enthusiastically. "We're totally on the same page here."

"Let me show you the software I like to use," Jackson says, pulling Xander aside.

"Okay, I think we lost them." Kenna laughs. "Let's just leave them to their own devices."

The rest of us continue on the tour, which doesn't take very long. Hudson shows us the commercial kitchen and shares his thoughts about various layouts and where to put the stage.

"We'd prefer to arrange the rentals ourselves for insurance reasons. I hope that's not a problem."

"Sounds like we'll save a bundle, actually," Kenna says. "We won't complain about that!"

"Want to see the patios and the roof deck now?" Hudson asks.

Hudson leads us to the opposite side of the building, and we are treated to a tour of the waterfront patio area. There's covered and uncovered seating, furnished with a combination of bar-height tables and sofa-style seating groups.

"We'll bring in space heaters for the event, of course," Hudson says. "Hopefully, the weather will hold for a few more weeks, but we can look into tents just in case."

"I love it!" Kenna enthuses. "I bet you have amazing light here at the golden hour."

"We do in the summer," Hudson says. He points out the waist-high fencing surrounding the patio. "As you can see, everything is also gated in. That should reassure the dog owners who plan on bringing their pets."

A gated staircase at the end of the patio leads to the second story, where the rooftop garden and penthouse lofts are located.

"Come on up." Hudson swipes a card to open the gate.

He leads the way up the stairs to a spacious, secret garden hidden from the street and riverfront promenade below. The view is spectacular.

"This is one of my favorite spaces. It's going to be reserved for our residents' exclusive use. But since I'm the only one living here at the moment, we'll open it up for the event."

Cookie immediately hops up on one of the outdoor couches and rolls onto her back. Tongue out, belly basking in the sun, she is completely blissed out. I can't blame her. This is a pretty sweet spot to hang. I plop down beside her to scratch her belly.

"Whoa, I think she approves." Xander whistles, coming up the stairs to join us.

"Who wouldn't love it here." I sigh. "It's pretty dreamy."

"I think we've figured out everything we'll need for the website and streaming." Jackson waves from the stairs. "We should be good to go. Don't forget we're taping tomorrow, Em. Xander is gonna pop in for the session."

Emily reads a message on her phone. "I hate to cut this short, but I have to call someone back about an assignment."

"Rome gig?" Jackson looks hopeful.

"You're flying to Rome for a story?" I ask. "How lucky are you?"

Emily grimaces. "Maybe. I've been asked to do a piece on a self-help guru. I'm just not sure it's a good fit. Celebrities aren't my usual beat."

"I'll give you a lift!" Angie says. "I'm headed back into town now. I want to hear all about it. You know, they have some really interesting dog breeds in Italy."

Emily takes Angie up on her offer, and Jackson follows closely on their heels, anxious to get back to coding.

Xander checks his watch. "I gotta hustle too. I have two more appointments this afternoon."

"Can I ride with you?" Kenna asks. "I've got to get back to the diner for the next shift."

"What, nobody wants to ride back with me?" I ask.

"Actually, Georgia, I was hoping you could stick around for a few more minutes," Hudson says.

Xander and Kenna both catch my eye.

"You good, G?" Xander asks.

"It's okay, you guys can go. I'm just gonna sit here for a little bit longer and bask in the bougie vibes," I say.

"I hope you'll come back sometime soon," Hudson says to Kenna and Xander. "Not just for this event. I'd love to have you all over for drinks sometime." He shakes Xander's hand.

"Let me know if you need anything from me," Hudson says as he walks them to the stairs. "Anything at all." I love the way he moves. He really is lithe like a cat.

And then it strikes me that we're alone on this rooftop. There's something strangely intimate about it, even though we're here in broad daylight. It's like we're on our own private island. The only people in the world. He walks back toward me, not appearing to be in any particular rush.

I want to say something, but I can't think what to say. I feel like I need a keyboard. My brain can't seem to make my mouth form coherent sentences right now.

This turns out to be fine because when Hudson joins me on the sofa, he isn't interested in speaking to me.

"I'd like to introduce you to someone, Cookie." Hudson strokes Cookie gently. She rewards him with a big, slobbery tongue bath.

I'm jealous. Watching his hands move over her ribs and torso, I'm wishing it was me he was stroking. I'm wishing it was me licking his neck, his jaws, his soft lips. The lower one is slightly fuller than the upper one, I notice. Too late, I realize I'm staring.

Hudson holds out a hand. I notice that his eyes look just like a satellite photo of the world. Flecks of brown and green swimming in a vast, blue ocean. I could get lost in that world if I'm not careful.

"Are you positive you want to do this?" I manage to ask. "I'm not sure it's safe."

"I'm pretty certain it's not," he agrees as he pulls me up and into his arms, "but I'm still sure I want to do it."

"What if it doesn't work out? What if they hate each other?" I ask.

"And what if they don't?" he whispers, before dipping his head to my neck.

Teasingly, he traces the curve of my collarbone with his lips. I moan. The touch of his tongue against my throat is pure fire. I'm melting into him, unable to separate myself from the sensation of our bare arms touching. I reach out to lift his shirt, and suddenly, he's carrying me in his strong arms and walking.

"Cookie!" I gasp.

"I got you," he says, and I glance down to see Cookie's leash is wrapped around his wrist. She is following obediently, tongue out, with the biggest, shit-eating dog grin I've ever seen in my entire life.

Hudson kicks open the door to the loft.

"Where's the cat?" I ask.

"He's in my bedroom, don't worry," Hudson says. He's addressing Cookie but he's speaking to me. "We can go as fast or as slow as you like, Cookie. We don't even have to do anything today, if you don't want."

I want. I want so many things. Including meeting the damned cat. But not just yet. I grab his shirt and yank. He helps me out by lifting it up and over his head, leaving me to delight in and explore his beautiful, broad chest.

My fingers trace the lines of his lean-cut muscles. I pause on a small series of nautical tattoos along his ribcage and look up at him to ask.

"I'm kind of into sailing," he says.

"And this one?" I trace my fingers over the axe.

"About that …"

"I don't even want to know." I silence him with a finger to his lips. "Because why on earth would you have ever let me win?"

He sucks the tip of my finger, smiling playfully. "You're a fearsome opponent."

"You have any runes tattooed anywhere that I should know about?" I ask.

"Runes?"

"Like Ragnar. I'm not entirely convinced you're not a Viking." I breathe out against him.

"Because you think I'm raiding and plundering your village?" he asks. He lifts me onto the kitchen counter and slowly unbuttons my shirt, holding my gaze the entire time. One button. Two buttons. Four. Then he peers down at my lacy bra and lowers his head to lick my breastbone. I prickle with wet, electric wanting as his chin stubble grazes against my sensitive skin.

"Come on, Baby Boy. Mommy's going to get you something yummy to eat." A high-pitched voice reverberates above us.

What the heck? I hear the sound of a door opening upstairs and clutch at my shirt. Hudson freezes, eyes wide and filled with thunder.

High heels clatter across the hardwood floor above, then clang against a metal staircase, coming down, down, down toward us in no particular hurry.

But I am. I slide down from the counter and frantically button my shirt. Hudson scrambles around on the floor for his tee and swiftly pulls it over his head. I should probably tell him it's inside out. No. No, I shouldn't. He's staring at my buttons, which are buttoned completely wrong.

Shit.

"Huds! You're home! Look at that, Ollypops! Daddy came home!" says the tall, blonde woman. The same gorgeous woman I saw in the Google search I did on Hudson.

"Ash, what the hell are you doing here?" Hudson stares at her. "And how did you get in?"

"The foreman gave me a spare key." She bats her lashes. "I was super tired. Major jet lag. I told him I needed to get in your bed ASAP."

"You should have called," Hudson says.

"I know, but I wanted to surprise you. I finished the London job early, and the team sent me here to handle the staging of the lofts. It's just perfect, isn't it, Babe? Now Ollie doesn't have to miss his mommy for another minute, does he? Do you, Olly." She glares at me before looking around for Oliver, who is nowhere to be found.

Suddenly, I hear whining coming from the living room behind us. Hudson and I spin around and take in the scene that's playing out before our very eyes.

Cookie is lying on the floor with her paws out in front of her. Her head is down and her ears are tucked back. Her tail is nestled between her legs. She's looking up submissively at the cat standing over her. Oliver, meanwhile, is totally unfazed. He's sitting calmly in front of her. So close that their noses are almost touching. Is he sniffing her snout?

Without any warning, Oliver licks her. He licks Cookie right on the nose. She startles a little but doesn't move. Tentatively, her tail loosens and thumps. I think she likes it!

Ashley groans.

"Is that your dog?" she asks, looking down at me disgustedly, then back at the wet spot Cookie is lying in. "Because I think she had an accident. Gross. You should probably get that cleaned up before it sets."

My face flames with shame and frustration. I cannot meet Hudson's eyes. Stupid, stupid, stupid. What was I thinking? That there might be something meaningful between us?

"Sorry about the mess," I say. "I told you she's afraid of cats."

"Uh … doesn't look that way to me," Ashley says. The nasal twang in her voice grates on me. She sounds like one of those stereotypically spoiled princesses from television sitcoms. She adds extra syllables. When she says me, it sounds like meee-uh.

I decide to ignore her. "Can I just get a towel or something? I'll clean up and get out of your hair. Seems like you two have some catching up to do."

"Thanks so much for understanding." Ashley shoots me a self-satisfied look.

"Absolutely not!" Hudson shouts. "The only person leaving the loft right now is Ashley."

"But Huds," she protests. "I told my driver to have my bags delivered here."

"Which was pretty damn presumptuous of you, Ashley," he says. "There's always room at the motel if you can't find anywhere better to stay. I'm happy to call you a cab. But you are NOT staying here."

"I'll just use these …" I grab a roll of paper towels off the counter and head toward the puddle, but Hudson catches my wrist and takes the towels.

"No, Georgia. You're my guest. I'll get that. And for the record, Ashley is not my girlfriend or my anything. She's just messing with you. The only reason she came here is for the cat."

"Rude!" Ashley rolls her eyes. She's glaring at Hudson now. "But typical." Now she turns to face me. "Word to the wise, or whatever you are. It's not going to work out. He's not into long-term relationships. Hudson Holm doesn't do commitments."

"Uber is on its way," Hudson says. "Do you need to grab anything, or are you good to go?"

"Fine. Whatever. You don't have to be such an asshole about it. I just wanted to see my cat."

"Don't go anywhere, Georgia," Hudson says. "I'm going to walk Ashley out, and then I'm going to clean up. Can you keep an eye on those two for a minute?"

Cookie is still eyeing Oliver warily. She seems almost afraid to move. She's looking desperately at me for reassurance. Oliver, on the other hand, has stretched out next to the dog and fallen asleep. He is snoring. Loudly. If it wasn't so ridiculous, it would be funny. Actually, it's still funny.

"Do you see them?" I ask Hudson.

"Right?" he answers and brushes his fingers down my spine. I sizzle.

"Um … it's a little chilly out. Can I borrow a sweater?" Ashley asks.

"No!" Hudson says, and he shows her the door.

Before Hudson can come back, I collect my things and clip Cookie's leash back on.

Who was that? An ex? Is it really over between them? Is she making a play to get him back? Obviously. Has he been watching her cat all this time as a way to keep her on the back burner? Friends with benefits? Doubt, suspicion, and a bunch of other emotions crowd to the surface.

Questions. So many questions.

Whoever she was, she seems like a jerk. Had she said Oliver was her cat? Who abandons their pet for weeks on end like that? I clench and unclench my fist. A not-so-small part of me wishes I had a socially acceptable reason to punch someone. In many ways, getting physical is so much simpler. A relief even. I know how to defend myself physically. I'd never run from a fight.

But this thing with Hudson isn't just physical, I'm starting to realize. And it has me spinning out, ready to run. What is it about Hudson Holm that has me wanting to run every time I see him? Either at him or away.

My body practically aches with the wanting. But no. Not tonight. Maybe not ever.

I reach the street just as he's turning to head back in. The Uber's taillights are sliding off into the night, vanishing along with our moment.

"I wish you wouldn't go." He tips my chin toward him and gazes down into my eyes. But he doesn't kiss me. He's searching for something, but I'm not sure I can give it to him. I look away.

"That was awkward," I admit.

"It was," he agrees, absentmindedly petting Cookie. "So, I can imagine what you're probably thinking."

"It's none of my business," I say.

"Yeah, but I want to tell you," he continues. "Ashley and I had a moment. Wasn't even a thing. More like a near miss. It was never going to be anything more. But she thought she could change my mind if she was persistent enough. She adopted a cat and put my name and address on the form, like we were a couple."

"Oh my God," I say. "That's crazy. Does that sort of thing happen to you a lot?"

"Yeah, it was crazy." He runs a hand through his hair. "Anyway, I couldn't send that poor beast back to a kill shelter, so I agreed to keep him while she went to work on a project in Chicago. I really had no idea the management company would choose her to stage the lofts here."

"No worries. You don't owe me any kind of explanation." I fish in my bag for the car keys.

"No, really, Georgia. I didn't know. I didn't want her to come. There isn't anything between Ashley and I, and I don't want there to be. She had the wrong idea about the nature of our relationship right from the start."

"Which was?" I can't help myself.

"No relationship."

"But that's not what she wanted, right? What was she looking for?"

"The phrase trophy wife comes to mind."

"And what were you looking for?"

Hudson sighs, then straightens and stretches in the lamplight outside the lofts, raising his arms above his head and doing a few neck circles. He's avoiding my gaze. And still, I'm mesmerized by the sliver of skin peeking out between his T-shirt and jeans. I have to look away.

"Your shirt's inside out," I say.

"Yours is buttoned wrong." He laughs, and before I can stop him, he is reaching out and unbuttoning me, quickly and deftly, correcting my mistake. There is heat from his hands. The brush of his knuckles against my throat gives me goose bumps. He finishes and steps back.

"Come to my sister's birthday party this weekend," he says. "Please?"

"I don't know if that's a good idea."

"I want you to meet Lilly in person. She needs more role models like you. Strong, independent, ass-kicking."

"Flatter much?"

"Lilly may be thirteen, but even she knows our stepbrother is kind of an asshole. You are her hero now. Plus, you would be doing me a huge favor. I could use a little help with my ex-stepmother."

"What's up with your ex-stepmother?"

"Eggplant emojis, for starters." Hudson shakes his head and looks at the stars. "Honestly, I haven't told this to anyone, Georgia, so you better not repeat it."

"Eggplant emojis?" I ask.

"Yes, eggplant emojis, flames, hearts, etc."

"Your stepmother sends you eggplant emojis, Hudson? You do know that's not okay, right?"

"I know, but it's always this gray area. Like was it an accident, or was she doing it on purpose? Like the eggplants are followed up with a random string of other emojis. And there was the butt grab that one time when she was walking behind me and 'tripped.'" He makes air quotes with his fingers.

"Sounds like she's gaslighting you." I frown.

"If you came with me, not only would Lilly be thrilled, but I'd feel much safer too," Hudson pleads. Then he pulls me into his arms, holding me close, gazing down.

"You don't actually need my protection from anyone," I say. "You're big enough to defend yourself."

"You might be surprised, Georgia. People are always trying to take advantage of me. Especially my family members. But also, people like Ashley."

"And how do you know I'm not yet another Ashley, hoping to hitch a ride on the … money train?" I ask. I almost said eggplant express but recalibrated just in time.

"That's the point," Hudson says. "I kind of wish you would take advantage of me. For once, I can't think of anything I'd like more."

I can feel his heart thumping, and for some reason, I believe him. There's something happening here. Something far scarier I should be running far and fast from.

"Fine, I'll come," I say, pushing him away with a decisive shove. But only because I know you let me win that axe-throwing match. Text me the details, and let me know what to bring."

I click the lock on my car and pop the hatchback for Cookie to jump in.

"Later, Holm Hater," he says.

"Hate You Later, Hudson," I reply.

I can see him in the rearview mirror as I drive away. He's still standing there, smiling, as I turn the corner.

hudson

. . .

WALKER'S FLIGHT IS DELAYED, which means I spend the better part of the next day in Seattle, working from a café. Fine with me. Now that Ashley's in town to stage the lofts, I'm happy to stay away and let her do her job. The sooner she's done, the sooner she'll be gone. Though I am a bit concerned about what she's planning to do with Oliver. She hasn't mentioned signing a lease anywhere. Meanwhile, I've instructed the crew that she's not to be allowed back in my place. Not under any circumstances.

"Is that all of your luggage?" I ask, surprised to see Walker coming through security with only a small duffel.

"You can't go your own way if you're schlepping a lot of baggage, son!" my father quips. I suspect he's referencing that new Blaze Smith book everyone is talking about.

"Mm-hmm." I nod.

"I've still got a full closet of clothes at the main house, anyway. I'll have Mel pack it up and send it over to me."

"Okay," I say, wondering where exactly he thinks that's going. It's a one-bedroom loft, and Bryce left behind a full wardrobe of his own stuff. I've barely got a foot-long length of rail in the closet for my own clothes.

On the drive back to Ephron, my father fills me in on his fishing and cooking successes. He tells me he's learned how to filet and cook several different types of fish during his private lessons with the onboard chef.

"Was she hot, then?" I ask, assuming the worst.

"She is a he, and it's the same chef we've used for a decade, Hudson. Honestly, as if I'd take advantage of staff!"

"Wasn't your third wife Bryce's nanny?" I ask, referring to Lilly's mom, Mel.

"That's different." Walker shakes his head. "She was an independent contractor. And Bryce's mom had already moved out."

"And she was twenty years younger than you," I point out, even though I know mentioning this will be pointless.

"She sure was." Walker grins shamelessly. "But the heart wants what the heart wants!"

"Yeah, the *heart*." I roll my eyes.

"No regrets, son. Look what came out of that relationship. Wouldn't change a thing. Can't believe Lilly is already a teenager."

I can't argue with this, so I change the subject.

"So where is my little brother now? Off to the Maldives to soothe a widow? Checking out a rave in Thailand?"

"Kenya, actually." Walker chuckles.

"Let me guess? He decided to take some girl on a safari?"

"Nope." Walker shakes his head. "He's not going to be able to afford anything like that for the foreseeable future."

"Really?" I take my eyes off the road for a moment to study my father's profile. He's got his seat leaned back and his eyes closed.

"I've cut him off. And don't you go lecturing me about how I should have done it a long time ago. I've always felt sorry for that boy. Both of his parents essentially abandoned him. That'll screw someone up."

I think of Georgia, and how she'd been let down by her biological parents and the foster system before fate led her to her adoptive mom, Joan. Only to lose her. This thought makes my heart ache. But Georgia had taken all that adversity and turned it into a triumph. The shop, the shelter, her own clothing line. She has so much to be proud of.

"Why Kenya?" I ask.

"There's an elephant sanctuary there where the workers care for orphaned baby elephants." Walker sighs. "I saw a documentary about it on the flight to Bora Bora. I had to pull some strings, but I secured Bryce a place on one of their rehab teams. He's going to be working one-on-one with the animals for the next year."

"Bryce agreed to this?"

"He did when I froze his accounts and told him it was this or he gets cut off forever." Walker tips his seat back farther and shades his eyes with his sun hat. "Aside from the lessons he's bound to learn shoveling elephant shit, I think he may benefit from working with orphaned animals. Teach him some gratitude."

"Blaze Smith book?" I guess. Those self-help books are always big on practicing gratitude.

"Great stuff." Walker agrees. "When it doesn't put me to sleep."

When we pull into the loft parking garage, I notice that Ashley's rental car is parked in the visitor spot. Shit. I was hoping she'd be done for the day and I wouldn't have to run into her.

Walker follows me into the loft and wolf-whistles. He hasn't been back to Ephron in a while. It's the first time he's seeing the transformation. "Jeez Louise. I can't believe this is the same old warehouse. Well done, son!"

"I can't take all the credit, Dad. Our teams have been working pretty hard for over a year now."

"But it was all your idea, your vision," Walker says. "You've pitched it every Thanksgiving since grad school."

This much is true. I've been pushing for this project for at least eight years.

The elevator bell dings, and the door slides open to reveal Ashley. The breeze from the garage blows her hair back, like she's in a shampoo commercial, and she shakes her head to prolong the effect, enjoying the dramatic entrance. As she steps out, her perfume—a synthetic-smelling, floral scent mixed with cotton-candy overtones—punches me in the nose. I note that she is wearing a skin-tight, bone-colored sheath dress, stiletto heels, and a full face of makeup. Perfect for a construction site.

"Who is this lovely vision before me?" Walker's face lights up. I can almost hear his rusty gears grinding as the notorious Walker Holm charisma revs itself up and cranks back online.

"You must be Walker! I'm Ashley." Ashley flashes her pearly veneers and sticks out her pink, acrylic-clawed hand. I hadn't really taken stock before of how much of her physical appearance is fake—fake hair, fake nails, fake teeth, fake boobs.

Rather than shake Ashley's hand, Walker reaches out and lifts it to his lips. It's just the sort of thing I can imagine Georgia decking someone for. But Ashley giggles like an antihero in an Austen movie, thrilled to be the center of attraction at last.

"Such a gentleman, Walker. I've heard so much about you from Hudson."

"Well, I haven't heard nearly enough about you."

I'd love to log on to the challenge portal as Oliver and tell Cookie about this whole exchange. I'd say something like, *"It was quite deplorable, Cookie. Such rampant buffoonery and a complete lack of decorum!"*

And then I expect Cookie would check me with something along the lines of, *"Lighten up, Furball. Whatever floats their boats!"* Or would she? What would she say?

Maybe she would me ask what I'd hoped to get out of a relationship with Ashley.

Nothing, apparently. Aside from a cat.

"Ahem! Earth to Hudson!" Ashley clears her throat and continues to smile her utterly insincere smile at me. "What do you think about my proposal?"

"Sorry, lot on my mind." I apologize. "And a long drive. I'm a little brain-dead."

"Looks like you need to get some good rest, Son." Walker claps me on the shoulder. "Ashley just suggested that I stay in one of the other model lofts she's staging. It's actually a two-bedroom place, and she was saying that she'd considered staying there herself, but she's not entirely comfortable staying alone with all the construction still underway on the building. I suggested we bunk up together." His voice has definitely dropped an octave, getting even deeper and more gravelly than usual. "In separate rooms, of course."

"That would really be so wonderful," Ashley gushes. "It's a commute to the Doubletree and I really would prefer to stay on-site." She smiles a little smugly at me, clearly pleased with herself. But if she thinks I care, she is sorely mistaken. This actually works out better for me. It gets both of them out of my hair.

I pretend to be thinking about their plan for a minute.

"Well, okay. I guess that makes sense." I shrug. "Especially if it speeds up the project timeline."

"Fantastic!" Ashley claps her hands victoriously. "I'll just show your dad up there now so he can get settled in." She eyes his duffel. "Is that all you've got? I'm so impressed with a man who travels light!"

"I don't believe in excess baggage, Ashley. Gotta live in the moment!" Walker asserts. "Shall we?" He places a hand on Ashley's lower back. I look over my shoulder to make sure there's not a brontosaurus ambling up behind me in the parking lot. Ashley doesn't seem to mind the invasion of her personal space one bit. She bats her lashes and smiles up at my father. I'm not sure whether I'm glad or horrified to see her humor him like this. Glad, I guess? It's one less potential lawsuit to worry about.

Ashley addresses me while still looking up at my dad. "I'll give you a full tour of the staging work we've done so far after we get settled, Hudson."

"No need. I can show myself around later this week," I say. "Just text me with any questions or problems."

"Will do!" Ashley waves cheerily over her shoulder. No mention of the cat, I note.

Walker stops for a moment and pauses, turning back toward me. "Hey, Hudson. They still got those chili fries at The Onion?" he asks.

"You bet they do."

"Then let's plan on grabbing dinner and drinks later. Eight o'clock work for you? I'm still on Bora Bora time."

"Sure, see you then," I say. I turn and head toward my own loft, relieved to be alone again—at least for the moment.

276

georgia

. . .

"I JUST WANT to read it one more time before I go," I say to Kenna, referring to the *Pet Friends* article. Emily dropped off a copy this morning, and I'm just sad I don't have time to laminate it before leaving for Lilly's party.

"We've already had three online orders this morning. Maybe I should stay here in case it gets too busy?"

"For God's sake, Georgia, it's just one day off. The shop isn't going to implode. I got this." Kenna tries to shoo me out of the store.

"Do you think Lilly will like these?" I hold up a gift bag full of graphic novels.

"Hudson said that's what she's into, right? Don't sweat it, G."

"What about my outfit. Is it okay?" I'm wearing cowboy boots, leggings, and a hand-pieced mini dress that I made out of a collection of vintage sweaters.

"You're look adorable. I love how you used the paisley pattern for the pockets."

"Thanks." I glance around, trying to recall anything I may have forgotten to tell her. "You can call if you need anything. You have my keys to lock up?"

"Yes! And I'll drop Cookie off at your place after. Got it!" Kenna sips her tea. "I can't wait to see who comes in. Maybe I'll meet a hot dude who rides a Harley with his Pomeranian. Can you imagine the itty-bitty helmet?"

"Careful what you wish for," I caution, thinking about how I had imagined a Viking raider in my store not long before Hudson appeared.

"Honestly, you know what would make the time pass faster?"

"What?" I ask. I owe her. She could ask for almost anything.

"If you let me read the texts between Cookie and Oliver."

"Good one." I laugh.

———

The Holm residence is a stately, historic mansion a few miles outside of town. It's familiar to most Ephron residents. So many civic and charitable events have been hosted there over the years, as well as community holiday parties.

Xander is already there when I arrive. I park behind his van on the long, circular, gravel driveway. There are a bunch of balloons attached to his side mirror.

I'm surprised to see Angie sitting on a folding lawn chair a few yards away, reading a romance novel. There's another bunch of balloons attached to her chair. She waves hello enthusiastically as I draw near.

"Oh, hey there, Georgia. Isn't this fun? Xander's over there showing off some of our social media success stories. We borrowed a few of the newly adopted, Tiktok famous, dogs for the day. Promised I'd stick around and babysit."

She points to a penned-in area on the side lawn, where Xander is holding court with a gaggle of preteen girls. I recognize the dogs immediately. One of the girls is taking a selfie with Mr. Miyagi, who is panting happily and enjoying the attention. Two other girls are showing their phones to Xander. There's a bulldog with a coach's whistle and striped ref's shirt sitting on his lap.

Xander looks up, waves, and mouths the word "Help!" Angie and I laugh because he can't keep the grin off his face. We're not buying it. He's clearly lapping it up.

"He's in his element," Angie says. "The grown-ups are around back. I almost forgot! I'm supposed to send you along."

I glance tentatively at the open gate and path beyond. "Are you sure I can't help out here?" I ask. "Get you anything to drink?"

Angie holds up her water bottle. "I'm good. I was just getting to the spicy part in my book, so …" She smiles and waves me away. "Shoo! Go on, then!"

The path dumps me out on another perfectly manicured lawn. A pavilion tent has been set up with round tables inside. The tables are dressed for a tea party. A few adults are gathered around a firepit near the pool. They must be the moms of Lilly's friends, I think. Or perhaps they are her mom's friends.

A small, black dog in a familiar-looking cop costume from my shop streaks across the lawn. He's trailed by a tall, athletic girl I recognize is Lilly. Her streaky, blonde hair is flying out behind her.

"Larry! You get your fat butt back here!" she yells.

"See? I told you I was shopping for my sister's dog." Hudson walks toward me, smiling, and takes the gift bag from me.

"You didn't have to actually bring anything!" He peeks inside before depositing the bag on a gift table in the tent. "I bet she'll love these though!"

"Phew! I had no idea if I was buying the right ones."

"Can I get you anything?"

I drink him in, feeling thirsty. How is it that I've only just met him, yet I've missed the sight of him since I last saw him? His deep-blue sweater brings out the dark blue of his eyes.

"Is that linen?" I cannot resist. I reach out to touch his sweater.

"No clue." He shrugs and catches my hand. He speaks low and close to my ear. "Maybe you need to run your hands all over it and let me know."

A plume of heat sweeps through me. Hudson watches my reaction, his eyes flickering with the same flame that lit me.

"Or, I could just read the label." I pluck my hand away, grateful for the cooling autumn breeze.

"You look amazing, by the way." Hudson's eyes are still on me, continuing to smolder. "Did you make that dress yourself?"

"Is it that obvious?" I look down, suddenly doubting my clothing choice.

"Only because I know how talented you are," Hudson says. His fingers lightly trace the seams of my pieced-together dress. "I like how you've assembled so many bits together and made something better from them all."

"Better than them ending up in the landfill," I say.

"Mm-hmm." He dips two fingers into my front pocket, stroking the soft, knit fabric between them and his thumb. My eyes close, as if it's me he's stroking. He smells so good again. It's not a cologne. It's just him.

"Hudson!" Lilly flies past me and flings herself at him. She's barefoot, wearing jeans and a faded, tie-dyed sweatshirt. She's a little bit taller than me already, and it's clear that she's going to be a giant, like her brother.

"Lilly, this is …" Hudson begins.

"Georgia!" Lilly finishes for him. She sticks out her hand. "We are going to be best friends."

"Okay." I smile.

"So, can you believe this bullshit?" Lilly asks us. "Mom still thinks I'm five. She insisted we do a tea party. And she thinks we're doing a stupid fashion show after. But there's no way my friends are dressing up. Look at this!"

Lilly drags us to the other side of the tent, lifts a flap, and points to an open part of the lawn where someone has set up racks of clothing, accessories, and photo props. There's a vanity table staffed by a couple of teenaged makeup artists, and a forty-foot-long red carpet. At the end of the red carpet is a photo booth with a celebrity style, step-and-repeat photo backdrop, emblazoned with Lilly's name and the number thirteen.

My mouth drops open. Lilly peers at me and nods.

"Right? You feel me? Xander and I came up with an alternative plan. But someone has to step up. I'm counting on you two. Do not let me down." She gives us a sidelong look before skipping off to her table.

"So that's Lilly," Hudson says, fondly watching his sister.

"She's amazing." I laugh.

"Everyone, take your seats, please! The tea party is about to begin!" A tall, willowy, dark-haired woman in a clingy caftan has teetered into the tent, high heels sinking into the grass. She's ringing a brass bell.

"That's Mel, Lilly's mom," Hudson says.

We take our seats at the far end of the tent at one of the tables designated for "grown-ups."

"Remember how I told you I needed your help today?" He looks around the tent and locates Mel, seating herself at the other table for grown-ups. She's flanked by two attractive men. The rest of the table appears to be populated by Lilly's friends' moms. "Looks like I'm safe. Mel's sitting with her personal trainer and the gardener." He raises his eyebrows significantly at me.

"Phew!" I wipe invisible sweat off my forehead. "I'm glad I won't have to defend your honor after all."

But Hudson suddenly seems distracted. He's looking warily over my shoulder now at someone else coming toward our table. He takes a deep and sudden breath, then lets it out slowly. I swivel my head around to see what he's looking at, then quickly turn back to face him. His face has become a neutral mask, completely unreadable. Under the table, he places a hand on my knee and squeezes gently.

"Well, now. This should be interesting," he mutters softly.

Ashley slips into the seat on the other side of Hudson. Her tight, off-white leggings leave nothing to the imagination. She's wearing them with a pink argyle twin set and a brand-new pair of designer tennis shoes to complete her "suburban" look.

Walker takes the seat beside Ashley. He appears to be wearing tennis clothes as well. Lilly sees him from across the crowded tent and waves excitedly. He grins and waves back.

"Ashley wasn't doing anything today, so I invited her along." He takes a drink from the server and tastes it, making a face. Then he pulls out a flask and doctors it up, offering the flask around to others. Ashley giggles and holds out her cup, waving cheerily at me as she does so.

Hudson leans in to brush my hair aside and whispers in my ear, "I'm so sorry, Georgia. I had no idea she'd be here."

"It's fine," I whisper back. I'm trying not to stare. Ashley is practically hanging on his father.

In my pocket, my phone buzzes with an incoming text. A covert glance shows me that it's Kenna.

The message simply says, *"Please call ASAP."*

A million scenarios play out in my mind as the adrenaline surge kicks in. What if the store was robbed? What if Cookie ran away?

"Excuse me," I say, "I have to take a call." I hastily make my way out of the tent onto the lawn, past the pool, and down another pebble-lined path toward a small pond.

"What is it? What's wrong?" I shout when Kenna answers.

"Oh, Jesus, G, chill. Nothing's wrong. I just couldn't find your house keys. But then I remembered where you keep the spare."

"That's it?" I ask, wondering how I'm going to expel this excess adrenaline now. Jumping jacks? I do a few quick twists and jump up and down a bit. I'm just slipping the phone back into my pocket when I hear the sound of crunching gravel and see Hudson coming down the path.

"Everything okay?" he asks.

"Yeah, just a little confusion about my keys."

"There's actually something I wanted to talk to you about," Hudson says.

"Oh?"

"It's about the clothing from the Farm & Holm site. Do you have any preferences for what we do with it?"

"What do you mean?" I ask. "I thought you said you were pulling it all."

"We did," Hudson says. "And we can have it all destroyed if you want. But there's another option I thought I'd run by you."

"Okay." I take a breath. "It does seem shameful for them to end up in the trash."

"We can remove the labels and donate the costumes to a charity. There are several orgs that would take them, but I thought perhaps you might want them to be distributed directly to pet shelters so there's no chance of resale and further brand confusion."

"Out of curiosity, how many of those costumes did you make?" I ask.

"About twenty thousand units, I think."

"As in TWENTY THOUSAND?" I choke. "You're going to donate twenty thousand dog costumes to charity?"

"Well, no. There's only about nine thousand left to donate."

"What happened to the rest?"

"They sold." Hudson smiles wryly. "They were actually doing pretty well for us. I'm sure you'll be getting a settlement offer from the legal team."

This is something I hadn't considered. I can't help but wonder how big that settlement might be. And how long it might take.

Meanwhile, I do some quick math in my head. Farm and Holm sold one hundred times more of "my" costumes in a few months than I've sold in my entire career.

"How will you even find someone to take a donation that big?"

"I'm sure we can locate international rescue orgs to work with. We'll look into it more if that's something you'd like to pursue. You don't have to decide this minute."

"Okay," I say. The idea has me excited now … the sheer volume of it and the impact it could have! "You know, I could sew all day, every day, for years, and I still wouldn't come close to being able to donate that many pet costumes." I sigh.

"Along those lines," Hudson says tentatively. "I know that our normal way of production doesn't necessarily appeal to you, but what if there was a way to meet in the middle? What if we licensed your original designs and had them sewn in small batches in ethical, sustainable shops?"

"You think you can do that?"

"I'd like to try."

"Maybe a portion of the proceeds could go to shelter pets too," I suggest.

Hudson nods. "Or we could even adopt a 'buy one, donate one' sales model."

"This is an intriguing idea," I admit, trying not to get too excited about it. He might not be for real.

"You can still talk to a lawyer." Hudson smiles wryly. "I would. Make sure you get what you deserve for the clothing that was sold. And then you could take that money and run … do something like this on your own."

"I wouldn't know how," I confess. "I don't have the head for that stuff. Perhaps I do need someone to catsplain a few things after all."

"You know what's funny?" Hudson reaches his hand out to mine and we spread our fingers, measuring ourselves against each other. "Right after you left the table earlier, I caught myself checking my phone."

"Expecting a call?" I ask.

"No," he says. "I was checking to see if I had any new messages from Cookie."

"I do that all the time too," I admit.

"It's a little crazy, isn't it?" he says, stepping closer.

"It is," I say.

"You are making me crazy, Georgia. And the weirdest part is that I think I was already starting to fall for you when I thought you were a dog."

"I don't even normally like cats," I admit, "but Oliver really grew on me."

Hudson draws me close and bends to place his lips on mine. This kiss is long and slow. There is no pressure. Time stops as his lips explore mine. Somewhere off in the distance, I'm aware of the waves lapping along the shore of the pond. I feel as if I've lost all sense of gravity, and then I realize he's lifting me … literally sweeping me off my feet.

My hands find the back of his head, tangling in his hair, pulling his mouth closer, kissing him back, harder. He groans, stops, and pulls away. I wonder if there's a boathouse or something nearby.

"I'm sorry. I don't know what came over me. We should go back," he says, and sets me down on my unsteady feet. His eyes are darker, and some of my lipstick has rubbed off on his lips. I trace them with my fingertips, wiping away the telltale red streaks.

"It appears I've rubbed off on you. I knew I could corrupt you."

He traces my lips with his finger and pulls me in for another kiss, quick and with a flick of his tongue that has me trembling. "You're a naughty girl. I'm going to have to keep an eye on you."

By the time we get back to the tent, it appears it is time for the fashion show.

———

Xander is tapping on a wine glass with a spoon, and Lilly is ringing her mother's brass bell to get everyone's attention.

"What's this? What's going on, Lilly?" Lilly's mother's teeth are gritted as she speaks through a large, artificial smile. Lilly merely shoots her a thumbs-up sign before jumping up onto a chair.

"Everyone knows what a fan my friends and I are of Xander Starr's pet transformations, right?"

Lilly's friends clap and cheer, along with Walker and a few of the moms in attendance.

"We wanted to treat you all to a different kind of transformation today though." She turns toward Xander, who steps up on a chair beside her.

"Today, instead of turning a pet into a superhero or movie character, we'll be reversing the process. We're going to be transforming my sister, Georgia, and Lilly's brother Hudson into their online alter egos. Did I mention that Georgia and Hudson both have shelter pets in their lives?

"The videos Lilly and her friends make will be posted with information about how to support the Kismet Pet Rescue Organization," Xander explains.

"And I'll be donating my birthday money to Kismet too!" Lilly chimes in.

"Get ready for an EXTREME makeover and quite a show!" Xander says. And then he and Lilly fist-bump, both looking at us defiantly.

"Those little shits," Hudson whispers under his breath.

"They are so dead," I agree.

———

After the party, we buy a packet of baby wipes, some eye makeup remover, and a bottle of toner. We bring it all back to my place.

"Stand still, Furball!" I admonish.

Hudson is sitting in my bathroom on the edge of my tub, and I am attempting to remove the caked-on makeup from his face.

"I'm so glad you knew what to buy," he says. He sorts through my bowl of bath bombs and sniffs. "Ooh, I like this one."

"Shall I run you a bath?" I ask sarcastically.

"Only if you're willing to join me."

"I thought cats didn't like water."

"You shouldn't stereotype, Georgia."

"Take off your T-shirt," I order, wiping my way past his beautifully carved jaw, down his neck, and toward his collarbone. "I need better access here."

"Yes, ma'am." He complies, pulling the shirt over his head. It's the first time I've had a really good look at his bare torso. As I wipe the last of the makeup off his neck, I can't peel my eyes away from the hard planes, smooth skin, and light dusting of blond hair in all the right places.

"Eyes up here," he says, tipping up my chin. His eyes are gleaming provocatively.

"Right. I think I got most of it off." I turn his chin back and forth to inspect my handiwork.

"Your turn, then." He jumps up and spins me to sit on the edge of the tub. "So, I just use this stuff and the wipes?" He gestures at the bottle of makeup remover and the face wipes on the counter.

"Yes," I answer, and I realize that I'm trembling. This is just so surreal. I cannot believe that I have this giant man in my bathroom right now.

Hudson kneels down in front of me and sits back on his heels. He gently wipes away at the layers of puppy-dog makeup the girls and the makeup artist piled onto me. He tosses wipe after wipe into the already overflowing trash can. Then he stops to admire his progress.

"So, this is what you look like without makeup." He smiles. "I like it."

"I don't usually wear a lot of makeup, just lipstick," I object.

"Then I guess I just like your face," he says, leaning in to plant light kisses at the corners of my eyes, the tip of my nose, my lips, and down my jawline. "But I think you better take off your camisole so I can get the rest of the makeup off your neck and shoulders here." He traces a finger along my collarbone. "May I do the honors?"

"Please," I say.

Hudson peels my cami away and leans back, taking in my lacy, red, balconette bra, which is barely covering my suddenly pebbled nipples. He runs a finger under one of the straps to move it aside as he strokes me with one of the wipes, and then his eyes look up to question mine. I nod, and he reaches one hand around to unhook me. I inhale deeply as he does, reveling in the warmth and clean, manly scent radiating from him. So close.

As the bra falls away, I sigh and lean back slightly. Hudson takes a sharp breath and moves his hands to my waist before bending forward and burying his head in my chest. He takes his time moving from left to right, giving each of my aching nipples ample and generous attention before moving to the other.

"Eyes up here." I run my fingernails through his hair and tilt his head up toward my face.

He gathers me in his arms, standing with me, kissing me urgently now. His tongue is doing things to mine, moving in circles that seem to be controlling my hips. With each tantalizing swirl, I'm gyrating, wet heat building, my need growing against his.

"Are we really doing this?" he asks.

"I sure hope we are. I don't know how much more I can take of your teasing," I say.

"You're calling me a tease, now? Shall I show you how I'd like to tease you?" Hudson kicks the door to my bedroom open with his foot and pauses in the doorway.

"Are you trying to torture me?" I ask, willing him to continue walking toward the bed. The bed is an island, and I am at sea. I want nothing more than to reach it with him, to be laid down on it, to be stripped bare, to feel his weight on top of me.

"I'd say it's the other way around, Georgia. From the moment you slammed into me outside The Onion, I haven't been able to get you out of my head. You've done something to me."

"Bed," I say, sinking my nails into his back. "Now."

He takes three long steps and drops me onto the bed. "Your wish is my command."

"For the record," I say, sitting up to undo his jeans, "I wanted you too. From the moment you strode into my store, acting like you owned the place, which, technically speaking, makes a lot more sense now." He groans as I undo his zipper, pulling his pants down and freeing him. "My Ragnar." I kiss a trail around his inner thighs and groin, delighting in the way it makes him strain.

"Jesus, Georgia."

"If you could just stand there for a moment?" I request. "I want to look at you. I've never had a real-life, naked Viking in my room."

"Undress yourself, then." Hudson tips his chin out and gestures at my leggings. "I'll stay here and watch."

"Okay." I stand on the bed and roll down my tights, taking my time, watching him and his obvious reaction to me. His eyes skate across my body, leaving every nerve ending alive and crackling, aching for contact. I'm down to nothing but my thong.

"Hudson?"

"Yes, Georgia?"

"Did you ever picture me when we were chatting as our pets?"

"I didn't dare picture you. But I hoped, Georgia. I really hoped it was you."

"I hoped it was you too," I whisper.

And then in a single step, a lunge, he's moving toward me, on the bed on his knees, walking me back up against the headboard. He uses his teeth to pull the front of my thong down, lingering for a moment to torture me with his hot breath.

I don't think I've ever wanted—no, needed—someone so much.

"Take this off." My breath comes out ragged, my words separated by gasps.

Hudson pulls my underwear away, and in the next moment, without hesitation, he pins me to the wall, plunging his tongue into my folds, kissing, teasing, and tasting me.

My legs are shaking. I'm so close, so close I don't want him to stop. But I also don't want to come like this. I want him inside me.

"I need to feel you, Hudson." He pauses and looks up at me, dreamy-eyed.

"How would you like to feel me, Georgia?"

"On top of me, inside of me." I slide down the headboard and reach forward to touch the part of him that appears to be in complete agreement. His skin feels like silk under my fingertips. Like something fine and magnificent. The firm length of him strains against my grip.

"There's a condom in the bottom drawer," I say.

I lean forward to lavish his tip with butterfly kisses, and he moans.

"I'm torn because I don't want you to stop," he says. "But I also don't want this to end." He reaches out sideways to dig in my bottom drawer and retrieves a foil packet.

"Found it." He walks to the foot of the bed and slowly unrolls the condom onto himself as I watch.

"On second thought, I think I'm with you on wanting to be inside you, Georgia. In fact, I don't think I can wait."

He leans down, grabs my ankles, and pulls me away from the headboard, all the way down to the foot of the bed till I am seated there, and then he sinks to his knees. His eyes are half-closed and his lips parted. A thick lock of blond hair has fallen forward across his forehead.

"I'm going to take you now." His tongue flicks the sensitive spot behind my ear, and he bites my lobe. He parts my legs with his hand and then reaches down to slide a finger inside me, then over my swollen bud. I'm so wet, so ready. I arch forward.

"Please," I beg. I don't ever think I've said that word in bed before. But at the moment, I may as well be begging for my life. If I don't feel him inside me, and soon, I might actually die.

"As you wish," he says, thrusting long and hard, and we both moan together because it feels so good. The sweet relief of it.

But that relief doesn't last. It's a moment, and then we are rocking backward together, at sea. The storm is gaining momentum with every thrust, the waves threatening to overtake us.

The power of it takes my breath away.

It's not like I've never had sex before. But never like this. Never in the middle of an ocean so deep, with a thirst so great. He lifts me, moving us both to the center of the bed.

"I want to feel you come, Georgia. Come with me," he rumbles. His fingers lace with mine and pin my outstretched arms over my head. It's all the invitation I need. The boat is tipping. We are flung together into that boundless abyss.

hudson

. . .

I AM TANGLED in the sheets, and there is a large dog sleeping curled up beside me. It takes a moment for me to remember where I am.

I'm in Georgia's bed. I spent the night in her house. We had sex. More than that. Sex doesn't seem like the right word to describe it. I've had sex before. I've never had that.

This isn't a normal, "just got laid" feeling. This is a sort of soul satisfaction that has opened up a whole other level of being for me. Clear skies. Birds are singing. Heaven? Oh shit, I really am a cliché.

My stomach is growling. Somewhere downstairs, I smell coffee brewing. I use the bathroom and pull on my boxers and jeans. I'm holding off on the makeup-stained tee for now.

Georgia's en suite bathroom is charming and spacious for an older home. Light spills through a large window lined with plants, and a prism casts rainbows all around the mosaic-tiled floor. Her slipper tub is massive, big enough for two. I'm definitely filing that detail away for later.

Wait, what? What am I thinking? Why am I even still here? I stare at myself in the mirror. Stubbled and satisfied, but not completely sated. The sight of the scratches on my back and the memory of what happened last night—all three times—has me more than ready to go again. I can't seem to get enough of her. I have an overwhelming need to do it all over again, to beat my own high score, to commit every curve and sigh to memory. As if I even could. When it comes to winding me up, she's gone pro. I can't predict what she'll do or say next. But I'm dying to know.

Normally, at this point in a hookup scenario, I'd be waking in my own bed. No unnecessary overnights. That's always been my rule. Normally I wouldn't be waking up spooning with a girl, and certainly not with her dog.

"You're in so much trouble, man." I speak to my reflection and head downstairs.

Georgia is in the kitchen, wearing an oversize tee and little else.

"Oh good, you're awake," she says. "How do you take your coffee? Sorry it's not egg coffee, just regular pod stuff." She looks at me and blushes. "Oh my God! Your back …"

"I better not let Oliver see those. I'm not sure he'd approve." I kiss her sweet and salty neck and take the mug from her hand. "Black is fine. Good morning, by the way."

"Mmm. Well, I guess you had it coming," she says. "I'd apologize, but it's more of a sorry, not sorry, situation."

"I'll heal," I assure her. "And then you can mark me all over again."

"You wish."

"Damn straight I do."

Her eyes hold mine, and the heat is back. I'm weighing my options between the kitchen counter and the table. Definitely the counter. The table is small and doesn't look sturdy.

Cookie barks.

"Shit," she says, checking the time on her phone. "I really gotta get a move on. I have to take Cookie to the dog park before I open. Not that I want to kick you out or anything. I don't really do breakfast."

"That's okay, I'll grab something later. I've got a full day too." I pull her close and kiss her. "But Georgia, I don't think we're done here."

She kisses me back with so much passion, I start to doubt whether either one of us is getting to work today. I leave my coffee on the table and drink her in, backing her up onto the counter. Her legs wrap around me, and I'm regretting the decision to put on my jeans.

But then suddenly, she stops and pushes me away. She holds me at arm's length and shakes her head, the look of frustration on her face unmistakable.

"Dammit. No. This has to stop. I really hoped that last night would do the trick, get you out of my system. But you're like one of those scary 'try it once and you'll get addicted, and next thing you know, you're living in a cardboard house' drugs," she says.

"Oh, *I'm* addictive now?" I question her. "Because I don't DO overnights. I was supposed to wake up in my own bed."

"Humph." Still holding me at arm's length, she pivots her legs to one side, then slides down beside me. "So, we're in complete agreement. This can't happen again. But before you go, I need you to try on the costume for the masquerade. Come with me." She takes my arm and drags me into a side room filled with sewing notions.

Wait, what? What did she just say?

"Georgia, I don't get it. I don't agree. I don't understand what just suddenly changed," I protest.

She takes a fur-and-leather vest off a form and proceeds to fit it onto my naked torso.

"Look, Hudson, I was wrong. You've proven to me that you're not the devil incarnate, as I originally suspected. Your sister is adorable. Your dad even seems semi-okay."

The touch of her hands is still doing things to me.

"Your brother is still an asshole though. I'm not ready to revise that assessment."

"Georgia, look at me?" I reach out for her chin and she adeptly steps aside, grabbing a ball of pins off a shelf. The walls are lined with sketches. One area holds a rack with scissors and cutting tools. There are rolls of fabric in the corner and two sewing machines on a large work table.

"No, really, Hudson. Trust me. It's better this way. For both of us." She pulls on the shoulder of the vest and swiftly pins it. "Hold still."

She steps back to evaluate if there's anywhere else that needs adjusting. "Look, last night was amazing. Mind-blowing even. But we both know it's not going to work. You're only in town till the warehouse project is done, and I've got to focus on my business if I've got a prayer of staying in the shop and continuing to support Kismet and, you know, keep doing what I do."

"But …" I have never wanted to kiss her more. The words I'm trying to form halt. I feel like a denied child, indignant and muttering. But, but, but!

"Plus, you know, you don't actually do …" She tugs the vest and pins the other shoulder.

"Relationships?" I finish. "According to Ashley?"

"Oh, come on, Hudson. It's all over the Internet what an uncatchable catch you are. The jury is out about whether you're even into girls, but I think I can vouch for you there."

"I'm into *you*," I say. My hand reaches toward her, but she ducks away again and I'm left to cuddle air.

"For now, maybe. But you'll get over it. Look, we've still got to finish the Petfluencer Challenge, and we're throwing this shindig in your space. I think the safest option is if we both do the adult thing now and decide to proceed as friends."

"With benefits?" I ask warily.

"Oh, Hudson." She sighs. "Just getting to feast my eyes on you in this Viking costume is a real benefit for me." Georgia has to stand on her tiptoes to set the horned hat on my head, and when her breasts brush against me, I have to close my eyes for a minute.

"It's perfect. I have a matching hat for Oliver too. See? Is this not the most hysterical thing you've ever seen?"

It is, actually, but I'm not inclined to give her the satisfaction.

"Great. Alrighty then, guess I'll be on my way." I shed the vest and place the hat back on her work table. I can't get out of here fast enough.

"You forgot something," she says.

"Excuse me?"

"You can't go home without a shirt."

"It's dirty. Keep it. I'm good."

"Don't be silly. Take mine." She pulls her faded concert tee over her head and tosses it at me.

"Are you fucking kidding me?" I catch the shirt and fling it back at her.

"What? It's not like you haven't seen me naked. I just don't want you to freeze and catch pneumonia and then have to cancel the masquerade." She places her hands defiantly on her hips. Her breasts are pert and hard in the cold studio. Her breasts are mocking me.

"Yeah, whatever. Don't worry. You'll have your event space," I mutter and make my retreat, holding out a hand to shield my eyes. "And just because I've seen you naked before doesn't mean you can just strip in front of me any old time— especially if you've decided we're just going to be friends now. That isn't … well, it just isn't proper."

"Fine, whatever." Georgia rolls her eyes at me and pulls her tee back on. "At least take a sweatshirt?" She grabs an over-size hoodie off a hook on the back of the door, but I'm already gone. I don't want her sweatshirt. I don't want to smell her. I don't want to be her friend, with or without benefits. I certainly don't want to be the loser just waiting to get a look at her tits when she decides it'd be fun to tease me.

She can go fuck herself as far as I'm concerned.

With a click and two beeps, I'm sitting shirtless in my car, and then I'm peeling out into the street. I'm burning up and freezing cold. I've got half a hard-on and a heart that feels like it just got tossed and drop-kicked. I don't care what direction I'm going, as long as it's away from that volatile little bundle of trouble.

Back at my loft, I take a long shower before making myself some breakfast and feeding Oliver.

The cat, while initially peeved, now seems extremely happy to see me. It's the first time I've left him alone overnight, and I guess it never really occurred to me that he wouldn't like that.

Cats are supposed to be fine with being left alone. Cats aren't supposed to give a shit, right?

Except, now that I think back on this, I realize what a crock that is. Pretty much every night since he came into my life, Oliver has slept on the foot of my bed. He's my shadow as I move through the loft daily, settling in a beam of light or on a fluffy cushion in whatever room I happen to inhabit. What had he thought last night? He must have been worried. Maybe he thought I was never coming back?

"I'm really sorry, Dude," I say, petting him and giving him a little extra food. Much to my chagrin, he doesn't judge me at all. Not even a dirty look. He just purrs excitedly and gives me those damned, blinking "lovey eyes."

Worse, I realize that I'm sitting here, blinking back at him.

I do the only thing I can think of to make myself feel better. I throw myself into my work.

There's only a week left till the masquerade, and while I trust that Ashley has made progress as promised on furnishing the models, I haven't had a chance to tour them. I stop downstairs and grab a cup of coffee from the countertop where the workers have set up a temporary coffee station.

"Have you guys seen Ashley? Or my dad?"

"Not today, Boss. She might be out shopping for more stuff. And Walker hasn't been down for coffee yet. Maybe check his loft?"

"Will do," I say. "No prob." Good thing I have a master key for all the units. I don't really need anyone to show me around.

I start with the loft my dad and Ashley have been occupying. It's convenient that they've both been able to stay close to the project, but I'm probably going to have to talk to both of them about clearing out before the event. At least for the night, so that we can show the unit.

"Knock, knock," I call out as I bang on the door. "Anyone home?" I hit the doorbell for good measure, hearing the chimes echoing inside the large, mostly empty space.

Unlike my loft, this one is a single-level unit. It has two bedrooms, an open-plan, central kitchen and living room, and oversize bathrooms. The view is incredible, as with all these units. A full wall of glass leads to a large patio with one of those glass-fronted Jacuzzis Bryce was so crazy about.

Assuming nobody's home, I let myself in. Ashley has outdone herself. The space is outfitted like an urban dream home. The central area is furnished with a massive, white sectional sofa. There's a modern, glass dining table and leather Eames chairs off to one side. The kitchen is loaded with the latest and greatest appliances. A brass faucet and hardware gleam like jewelry. But the counters are littered with take-out containers.

I flip on the lights to assess the mess. The shades are all drawn, which is actually a good call both to keep the furnishings from fading and to conserve energy.

More incriminating evidence of Walker's stay in the unit includes a pile of pistachio shells on the glass coffee table and a pair of his loafers kicked off under one edge of the sofa.

Ashley's designer purse is tipped over on its side on the end table. I can't help but notice there's an unfolded sleeve of condoms spilling out. Nice. Well, who am I to judge? Looks like we've both moved on.

"Hello?" I call out again tentatively and check the first bedroom. It's immaculate. The white, platform bed has a white coverlet and sunny, yellow throw pillows. The panoramic windows also have their shades drawn. But the light pouring in through the open upper windows illuminates the large, abstract canvas above the bed. Ashley's clothes are hanging in the closet, and I'm glad to see she had the good sense to make her bed.

Finally, I make my way into the other larger bedroom, presumably where Walker has been sleeping. Not surprisingly, this room is a mess. The bed is rumpled and unmade, and there are at least six glasses of various beverages sitting on one nightstand, as well as another take-out container on the other. There's clothing on the floor too.

I make a mental note to ask Ashley to look into a cleaning crew and make reservations for herself and my father at a hotel for the night of the event next week.

Then I hear it. Laughter and splashing. Someone's out on the patio. In the Jacuzzi, probably.

There are windows and a door to the patio from the master, but the electronic shades are also drawn in here and I cannot see outside. I look around for the remote but can't seem to locate it. I do, however, find a second sleeve of condoms in my dad's nightstand drawer. Gross. Same brand as Ashley's, and I can't help but wonder if he'd have the nerve to ask her to pick them up for him.

Turning the latch, I head out onto the spacious patio. It's been furnished with a small seating group, cozied up to a tabletop firepit. There are sticky skewers here and crumpled wrappers. Marshmallow drippings are all over the table. Someone's been roasting their marshmallows and eating them too. Seriously, Walker?

Again, I hear splashing coming from the nook in the far end of the patio. Is that my dad in the Jacuzzi? Does he have a girl in there? Ugh.

I clear my throat loudly and approach warily. "Walker, is that you in there? Everybody decent?"

I needn't have asked. In the next instant, as I round the corner, the answer to my question is more than apparent. They are not decent. And their lack of propriety is on full graphic display in the glass-fronted hot tub. They don't even have the respectability to be running the jets. Nope. My dad and Ashley are sitting buck naked in the pool, feeding each other strawberries. Their nudity couldn't be more perfectly on display if they'd set up shop in a department store window. In fact, the display kind of reminds me of a department store window.

I'm officially questioning everything in my life that led up to the decision of this particular hot tub in this particular loft. Then I remember that Bryce chose it. Of course.

Neither of them has the decency to even look embarrassed either. In fact, my dad laughs. Ashley ducks under the water, her long, blonde hair fanning around her.

"I'm not sure what to say," I remark, willing myself to look anywhere but at the two of them.

"Don't be a prude, Son," Walker says. "We're all grown-ups here. Have you ever heard of knocking?"

"I knocked!" I defend myself. "I rang the bell. I knocked. I called out. I only let myself in because there was no answer."

"What made you come in?" Walker challenges.

"I'm checking the progress"—I gesture in Ashley's direction —"HER progress on the staging."

"Well, I could have told you she's making great progress," Walker booms. He pulls Ashley's hand and she floats to his side, sitting sideways with her long legs across his lap. I'm trying to keep my gaze above the waterline, but it's impossible not to see what's going on inside the fishbowl. I'm going to need more therapy, probably. Years of it.

"In fact," Walker continues, "she's done such an amazing job that I've decided to purchase this unit. So, you didn't have to check it out after all. It's no longer for sale. I'm buying it. We're going to be neighbors!"

"Isn't that great, Hudson? Now we can share custody of the cat. Maybe we can make a little passage for him to go between our lofts," Ashley pipes up.

"Sorry, Baby Girl." Walker shakes his head sadly. "That is not happening."

Did he really just call her 'Baby Girl?'

Ashley pouts. She literally sticks her lip out and pouts. I feel itchy.

"But Walker," Ashley says, "I can't just abandon him. I made a commitment. Some of us aren't afraid of taking that leap." She glares at me with what appears to be pity.

"I know you promised, Baby, but it's impossible. I'm allergic." Walker shrugs. "Figure out a different plan. Board him or something."

My skin is crawling. Walker may be allergic, but I'm the one breaking out in hives.

"Just … shut up! You can't have him," I shout. "And nobody is boarding my cat." I can't believe Walker even had the nerve to suggest it.

"Well, Son, that's not exactly up to you. Ashley and I have discovered something that I think is really special, and I'm too old to just let that kind of thing slip through my fingers."

He pulls her onto his lap. She doesn't even bother to hide her glee. Under the smug self-satisfaction, there's something girlish and giddy about her that I don't even recognize. Whatever. This is a message from the universe that I should probably take a vow of celibacy or something. Why do I keep looking at them? It's like a train wreck.

I don't want to see it. I can't look away.

"Jesus Christ. I'm not talking about you, Walker. I'm talking about Oliver. The cat. MY cat. She abandoned him"—I point accusingly at Ashley—"and I'm not willing to share. He's mine. All mine. Not negotiable."

And then I do a one-eighty and walk out.

georgia

. . .

I SPEND the rest of the week sewing. Thanks to Emily's article, there's been a run on costumes in the shop, and I can barely keep the rack full. And then there's the costumes for Hudson and Oliver. Even though I'm no longer sure he'll want to wear them.

I honor my promise. I finish the costumes the night before the masquerade. I take a photo of Oliver's suit before wrapping it up in plastic. Then I put on Hudson's discarded tee—I've been sleeping in it all week—and crawl into bed.

What do you think, Furball?

I text the photo. I don't know what I'm expecting back from him.

Great. Will you bring it by?

That's all he says.

It's the only communication we've had all week, although both of us have continued to complete our prompts and like each other's posts. There are still marks in my driveway from where he peeled out.

On the morning of the masquerade, Kenna comes over to help me wrap gift baskets for the silent auction. We sit on the floor, making our way through the piles.

"Check this out!"

Kenna holds out her phone to show me a photo the uncles have texted. They are already over there, helping with setup and doing food prep. The tables and chairs are already draped with black tablecloths. There are colorful dog treats scattered like confetti on every table.

"Looks great," I reply.

"The event website is getting traction too. People are already bidding on the silent auction items. And we sold out on the tickets."

"Jackson and Emily really came in clutch," I say.

"Not to mention Xander's fans and Lilly Holm's friends." Kenna points out. "But none of this would have happened without you, G."

I want to believe her, but I still feel deflated. It's a feeling I haven't been able to shake since the awful "morning after? with Hudson.

"This is some premium swag." Kenna ties a bow around a basket stuffed with everything a dog owner might want to spoil their pet.

"Our vendors were super generous with the donations," I agree.

"I heard Xander is auctioning off grooming sessions, and the HS track team is offering free dog-walking during the event."

"Yes! They're setting up a dog valet service." It is such a cute idea.

"Have you talked to Hudson today?" Kenna asks tentatively.

I shake my head. His name is still salt in my wound. My self-inflicted wound. But that doesn't mean it hurts less.

"He asked me to bring the costumes over for him."

"How did they turn out?" Kenna asks. "Show me!"

"Okay." I sigh and head to the back. I flip on the now functional lights. The costumes are hanging on a metal shelf. Every time I touch them, I relive Hudson storming out of my house. His face.

"Here they are." I hold up the matching Viking outfits for Kenna to inspect. They include shaggy fur vests, faux deerskin leggings, lace-up boot covers, loose muslin shirts and, of course, horned helmets. Oliver's helmet has a chin strap.

"Oh my God!" Kenna holds a hand over her mouth. "Has he seen these?"

"Not since I finished. He just saw them for a minute last week."

"Last week when he was at your house?" Kenna asks delicately. She's given me a hundred opportunities to talk, but I haven't been ready. She wants to ask me more. I know she does. But she is giving me space.

"Yep." I sigh and lay the costumes on the counter. I may as well pack them up in one of the gift bags. That way, I can leave them for Hudson, hang them on his door or something. The less contact I have with him, the better. I just have to get through tonight. And then I don't have to deal with him anymore.

This thought doesn't bring me any relief though. Instead, it makes me feel like hyperventilating. I blink away a few stupid tears.

Kenna seems to make a decision, and then she speaks.

"Are we ever going to talk about what happened? Xander seemed to think you and Hudson were really getting along at Lilly's party. I swear, if that bastard fucked with you, I'll put arsenic in his coffee."

"You don't need to poison him." I sigh. "Nothing happened. I mean … well, something happened. Something amazing." I stand up and pace around the shop.

"Okay." Kenna gives me space, waiting patiently until I'm ready.

"The sex was mind-blowing," I admit. "I basically thought I saw God. But then I told him we should just be friends. Because … you know." I gesture lamely around the shop, as if this makes sense.

Kenna blinks at me, biting her lip.

That's the thing about speaking your fucked-up truth. It doesn't make it truthier. It only serves to highlight what an idiot you are. The lump in my throat is painful. My eyes burn with the unshed tears.

"Go ahead, say it."

"I don't know what to say, Georgia. I'm just going to give you a hug, okay?" She wraps me up in her arms, and I rest my head on her bony shoulder.

When she releases me, I sink to the floor and toy with a pair of scissors, snipping the uneven ends off the bows waiting to be added to the wrapped baskets.

"Maybe it's not too late." Kenna pats my shoulder. "Tell me exactly what happened. What made you tell him you just wanted to be friends?"

"I don't know. One minute, we were in the kitchen. I was making coffee. He came downstairs. I was hungry. I wanted a big bacon breakfast, I wanted him, I wanted everything, and I felt like, for once, maybe I could actually have it. It was like my heart was waking up from a bad dream, and the sun was shining. But my pantry was empty. I really haven't cooked anything in the kitchen since my mom died, you know. I never eat breakfast at home."

Kenna nods. "I know. Why do you think I always bring you food?"

"So, we started making out. I knew he was starving because his stomach growled, but I thought, *We can't have breakfast here. He's going to have to leave me to go get some food.*"

I'm not even sure how to explain this, but I try.

"The thought of him leaving in that moment, Kenna … I don't know. I just felt so sure that he was going to leave me and never come back. I thought, *What if he changes his mind now that he's slept with me? What if he decides to go back to Seattle and get on with his super-rich life and his trophy wife-style girlfriends?*"

"Oh, Georgia," Kenna reprimands me, "cut it out. You don't give yourself nearly enough credit."

"Okay, then what if he got in a car accident?" I ask. "What if he simply went out for eggs and got t-boned and never came back?"

Kenna doesn't have an answer for this, but she understands. We're both orphans.

"I don't want to be his 'friend with benefits.'" Now the tears are falling for real, and I wipe my eyes with my sleeve. "I mean, he mentioned it, at one point, and I considered it for a second, but I don't think I could do it."

"You considered it?"

"Yeah, I was such an idiot. I took my shirt off."

"What? Why?" Kenna is shaking her head.

"I guess I kind of just wanted to see what he'd do? Like I wanted to wind him up a little. I don't know what I was thinking. It was so stupid. I was desperate for him not to go."

"But you asked him to go," Kenna says. "Have you talked since then?"

"No."

"Not even as Cookie and Oliver?"

"Just the one message. He asked me to bring the costumes by. The challenge ended this week anyway."

Kenna frowns.

"I don't know what's wrong with me. He was always going to leave town when the warehouse conversion was complete. What was I thinking, getting in bed with him?" I hug my knees, resting my head against them. "Maybe it's better this way."

It's miserable this way.

Kenna offers me a hand up from the floor. "You know what they say, Georgia?"

"Don't mix stripes and plaid?" I quip. "Because that's bullshit."

She cracks a tiny smile. "Nope, that's not the one."

"Don't eat before you swim? Also bullshit." I take her proffered hand.

"No, Georgia. I'm referring to your situation here."

"Fine. What do they say?"

"Love makes people do crazy things. Heatstroke, too, apparently, but I don't think that's your issue."

"Nobody mentioned the L word here."

I busy myself, snatching at scraps of cellophane and snipped ribbons on the counter and the floors, shoving them into the trash.

"I've known you for a long time, Georgia. I'm your best friend, and I love you like a sister."

I shove sheaths of packing materials back into their cubbies behind the counter. "I wish I never met that man."

"No, you don't." Kenna drops in the chair and swings her legs over the arm. "You're just scared because you're not used to feeling this way. But Georgia, you're not a coward. You'll never forgive yourself if you don't tell him how you really feel tonight. So, stop stress-cleaning and show me what you're going to wear."

hudson

. . .

THE EVENT SETUP is about to kick into overdrive when Walker pulls me aside to tell me something "important."

"I'm planning to propose to Ashley and make her wife number four." He opens his jacket to give me a peek at the ring box. "You snooze, you lose." He winks at me.

Seriously?

"Shouldn't you maybe get to know her a little better, Walker?"

Walker just shrugs. "Nah, what's the point? When you know, you know."

I don't know exactly what to say, but I offer up a silent prayer that Ashley never sends me an eggplant emoji text. For both our sakes.

"You'll get her to sign a prenup, though, right?"

"I'm in love, Son. I'm not an idiot." Walker rolls his eyes and straightens his Mad Hatter top hat. He gives zero fucks what anybody thinks about him. I'm never going to be sure whether I should be impressed or horrified by him.

"I didn't want you to be blindsided, but don't say anything. I want it to be a surprise." He taps his nose and then remembers something.

"When's Georgia getting here?" Walker looks around.

"I don't know." I shake my head. "But I hope it's soon. She's bringing my costume, and I need to talk to her."

"Hey Hudson, can we get you for a soundcheck?" Jackson calls across the lobby. People are really starting to stream in now, carrying gift baskets and flyers, running wires, and setting up speakers.

But no sign of Georgia or my costume. All around me, people are trying to grab me to answer questions, show them the fuse boxes, or direct them to the restroom. I'm pulled in a million directions.

After the soundcheck, I flag down Ashley. She's seated by the front door, manning the loft's check-in table. She hasn't seen Georgia arrive with my costume yet either.

I have an idea. I check my watch. There's just enough time if I go now.

I locate Jackson and tell him I've got to run a quick errand.

"I want to pick something up for Georgia," I say. "We had an argument."

"Just go, Hudson, get outta here. Do what you gotta do." Jackson shoves me out the side gate.

He pantomimes chucking an axe at me.

"Stop it," I say.

"Listen, Dude, if you don't go after her tonight, I am just folding up shop and giving up. I've run the numbers, and I actually think the two of you were made for each other."

"What numbers?" I ask. "You're totally full of it, Jackson. You don't have any data on Georgia or me that you could possibly be using to make such a prediction."

Jackson taps his head. "It's all up here. It's like the AI, minus the A."

"Okay, whatever." I laugh. "Just go do your thing and livestream the shit out of this, okay?"

I'm not sure if I'll be able to salvage things with Georgia tonight, but at the very least, we're going to save that shelter.

georgia

. . .

THE SUN HASN'T EVEN SET YET, but the warehouse is abuzz with activity. Dozens of people are scurrying around making last-minute adjustments, setting up information and check-in tables. Delicious smells are coming from the kitchen, where the uncles are prepping food to be passed on trays. Uniformed bartenders are stocking the two bars that have been set up on opposite ends of the space.

Jackson waves to greet me from his station by the makeshift stage. He's manning some sort of a console and making adjustments on four different computer screens.

Near the coffee bar in the middle, Xander is unloading the silent auction baskets he's brought over from the store in his van.

Emily dives in, helping to hang a banner, and Kenna takes off with her camera to get some shots outside. I check Cookie into the doggie valet area with the volunteers so I can help out with any remaining setup.

"Thank God you're here," Xander says, pausing to glance my way. "Nice costume. What is that exactly?"

"Punk fairy. You?"

"Ferris Bueller." Xander waves at one of the helpers setting out clipboards for the silent auction. "Over here. We need those here, please."

"Oh hey, Hudson mentioned you were bringing his costume?"

"I have it right here." I hold up the bag.

"Perfect. I just saw him on the other side over there, up by the stage."

"Check, check." The sound system comes on with a screech and a buzz as a tech taps on the microphone. Hudson unfolds himself and steps up to the microphone, adjusting the height. The sun is streaming through the windows. It paints him gold, like he's been dipped in honey. He squints. I don't think he can see me. I suck in my breath and gather my courage.

My plan is simple. I'll hand him the bag and ask him if he has a minute to talk. I just have to explain to him that I got spooked. I'll say I understand if he doesn't want to continue or whatever, but …

I haven't worked out the rest.

Having checked the mic, Hudson turns and bounds down from the stage, taking the steps two at a time. I see him check his watch and check in with someone arranging glossy brochures on the table by the door. When she stands to grab something out of a box, I see that it's Ashley.

Ashley has on an *Alice in Wonderland* costume that I suspect she purchased from one of the naughty costume catalogs. Striped thigh-highs, blue garter bows, and a lace-up pinafore. A label dangling from her bodice reads "Eat me."

I feel frumpy by comparison. I'm wearing a black bodysuit and a pair of iridescent, green wings. My hair is spiked with glitter gel, and my hot-pink fishnets are torn in several places.

Ashley is wearing false lashes and a padded push-up bra. I'm wearing wiggly antennae and a spiked dog collar.

I watch as Hudson leans down to go over a list with her. She points at something. He leans in closer to take a look, then shakes his head and laughs.

I try to make my way to the table, but there are so many people darting in front of me. I step aside to make room for some workers to get by with a pair of giant speakers. By the time I get to the table, he's gone again.

"Georgia!" Ashley trills and waves at me. "Is that Hudson's costume? He said he was waiting for you to get here with it so he could go up and get changed. You want to leave it with me? I'm just about to head upstairs and make sure everything's ready to go. I can drop it by his place."

"No, that's okay," I say. "I'll bring it to him. Where'd he just go?"

"Oh, he ran out to get more food or something. I don't know. Last-minute errand? Just leave it with me. I promise it'll get to him." She stands up and reaches out to grab the bag handles. I don't let go. Neither does she. It's like we are playing tug-of-war. Finally, I release my grip. She teeters backward as I let go but doesn't give me the satisfaction of falling down.

"Tell him I'm looking for him if you see him?" I urge.

"You bet!" She flashes her veneers at me and sashays confidently toward the elevator, passing the bar on the way. I see Walker there. Like half the other men, and a few women in the space, he seems mesmerized, watching Ashley make her way toward the elevators.

The bar appears to be open, and I could use a drink.

"Hey, Walker." I interrupt his reverie. He's holding a green top hat with an orange wig attached.

"Some party!" he says. He slips a bill into the tip jar and palms his whiskey. "We should do this every year!"

"It would really make a difference for the shelter," I say. I order a vodka soda and drink half of it down as soon as it comes.

"Have you seen Hudson?" Walker asks.

"Ashley mentioned he went on an errand?" I shrug.

"Georgia!" Lilly runs over and flings herself at me, ambushing me with a hug. "I love your look!"

"You look pretty cool too!" I say. She's wearing Cheshire cat pajamas and carrying her little dog, who looks just adorable in the doctor scrubs Hudson purchased in my shop.

"I wanted to dress up like a patient from *Botched*, but my mom wouldn't let me. Whatever. I'm already in pajamas, and Dad said I can sleep over in his loft tonight." Her grin matches the feline on her pajamas.

hudson

. . .

THERE'S a gas station and a convenience store in the warehouse district. Both of them have thirty-seven different kinds of spicy chips, but that's not what I'm looking for. The corner market by the highway doesn't have it either.

I have to drive all the way into the center of town to a proper supermarket.

I just hope that with this peace offering, Georgia will hear me out.

How had our morning deteriorated so quickly? When I replay the actual words that she said the other day, none of them make sense. One minute, we're making out, and the next, she just wants to be friends because it's the rational thing to do? And she pulls off her shirt? It's the opposite of rational.

Frustration is still coming in waves, but I'm calmer now. Getting sent away had made me angry, but I'm angrier with myself for leaving and not sharing my feelings. I don't want to be relegated to the rank of friend—with or without bene-fits. I want more.

But I'd been too chickenshit to tell her.

For the first time, possibly ever, I know exactly what I want. Without question, without hesitation, without excuses.

If I don't tell her what I actually want, how I really feel, then I'll never know for sure. Perhaps Walker did have one point.

When you know, you know.

———

I pull into the covered parking lot, making sure to leave room behind me for service vehicles. Then I exit onto the street. Xander corners me outside the building.

"We doing this?" Xander asks.

"We are!" I return his fist bump. "Where's Georgia?"

"She's inside, getting some ice for one of her vendors, I think," Xander says. "I wanted to talk to you about her for a minute, just the two of us. Man-to-man."

"Okay." I don't know why I'm suddenly nervous, but I am. Xander has been nothing but friendly to me, and he's been a hero for Lilly. But suddenly, I get the feeling that as great as it might be to have Xander in your corner, he's not someone you want to cross.

His sunny disposition is darkened by clouds of suspicion. If he wasn't wearing a Ferris Bueller costume, he'd be genuinely intimidating.

"What's going on between you two?"

"I think that's between us," I say.

"You know my sister is very special to me," Xander says. "And she's not as tough as she looks. She's going to test you. She has a hard time letting people in. We both do. And I swear to God, if you do anything to hurt her … well, I don't care who the hell you are. I can do some scary shit with my clippers."

"I don't doubt that." I bite my lip because, although I'm sure he's being sincere, the Ferris Bueller costume is ruining it for me.

"But Xander, it's not just up to me. It's up to her. I'm crazy about her. If I haven't made that clear enough already, I intend to do my best to remedy that."

"Good," he replies. "We're good. Now you better get your ass into that costume she made for you before the guests start knocking the door down."

He's right. There's a line forming out front.

Once inside, I look around for Georgia. Is there time to talk to her before the event begins?

"Hudson, you better get dressed! I put your costume in your loft." Ashley is carrying a clipboard with sign-up slots for loft tours.

"Go light some candles in the breezeway! We're almost ready to begin." She barks an order at one of the interns from the management team.

Then Ashley shoves me inside the elevator. In the last seconds before the door closes, I see a green-winged fairy flit by and I recognize her. My battle pixie. But the elevator is already on its way up, and I'm already running so late. I need to get into my costume.

Perhaps she'll like me better when I'm dressed up as her Ragnar.

THE NEXT HOUR IS A BLUR. The uncles have me plating food. Emily asks me to sprinkle confetti in the bid envelopes. I fetch ice for a cooler full of "pupcicles" and grant permission to one of my cat toy vendors to place tins of catnip-stuffed "anchovies" on each table.

Angie asks me to help her tie her den mother kerchief and then excuses herself to check on the pet valet attendants. Someone scanned her entire photo album for a slide show. Kismet's greatest success stories are being projected on giant screens all throughout the venue.

As we get closer to opening the doors to the public, Jackson and the livestream crew make their rounds from area to area. Periodically, they give me the thumbs-up sign, which I take as a good sign.

I'm too busy to check the site, but Xander assures me it's all set up for the livestream, online bidding, and the costume contest.

The only person I haven't run into again is Hudson.

When I make my way back to the table up front, Xander grabs my arm. "Thank goodness you're here. We need more help with check-in!"

"I should probably check on Cookie," I protest. "She's been up in the roof garden for a couple of hours already."

"I'm pretty sure Cookie is having the time of her life." He points to a chair, inviting me to take a seat. "I was just up there, and she had four people playing fetch with her. We need you here, G. It's showtime!"

"Wait, where are you going?" I ask.

"To greet my fans!" Xander rolls his eyes. "Can you believe Mac made me a step-and-repeat banner? I'm doing photos and signing autographs."

Out front, I spy Mac's flaming-red hair, which even a surgical cap cannot fully contain. He's rocking a sexy doctor costume. I wave hello to him, and he smiles widely and waves back.

"He sold so many tickets," Xander gushes. "He hit up all of his patients."

"Mac's been so generous. I don't know what we would have done if he hadn't opened up space in his clinic for the last few months."

"He's all right." Xander smiles. "I think he's actually going to miss it a little when the shelter reopens."

"I'm so happy you have him," I say. "At least I don't have to worry about you being homeless if all this doesn't pan out."

"Are you kidding me?" Xander's mouth is hanging open. "Are you really sitting here, still worrying about losing the house?"

"I know everyone's doing their best," I say, "and I think it's awesome. But do you have any idea how much it costs to relocate a shelter?"

"Uh … yeah, I have some idea," he says.

"I'm just not sure it's realistic." I continue. "I mean, this party's definitely going to help but—"

"Let me show you something, Georgia."

Xander pulls out his phone and swipes up. He selects a page that is showing the same slideshow currently running on the screens in the loft. Then he clicks in the corner on a running total that makes my eyes bug out.

"We made that much already?" I ask.

"This is just ticket sales and pledges. We just opened up the auction, and we haven't even started the costume contest yet."

"Holy shit, Xander," I say. "You did it."

"Kismet is coming back better than ever! And nothing's happening to the house." He smiles. "I told you not to worry, Georgia."

"I don't know what I'd do without you, Xander," I say. The relief is overwhelming, and I'm trying not to get too choked up. "None of this would have happened without you."

"And I wouldn't be here without you," Xander points out. "You've always taken care of me. Feels pretty damned good to pay it forward. Thanks for letting me be the hero for a change."

"You're welcome," I say, and then I accept and reciprocate his hug because resistance would be futile.

"I wish Mom was here." I sigh.

"Me too," Xander agrees.

"She'd be taking terrible photos with her flip phone," I say, and we both laugh.

"Doors are opening in two minutes!" a volunteer booms out. Mac waves both arms over his head to beckon Xander back to the banner.

"Tell Mac thanks again, from me," I tell Xander before he turns to go.

"Are you going to come clean about your feelings for Hudson?" he asks. "Or are you going to grow old alone with your cats?"

"Dogs," I say. "He's the one with the cat."

Xander rolls his eyes at me. "You deserve nice things, G. Don't you forget it."

hudson

. . .

THE INTERN STOPS me in the breezeway as I'm exiting my apartment.

"Whoa! Cool costume. You look so Viking-y!" he says. "You're Hudson, right?"

"Yes," I say. I'm looking past him toward the elevator. There's still time to find Georgia before I have to make my speech.

"I'm supposed to ask you about the space heaters?" he says, uptalking the statement into a question.

"What about them?"

"We need help turning them on."

Shit. I take the stairs and survey the outdoor areas. Nobody has put the propane tanks into the space heaters on the roof deck and patios, and the temperature is dropping quickly.

Cookie runs over to greet me, and I scratch behind her ears. She licks my face. Her iridescent-green fairy wings, rhine-stone-studded collar, and hot-pink fauxhawk are adorable. I snap a few photos of her and add them to my Instagram story, tagging her account.

"You really are the goodest girl," I tell her affectionately. "Even though you drool."

With the help of the intern and two of the larger teenaged volunteers, I start the laborious process of hauling propane tanks over to heaters and getting them lit.

It takes a lot longer than expected. By the time we're done, I'm a sweaty mess and most of the guests are checked in.

Kenna comes out onto the patio to snap photos of the pets. I grab her. "Have you seen Georgia?" I ask.

"Oh my God!" She puts a hand to her mouth.

"That bad?" I look down at my costume, which is drenched with sweat.

"No, no"—she giggles—"that good. You look ... authentic. I have to get a shot. Has Georgia seen you? I mean, have you talked?"

"I've been looking all over for her. I thought I saw her for a second earlier. Is she dressed as a battle pixie?"

"I think it was a punk fairy, technically," Kenna corrects me. She hesitates a moment before speaking again. "Listen, Hudson, go easy on her, please? Hear her out?"

"Excuse me?"

"I mean, this is totally middle school of me, but I think she has the feels for you."

"The feels?" My heart skips a hopeful beat. First Xander, now Kenna. Is it possible that the feelings I'm feeling could actually be mutual?

"I've already said too much." Kenna puts her hand over her mouth. "How's your cat? Where is he? I want to meet the famed Oliver!"

"He's up in my loft. Here's a pic of him in the costume, except I couldn't find his helmet." I show her the photo of Oliver in his costume and the selfie I shot of the two of us together. I can't suppress my grin. I've been waiting all night to show this photo to Georgia. I look over Kenna's shoulder to see if I can catch a glimpse of Georgia in the crowd inside.

"You should totally post that one." Kenna grins back. "Just go, Hudson. She's working the front table."

I bound down the stairs, looking between the table and the bar. Finally, I see her. She's stomping toward the elevator in her hot-pink, fishnet tights and combat boots. Her wings are flapping, and she looks like she means business. She slips into the doors just as they are sliding shut. By the time I get there and press the button, the elevator is already well on its way up.

Damn.

I'm about to run up the stairs to catch her on the other end, but someone grabs my arm and tells me it's time to make the announcements. I fumble in my pocket for the speech I've prepared. Thank God it's still there.

Hopefully, Georgia will like it. We can speak afterward.

georgia

. . .

FOR THE NEXT FORTY MINUTES, I'm checking in guests. So many guests. Even after all the guests who have pre-purchased tickets arrive, more last-minute guests keep coming.

"We heard about it on the *Lit Lovers* podcast."

"We saw it on Instagram."

"I follow Xander on TikTok."

"I buy my pet iguana's wigs at your shop!" That last one is the most gratifying. I file the iguana owner's Instagram account info away for future collabs.

The DJ is spinning, the guests with pets are mingling outdoors, and everyone is having a great time. Except for me. I still haven't found a moment to speak to Hudson. I haven't seen him at all. As I stand to go and look for him, I kick something from under the table. Much to my shock, it's a tiny Viking helmet that I immediately recognize as part of Oliver's costume. It must have fallen out while Ashley and I were wrestling with the bag.

Grabbing the miniature Viking cat helmet by the horns is not exactly the same as grabbing a bull, but I suddenly feel fortified with a similar determination.

I can't go another minute without finding Hudson and talking to him!

Since I haven't seen any sign of him in the main event space, I assume he's up in the loft. I stomp toward the elevators and tuck in behind a group that's heading up to the roof garden.

He's got to be up in his place or one of the other lofts that are open for tours.

When I get to the breezeway, I see that Ashley is walking toward Hudson's door. I press myself against the wall, taking cover behind a plant so she doesn't see me. She's got her cell phone to her ear. She looks over her shoulder to see if anyone is watching, kicks off her heels, swipes a keycard, and ducks in.

I creep toward the door, which is slightly ajar, and I can hear her talking.

"Yeah, yeah," she says. "I'm pretty sure it's a done deal. I mean, he went ring shopping yesterday. He didn't think I knew, but I set up his cell to share his location with mine."

I wonder if Oliver is in the loft and worry that he might get out.

Ashley laughs at something the person on the other line must have said and continues.

"Right? Who would have thought after that first night he would have invited me to stay in the lofts? But what can I say? You can't stop the course of true love. Looks like I'm destined to be Mrs. Holm after all."

I freeze. The lump in my throat feels like I've got a porcupine stuck in there. I can't breathe. I've got to get Cookie. I've got to get out of here.

I drop the helmet on the ledge outside the door and turn to run.

Instead of taking the elevator, I head to the roof garden and make my way down the stairs to the pet valet area where Cookie is playing with the volunteers. She's having so much fun she doesn't want to leave, but I force her, dragging her behind me.

We exit the party via a side gate.

Tears stream down my face as I pause on the street outside the building.

Inside, everyone is having a wonderful time dancing, laughing, toasting. Walker is spinning his daughter on the dance floor. There are crowds gathered around the small tables, bidding on the silent auction items. Kenna is circulating among the guests. I find her easily by following the bursts of flashes. Jackson isn't far behind, shooting video. Emily, Xander, and Mac are standing with a group of people I don't recognize, laughing at some joke.

And finally, I spot Hudson.

Hudson Holm is taking the stage, resplendent in his Viking costume. He's about to make an announcement, but he's searching for someone. Someone who is obviously not me. Because I'm on the outside again, looking in at all the happy people who belong to someone. It's just me and Cookie on a foggy, starless night.

hudson

. . .

"GOOD EVENING, everyone. I am Hudson Holm, and I have the honor and distinction of being your emcee for tonight. I'd like to start off by thanking all of you for being here and for your generous contributions to Ephron's local pet shelter. Tonight, we're rallying to raise enough money to help hundreds of pets be treated, vaccinated, spayed, and neutered and, most importantly, to find loving homes.

"Most of you know Xander and Georgia, whose mom, Joan, founded Celestial Pets. Joan was a beloved member of our community, and this masquerade honors her lifelong mission to bring people and their pet soul mates together.

"I never really believed in soul mates—animal or otherwise—until recently. That's when I met eleven-year-old Oliver, who incidentally was also a shelter pet."

I pause here to connect my phone to the computer running the projector so I can share the photo of me and Oliver in our matching costumes from earlier this evening. Predictably, this photo gets a lot of oohs and aahs.

"Pretty amazing photo, right?"

I proceed to tell the crowd about how unexpectedly Oliver came into my life and how he carved out a place for himself, becoming such an important part of my life.

"I finally had to come to terms with it," I confess. "I'm a cat person. This is my cat, and I love him."

There's a quick bit about the lofts and how the space we're in will soon be a part of a vibrant, pet-friendly, live/work community. I encourage everyone to take a tour of the models.

From there, I go on to thank all the sponsors, mention all the businesses that donated items for the silent auction, and play a quick video showing some of the ways the local shelters will use the donations that are collected tonight.

While the video is playing, I scan the crowd, unsuccessfully, for Georgia. I spy Walker, with his arm around Ashley. He gives me the thumbs-up sign.

"Some of you might be wondering why a large pet supply company like Farm & Holm is hosting a small, local business like Celestial Pets tonight. On the surface, it seems like we shouldn't be allies, we should be rivals."

I see Emily sitting in the crowd, notebook out, taking notes. She waves at me.

"And in the past, maybe that would have been true. But coming home to Ephron—the town where our family's business was founded—has really driven home the importance of communities. It's taught me the value of shopping local and supporting local businesses and artisans. That's why, moving forward, Farm & Holm will be highlighting independent artisans and smaller, local shops on our site each month. These shops and vendors will have the opportunity to participate in an incubator and receive training and capital to help them grow and scale their companies."

Someone in the crowd whistles, and there's clapping. I catch Xander's eye, and he's nodding approvingly, conferring with his partner. But where the hell is Georgia?

"We'll be working closely with pet influencers as part of our discovery and promotion of these companies, and we hope to see a significant portion of the profits turned over to shelter projects in communities like ours all over the country."

There's a round of applause now, and a few people stand up.

"But I don't want to make tonight about Farm & Holm. We're honored to have been given the opportunity to play host to this event. And now, I'd love to introduce you to Georgia Starr, the owner of Celestial Pets and daughter of Joan Starr. None of this tonight would be possible without Georgia. She's certainly been my muse since I arrived in town. She sparked this idea, and honestly, she's sparked so much more. Georgia? Won't you come up here?"

The crowd looks expectantly from side to side, searching for her.

"Anyone seen a five-foot-two fairy?" I joke.

Silence. Then a bit of confused murmuring. She isn't here. At least, she isn't inside the building. Outside on the street, I think I catch a flash of iridescent green. Was that just my imagination playing tricks on me?

"Excuse me for a moment," I say, racing down the steps and toward the door. By the time I get out to the street, however, she is gone. There's no sign of her.

Tap, tap, tap. In my absence, someone is putting a finger to the microphone. "Speaking of soul mates …" Walker is talking into the microphone. "I wonder if you'll all let me hog the mic for a moment for a little personal business. I'm Walker Holm, and this here building was my family's warehouse once upon a time. I remember flying paper airplanes in here when I was a kid. I spent so much time here with my dad that sometimes I felt like I lived here. And now I do! I've purchased one of the lofts in this building and can't wait to meet my neighbors. And there's one neighbor in particular I can't wait to see, hopefully each and every morning. Ashley?"

Walker is attempting to get on one knee when Xander grabs me.

"Come on," he says. "Looks like she's on her way back to the store."

"How do you know?" I ask.

"I made her share locations with me when she got the new phone. She may be my big sister and have a black belt, but I'm still bigger and badder, and when push comes to shove, I can hit harder," he says. And then he raises an eyebrow at me, as if I need reminding about our earlier conversation.

"I'm parked in." I run my fingers through my hair in frustration.

"We can take the van. I parked around the corner," Xander says. "I'll just tell Mac I'm leaving for a bit."

"Let me grab something from upstairs?"

"Okay, meet you out front," Xander says.

I dash up to my loft. On my way in, I notice Oliver's tiny Viking helmet sitting by my door. There it is! I was wondering where it was. How did it ever get out here? I set it down on the dining room table in the loft and throw my supplies in a paper bag.

Oliver, who has been watching people coming and going all night from the window, jumps on the table to sniff the hat. He flicks his tail.

Impulsively, I grab the helmet, pop it on him, and snap a close up photo of him in it. He doesn't even have a chance to protest before I pet and praise him lavishly.

"Wish me luck, Oliver!" I say. "I promise I'll be back."

He meows reassuringly at me.

I'm pretty sure he is, in fact, saying "Good luck."

georgia

· · ·

IT'S AROUND four miles back to the store, where my car is parked, but that doesn't deter me. The night is cool and clear, and it feels great to stretch my legs. My heart is pounding and my wings are flapping. Cookie trots alongside me.

"What was I thinking, Cookie?" I ask her.

It was just temporary insanity induced by our mutual lust. But in the end, that's all it was. Animal attraction. If it was more than that, he wouldn't be proposing to Ashley. Possibly right at this very moment. He was proposing and they would be leaving town, and that would be the end of it.

For a horrified moment, I consider that they might not leave town. They might settle permanently in the lofts. I might have to see them all the time, strolling through Holm Square in matching cashmere tennis sweaters. I feel like hurling. I feel like punching something. I wish I had an axe to throw.

My phone dings with a notification from the event's hashtag stream. It's a photo of a woman's hand with a massive rock on it and the caption: *"She said yes!"*

Motherfucker. I knew it! I pick up the pace, blinking back the tears.

Was I just jealousy bait? Had he been using me as part of a ploy to win Ashley?

My phone dings again and I check it. It's a message from Xander.

> Where are you?

> Needed some air. Heading home. Carry on without me.

And why shouldn't they? The event's been handled, the evening is a success, and nobody needs me there—for anything. Turns out I'm not so indispensable after all.

> Heading home? On foot? You sure you're okay?

> I will be. Just a little emotional seeing it all come together. Thanks, X.

I plan the rest of my evening. I'll go back to the store and get my car. Then I'll go home and get into a nice hot tub. Maybe light some candles.

And cry. Definitely cry.

Cookie nudges me, and I scratch her ear.

"I'll be okay girl," I tell her. "I'm used to being alone. I was just being silly. I got swept away with the whole Viking thing."

My phone dings again. It's a photo from Kenna this time. The time stamp indicates it's delayed. The photo is from over an hour ago. It's Hudson in his costume, standing outside on the patio with Cookie. She's added flaming stickers all around him. I text her back.

She texts me right back.

Enough. I drop the phone into a pocket in my tulle skirt.

The streets are empty in this area, but I don't feel unsafe. It's quiet. Peaceful even. I can hear myself think.

Thank goodness I hadn't had the chance to tell Hudson how I felt. If I'm being honest, how I still feel about him. At least I'd been spared that mortification.

My phone bounces against my thigh as I walk. It continues to light up, buzzing like a winning slot machine. I'll have to give this phone back to Hudson. What a pain in the ass that is going to be. I only just got all my contacts transferred. And there's all the photos of Cookie I've taken on it.

I pull it out again and open the camera roll. I barely took any photos tonight. Just the one of Cookie for the costume contest, and another of Xander by the gift baskets. I scroll back over the rest of the photos till I get back to the first one. It's the thumbnail of the video set to the *Toy Story* theme. My eyes water and my finger hovers over the delete button, but some-how, I can't bring myself to do it right now.

"Need a lift?" A jeep pulls over, and I recognize some of the teenaged volunteers from the event.

"No thanks, I'm good!" I wave them on, despite the fact that I can feel blisters starting to bloom on the backs of my heels. The pain is distracting in a good way. It gives me something physical to focus on instead of the excruciating way my heart is aching in its lonely hollow.

Besides, I'm almost there.

hudson

. . .

XANDER TAKES an alternate route to the store from the one that Georgia is walking.

"Shouldn't we just pick her up?" I ask.

"No, man, trust me. She's gotta cool off. Besides, I sent some of the kids from the pet valet to offer her a lift. They just texted me that she said no."

We get to the store before her. Xander pulls to the curb. I get out and walk around to the driver window.

"This is where I leave you. Good luck, Dude," he says.

"You're not going to stick around?"

"No. This is between the two of you, like you said before. Plus, I don't need to see all that stuff like the other night. Maybe save it for somewhere with blinds?" Xander waves as he takes off.

"Gotta get back to the party!"

I wait for what feels like forever, sitting on the sidewalk outside Celestial Pets. The block is dark, save for a couple of streetlights. Normally, the diner would still be open, but they've closed early due to all the staff being busy at the masquerade.

Across the street, at the center of the park, I can see a light on in the gazebo near my great-great-grandfather's plaque. It's familiar … and reassuring. This town, this street. I realize that this is the exact place I've pictured in my mind each and every time I've ever been asked, "Where are you from?"

I swing the bag from hand to hand and count to three hundred. Then I go online and pay to vote in the costume contest which is finally live. Ten times for Cookie and eleven for Oliver.

But still no Georgia. Where is she?

Frustrated, I log on to the challenge portal. Although it wrapped earlier this week, we've still got access. I pull up the photo of Oliver in the Viking helmet and send it to Cookie. "I missed you tonight."

And then I see her tiny, winged form in the distance. She's walking on the other side of the park, illuminated by the light of her cell phone. The green wings of her costume, bobbing in the night, look ethereal, like a firefly or a spirit.

This is it. She'll be here any moment. I'm doing this.

Except she isn't coming this way.

Georgia pauses, presumably pressing something, and the light on her phone goes out. I can barely track her progress as she continues across the park, heading toward a dark alley between two buildings. The parking lot. She must be headed to her car.

Stupid, stupid, stupid! Why would she be coming to the store at this hour? She was just headed here to fetch her car so she could go home.

She hasn't seen me sitting here in the shadows. She's walking at a pretty fast clip, and she isn't looking back. Cookie is trotting along beside her.

I have to catch them before she drives away!

Leaping to my feet, I jog after her. Fortunately, I'm wearing my trainers under the faux lace-up boots of the Viking costume. The leggings and muslin shirt are quite comfortable. And the fur vest has done a fine job of keeping me warm.

There's no time or space to shove my helmet in the paper bag, so I just run with it on. It's surprisingly well balanced. Perfect for battle, I muse.

She's halfway through the alley by the time I catch up to her.

"Wait! Georgia!" I call out her name. She freezes, crouches, and pivots to face me. There's no time to read her expression before she punches me. Hard. Square in the jaw.

georgia

. . .

BECAUSE MY HAND is curled into the perfect fist—thumb outside, fingers straight—it really doesn't hurt too bad when my knuckles slam into Hudson Holm's jaw. His Viking hat hits the brick wall beside us and goes clattering to the pavement.

Cookie barks and whines.

"Hudson!" I gasp. "Oh my God! What? What are you doing here?"

"I probably had that coming, sneaking up on you like that." He bends to retrieve the helmet and leans against the wall, gingerly stroking his jaw.

I'd heard him running behind me in the alley and hadn't stopped to look back. Operating purely on instinct, I'd attacked.

"Are you okay?" I ask. I want to touch him, to see if he's bleeding. I want to … Holy hell. He's wearing the costume, and dammit, he looks incredible, even in the dim light of this back alley.

"I'm fine," he says. "Better than fine now. I've been looking for you all night."

"You have?" I ask. "Why?" I'm genuinely confused. Shouldn't he be with Ashley right now? Snapping photos and commemorating the moment?

"Because I wanted to talk to you, Georgia. I have things to say to you."

"Say them, then," I say, sticking out my chin. I jerk Cookie's chain, forcing her to heel. I can tell she's dying to lick Hudson, and she can get in line. If I can't drool on him, neither can she.

"Not here," he says, attempting to wipe away the blood that's starting to drip from the small cut my punch left behind.

"Oh shit, you're bleeding," I say. "I'm sorry, Hudson. But you really shouldn't—"

"Sneak up on a woman in a dark alley? Yeah. My bad. I'll live. But do you think maybe we can go somewhere else to talk? Preferably somewhere with a sink and a first aid kit so I can take care of this first? I don't have a car, and it's a long walk back to the lofts."

"Fine." I exhale. "Just come back to my place with me. I'll clean you up."

"Thank you, Georgia," he says, and the sound of his voice laps over me like waves on the shore.

"You might want to take off the helmet," I say when we get to the unicorn. "Unless you plan to impale the roof of my car."

Hudson removes the hat. He puts it and his paper bag in the back seat with Cookie. She sniffs the contents curiously. Then he pushes the passenger seat back as far as possible before getting in. We don't speak in the car. The only sound is both of our phones blowing up with messages and texts—messages and texts that we both pointedly ignore.

I park in the driveway.

"Come in. I'll get my first aid kit."

"Thanks." He retrieves the helmet and puts it back on, then grabs his bag.

I have him sit on a stool by the kitchen counter. Memories of the last time he was in my kitchen replay in my mind. Hudson lifting me onto the counter. Hudson sticking his tongue in my mouth.

Hudson thrusting.

His eyes meet mine. Amber flecks are flashing in that sea of blue, and by the way he's biting a lip and looking hungrily at me, I get the impression that he's streaming the same episode in his memory as I am in mine.

I finish cleaning the cut and put a tiny, round Snoopy bandage on it. There. Nobody can look sexy with a Snoopy bandage on their jaw. Can they?

Nobody but Hudson, apparently. It only compromises the Viking costume a little.

"So, Ashley," I say. "I suppose I should congratulate you."

"Me? I mean, I really had nothing to do with it. And ultimately, I don't really think it's that big of a deal." Hudson lays a hand on my arm. I recoil.

"You don't think getting married is a big deal?"

I'm confused. Does he intend for me to be his piece on the side? Can that be what he's come to talk about with me?

"It's totally a big deal. For Ashley. And my dad. Not so much for me."

"Wait, what?" I shake my head. "Hold on a minute?"

"You didn't think that I was marrying Ashley, did you?"

"But I heard her, saying that staying in the lofts was the best decision ever, bragging to someone that she'd finally bagged a Holm."

"Not this Holm." Hudson tips my face to look at his. "Ashley is marrying my father, and I wish them both well. But that's not what I'm here to talk to you about, Georgia."

"You're not?" My brain is still trying to piece things together, and his touch makes it much harder to think.

"No." He shakes his head, and I feel myself swimming in his gaze.

There's that gravity issue again. It's going in the wrong direction. Hudson is not marrying Ashley. My jealousy drifts off like so much space junk. I'm still dizzy though. Dizzy and drawn in his direction by some kind of magnetic anomaly.

"Are you hungry?" he asks.

My stomach growls loudly and comically in response.

"How about I make us something to eat?" He holds up the paper bag.

"Isn't it kind of late?" I protest.

"You've been working like a dog all day. Why don't you go get into that glorious tub of yours and let me heat up something for you?"

He's already heating something up for me, I think. But it's not something in that bag. I want to go to him. I want to run away.

"Okay," I say, grateful for the chance to retreat and gather my thoughts. It's impossible to think clearly with a Viking standing in the middle of my kitchen.

"Shall I knock when it's ready?" he asks.

"Sure," I say. I remove Cookie's wings and fill her bowl with water before heading upstairs.

"Do me a favor?" he says. "As a friend? Don't throw those wings away just yet."

"You planning another party?" I ask.

"You never know," he says with a winsome smile.

———

I run the hottest bath I think I can stand and pour a lavish amount of lilac-scented bubble bath in. Then I light some candles, order Alexa to play a jazz channel, and dim the lights. Hudson isn't marrying Ashley. He's right downstairs, in my kitchen.

When the tub is full of frothy foam, I strip off the fishnets, my skirt, my bodysuit, and the hot-pink underwear I'd selected earlier, back when I'd imagined the possibility of a very different sort of night. I hang my fairy wings on a hook on the door. Finally, I slip my naked body into the bubbly heaven that's awaiting.

I attempt to empty my mind of all thoughts and float.

"Knock, knock." Hudson raps on the bathroom door. "Okay to come in?"

I look down at the tub, which is still so full of bubbles that he's not likely to get an eyeful. "You sure that's safe?" I ask.

"I won't look, Scout's honor," Hudson says. "I just don't want to make you get out of your bath."

"You can come in," I say. "And don't worry about your virtue. You'd need X-ray vision to see through all the bubbles."

He enters the bathroom, holding my favorite mug. It's steaming, and there's a spoon standing upright in it. He sets it on the counter and pulls up a stool next to the tub.

"I have news for you, Georgia. I don't need X-ray vision. I've got a photographic memory."

He's lost the helmet, but he's still wearing the vest. I sink deeper under the bubbles and allow my eyes to slide closed. My memories are currently more pornographic than photographic.

"Nice choice of music, by the way. Now, do you want to talk?"

"Actually, there's something I need to get off my chest." I sit bolt upright, forgetting for a minute and exposing myself. He shakes his head and laughs. I realize I'm blushing, and I cross my arms over my chest and slide back down under the water.

"I was actually looking for you earlier too," I say. Suddenly, it seems really important that whatever he has to say, I'd better say my piece first. I've been granted a second chance by some miracle, and I'm not going to waste it.

"Okay," Hudson says. "Hit me. Only, maybe don't actually hit me this time?" He fiddles with the wings hanging on the door.

"I don't want to be friends with you, Hudson."

"You don't?"

"And I don't want to be 'friends with benefits' either. Although this benefits package is super tempting." I gesture toward him.

"You like my package?" He grins.

"Oh, shut up." I splash him. He pretends he is shocked.

"Now look what you've gone and done. I'm soaked! I'm going to have to take this off."

He stands and peels off the vest and the muslin top. I find myself counting the ridges in his six-pack and staring at the pale-blond treasure trail that is right about my eye level right now. If I splash his pants, will he take them off too?

"You were saying?" He reaches across the tub and grabs a sponge. "May I?" he gestures to my back.

I lean forward and close my eyes as he pushes my hair to the side and proceeds to wash my back with slow, sweeping strokes. His hand dips down into the water to wet the sponge, and he squeezes it out along my spine.

"Ugh … stop it. I can't think. That just feels too good." I moan. My nipples are hard. My toes are curling involuntarily. I don't think I've ever been so simultaneously aroused and relaxed.

"So, don't think." His lips tease my earlobe as he leans across to whisper in my ear.

"I think I'm falling in love with you!" I blurt it out and duck under the water so I don't have to see his reaction.

How long can I realistically hold my breath? I've never been very good at it. But this, I think, is the perfect time to go for a personal record. I stay down as long as I can, only emerging when my lungs are screaming. I open one eye slowly. The stool is empty, but the pile of clothes on the floor has grown. I sit up straight and look over my shoulder.

There he is. Looking more like a bold Viking warrior than ever, without a stitch of clothing on.

"Scoot forward," he says, easing into the tub behind me and wrapping me up in his long, strong limbs. "You were saying?" He nibbles at my neck and cups my breasts.

"No, you." I moan a little. "I said what I had to say. Your turn."

"So, funny story," he says. "But once again, I think you've beaten me to the punch."

"I'm sorry I punched you, Hudson."

"You can punch me again, if you want, if you'll just say you love me again." Water sloshes over the rim of the tub onto the floor as I roll onto my belly and wrap my arms around his neck. He sits us both up, and I drape my legs around him, rocking against him, slowly.

"Stop." He groans. "It's my turn to talk, and now you're not making it easy for me."

"Mmm …" My hips have a mind of their own, and they won't stop grinding. He reaches around to grab my ass and makes me stop though.

"I don't want either one of us to be underwater or incapacitated when I say this, Georgia. I want your full attention."

"Say it already, then." His efforts to literally bring me to a grinding halt have done little to quench my desire.

"I'm falling in love with you, too, Georgia Starr. And I really wish you'd let me go first. Because I had a whole plan."

"I like this plan." I smile coyly, sliding against him.

"This is exquisite torture. But it wasn't the plan. I made you dinner, remember?"

"Dinner was your plan? In a mug?"

"Not just any dinner. Wait a minute. Don't move a muscle."

He's up and out of the tub, and back, so quickly and lithely that he barely has time to drip on the tiles.

"You know what they say, Georgia."

"Don't knock it till you've tried it?" I guess, spying the mugful of my favorite comfort food.

"Truth." Hudson smiles. "But I was thinking of another phrase. It goes more like this: 'If you like it, then you better put a ring on it.'"

My mouth falls open. Hudson places the mug on the stool beside the tub.

"Are you kidding me? Are you proposing to me with pasta right now?"

"I guess so, in a way." He laughs and lifts the spoon. "I'm proposing that we give this—us—a chance. What do you say?"

I'm speechless, so it's just as well that my mouth is full of food. I swallow slowly.

"Look, I know it's early days, but a not-so-wise man said something to me earlier today."

"Who was that?" I manage to get out.

"It was Walker, of course. He said, 'When you know, you know.'" Hudson reaches over, pulls a spaghetti ring from the mug, and raises it up to the light. I hold up my pinky finger, and he slips it on the tip.

"He does have a point." I lift up my hand to admire the decoration, but Hudson leans forward to grab it and slurps it off, teasing between my fingers with his tongue.

"Hey, that was mine!" I protest.

"Mmm … I couldn't resist," he says, licking his lips.

"Later, Hater!" I push away from him and retrieve the mug of pasta from the stool, feeding myself another spoonful.

"I really thought you hated me," he says. "Which was a problem, considering the way I was feeling about you."

"I thought you hated *me*!" I laugh.

"I kind of did, to be honest. Or at least I hated the way you made me feel completely out of control of my emotions."

"Same." I nod.

"I don't want to waste any more time, Georgia. I knew it the first time I kissed you. It was like coming home."

"How are we going to tell Cookie and Oliver?" I ask.

"I think we should offer them a collab," Hudson says. "They can be the faces of that new pet clothing collection, if you'll still consider it. I'd love to help you find a way to scale and distribute your designs—without compromising any of your values."

"Did you really come here to talk shop?" I ask.

"Not exactly," he says, pulling me closer. "Mostly, I just wanted to tell you how much I admire you. And how much I'm looking forward to whatever the future brings."

"So, does that mean you'll be sticking around in Ephron, then?" I ask.

"If you'll have me," he says, placing another pasta ring on my finger and lapping it off.

"I will," I say, planting a ring on the back of his ring finger and then using my tongue to clean it off.

Hudson takes the mug from my hands and positions it back on the stool before kissing me slowly and deeply.

"Welcome home, Hudson," I murmur before wrapping my legs around him.

THE END

author's note

Dear Reader,

I enjoyed writing this book so much and hope you've enjoyed reading it too. If you did, I'd appreciate you leaving a review to let other readers know about it and/or a shared link on social media. Don't forget to tag me if you share.

Your feedback is so important to me!

Xo, Ciara Blume

Want to find out what's next for Georgia, Hudson, and their furry friends? Sign up for my newsletter by scanning the QR code above and I'll send you a bonus chapter. You won't want to miss the *Lit Lovers* podcast episode where Georgia and Hudson discuss what it's like to discover that your secret soul mate is someone you think you hate.

Please enjoy a sneak peek of Theater Lovers, Book 3 in the Lit Lovers series, included at the end of this edition.

theater lovers: prologue

Fifteen years ago …

I wait with Dean in the wings of the theater. This scene is my favorite part of *Little Shop of Horrors*. It's the moment when Audrey and Seymour finally kiss. But that's not why it's my favorite scene. It's my favorite because it lasts for almost seven minutes. And during those seven minutes, I get Dean all to myself. Just the two of us, alone in the dark.

Seven minutes in heaven.

It's the opening night of the high school theater's limited run, and I've made an important decision. I'm not going to wait around for the cast party. I am finally going to go for it. I'm going to kiss him.

I shift nervously and bounce on my toes in my black jazz shoes, chosen specifically for this occasion. I'm no dancer, though. I wish I had the grace and rhythm of Brittany, the popular senior who is currently standing centerstage, awaiting declarations of passion and a theater-worthy kiss from her costar. Why do things seem to come so easily to the Brittanys of the world? Brittany will probably also be prom queen.

I, Chelsea Porter, on the other hand, am an expert at flying under the radar and blending into the scenery. Hence the black jazz shoes. Perfect for stepping silently during scene changes. My clothing helps to make me invisible as well. I'm wearing black leggings and a baggy, old, oversize, black sweatshirt that used to be my dad's. There's a faded picture of him and his bandmates, all big hair and '80s' rocker clothing, reflected by the cracked and peeling tour dates below the image. They hadn't been on the charts for very long, but that one song had been a bona fide hit in '87.

I tug on the black beanie covering my mousy-blonde hair.

Even my underwear is black. Not that it matters what I'm wearing in the near-pitch shadows I'm currently inhabiting with Dean. But it boosts my confidence knowing I've got on something "sexy" underneath my cloak of invisibility. I can feel the itch of stiff, synthetic lace against my recently sprouted boobs. I know Dean has noticed them as well. I caught him staring at my chest during one of the dress rehearsals. I'd just been wearing a tank and no bra. It was freezing cold in the theater that night, and when the lights came back on? My headlights were definitely on. I was mortified. Dean had handed me his jacket. His *letter* jacket. I hadn't wanted to give it back.

The thong is giving me one hell of a wedgie. I squirm and consider picking it out but ultimately decide against it. It's dark, but Dean still might be able to tell. We use other senses in our inky, velvet-curtained cocoon. I can tell exactly how close he is with my eyes closed. Eight inches at the moment. That's the size of the air pocket behind me, between us. I just have to turn around and lean in.

The audience bursts into laughter, signaling me that I only have two minutes left until the onstage kiss. This is when I'm going to do it. My heart thumps even faster and harder. Can Dean hear it? Can I hear his heart? I'd like to think I can. I close my eyes and listen. Nothing. Just the faint and steady sound of his breath. If I concentrate, I can feel it faintly on the back of my neck. And I can certainly smell him. Dean smells like Old Spice, grass, and sweat. He'd probably been playing football right up to the minute he got to the theater. The smell of him is easy to isolate. It stands out from all the other smells in the theater, as if lit by a spotlight. Somewhere in the background, there's also the dust and must of thrift-store wardrobe items, the cold pizza we hastily snarfed for dinner, and the woodshop and paint smells of the flats we're waiting to swap. But all of that fades to black when Dean steps closer. Six inches?

I can feel the warmth radiating from his skin. Warmth and goodness. Not everybody knows what a good guy Dean Riley is, but I know. I know the real Dean because he's my big brother, Jackson's, best friend. And he's my friend, too, though most people don't really see that. They don't see Dean watching movies with me while Jackson messes around on his PC, or Dean helping me pick out the paint colors for the mural in my bedroom. Sometimes I think Dean is more *my* friend than my brother's. Not that I'd say that out loud. Who would believe me?

Dean and Jackson are legends at Ephron High, unarguably the coolest guys in the senior class. Brains and brawn. The most eligible bachelors.

Somehow, they've both managed to remain single almost all the way through the fall term. Not that Dean hasn't hooked up with anyone. From the rumors, he's been hooking up with a different girl every weekend. He even made out with a freshman cheerleader last month. I wanted to hate her, but who could blame anyone for wanting to kiss Dean Riley? Those lips, and the way he smiles at you, like everything is a private joke. Irresistible.

I also can't be jealous. I know that Dean thinks the girl is bonkers. She practically stalked him, asking him for a commitment after the party, and they didn't even make it to third base. This, Jackson says, is why he never makes out with freshmen.

Yuck. I *really* don't want to think about what my brother is up to. My guess, though, is not much. He says he isn't interested in seriously dating anyone till his frontal lobe firms up a bit more.

On the other side of the curtains, an anticipatory hush settles over the audience as they wait to see what happens next. It mirrors my own tension. I feel as taut as a drawn bow.

As I wait for the big moment, I run down the "Perfect Man" checklist in my head. It's like a mantra. Dean checks every box.

My Perfect Man: A List by Chelsea Porter

1. Doesn't put up with bullshit from anyone—check! Dean doesn't care what anyone thinks. He stands up to bullies and calls it like it is.

2. Good with his hands—check! Dean can fix anything. He built the entire Little Shop of Horrors set from scratch.

3. Knows how to ride a motorcycle—check! Dean says it's a life skill.

4. Has piercing, blue eyes—check! Aquamarine, but close enough.

5. Has great hair—check! Thick, wavy, auburn hair, bonus points for the unusual color and shine.

6. Has a great sense of humor—check! Although, I could do without the practical jokes he and Jackson are always playing on me.

7. Good at sports—check! This is mostly because my future kids certainly won't get that from me. I have two left feet.

8. Popular—check!

9. Has a great bod—double check!

I'm just about to do it, when Dean unexpectedly leans forward and wraps his arms around my waist. The audience gasps, and so do I.

He leans his chin on my shoulder and whispers in my ear.

"What do you think, Chels? Should I ask Brit?"

There's no time to spare. I have to do it now. I spin around to face him and reach up to tangle my hands in his hair. Oh, God. It's just as soft as I always imagined.

I pull his lips to mine. Someone in the audience wolf-whistles.

At first, Dean freezes. His hands drop to his sides. But then, something switches on, and he's pulling me closer, kissing me back tenderly and passionately as the orchestra music rises to a touching crescendo.

But just as suddenly, when the music stops and the curtain drops, he shoves me away.

"No!" he asserts. "No. No. No. NO! This cannot happen! What the fuck, Chels? Did Jackson put you up to this? Are you pulling a prank on me?"

All around us, there is motion. Brittany and her costar have rushed off to change, and crew members are wheeling the flats from the last scene offstage, opposite us. It's our job to get the new pieces into place. Now.

"We gotta get this out there. Grab your side," Dean whispers, positioning himself on the far end of the flat, back to the stage. He takes a step back, pulling the huge, unwieldy set with him. He's doing most of the work of moving the large pieces. It's my job to look for the reflective tape marks and guide him.

I'm still buzzing from the kiss, but we've rehearsed this, done it dozens of times.

"Keep going. Left a little. No, right," my voice barely audible in the dark. My hands are shaking. The wooden backdrop wobbles ominously, falling toward me.

"Shit!" Dean says as he scrambles to steady it. I can hear the panic in his voice. It's loud enough for the audience to hear as well, and a small sneaker wave of snickering washes over us.

"It's okay, Chels, you're safe. I got it," he whispers a second later. He stops in exactly the right spot and quickly folds down the braces to secure the set in place. He doesn't look up till he's done, but when he does, he isn't looking at me. He's looking over my shoulder at the backstage area of the wings where Brittany is standing, mid costume change, wearing nothing but a tiny bikini to protect her so-called modesty. There's not a lot of light back there, either, but to our light-starved eyes, she may as well be basking in a ray of golden sun. She wiggles her fingers in a cute, girly wave at Dean, and I watch as he smiles, nodding back at her.

What had he been saying before I kissed him?

"Should I ask Brit—"

Ask Brit. Ask her what?

Oh. Oh? OH! Understanding doesn't dawn gently. It peels off me like a deceptively pleasant, hot wax strip when it's suddenly torn away from your sensitive hairy bits. I want to howl, but I can't.

"You want to ask *Brittany* to prom?" I ask, barely above a whisper, but louder than it should be. Dean's eyes widen, the whites catching the light as his head whips back to my face.

"Shh." He holds a finger over his lips.

But I'm already running away, not paying attention, not watching where I'm going. I trip and slide on my ass, straight into the sets that have just been wheeled offstage. My brand-new, "sexy" thong catches on something, dragging and cutting into my flesh, giving me a rope burn that's only slightly less painful than the blow to my pride.

And then the stacked sets fall like dominos, landing on my left leg, leaving it fractured in two places.

———

After the show has ended and I've been X-rayed, Dean stops by the hospital with a big bunch of roses. He sends my mom and Jackson down to the cafeteria to get some food and sits with me while I wait to get my cast. I still cannot look at him.

"Way to steal the show," he says, laying the roses on the table.

"Sorry I couldn't help with the third act," I say, pretending to be tough.

"I'm sorry I couldn't come sooner." He shrugs. "But you know what they say … 'The show must go on!'"

I snort. "Right. But first, they say, 'Break a leg.'"

"You know you're not literally supposed to break a leg, kiddo? It's just an expression." Dean attempts to take my hand, and I yank it away. *Kiddo?* He's never called me that before.

He paces around the room, examining rolls of plaster and tape. He fiddles with a frightening pair of oversize scissors.

"Hey, I don't think you're supposed to touch that stuff," I say primly.

"I'm just interested to see how it works. Mind if I watch while they put your cast on? I've never worked with fiberglass before."

"Is that why you're here?" I pout. "Because you're dying to do crafts with medical supplies?"

"No, Chels," he says, putting a hand on my face and turning me to face him. "That's not why I'm here. We should talk about what happened."

"No need. It was just an accident. A stupid accident. Best if we all forget about it," I say. "And the sooner the better."

"I don't know, Chels. I don't think anyone is going to forget tonight's performance," Dean says, barely suppressing that knowing half smile of his. "Especially me."

I fold my arms across my chest, hugging myself protectively, trying to ignore the pain from the uber wedgie between my butt cheeks as I lift my chin higher, attempting to muster whatever scrap of dignity I have left. There's only one thing I need to know.

"Did you ask Brittany to prom?" I ask.

Dean shrugs. "Nah, she asked me first."

"And you said yes?" I ask, incredulously.

"Sure, why not. She's hot." He smiles that rakish smile again, and I feel like smacking him suddenly. Why is he torturing me like this? It's one thing to reject me, but calling me kiddo after he kissed me back and then telling me someone else is hot? What the actual fuck? A fresh wave of outrage crests and breaks over me.

"But you kissed me back!" I spit out, tears starting to collect in the corners of my eyes. "How long after the ambulance left did you wait to make out with her?"

I'm suddenly impatient to get my cast and get out of here. And not just this room. My whole life. Clearly, I can't go back to school for the rest of the year. Perhaps I can apply for an inter-district transfer to another high school. Better yet, maybe I can apply to a fancy Swedish boarding school like Jackson's old best friend, Hudson Holm. Surely there are scholarships for special cases like mine?

Dean uses his thumb to wipe a stray tear from the corner of my eye.

"You're too good for me, and you know it, Chelsea. Also," he says more seriously, "too young."

"I'm not a little girl anymore, Dean," I argue, pushing myself up on my elbows. My oversize hospital gown gaps and slips off my shoulder, revealing the lacy, black bra I'd worn under my sweatshirt just in case.

"I can see that, Chelsea." Dean pulls up the gown, looking away pointedly.

"Then why? Why are you doing this to me?" I whine, realizing a moment too late that I sound exactly like the child I don't want him to see me as.

"Because I don't want to take you out of the oven when you're only half baked." He smiles. "Not to mention my own mushy frontal lobe. Just ask Jackson. We're both still wobbly. Can't be trusted to make good decisions."

"So, kissing me was a bad decision, then?" I narrow my eyes.

"No. I mean, yes. Your friendship means so much to me. It's too special to risk it." Dean's eyes are imploring.

"Or maybe I don't mean enough." I turn my head to face the wall.

"Cut it out, Chelly Belly." Dean sits on the edge of the exam table next to me, calling me by the stupid nickname my mom used to have for me when I was little. I'd made her stop calling me that when I was ten. Right around the time Dean and Jackson started hanging out. They still bust it out from time to time when they want to annoy me, though.

"Fuck off. You cut it out." I attempt to elbow him away, forgetting for a moment that my left leg is broken. Crushing pain shoots through my whole body, making me freeze with pain.

"Shit!" Dean exclaims, jumping up. "Did I hurt you? I'm so sorry. This is all my fault."

"Honestly? My pride hurts a hell of a lot more than my leg, Dean. Maybe you should just go," I say. "I don't want to hear any more bullshit about being a half-baked cake. I get it. You're not into me. Now leave me alone."

"Look at me, Chels." Dean stands patiently by the table and waits. "I mean it, *look* at me."

I know how stubborn he is. He's not leaving till I do it. I force myself to meet his eyes, my tears still streaming.

"There you are," he says, when I do. I am surprised to see that his eyes look a bit teary too.

"You know me well enough to know that if I simply wasn't into you, I would say so, right?" he asks.

Slowly, I nod. I do know him well enough. Almost as well as I know my own brother. Possibly better.

"So why can't you believe me when I say it isn't that? Why can't you trust me when I say that if you were my age or, God help me, if you weren't my best friend's little sister …"

Dean leans over and traces my lower lip with his thumb while staring into my eyes. I feel my lids growing heavy, my eyes beginning to close, as if he's about to kiss me. Which he isn't. In the next instant, he's spinning away and pacing again.

"I tell you what. I just had an idea. Let's make a deal."

It takes me a moment to catch my breath. "You want to make a deal with me?"

"Yes. Here it is—check back in with me when you're my age."

"You want me to 'check in' with you when I'm seventeen? Why? You think we'll be fully baked by then?"

"I don't know how baked we'll be, but the difference between seventeen and twenty isn't nearly as tricky as the difference between fourteen and seventeen, is it? I'm guessing that by the time you're a senior in high school, you'll have a trail of broken hearts in your wake and you won't even remember my last name."

"Probably," I say, thinking *never*.

"If, for some reason, you find yourself single and in need of a prom date for your senior prom," Dean says, "I'll be there. With bells on. Chels bells. Scout's honor," he swears, smiling wryly and performing a Boy Scout salute.

"Deal," I say. "On one condition. We never tell Jackson about any of this." I hold out my hand to shake.

A man walks into the room carrying a clipboard and asks, "Ready to pick a color for your cast?"

"And you have to let me be the first one to sign your cast," Dean says, before grasping my outstretched hand.

We shake on it.

When the cast is done, Dean signs my cast along the top edge, toward the inside, halfway up my thigh. He writes his name, draws a heart, and writes the last two digits of the year I'll be graduating. Then, as if swearing an oath, he kisses his thumb and presses it to the heart he's just drawn. His hand grazes my inner thigh as he strokes his thumb along the top edge of the cast. But then Jackson has to ruin everything by laughing loudly about something in the hallway.

Dean pulls his hand away quickly, just before my mom and Jackson walk back into the room.

Perhaps the night wasn't a total loss after all. Dean Riley just asked me to my senior prom.

acknowledgments

This book would never have happened without my friend Carla Young, with whom I spent many Friday mornings plotting and dreaming about the residents of Ephron.

I owe multi-award-winning author Tara September for her generous advice, support, and intros to my editors—my developmental editor, Anya Kagan, of Touchstone Editing, and my copy editor, Joyce Mochrie, owner of One Last Look, who worked their magic, making this book so much better. Jillian Liota of Indie Graphic is the rockstar who made my cover judgement worthy.

Writing is a lonely biz, but I'm so fortunate to have Jessica Rosenberg, whom I can text with and share choice expletives about the "process" as well as victory gifs when we solve plot problems. She gets it. Thanks also to Angela Camacho, Katherine Kotkin, Stacey Craven, Debbie Bookstaber, Jill Parkin, and Marcie Taylor for the daily sanity checks and pep talks. You are my people.

To my mom and my kids who challenge, encourage, and continue to put up with me. Thank you for giving me the space and time to do this. ILY. You have my permission to skip over the spicy parts.

Dad, I hope you're watching and you're proud.

Last but not least, thanks to my beloved pets over the years, including OG Oliver, Stinky Kitty, and Jasper the mutt. HK, my eleven-year-old, odd-eyed Persian cat, would like to take full credit for this book. She's spent almost as much time sleeping on my laptop as I have spent writing on it. Her Instagram account can be found @petfluential.

www.ingramcontent.com/pod-product-compliance
Lightning Source LLC
Chambersburg PA
CBHW021415310726
48971CB00005B/1349